PENGUIN

Scent of a

Scent of a Killer

KEVIN LEWIS

PENGUIN BOOKS

PENGUIN BOOKS

Published by the Penguin Group
Penguin Books Ltd, 80 Strand, London WC2R ORL, England
Penguin Group (USA) Inc., 375 Hudson Street, New York, New York 10014, USA
Penguin Group (Canada), 90 Eglinton Avenue East, Suite 700, Toronto, Ontario, Canada M4P 2Y3
(a division of Pearson Penguin Canada Inc.)
Penguin Ireland, 25 St Stephen's Green, Dublin 2, Ireland (a division of Penguin Books Ltd)
Penguin Group (Australia), 250 Camberwell Road, Camberwell, Victoria 3124, Australia
(a division of Pearson Australia Group Pty Ltd)
Penguin Books India Pvt Ltd, 11 Community Centre, Panchsheel Park, New Delhi – 110 017, India
Penguin Group (NZ), 67 Apollo Drive, Rosedale, North Shore 0632, New Zealand
(a division of Pearson New Zealand Ltd)
Penguin Books (South Africa) (Pty) Ltd, 24 Sturdee Avenue,
Rosebank, Johannesburg 2196, South Africa

Penguin Books Ltd, Registered Offices: 80 Strand, London WC2R ORL, England

www.penguin.com

First published 2009
2

Set in 11.75/14 pt Monotype Garamond
Printed in Great Britain by Clays Ltd, St Ives plc

ISBN: 978-0-141-03011-1

www.greenpenguin.co.uk

To Jackie, Charlotte and Nathan,
AKA 'The Groovy Gang'

Prologue

At first he thought he must be dreaming. Then, as the fog clouding his mind began to lift, he started to feel uneasy. Finally, with the full reality of his situation slowly becoming clear, Raymond Chadwick started to panic.

The brightly lit room he had woken up in was eerily quiet and smelled of antiseptic. He had no idea of where he was or how he had got there. The only thing he knew for sure was that something was terribly, terribly wrong.

The overhead lights were dazzling, like staring directly into the sun, but when Chadwick tried to shut his eyes and turn away nothing happened. He couldn't move. For some reason his whole body seemed to have stopped working. His arms, legs, fingers, toes, lips, tongue – they were all useless. He couldn't even blink.

What on earth was going on? The last thing he could remember was sitting in the passenger seat of a fast-moving car. After that, everything had suddenly gone blank. And now he had woken up in . . . a hospital? That was the only thing that made sense. There must have been a crash, some kind of accident. How badly hurt was he? Was he going to be paralysed for the rest of his life? Please God, no! Anything but that.

Chadwick forced himself to calm down, to concentrate, to slow down his racing heart and take in as much as possible about his situation. He knew he was lying on his back, naked from the waist upwards – he could feel the cold air against his skin – but nothing hurt, he wasn't in any kind of pain at all.

His fuddled brain searched desperately for an explanation. He still felt as though he was waking up from a deep sleep so perhaps he had just undergone an operation and was coming out of the anaesthesia. That too seemed to fit the facts. But if that was the case, why was there no one here with him? Why had he been left all alone?

Then another thought came into his mind and terror started to rise within him. What if the operation had not yet started? What if he remained awake during the whole procedure? He had read about cases like that and they had become the stuff of his nightmares.

Then, from somewhere off to his right, came the sound of footsteps. Solid shoes against a tiled floor. A steady clip, clip, clip, coming closer and closer. The footsteps clipped their way around the room, moving to one side, pausing for a few seconds, then moving back. A few moments later came the sound of a voice, a gentle, slightly muffled voice repeating his name over and over, assuring him that everything was going to be all right, that there was nothing to worry about.

A sense of ease slowly washed over him. The physical presence of another human being in the room was all the proof Chadwick needed that he had not been forgotten, that he was being cared for.

And there was more. The fact that the doctor was talking to him meant they knew he was conscious. Also, the fact that he was being reassured meant he was surely over the worst and on the road to recovery.

As he began to calm down he focused on the voice. There was something familiar about it. Chadwick knew he had heard it before but struggled to place it. Just then something appeared at the bottom of his field of vision. A head, covered in a tight-fitting green cap, was leaning over his torso, examining him. As the head moved along his body he could see the edge of a surgical mask covering the lower part of the face, leaving only the eyes visible.

For a brief moment the eyes looked directly into his. They were cold, detached. He could sense no emotion in them as the head vanished out of view.

A clatter of metal against metal was followed by the return of the head and a warm sensation on Chadwick's chest as a soft palm pressed down on to the space between his nipples.

The muffled voice spoke again. 'Don't worry, Raymond. It's all going to be okay. I'm going to make it all okay.'

The fingers were spread wide and felt good against his cold skin. A thumb started to slide back and forth across his sternum, pushing his chest hair aside. Slowly the hand began to press more firmly until it was forcing his shoulder blades flat against the bed beneath him.

Then a new sound. A muffled giggle. A laugh. The tone of the voice changed, becoming harsher, rising with excitement. 'You really thought you were going to get away with it didn't you?' the voice said. 'You truly believed that no one was ever going to find out. But you were wrong, Raymond. So wrong. You can't go around treating people like that. You just can't. Now you're going to have to pay. You know what I'm going to have to do to you, don't you?'

Chadwick's heart began to race. He tried to move but found himself still paralysed. He stared back at the eyes, which were now wide with excitement, and he could sense a smile beneath the mask.

Then came something new. Something awful. It was at once white-hot and ice cold, a pin prick of intense pressure that seemed to pierce downwards, moving deep inside him, becoming more and more agonizing by the second. The pain was like nothing he had ever known. He felt his skin tearing, his muscles ripping, as the razor-sharp surgical scalpel sliced into him. He felt the fountains of warm blood spilling out over his sides, the pinch of cold air against his exposed internal organs. Chadwick tried to open his mouth and scream, but no sound came out.

The hands were deep inside him now, pulling, twisting and wrenching his organs apart. It couldn't be happening, but it was. He was being cut open by someone who was only too well aware that he was still awake. This was no mistake, this was no innocent error. He was witnessing his own cold-blooded murder.

The voice that had once gently called his name was now breathless with excitement. The sound of euphoric laughter was still ringing in Chadwick's ears as the life seeped out of him and the bright lights slowly faded into absolute, eternal darkness.

'I know the drill.'

Detective Chief Inspector Neil Barker looked across the table and stared hard at the stern-faced woman sitting opposite him. 'Then you know that we have to go through it anyway,' he said, trying hard to hide his irritation. Then, as he looked around the room, his face seemed to soften slightly. 'Listen,' he said quietly. 'No one likes being on the receiving end of all this. Let's just get through it as best we can.'

'Whatever,' came the surly reply.

DCI Barker shuffled the sheaf of papers in his hands, cleared his throat and began. 'For the benefit of the tape, please state your full name, your warrant number and the unit to which you are currently attached.'

'Stacey Elizabeth Collins. 177265. MIT South.'

'Thank you. I am Detective Chief Inspector Neil Barker, attached to the Anti-Corruption Unit of the Directorate of Professional Standards. My colleague is ...'

Barker switched his gaze to the black woman in the neat grey trouser suit sitting on his right.

'Detective Inspector Karen Willis, also attached to the Directorate of Professional Standards.'

'Also present on behalf of DI Collins is a Federation representative. Could you introduce yourself?'

'Alan Matheson. Police Sergeant 383, posted at Plumstead Police Station.'

'Thank you,' said Barker, nodding in the man's direction. He then twisted his body to face the middle-aged man behind him. 'And the final person in the room is . . .'

The man leaned forward so his soft Scottish accent would carry across to the microphone. 'Detective Chief Inspector Warren Milton. Serious Organized Crime Agency.'

Barker turned back and continued. 'The date is Thursday, 13 May, and the time by my watch is now 5.32 p.m. We are in an interview room at Peckham Police Station. At the conclusion of this interview I will explain the procedure for dealing with the tapes and your access to them. Do you understand?'

Collins raised her eyes to the grey-flecked tiles of the suspended ceiling. 'Of course.'

'Before I say anything further I will caution you that you do not have to say anything but it may harm your defence if you do not mention when questioned something which you later rely on in court. Anything you do say may be given in evidence. Do you understand?'

Collins understood only too well. After eighteen years in the police force she had given the same warning on hundreds of occasions – every time she made an arrest. And, as one of the Met's leading detectives, Collins made more arrests than most. This was the first time she had ever found herself on the opposite side of the interview desk, and it was an experience she would have happily gone without.

Normally she would have been sitting in one of the comfortable wooden chairs, not the flimsy plastic one that flexed every time she moved and was almost impossible to relax in. It was, of course, just one of a number of ploys used to give officers an edge over suspects during interviews.

Don't rise to the bait. Don't let them get to you.

'I understand,' Collins said softly.

'Then let us proceed.' Barker jerked his head towards Willis, who opened a slim manila envelope and pulled out a series of grainy colour photographs. She slid the first across the table towards Collins. 'This was taken by SO11 officers involved in long-term surveillance of the main target in a drug-trafficking investigation,' she said. 'You will see there is an obvious cause for concern. This is your chance to explain.'

Collins glanced down at the print and needed no time at all to take in all its details. After all she was in it. She had lived it. Taken at dusk using a powerful telephoto lens, the photograph showed her speaking to a man called Jack Stanley in a park near the ruins of an old manor house in Chiselhurst, Kent.

Collins had known Stanley for just about as long as she had known anyone in her entire life. And for just about as long as she had known him, Jack Stanley had been on the wrong side of the law. Over the years he had progressed from a petty criminal on the Blenheim Estate, where he and Collins had grown up, to a leading figure in the South London criminal underworld.

When Collins joined the police service she quickly reached an agreement with her childhood friend. Stanley provided her with tips about the activities of drug gangs and armed robbers, and even helped her to recover stolen goods. In return Stanley received subtle hints about potential police investigations into his growing criminal empire and detailed explanations about the latest forensic techniques that might be used against him.

It was a covenant with the Devil that saw Collins's career go from strength to strength as she developed a reputation as an outstanding and highly effective officer, but Stanley benefited even more. The majority of his tip-offs led to arrests of members of rival gangs who were trying to muscle in on his patch, thus clearing the way for his own people.

What Stanley didn't know was that Collins had, for the most part, always managed to avoid doing anything illegal. The hints about police investigations amounted to little more than underworld gossip, while details of new techniques and technology could all be found in publicly available sources, just so long as you looked hard enough. But there were plenty of times when Collins sailed too close to the line or briefly stepped over it. It was, she told herself time and time again, the only way she could do her job. It was a necessary evil.

Collins cut her ties with Stanley soon after he was arrested as the prime suspect in a gangland slaying. He was acquitted after all the key prosecution witnesses suddenly and mysteriously withdrew their statements and developed collective amnesia. In the years that followed, Collins always knew there would come a time when their paths crossed once more.

The meeting in the park where the photographs had been taken was the first time they had seen one another in several years. Collins had run into a brick wall while investigating the case of a young boy named Daniel Eliot, who had been kidnapped and murdered. Thanks to his criminal contacts, Stanley had been able to help out, but in return he had wanted Collins to help him uncover an informant in his organization. Collins had refused point blank, as it was clear that Stanley would have immediately had the grass executed and Collins didn't want blood on her hands. But soon afterwards her daughter, Sophie, had gone missing and she had needed Stanley's help once more.

Collins had been trying to stall Stanley ever since, but now the demons of the past were coming back to haunt her. Not even her closest colleagues knew just how much assistance this gangland figure had provided for her over the years. And they could never know. While she could justify her behaviour to herself, allowing the whole truth to come out would mean instant dismissal and possible prosecution. If she was going to get out of this with her career intact, she was going to have to tread very carefully.

Collins looked up at each person in the room in turn before fixing her gaze on DCI Barker. 'I've known Jack Stanley my whole life,' she began. 'We grew up together on the same estate. When I joined the police he became an unofficial informant. As I'm sure you're aware, a lot of that kind of thing went on back then, before the regulations were tightened up.'

'That's ancient history,' interrupted Willis, her dark eyes flashing with irritation. 'This photograph was taken three months ago – '

'I was just getting to that,' said Collins, turning her gaze to meet that of her accuser. 'I haven't seen much of Stanley since I joined MIT, but I looked him up when I was working on a kidnap case. The money drop had been due to take place on the Blenheim and I thought some of Stanley's people might have seen something.

'I know that, technically, it was a breach of protocol, but we were up against the clock and there was no time to go through official channels. As it turned out, Stanley was able to provide some crucial information that had a significant impact on the resolution of the case.' She was doing well, sticking as close to the real truth as possible to keep her story convincing and her delivery natural.

Willis nodded slowly. 'We're fully aware of your

role in the Daniel Eliot case and I can see that someone in Stanley's position would have been well worth talking to.' She slid three more photographs across the table as she spoke. 'But that still leaves the question of why you went to see Stanley again three weeks later. And exactly why on earth you felt the need to take your thirteen-year-old daughter with you.'

Collins breathed in slowly and deeply through her nose, attempting to fill her lungs with a much needed calming breath without letting it show. She had expected the pictures of her and Stanley in the park. She had not expected these new shots. All her earlier responses had been carefully rehearsed. Now she would have to do it on the fly.

Don't rise to the bait. Don't let them get to you.

She carefully studied each picture. The first showed Collins getting out of her car in front of a set of large metal gates, the entrance to Stanley's palatial home. Inside the car, clearly visible in the passenger seat, was Sophie. The second photograph had been taken a few moments later. The gates were open and Jack Stanley was leaning casually against one of the posts. The third photograph showed Sophie out of the car and Jack Stanley smiling broadly at her.

Collins could sense that every pair of eyes in the room, including those of her Federation rep, were staring intently at her. She looked up from the photographs and met the gaze of DI Willis head on. 'It's completely innocent,' she said softly.

'Sophie had gone missing during the course of the kidnap investigation. I was distraught because the kidnapper had uncovered some personal information about me, and there seemed to be a possibility that he had snatched my daughter. I knew she had last been seen on the Blenheim, so I asked Stanley to help find her. A couple of hours later he delivered her safely to my parents. The day these photographs were taken, Sophie and I had simply gone there to thank him.'

There was an uncomfortable silence after Collins had finished her explanation.

'That seems a little unlikely,' said Willis, leaning back and folding her arms in front of her. 'And, might I say, pretty bloody convenient, considering what you are being accused of.'

'And what exactly am I being accused of?' asked Collins.

Willis looked across at Barker, who leaned forward, placing his elbows on the table in front of him. 'We are investigating allegations that you have been passing police intelligence to Jack Stanley.'

Don't rise to the bait.

'I have never done any such thing. I never would.'

'During the time he was an unregistered informant, did Stanley ever ask you for intelligence information?' asked Barker.

'Of course not.'

'Have you ever offered Stanley intelligence information?'

'No. Never. Absolutely not.'

'And what about during these two meetings? Did he ask you for anything in return for the assistance he had given you?'

At that moment Collins slowly, deliberately, swept her eyes across to her right in a move she had practised to absolute perfection.

Years of training and experience had taught Collins, along with other officers, common ways of telling when people are lying. When a person remembers something that actually happened to them, their eyes usually move to the right, an outward manifestation of the brain activating its memory centre, which is located in the right lobe. By contrast, when a person tells a lie, their eyes move up and to the left as their brain activates its cognitive centre to enable the person to create a false story.

Collins knew that looking to the left while she gave her explanation about the photograph would be an indication that she was making up her answer. But if she was going to survive this encounter with the DPS and SOCA officers unscathed, she was not only going to have to lie but she was also going to have to get away with it. Few could fake their eye movements as well as Collins could.

'No. He didn't ask me for anything. He wouldn't do that.'

DI Willis sat forward again and exhaled noisily. It was clear that she didn't believe a word of what she was hearing. 'This could all be bullshit. Is there anyone who can even confirm that your daughter had gone missing in the first place?' she said, a sarcastic tone evident to all in her voice.

Collins could feel the muscles tightening in her chest and her hackles rising. 'What are you trying to say? Are you calling me a liar? You asked me to explain why I had my daughter with me and I'm doing just that. At least do me the courtesy of hearing me out.'

'I did listen. I heard every one of your lies loud and clear and I don't care to hear any more.'

Don't rise to the ... ah hell with it.

A red cloud of mist seemed to fill Collins's eyes, and she slammed her fist down on the table in front of her. 'How dare you? Yes, there are other people who knew about Sophie being missing. I was desperate. I called everyone. Check with James McNultie, check with DS Woods, check with my parents, for God's sake.'

'We will, we'll check with them all. You bet we will.'

'You do that, and then you come back here and apologize when you realize I've been telling you the truth.'

'I'm just doing my job,' snapped Willis.

'What job is that? Spreading so much fear and mistrust among the rank and file that honest coppers are too scared to stick their necks out.'

'Anyone who sticks their neck out too far deserves to get it chopped off.'

Collins leaned towards Willis.

'Are you threatening me? You pissy little . . .'

Barker raised both his hands in the air. 'Okay, okay. Calm down. Both of you. I'll tell you what's going to happen right now, DI Collins. At this time there is no intention to charge you with any offence and therefore you will be free to return to your duties. You are not suspended. You'll be joining a new murder squad reporting to DCI Anderson. Per my orders, he'll be keeping a close eye on you. And if you want to use Jack Stanley or anyone else as an informant of any kind, you'll have to register them. I also suggest that in future any meetings with him – accidental or otherwise – should be logged with DCI Anderson or another senior officer.'

Collins shook her head. The time had come for her to make her closing statement, to wrap this up in a neat package. 'It was just a one-off, based on the circumstances of the time. There's no reason to think I'll be meeting up with Jack Stanley ever again. He was part of my past and, during the Eliot investigation, he briefly became part of my present, but I can assure you he has no place in my future or in that of my daughter.'

'Probably just as well,' said a voice from the far corner of the room. DCI Milton was speaking for the first time. 'SOCA are getting ready to make a move against Stanley's criminal empire. It's going to be a devastating blow. You wouldn't want to be anywhere near him when that goes down.'

Barker, Willis and Milton watched Collins and her

Fed rep walk out, shutting the door of the interview room behind them.

'So, what do you think?' asked Willis.

Barker sat back down and placed the tips of his index fingers at the base of his nose. 'She's hiding something. I'd put money on it. Covered it up well at the beginning, but it showed through when she lost her temper. Tell you what, Karen, you've got that annoying sceptical tone down to a tee.'

Willis giggled like a schoolgirl. 'There's nothing like a good wind-up for loosening the tongue. I'm not convinced she's passing information, though. She's way too savvy for anything like that. I'm inclined to believe her.'

'But pictures don't lie.'

'No, but we had that DI on her unit' – she checked her papers – 'Drabble, who was keeping an eye on her and she didn't come up with anything. I've reviewed her last few cases and as far as I'm concerned she's clean. Not totally flawless but clean enough.'

DCI Milton moved to the centre of the room and perched on the edge of the table. He wore glasses and had a neatly trimmed full-face beard that was just beginning to go grey at the outermost edges. Barker looked up at him. 'Being a bit free and easy with the old intel there, aren't you? I wasn't aware that SOCA had a raid planned; I didn't think you'd got that far.'

Milton smiled. 'We haven't. There's nothing

planned,' he said. 'But I want to see if any news of it gets back to Stanley. If it does, it can only have come from one place. And we'll know for sure if Collins is dirty or not.'

2

Stacey Collins emerged from the basement exit of New Scotland Yard and headed towards her BMW in the far corner of the underground car park. She switched on her mobile and checked the time, then hit a couple of buttons and held it up to her ear.

'Hi, Mum.'

'Stacey! I thought you were going to be tied up all morning.'

'So did I! The meeting finished early, so I'll head over and pick up Sophie now. See you in ten minutes.'

'Oh.'

'What do you mean "oh". What's going on?'

'It's nothing, dear. It's just that . . .'

'What, Mum? What's happened?'

'Promise you won't swear.'

'What is it? What's happened?'

'Jack's here.'

'Oh for fuck's sake. Mum!'

Her mother's voice dropped to a whisper. 'He's her father, Stacey. He has a right to see her. And she has a right to see him.'

'Not like this. Not behind my back. You have to let me deal with this my way, I told you that. Jesus

Christ. Do you have any idea how much trouble you could get me into?'

'What was the point of telling her, of telling all of us, and introducing them if you're not going to let him be part of her life?' Her mother was moving through the house with the phone now, trying to find a quiet corner to continue the conversation. 'You can't give with one hand and take away with the other. It's just not fair. It's not right.'

'You don't understand.'

'You're right I don't understand. Nor does your father. We don't understand why you kept this from us for all these years. Why did you keep it from her? What on earth were you thinking?'

'I wish I'd never told you anything. Any of you.'

'Well, that just says it all. You have no idea how much you've hurt your father, do you? You don't even care.'

Stacey bit her lip. The words cut her to the quick. She could hear her father in the background, grunting from the effort of manoeuvring his wheelchair around the furniture. She and her mother had offered to rearrange things to give him more room, but John Collins was as stubborn as a mule and had refused every time. Being in the wheelchair was one thing; living in a house that screamed disabled access rather than normality was more than his pride could take. 'You know that's not true,' Stacey continued. 'Look, I'm on my way. Don't let him leave until I get there.'

*

Jack Stanley was in the living room sharing a joke with Sophie and Stacey's father when she let herself into the house. She kissed her dad softly on the cheek but did not return Jack's cheerful smile when he looked over at her. All she could manage was a terse: 'We need to talk.'

Their physical relationship had been brief, a matter of a couple of weeks of playing around, followed by a single drunken night that Collins had long ago dismissed as a moment of weakness. She had discovered she was pregnant soon after Stanley's arrest for the gangland murder and, feeling certain that no father at all was better than one in prison, had kept it from him.

Sophie had been born while Jack was still on remand. After his release he had asked her only once about the child. Stacey had lied about Sophie's age to throw him off the scent, and Stanley had been kept in the dark ever since. She had finally revealed the truth a few weeks earlier.

Her parents' bedroom was far from ideal as a venue for a difficult conversation, but with the door firmly closed it was the most private place in the flat.

'You shouldn't be here, Jack.'

'Don't worry, Princess. I wasn't followed. Give me more credit than that.'

Stacey's eyes widened.

'I know I've been under surveillance,' Jack continued. 'But they're easy to get rid of.' He noticed the look on Stacey's face and smirked. 'What, you think you're my only police source?'

'I'm not your source at all,' she protested. 'This has got to stop. You can't see Sophie any more. Not like this anyway.'

'What are you talking about? No one is going to find out.'

'They've already found out. They have pictures of the three of us together. That day we came round and I told you about her. I've had internal affairs on my back all afternoon. They could be outside right now. If they find out you're here, I could get sacked.'

Stanley's eyes fell to the floor in thought. 'But if they already know . . .'

'They don't know you're Sophie's father and I don't want them to know. It's one thing having you as an unregistered informant; there's no conflict of interest there. I can still be trusted. I can still do my job. I don't think anyone is going to feel the same if they find out you're the father of my child.'

'You owe me,' snapped Stanley, his voice getting louder. 'I saved your arse with that kidnapped kid case. Let's face it, you've built your whole fucking career on the back of my graft.'

'And you've built yours by breaking the law. You'd be banged up if it wasn't for me.'

They stared at each other for a few moments, breathing hard, neither one willing to back down. Finally Stanley waved a hand in the air dismissively.

'Oh, this is ridiculous. This is my daughter we're talking about. You keep her a secret from me for thirteen years. Then, when you finally tell me and invite me to be part of her life, you get cold feet about it. You can't turn the clock back. What's done is done. You're just going to have to find a way to deal with it.'

Stanley glanced at his watch. 'Enough of this bollocks. I've got to go. I've got somewhere I need to be. But this isn't over. Finding out that I have a daughter is the best thing that ever happened to me and I intend to make the most of it. Now I'm willing to be careful, I'm willing to take precautions, but that's as far as it goes. You try to come between me and Sophie, and I'll give you more trouble than you can handle.'

With a grim snarl on his face, Stanley pushed past Stacey, knocking into her shoulder as he headed for the door. When he pulled it open, Sophie was standing directly outside. Stanley's face immediately broke out in a huge smile.

'Hello, Princess. I was just coming to find you. I'm gonna have to go.'

'Do you have to? It feels like you only just got here?'

'My business won't run itself. But cheer up. I've got a present for you. It's in my bag in the living room. Come on.'

Before Sophie followed, she turned back and stared into the eyes of her mother. She would never admit anything, but Stacey knew she had probably heard every word of their conversation. Stacey opened her mouth to speak, but Sophie had already gone.

Three hours later and back at her own house, Stacey Collins stood outside Sophie's bedroom, trying to summon up the courage to step inside.

She was racked with guilt and convinced that she was without a doubt the most terrible mother in the whole wide world. For years now the worst of her arguments with her daughter had almost always revolved around the fact that Sophie desperately resented not having a father in her life. Time and time again Sophie complained about the fact that her mother worked such unsociable hours and always, always seemed to put her job first. 'But none of that would matter,' a tearful Sophie would sob, 'if I had a dad.'

Stacey had grown up with two parents who were always there for her, and, even when their own relationship hit a few bumps, stayed together for the sake of their daughter. Sophie had known no such security, and for years Stacey had decided that it was better to lie than to face the truth: that Sophie's father had been right under her nose all along. But now that she had brought the two of them together and it was too late to turn back, Stacey found herself wondering whether, despite the aggravation, her original instincts had been the right ones.

Was a gangland father really better than no father at all?

She was only too well aware of the extent of Stanley's criminal enterprises but she had purposely blinkered herself off from his activities. Now for the first time she had to accept that her daughter shared DNA with a man capable of the most inhuman acts possible. And the thought made her shudder.

There was no doubt in Stacey's mind that Jack Stanley was fully capable of carrying out cold blooded murder. She was a hundred per cent certain that he had only been acquitted in the earlier case because the witnesses had been left terrified. God only knew how many other killings and deaths he had had a hand in. Yet all that Sophie could see was a man who bought her presents and had the time to spend with her that her mother did not.

She had finally relented to Sophie's demands in a moment of emotional weakness, and at the time she had been convinced that she was doing the right thing. But now she was far less sure. What if Sophie found out the truth about her father? What if he ended up in the dock on another murder charge? Sophie could find herself despising them both.

Stacey's mind drifted back to the forthcoming raid the SOCA officer had mentioned. Could it be true, and if so why mention it to someone who is suspected of passing on information to the target? She had said nothing to Stanley and had no intention of doing so. Her instincts told her it was a test, a kind of trap, but a part of her hoped it was for real. An arrest for drug trafficking would be the lesser of numerous evils. Sophie would be upset but at least she would get to know the truth about her father before the bond between them got too deep. It would be for the best.

Stacey knocked on the bedroom door and gently pushed it open. Sophie was sitting up in bed on top of the covers, her eyes shut and her head slowly bobbing back and forth.

'Sophie, can we talk?'

There was no response. Ever since Sophie had become a teenager, Stacey had become used to the silent treatment. But upon closer inspection she realized there was another reason that her daughter had not heard her: two thin white wires led down from under her hair on either side of her chin and into her lap. Sophie was listening to the brand-new iPod Touch that Jack had given her.

Stacey moved forward and touched her daughter gently on the shoulder. Sophie's eyes opened with a start, and she fumbled with the controls on her music player to turn it off before pulling the headphones from her ears, one at a time.

Stacey sat down on the bed alongside her.

'Listen, Sophie, I don't know how to say this. There's no easy way, so I'm just going to come out with it. I don't think you're going to be able to see your father any more. Not for a while anyway.'

'Why, what's happened?'

'Nothing, nothing's happened, but it's just . . . there are things going on, things going on at work that you don't know about, things I can't really explain to you that mean it's difficult, actually impossible right now.'

Sophie eyed her mother cautiously, weighing up her words. 'You're jealous?'

'Don't be ridiculous.'

'Who's being ridiculous? You are jealous. Of course you are. That's why you never wanted to introduce him to me before. That's why you want me to stop seeing him now. It's because you can see how close we're becoming, because he treats me like an adult, not like a little girl, he shows up your failings, it's because – '

'Just shut up and listen. You don't know that man the way that I do. Jack Stanley is . . . he's done some bad things in his life. Things that could get him into a lot of trouble. With my job, I can't be seen to be associating with someone like that.'

'But you're not, Mum. I am.'

'It affects me too.'

'You just don't want us to be together.'

'That's not true, darling. If I didn't want that I would never have introduced you to him in the first place.'

Stacey sighed deeply and ran her fingers through Sophie's hair. 'I know you feel like you've missed out your whole life by not having a father around. And now that he is in your life you must feel as though

I'm trying to take that away from you, but that's not the case.'

'It does feel like that.'

'You have to understand that there are things about Jack, about your father, that you don't know about. Things that have happened in his past that — '

'Like him being in prison? He's told me all about that. And you're right, it's in the past.'

'There's more to it than that. It's dangerous.' Stacey tried to think of the best way to put this, a way that wouldn't give her daughter nightmares. 'Some of the things that your father has done in the past, they're the kind of things that can make a lot of people angry. I worry about you, and at the moment I just don't know if it's safe for you to be seen with him.'

'But nobody sees us, not if he comes round to Nan's.'

'I'm sorry, Sophie. I just can't allow that.'

For a moment it looked as though Sophie was going to cry, but then her resolve stiffened. She looked directly at her mother, tiny traces of moisture in the corners of her eyes. 'I don't want to do anything to upset you or get you into trouble, Mum. I mean, it's great having a dad and everything after all this time, but I'll never forget that you're the one who brought me up. You're the one I owe everything to.'

'Thanks, Sophie.'

'Though if you'd told him about me earlier, then

he probably would have been around a lot more.'

'Sophie!'

'I'm just saying.' Sophie looked down at the iPod in her lap. 'Okay. I don't really understand why but, if you really think I shouldn't see Dad for the time being, then I won't. But it can't go on for ever. I want him in my life. I really do.'

'And he will be one day. I promise.'

'Okay.'

Stacey smiled, reached out with both arms and pulled Sophie into a huge hug. Their bodies pressed together and their chins rested on each other's shoulders as they held each other tightly.

'Thanks, Sophie. I love you. You're the best.'

'I love you too, Mum,' said Sophie, rolling her eyes up to the ceiling.

3

Tunde Okuma pointed a short, stubby finger towards the end of the line of cars parked along the quiet Peckham side street and sighed. 'One day,' he said with his thick Nigerian accent and a dreamy look in his eyes, 'one day, my friend, I am going to have one of those for myself.'

His colleague Matt Dunn squinted over at the gleaming silver Mercedes and grinned. 'You mean you're going to give up work and start stealing cars for a living?'

'Funny. But you won't be smiling when my dream comes true.'

As long-suffering traffic wardens for the London Borough of Southwark, Dunn and Okuma always saw more than their fair share of cars. But in such a deprived area, luxury models like the Merc were something of a rarity. The local drug dealers and pimps had long ago learned that flashy motors brought too much police attention, while any resident able to buy one legitimately would do so only if they had a garage to park it in.

Up until then it had been a good morning. Between them the pair had issued five PCNs apiece, their first break was fast approaching, and to top it all off the sun was shining. However, the side street looked as though it was going to be a dead loss until Okuma reached the Mercedes. His eyes lit up immediately when he saw there was no ticket displayed on the windscreen.

'Result,' he said eagerly, reaching for the machine hanging from his belt.

'Wait up,' said Dunn, hurrying over from the other side of the road. 'Better make sure it hasn't dropped down somewhere.'

'Who cares?'

'It's a nice car. And you know the rule. The nicer the car, the bigger the prick behind the wheel. I don't want any trouble if the driver turns up and we're still on scene.'

Trouble was something both men had come to expect as part of the job, but Okuma was by far the more wary of the two. The previous day he had been on patrol at a local authority car park near a busy shopping centre. He spotted a young woman in a filthy VW manoeuvring her car so badly that she ended up taking up the space of two bays. Okuma made his way over to her just as she was climbing out of the car, planning to ask her politely to repark her car so that he wouldn't have to give her a ticket.

She wore ill-fitting lycra leggings and a faux leopard-skin top and turned to face him as he approached. He had barely opened his mouth when the woman began screaming at him, a stream of abuse and filth pouring out of her mouth. He was a prick, an arsehole, a fucking Nazi and more. She would not shut up and would not listen to anything he had to say. It was impossible to get a word in edgeways to explain that he was only trying to be nice.

Eventually, with a menacing-looking crowd beginning to gather in order to see what all the commotion was about, Okuma gave up and walked away, leaving the woman to think she had managed to get out of a ticket that Okuma had had no intention of issuing in the first place. It was the sort of incident that seemed to be happening more and more often, especially when the driver concerned had a nice car.

Since becoming a warden, Okuma had been kicked in the shins, spat at, had a tin of processed peas thrown at him and been called every name under the sun along with a fair few that seemed to have come from an alternative universe. The last time he'd ticketed a Merc the burly owner had threatened to cut his balls off. If Dunn wanted to hang about, Okuma decided it would be better for his colleague to take the lead.

Okuma stepped back as Dunn cupped his hand against the side window and peered inside. A fraction of a second later Dunn leaped back in surprise. 'Fuck! Scared the shit out of me.'

'What is it?'

'There's someone inside. On the back seat. Looks like they're sleeping. Must have been out on the town and got too pissed to drive home.'

Okuma stepped forward to see for himself. There was no mistaking it. A figure was curled up on the rear seat in the foetal position. The upper half of the body was covered in a thick woollen blanket. Two legs, visible only from the knees downwards, emerged from the other end. They were clad in dark trousers, grey socks and finished off with polished Oxford cap shoes.

Okuma began tapping at the window. 'Sir, excuse me, sir, but you can't leave your car here without a valid ticket.' There was no response. He tapped louder. 'Sir? Sir!' Still nothing.

It was then that he noticed the small black cylinder on the inside of the window was in the raised position: the door was open. He tugged at the handle and was immediately hit by a wave of warm, fetid air. The smell of soft leather and wood polish was mixed with something unspeakably awful. Something unmistakable. Something no longer alive. The smell of decay. The smell of death.

'Oh, Jesus,' he gasped.

Okuma was almost in a trance as he reached forward to grab the edge of the blanket with trembling fingers. He pulled it back. His eyes needed only an instant to take in the ragged skin at the top of the neck, where a grey ooze seeped out in place of a head, the cavernous opening in the centre of the bloated chest and the stiff arms ending in bloody, mutilated stumps.

Okuma turned away and threw up violently,

gulping down desperate lungfuls of fresh air. Then he reached for his radio.

When the call about a headless, handless body had first come into the Murder Investigation Team office at Peckham, Collins had not been surprised that it had been assigned to one of the other DIs on the unit. It had been more than six weeks since her interview – or should that be interrogation – with the DPS; yet, despite receiving assurances that she would face neither criminal nor disciplinary charges over her dealings with Jack Stanley, she knew that she remained firmly in the doghouse so far as her superiors were concerned.

It was clear that DCI Anderson, the newly appointed head of the MIT, did not rate her as a detective at all, and the two cases she had worked on since he began had given her precious little opportunity to stand out from the crowd.

The first had been a so-called 'self-solver' – one of those murder cases in which the identity of the prime suspect is known from the outset and a full confession is blurted out soon after the moment of arrest. Even the most junior, inexperienced detective could not fail to get a result under such circumstances.

The second case had involved the drive by shooting of a shady businessman who had made so many enemies that it was almost impossible to whittle down the massive list of potential suspects. To make matters worse the victim himself, only lightly injured in the attack, had refused to cooperate, rapidly forcing the attempted murder investigation into a stalemate.

All of which made it hugely surprising that, less than an hour after his arrival at the latest murder scene, DCI Anderson had put in a request for DI Collins and other members of the team to join him there.

The obvious question – why? – played on her mind as she steered her BMW through the South London streets. In Collins's experience, such an early call for more resources could mean only one thing: that the victim was a celebrity, somebody who mattered, and that maximum manpower was being called in to crack the case.

The first forty-eight hours of an investigation are by far the most crucial. Memories of potential eye-witnesses are still fresh, forensic samples have not degraded, and those responsible for the murder are still likely to have crucial evidence in their posses-sion. By bringing in the whole team, Anderson was clearly hoping to get a quick result and therefore cement his position as the new team leader. Collins thought back to the Jill Dando murder inquiry, when more than a hundred detectives had been brought in to track down the killer of the popular BBC presenter.

Having parked at the end of the cordon, Collins made her way towards the line of blue-and-white tape that was stretched across the road. A crowd of nosy onlookers watched jealously as she ducked underneath and showed her ID to the Community Service Officer on guard. 'DCI Anderson is waiting for you over at the mobile command unit,' he said flatly.

Collins quickly spotted Anderson in the midst of a group of other officers outside the small Portakabin decked out in police colours that would be the team's base in the early hours of the inquiry. Her own DS, Tony Woods, was already there, as were DS Richard Porter and DI Leonard Hill, the two officers Anderson had brought with him to the murder team. There were also a few DCs, and Collins silently cursed herself for being one of the last to arrive. The presence of a mobile command unit meant they were in for the long haul. She would have to call her parents and get them to look after Sophie for the evening.

Anderson was in his mid forties, well over six feet tall with the kind of slim, athletic build that suggested he either spent hours in the gym or was a sports fanatic in his spare time. Clean shaven, his dark, wavy hair had been styled into a smart-yet-fashionable cut. His deep hazel eyes seemed to flash with irritation as he spotted Collins coming towards him, and he took a long drag on the cigarette he had been smoking.

'I got here as soon as I could sir,' said Collins. 'What's going on? Who's the victim?'

Anderson said nothing for a moment but just eyed Collins carefully as a stream of smoke slid out of his nostrils. 'Don't know,' he said at last. 'Haven't got a positive ID for any of them yet.'

'Them? I thought there was only one.'

'That's because you're late. Follow me, Collins.'

He set off at a rapid pace towards the large white incident tent that had been erected to cover both the car and its immediate surroundings. A box of protective paper suits, along with their accompanying masks and overshoes, sat outside the entrance.

Anderson and Collins both suited up before he led her inside, reminding her to stick to the makeshift path of plastic planks that had been laid out to avoid the crime scene being contaminated. Spotlights blazed away from the corners of the tent. Grim-faced forensic officers wearing knee pads carried out a fingertip search of the ground around the vehicle, while others dusted the doors and windows for prints. Blowflies were swarming all around and the stench of death was everywhere. Collins knew she would smell it in her hair and taste it in the back of her throat for the next few days at least. Every now and then there was a huge flash of light as the police photographer took another snap of the remains. Anderson steered Collins towards the back-passenger side door of the car, which was wide open.

'This is victim one,' he said. 'Found by a couple of traffic wardens. Hasn't been touched apart from having the blanket that was covering the upper half of the body pulled away.'

Collins held her breath and leaned towards the car

to get a better look. With its missing head and open, empty chest cavity, the corpse looked more like a cattle carcass from a meat market than like anything human.

She could see the white of the bones along the edges of the hole where the ribs had been ripped apart and the ragged flaps of muscle and tissue hanging down inside like shredded curtains. There was no sign of the missing organs in the footwell or elsewhere on the backseat and precious little blood anywhere – a firm indication that the victim had been killed elsewhere.

The body was naked from the waist upwards. The lower half was clad in trousers that had been pushed down to just above the knees. In the place where the genitals should have been Collins saw only another gaping hole.

Having taken in all she could, Collins stepped back and Anderson led her towards the rear of the car, where the boot lid had been raised. Inside Collins saw two more figures that had once been human beings but were now reduced to something almost unbearable to look at.

The bodies, both naked, had been arranged top to tail, the limbs twisted into awkward angles to fit into the available space. Once again both were missing heads and hands, but this time Collins had a close-up view of the decapitations.

The tissues of the neck were severed all around down to the bone. The remaining bright red flesh had become wet and slimy, and seemed to pulse slowly as thousands of tiny white maggots moved across its surface.

Collins held her breath and gulped air in through her mouth to prevent her from throwing up.

'Jesus,' she gasped.

'Looks like the MO's the same on all three victims. Best I can tell they are all men of a roughly similar age. IC1s. I've seen this level of decomp before and it's the same for all three. I'm working on the assumption that the bodies are a couple of days old at most. It's gonna be a right git of a case. Triple killings like this are as rare as rocking horse shit.'

'Do you think it could be some sort of gangland vendetta, a drugs hit maybe?'

'That was my first thought, but that doesn't square with the open chest cavities. The organs could have been taken as trophies or for some kind of ceremony. Either way, we're looking for a seriously sick bastard.'

Collins cocked her head to one side as she looked at the corpses. Outside of the drugs world, the usual pattern for a serial killer was for the murders to take place one at a time and for the rate of killing to escalate over a period of months or years. For someone to begin with a triple homicide was unprecedented.

'No one starts out like this,' she said, thinking out loud. 'We should check the cold case files to see if there has been anything like this before.'

'Already been done and we've drawn a blank,' said Anderson. 'Plenty of headless bodies and a few corpses with missing organs, but never the two combined. We're breaking new ground here. Lucky us.'

Anderson glanced at his watch. 'Initial briefing in ten minutes inside the MCU. Try not to be late again.'

'Yes, sir.'

As she watched Anderson leave the tent, Collins briefly pondered the fact that it was a shame he was such an arsehole. If not, he would almost be her type. Just outside the entrance, Anderson was stopped by a tall, slender woman with chestnut-brown hair peeking out from behind the confines of a white-paper hood. Collins immediately recognized her as Dr Jessica Matthews, the Home Office pathologist with whom she had worked with many times before.

Anderson could only summon up a tight smile and brief handshake in response to the doctor's cheerful greeting. Matthews entered the tent, closely followed by the Crime Scene Manager. Collins couldn't help but notice that the pathologist even managed to look good in her protective disposable white boiler suit.

Although the situation continued to improve, the police force was still dominated by men and male values, and many of the women working within it seemed to think the only way to get on was to have bigger balls and more testosterone than their male counterparts. He-bitches, Collins called them. But Jessica Matthews was different, far more like Collins herself. Resolutely professional and with an air of absolute authority, she walked her own path and refused to be led by those around her. Collins liked and admired her enormously as a result. She was one of the few women she came across during her working life that she considered to be a friend.

'Hi, Jessica.'

'Hey, Stacey, lovely to see you.'

Collins looked over her shoulder towards the bodies in the boot. 'Hardly lovely circumstances.'

Matthews smiled, showing a row of perfect teeth. 'Come, come, Stacey, we only ever meet at crime scenes or at the mortuary. There's always a dead body or two close to hand.'

Matthews leaned in close over the two bodies in the boot and then did the same with the remaining corpse, her eyes dancing around as she quickly took in all the details. Collins was rooted to the spot, fascinated by the sight of the pathologist at work. Matthews half climbed into the back of the car, resting her knee on the edge of the seat and leaning forward so she could run her gloved fingertips lightly over the edge of the open chest cavity. 'Well, no stomach, so no contents for me to look at, and no liver for me to take a reading from,' she said out loud. 'No head means no eyes, so no chance of a fluid check. Not enough blood on the seat to suggest death was in situ so there's little point in checking lividity.' She looked back at Collins. 'Nothing like a challenge to brighten your day.'

The pathologist looked around the tent, seeking out the police photographer. 'Have you got all angles on this?'

The man nodded. 'Stills from both sides and on top. I also shot some video. I've got all I need. The CSM says it's fine for you to move them if you need to.'

Matthews nodded and turned back to the body. She reached forward, gripped the edge of the severed forearm and tried to pull it straight. It did not budge. 'Rigor mortis,' she said to no one in particular. 'That puts time of death somewhere in the last twenty-four hours. Fits in well with the level of putrefaction when you factor in the open wounds.' She reached into her bag and pulled out a long, slender, rectal thermometer.

Collins winced. 'I really don't know how you can do your job,' she said softly. 'I mean, I see dead bodies occasionally, but to have to deal with them so intimately day in day out, I don't know how you cope. Especially when they're in this sort of condition.'

Matthews looked up and smiled. 'It's not so bad. I see myself as the victims' last hope if they're going to get justice. The blood, the gore, the bodies – none of it bothers me. But what does is trying to get my head round what goes through the minds of the people who can do such terrible things to another human being. I want to get as much evidence as I can to help you guys catch whoever was responsible.'

She paused and began prodding at the skin of the corpse's thigh with her index finger.

'I'm really glad you're working on this job. I never know who I'm going to be dealing with from one case to the next until I get to the crime scene. There are so many slimy coppers out there, it's good to have you on board. How are you finding the new DCI?'

'Seems efficient enough.'

Matthews turned, her eyes wide. 'That's a very diplomatic answer, Stacey. You two not getting on?'

'I think I've managed to work my way into his bad books already.'

'Between you and me, I hear he doesn't like working with women. Thinks we should all be at home in the kitchen or something like . . .'

Matthews stopped speaking. She had removed the thermometer and was staring hard at it, her forehead creased with a frown.

'What's wrong?' asked Collins.

'Doesn't make sense. I've just taken a reading. This guy has early-stage rigor mortis but his core temperature is lower than ambient.'

'What does that mean?'

'Bodies normally cool down to room temperature after death, but at ten degrees Celsius, this one is well below the temperature of his surroundings, so he's actually warming up. I'd need to check the other two, but my guess would be that the bodies have been kept in cold storage.'

'You mean frozen?'

'Possibly, but not necessarily frozen solid. Just somewhere cold enough to retard the normal death processes. I'd need to do more tests.'

Collins's mind was buzzing. 'So how long ago could they have been murdered?'

Matthews laughed. 'There's no crystal ball in my bag, Stacey. I have no idea at this stage. I'm just telling you what the initial evidence suggests. Could be hours. Could be days. Could be weeks. I really couldn't say.'

'Well, that means they might not have been killed at the same time. They could be months apart.' Collins stepped forward and took another look at the two bodies in the boot. 'We could be looking at a serial killer.' Collins glanced at her watch. 'Shit. I'd better go. I don't want to be late for the briefing. Thanks for that, Jessica.'

'Good luck.'

Collins took a few steps towards the entrance of the tent, then stopped and turned back. 'We should do it, you know.'

Matthews was puzzled. 'Do what?'

'Meet up again, without a body. The last time was what, a year ago?'

'More like a year and a half. It was after that serial rapist case, wasn't it? Christ, that makes me feel old.'

'You and me both.'

'That's right, we went to that Italian place, do you remember?'

'I do now.'

'Let's sort something out. I'll call you once I've got the PMs out of the way, some time towards the end of the week.'

'You're on.'

'Nice of you to join us, DI Collins,' Anderson said glibly as Collins squeezed her way on the edge of the semicircle of officers that had gathered around him inside the small room. Tony Woods shot her a weak smile before turning his eyes back to the boss.

'Another key field I want to get on right away is CCTV,' Anderson continued. 'This car can't have been there more than a few hours. The traffic and congestion charge people are already looking into it but I want to gather CCTV from this area as well. We want to see if we've caught any images of the driver decanting. We need to move fast – these private cameras tend to erase their stuff in a few hours and my nose will be seriously out of joint if we lose anything because we weren't quick enough off the mark.

'I want uniform carrying out house-to-house for the same reason. And let's track down the drivers of the cars that were parked in front of and directly behind this vehicle at the time the bodies were found, see if they remember anything.' Anderson sighed as he saw Collins raise a hand in the air. 'What is it, Collins?'

'Sir. I was just talking to the pathologist. It seems highly likely that the bodies are older than they look.

I think they may have been kept in cold storage. It means they might not even have been killed at the same time. The deaths could be days, even weeks apart.'

A murmur ran through the crowd of officers, and Woods began shuffling uncomfortably from one foot to the other. Anderson thumbed the end of his nose, then folded his arms and stared hard at Collins. 'And for your next trick you can come round to my house and teach my granny to suck eggs!'

Collins looked around, bewildered. 'I don't understand.'

'We'd already worked that one out, Collins. DS Porter, for the sake of our latecomer here, why don't you recap what you told us all a few minutes ago?'

Porter, a heavy-set blond man with small beady eyes, flicked through the pages of his notebook before he spoke. 'The car belongs to a Mr Raymond Chadwick, forty-four, a property developer, reported missing by his wife approximately six weeks ago. Described as five feet ten, heavy build, IC1. Last seen wearing a charcoal double-breasted jacket, matching trousers and black Oxford cap shoes. No mobile phone, bank or credit card activity reported since his disappearance. No ransom demand received by the family.'

Anderson nodded as he listened to the details, then cleared his throat. 'Working on the assumption that Chadwick is the man on the back seat – though we'll need DNA confirmation before we can be absolutely sure – it seems unlikely that he went awol for the best part of two months, vanished off the face of the earth, only to get himself killed just twenty-four hours ago.'

Anderson looked at the officers gathered around him before fixing Collins with his glare. 'Three bodies at once would be bad news. This is even worse. Three bodies from three different times with a cooling-off period in between. Looks like we've got a serial killer on our hands. Not only that, we've got a serial killer who wanted us to make a link between three separate killings. They needed to be sure we knew what was going on right from the start.'

Collins felt as though all the wind had been taken out of her sails. She wanted to kick herself as she listened to all the prime assignments connected to the case being handed out to those around her. She felt particularly cut to the quick when Woods was told to gather background information on Chadwick in order to expand the victim's profile. Soon it seemed she was the only one on the team with nothing to do.

'What would you like me to work on, sir?' she said meekly as the other officers began to drift away.

'News of the find has been broken on the after-noon TV bulletins,' said Anderson. 'That means we've had a couple of confessors come in already. I want you to take their statements and eliminate them from the inquiry.'

Every major crime always attracted a group of 'confessors' who came forward, admitted involvement and desperately wanted to be punished. Although they were regulars, they still had to be interviewed and their statements logged so they could be eliminated from the inquiry. This was always a relatively simple matter, as they knew almost no details of the crime other than whatever they had managed to glean from the TV and newspapers. They were a necessary evil in every incident room, but dealing with them was normally a task for some of the most junior officers on the team, not a DI.

'With respect, sir, I think I'd be more usefully employed elsewhere on this job – '

Anderson cut her off sharply. 'If you want my respect, Collins, then I suggest you start out by doing what I say and not questioning my authority.'

Collins bit her lip and took a deep breath. She had to calm down fast before she said something she wouldn't be able to take back. Or worse still threw a punch. The last thing she wanted was to be hauled back in front of the DPS. She pushed her anger way down into the pit of her stomach and spoke as calmly as she could.

'Yes, sir.'

4

DCI Anderson had asked the entire team to gather in the incident room at 9 a.m. the following morning for a briefing. Collins had arrived almost an hour earlier to write up her notes on the interviews she had conducted the previous evening with the confessors.

She had barely been at her desk ten minutes when Anderson arrived. He acknowledged her presence with a small nod and a half-grunt before making his way directly to his office in the corner of the room and shutting the door firmly behind him.

Over the next half hour other members of the team began to arrive and the skeleton crew who had been manning the incident room overnight left to head home.

As Collins peered at her computer screen, a shadow fell over her desk.

'Cheer up, it might never happen!'

Collins looked up to see the smiling face of Tony Woods looking down on her.

'Too late. It's already happened,' she replied.

Woods perched on the edge of her desk and leaned towards her, lowering his voice to a whisper. 'I don't know what he's playing at. I honestly don't. I tried having a word with him yesterday, saying he was wasting a valuable resource by keeping you on the edge of the main investigation, but he just wouldn't hear it.'

Collins smiled weakly. 'Thanks, Tony, but I think I'm on my own for this one. If I get a good break on the case, he'll probably start trusting me, but until he starts trusting me, I won't be in a position to get a break on the case. Catch-22.'

Woods was nodding slowly. 'You could always try sleeping with him.'

Collins didn't miss a beat. 'Well, it certainly helped when I applied for my last promotion.' She looked up at Woods and allowed her face to break into a full smile. 'I'm kidding,' she said.

'I know,' said Woods. 'So was I. What about talking to Higgins?'

'No, that would really piss Anderson off. I know I'm being kept out of the loop because of the trouble with the DPS.'

'But you haven't done anything wrong,' said Woods.

'I know, but when people start throwing mud around, some of it is bound to stick. Just being called in by the DPS is enough to convince most people you must be bent, regardless of whether there's any actual evidence.'

She swept her hand back through her hair. 'How did you get on with the backgrounder?'

Woods shrugged. 'Nothing that runs the flag up the flagpole. Married, couple of kids, one sister and two brothers. Both his parents are alive but divorced. Worked as a commercial property developer at some bigwig firm in the City. Not so much nine to five, more eight to eight, which is why he got the big bucks. The Merc was a company car.

'No evidence of financial worries, nothing to suggest problems with drink or drugs. Small circle of friends. Enjoyed his job. No enemies. Pretty unremarkable by all accounts. I'm going to see the widow later this morning.'

'Are we treating her as a suspect?' asked Collins.

'The DCI told me to keep an open mind, but we both agree it's pretty unlikely. I managed to track down a few of his work colleagues and one of his siblings. It wasn't the happiest marriage by all accounts, and there seems to be pretty strong evidence of at least one affair going back over the years. The wife's in line for a pretty good insurance payout, but to be honest it's a fair bit below what she would have got if she had divorced him. It's not really motive. We'd be looking at her a lot more closely if it was just Chadwick who had turned up dead.'

Collins nodded. 'I know what you mean. Once you get more than one body involved, it stops being a simple murder. When you have three with the same MO, there doesn't have to be any rhyme or reason behind it.'

'So what's your theory, then?'

'Haven't really got one yet. It all rests on who the

other two victims are. Everyone who gets killed gets chosen one way or another, even if it's just completely random. If we find out what criteria the killer is using to choose victims, that might lead us right to him.'

DS Porter and DI Hill bustled into the incident room and Collins eyed them warily. Anderson had brought them on to the team after having worked with them on his last two assignments. As a consequence they usually got to work at the sharpest end of a case, and Collins wasn't the only one who resented them for it.

'I can't believe you're still stuck on confessor duty,' said Woods.

A few moments later the door to Anderson's office opened and he stepped out, taking a moment to mentally check that everyone from the team was present, before making his way to the notice board on the far wall.

He pinned up a sheet of paper with RAYMOND CHADWICK printed on it in large block capitals.

'This is victim one. I've just been on the phone to forensics and they've matched the remains found at the scene with DNA recovered from his home.' He looked around the room until his eyes found those of DS Woods. 'Tony, when you see the widow, try to get hold of a picture of him so we can put one up here.'

Woods nodded.

Anderson stepped to one side and pinned up a

second sheet of paper, this time with the name EDWARD MILLER printed on it.

'This is victim number two. We've had a bit of a lucky break. Mr Miller got himself convicted of GBH three years ago, so his DNA was on the database. Now I can see all your little brains buzzing away and getting ready to ask the obvious question – could this be linked to his death? The short answer is, of course, and it's a line of inquiry some of you will be pursuing vigorously during the course of the next few days.'

Collins sighed quietly. She would have cheerfully bet money that she would not be one of those chosen to pursue that particular line of inquiry.

'What's interesting about Miller is that he has been missing for the best part of two years.' Anderson paused to let this sink in with the members of the team. 'Yesterday we were working on the theory that the deaths might have taken place a few weeks apart, but this massively expands that timescale. This killer clearly has access to cold-storage facilities, and, according to the experts, under the right conditions a body can be preserved pretty much indefinitely. It's going to make the search for victim number three that much harder because we'll have to go back as far as we can. And it goes without saying that we drew a blank on the DNA database so far as the third victim was concerned.'

Anderson pinned up a third sheet of paper, this time with a large question mark printed on it. He stood back and looked at the names on the board, then turned and faced his team.

'At this stage, in the absence of any firm leads, we're going to get things moving by looking very closely at the two victims we have managed to identify. I want to know every single thing there is to know about them. Habits, routines, likes, dislikes. Shoes sizes, fetishes. I want to know how they vote, how many sugars they take in their tea and the name of every single person they ever associated with. We're looking for anyone who might make us think they are worth looking at more closely.

'Now that it seems certain that we're looking for a serial killer, I'm going to be getting a profiler in. That will hopefully give us some valuable leads. I'm also hoping they might be able to narrow down the geographical area our killer is likely to be in.

'The street where the bodies were found is a little way off the beaten track, quiet enough to ensure they wouldn't be discovered immediately. That takes local knowledge. It might well be that that particular street was chosen as the dumping ground for a specific reason. The profiler might be able to cast some light on that too.

'Dr Matthews has given me a preliminary verbal report, but the full post-mortem and toxicology write-ups won't be available for at least forty-eight hours. Although we have three victims, the post-mortems will be quicker than usual because of the lack of heads, hands and internal organs. It means they have much less work to do. Unfortunately it also means we are going to have a lot less to go on from forensics.'

Anderson leaned back against the wall and shoved his hands deep into his pockets. 'I don't want to be patronizing but I want this done by the book. This is going to be a major inquiry and I don't want to leave any stone unturned. I don't want a review squad coming in here in six weeks' time because we haven't got a result and telling me that we've missed a load of obvious leads.

'I expect you to submit your intelligence reports into the HOLMES system a.s.a.p. so that I can see what progress is being made. But I find the quickest and easiest way to make sure that everyone on the team is up to speed is for you all to summarize your positions in regular morning briefings, or "morning prayers", as I like to call them. That way everyone can stay cross-referenced with what every other part of the team is doing without having to spend hours trawling through the system to dig up every statement. So who wants to go first?'

DS Porter stood up and opened his notebook. 'Myself and DI Hill have collected approximately twenty-two hours' worth of CCTV footage from a variety of sources, covering streets close to where the bodies were found and some of the main roads leading to it. But there are no images of the street where the car was actually parked.

'Some of the cameras show foot traffic in the area

and we might have caught the driver on film, but several hundred people walk through the area each day. Without some kind of description of whoever it was behind the wheel, we can't begin to eliminate anyone from our inquiries.'

Porter sat down and the officer beside him stood up. And so it continued around the room until each officer had given a short presentation of their work so far. Anderson made notes and asked a few questions. The breakthrough he had been hoping for was yet to emerge. Dozens of lines of inquiry were still being followed and hundreds of 'actions' were being dealt with. Nothing was being overlooked and, so far, nothing conclusive had been found.

When all the presentations were complete, Anderson threw the floor open for discussion. Collins put her hand up. She saw the DCI's jaw tighten as he nodded at her.

'The initial pathology report confirms that some of the internal organs of all three victims have been removed,' she said.

'That's correct, yes.'

'Do you therefore think that we're looking for someone with medical training?'

Anderson shrugged. 'Possibly. It depends on what you define as medical training. Even a schoolboy knows the difference between a heart and a kidney. And you can get all sorts of stuff off the internet these days. A doctor or surgeon or someone similar may well be behind all this, but I don't want that to be our only focus. And I certainly don't want to exclude suspects that have no link to the medical profession, not at this stage.'

A few other members of the team asked questions of their own until the energy in the room started to fade. 'Okay. Let's not stand around talking. Let's get to work.' Anderson began handing out assignments for the day and once again Collins found herself sidelined from the heart of the investigation.

Her task was to work with staff at the National Missing Persons helpline and compile a list of potential names for victim number three. Both Chadwick and Miller had been listed as missing at the time their bodies were found, so there was a good chance that the same would be true of the third victim, but Collins quickly discovered that the task was far more daunting than she could ever have imagined. After teenagers, middle-aged men are the most likely group to go missing, usually as a result of some kind of financial or emotional crisis. The initial list she was presented with contained thousands of names. It was clearly going to be another long day.

With an approximate height and weight as well as skin colour for the victim provided by the initial report of the pathologist, Collins could instantly eliminate those who were clearly too big or too small or from the wrong ethnic group, but it still left hundreds of names that had to be added to the 'maybe' pile.

And the pile seemed to be growing by the minute.

Stories in most of the day's papers giving vague details of the find ensured a stream of calls came into the incident room. Many were from distressed relatives wanting to know if their missing loved one could be among those found inside the vehicle.

Every time a new call came in, Collins's colleagues passed on the name of the missing man for her to check and cross-reference.

As the day went on, so Collins's level of frustration grew. At first she had assumed that the reason Anderson was being so awful to her was because he had his own DI and DS that he liked working with. But now it dawned on her that Anderson had not only been told to keep her on a tight reign by the officers from the DPS but had also been informed about the reason for her being interviewed in the first place. She couldn't tell if Anderson had actually made up his mind about whether she was a corrupt officer or not, but it seemed clear that he had decided to err on the side of caution.

It was gone eleven o'clock by the time Collins clambered into her BMW and pulled out of the police station car park. She longed for a long, hot bath to ease away the stress of the day. The sooner she got home the better.

At the first set of traffic lights she stopped at, an old but tidy Vauxhall Vectra being driven by a man who fitted the same description pulled up alongside and stared across at her. After a quick glance, Collins continued looking forward and ignored him, her mind filled with thoughts about the case and about Anderson. The lights changed and the Vauxhall shot off. She was so distracted that she did not even notice that it soon pulled over to the side of the road to allow her to pass.

The sound of a horn snapped her out of her daydream. Dazzling headlights suddenly flashed in her rear-view mirror. She looked up to see the Vectra moving dangerously close to her rear bumper. She sped up a little out of instinct, but the driver matched her. What on earth was this idiot trying to do?

Collins pulled closer to the kerb to allow the car to go past, but the Vectra simply stayed tight on her bumper. She tried speeding up again, and at that moment the car suddenly shot out into the middle of the road and blazed past her, only to cut in front just inches from her bumper and screech to a halt. Collins stamped her foot on to the brake and came to a halt just inches from the man's car.

Flaming with rage, she opened the door of the car and stomped out to give him a piece of her mind.

'What the hell do you think you're playing at?' she said, reaching for her warrant card. 'You have no idea how much trouble you have got yourself in . . .'

The window of the Vectra hissed as it rolled down, and the man reached out of the window and held up a mobile phone.

'My boss wants a word with you.'

Collins snatched the phone knowing exactly who

would be on the other end of it. The man's tactics suddenly made perfect sense. He had been checking that no one else was in the car with her and that she was not being followed.

'Hello, Princess,' said the voice of Jack Stanley.

'This your idea of a joke?'

'Do I sound like I'm laughing? What the hell do you want?'

'I want to know when I'm going to see Sophie again.'

'And for that you try to get me run off the road?'

'You're the one who says it's too dangerous for us to be seen together. This seemed to be the best way.'

'You don't deserve to be a father, not the way you're behaving. You're still a child yourself.'

'Save the lectures for someone who cares. I want to see my daughter. It's been more than a month. I'm fed up with playing your silly little games.'

Collins took a deep breath. She needed to calm down. 'Look, Jack, it's just too dangerous. There are too many things going on right now.'

'Nothing that we can't handle. I managed to keep my face off the radar up until now. I don't see how it makes any difference. I can take the same precautions.'

'I'm sorry, Jack. I just can't allow it. I've spoken to Sophie – '

'Don't give me any crap about her not wanting to see me. I know that won't be true.'

'You're right, she does want to see you, but I've

explained the situation to her and she understands that for the time being it just can't happen. Now if she can understand that and she's only thirteen, why can't you?'

Jack Stanley slammed his thumb against the red button on his phone to end the call and stood fuming for a few moments in the back office of his night club.

He was having a hard time concentrating on the business end of things. Ever since he had learned that he had a daughter everything in his life had seemed to change. The idea of a family and that kind of domesticity had never appealed to him and he had gone out of his way to avoid it, but this was different. Here was a ready-made teenager who wanted him to be part of her life. It was as if he was catching up on everything he had missed out on. And he was loving it.

He tossed the phone into a drawer and went out into the main bar area. More than three hundred teenagers and youngsters were gyrating to the latest UK garage sounds in the middle of the dance floor. Stanley made his way through them and headed to the bar, where his right-hand man, Danny Thompson, was leaning back nursing a scotch and soda.

'You all right, Jack? You look like you've swallowed a wasp.'

'I'm fine.'

'You don't look it, boss.'

'Leave it. I'm fine.'

'Woman trouble?'

'Yeah, you could say that.'

'That's why I stick with lapdancers and the like. Don't have enough brains to cause any trouble. You want to talk about it?'

'Nah.'

Thompson took a long slug of his drink and eyed his boss carefully. They had been friends since childhood and he knew him well enough to know that something was really bugging him, but also well enough to know that there was no point in pressing him any further about it. If he wanted to talk, he would do so in his own time. Instead, Thompson waited until Stanley had got a drink of his own and then decided to change the subject.

'I was speaking to Mitch on the Peacroft today. Said a couple more of the Albanians turned up, trying to undercut our dealers.'

Stanley slowly turned to Thompson. 'Any trouble?'

'Bit of a scrap. One of them went away in an ambulance. I don't think they'll be back.'

'That's what we thought last time.'

'True.'

'I don't think this is just a bunch of chancers any more. They're too well organized. They know too much about our prices and dealing set-up. The way they're probing, I think they're looking for a weak spot so they can make their move.'

'You think they're trying to take over the Peacroft?' asked Thompson.

Stanley shook his head. 'I know a little about the Albanians. I think their ambitions go a bit further than that. Their classic tactic is to establish a small foothold somewhere and then use that as a base from which to expand their operations. If we're not careful, they could end up coming after everything we've got. They don't work like us. The whole lot of them are cousins and brothers and uncles, it's like the fucking Mafia.'

'What are you saying?'

'I'm saying that blood is thicker than water and this lot have got it by the bucket load. They can call on people and rely on them in a way that we could never hope to do. I can get a man to do a job for a fair price, but I can't expect him to do it just out of loyalty.'

'So what should we do?'

'Not sure. They've got to be getting information from somewhere. One of our dealers must be feeding them stuff, but it must be someone low down. From what I know, they're trying to find out who's in charge of the operation so they can work out a way to take out the top man. The thing is, I'm too well insulated. Even most of the dealers on the Peacroft have no idea who they're working for, so the Albanians aren't going to get anywhere with that strategy.'

'What do you suggest?'

'We need to reassert our authority on the place. I want to hit them hard, a decisive blow so that they get the message they can't fuck about in our territory, but before we can do that we need to plug the gap. No point in planning a major action if they're going to find out about it in advance. They'll be waiting for us.'

'So we're still back to square one. Looking for the leak. Any new leads?'

'Nah. And my sources at the Yard seem to have dried up for the time being. Something will come. In the meantime, double the workforce on the Peacroft and put more lads down there, just in case they come back.'

'Tooled up?'

Stanley thought for a moment, then shook his head slowly. 'Put a couple of shooters in the safe house just in case but I don't want anyone carrying on the street. At the moment it's off the police radar. It won't stay that way if people start turning up dead.'

'I think we both know that's inevitable. You need to start watching your own back too.'

'Don't you worry about me.'

Thompson took another sip from his glass. 'You know you've been letting things slip. You don't want to appear weak.'

'Not a chance, Danny Boy. I'm stronger than ever.'

5

'You don't mind if I listen to my iPod on the way, do you, Mum?'

It wasn't really a question. By the time Sophie Collins clambered into the passenger seat of the car for the school run, she had already fitted one of the slim white earpieces and was in the process of doing the same with the other.

Stacey forced out a sweet smile. 'That's fine, love. In fact it's perfect. That way you can listen to your music, I can listen to the news, and we won't get on each other's nerves.'

Sophie smiled back, finished inserting the remaining earpiece and switched on the controls. She then sat back in her seat and closed her eyes. Stacey knew there would be no more conversation until a brief goodbye when they arrived at the school gates.

Ever since they had had their conversation about Jack Stanley, a certain chill had descended on her relationship with her daughter. They still got on well enough on a day-to-day basis, but it felt as though Sophie was keeping her mother at arm's length. The iPod in particular had become something of a wedge between them, driving them apart even when they were physically together.

When Stacey questioned her daughter about the way things were, the teenager insisted that all was well and that her only problem was an increasingly heavy workload at school, but Stacey's motherly instincts, honed by years of detective work, told her there was far more to it.

Although Sophie had agreed not to see Jack any longer, Stacey knew the decision was not a happy one. Once again Stacey cursed herself for backing down in the first place and giving in to her emotions in order to introduce father and daughter. It was, she felt sure, a decision that would haunt her for years to come.

And it wasn't as if Stacey didn't have enough problems of her own to deal with. Her mind was swimming with the names, measurements and descriptions of countless missing men whose details she was trying to match with the mystery corpse from the triple murder case.

Having obtained the victim's shoe size from the mortuary, Stacey had been able to reduce her list of possible victims significantly, but it still contained hundreds of names. She was looking for a needle in a haystack and was becoming increasingly convinced that, to all intents and purposes, the task that Anderson had assigned her was essentially impossible.

The whole team was coming under increasing pressure. The first twenty-four hours had now passed, and all they had managed to do was to identify two of the victims; they had not found any kind of motive for the murders or uncovered a single clue about the killer.

Morning prayers brought little relief. Woods reported that he had interviewed Patricia Chadwick, but she had said nothing that would justify any further investigation of her. She had also not been able to pinpoint anything in her husband's life that could have led to his death.

After Woods had finished bringing the team up to date, Anderson asked Collins for her own report. She could feel herself getting increasingly self-conscious as she explained that she had nothing at all to say and that her line of inquiry could take several weeks to complete. Anderson dismissed her with an impatient wave of his hand and moved on.

The team then learned that a thorough examination of all the CCTV footage had resulted in just two brief, blurry images of the Mercedes. They now knew that it had been driven into Peckham at around 10 p.m. the evening before the bodies had been discovered. It was too dark and the pictures too grainy for them to make out the features of the driver or even to tell how many people were in the car at the time.

The only thing they knew for sure was that Raymond Chadwick could not have been behind the wheel at the time the footage was filmed. The evidence showed that, even if he had been kept in cold storage, his body had been taken out and allowed to thaw at least twenty-four hours before it was found.

A slightly more promising line of inquiry had come out of DI Hill's interview with Edward Miller's former partner. Sandra Miller had revealed that the GBH for which Mr Miller had been charged related to a fight between him and her lover. Miller had arrived home from work early one evening and caught the pair in a state of undress in the middle of the living room. Miller had flown into a rage and attacked the lover but, being much smaller and weaker, he had taken a bit of a beating. A few days later, Miller tracked down the man and knocked him unconscious with a baseball bat.

'How long had the affair been going on for?' asked Anderson as DI Hill made his presentation.

'About four months. And the assault took place three months before Miller went missing.'

'Do you think the wife or the lover had enough motive?'

'The wife told me they had been drifting apart for years,' said Hill. 'According to her, he'd dipped his wick on more than a few occasions. She hadn't caught him red-handed, but it was obvious that he was playing away from home. She said he was trying to' – he flicked through the pages of his notebook to find the exact phrase – 'replace her with a younger model.'

Anderson scratched his chin thoughtfully. 'Two unhappy marriages. As a twice married man I can tell you that doesn't mean much. Tell me about the man she was seeing.'

'Ex-amateur boxer. Still goes down the gym on a regular basis. I know from experience that people in that sort of world can have some pretty dodgy connections. He had good reason to be bitter. She dumped him after hubby gave him a hiding. Miller made him look like a fool. He went around telling people he'd get the bastard back, that he'd rip his head off.'

Anderson nodded. 'I think we should bring the man in for questioning. Softly, softly, though. The jealous lover thing is good motive and could even explain the mutilated genitals. I think it's unlikely that he has a link to all three men, but I want to be able to eliminate him from our inquiries. What's his name?'

Hill flicked back a couple of pages in his note-book. 'Banks. Leroy Banks.'

'Ah. Works in finance, does he?'

Hill squinted at his notes. 'No, sir, he's – '

'I was kidding, Len. Bring him in this afternoon.'

DS Porter raised a pencil in the air.

'What is it?' asked Anderson.

'I was wondering if this could be a Mafia thing. They've been known to remove genitals. I was reading up on the origins of the Mafia last night. It's a sign that the victim offended the wife of another member of the clan.'

Anderson raised an eyebrow. 'You think Leroy Banks is Italian?'

'No, but some of the Yardie-style gangs that have

a predominantly black or mixed race membership are known to model themselves on the Cosa Nostra. When I was attached to Trident we had loads of cases where the perpetrators had carried out attacks based exactly on scenes from *The Godfather* or *Goodfellas*. They're really into that kind of symbolism. There have been a few Mafia cases in which bodies have been found with hands and heads cut off or with the genitals removed and stuffed into the mouth.'

'Okay, I'll accept it's a possibility, but, let's face it, it's an outside one,' said Anderson, a small smile curling at the corners of his mouth. 'Of course, we're somewhat hampered by the fact that we don't have the heads and hands so can't check to see if that's where the missing genitals are. But if they turn up in that state, we're all going to owe Porter a good few pints.'

A ripple of laughter worked its way through the members of the team before Anderson dismissed them and they headed off to start the day's work.

Collins sat at her desk and opened up the file containing the next set of missing person reports. Everyone was under such pressure to catch the killer, chasing one lead after another until they were exhausted. Yet she felt as if she had her hands tied behind her back.

She had been stupid to meet up with Jack Stanley and even more stupid to take Sophie along to his house to introduce them. It had seemed like a good idea at the time, but there was now no way she could tell anyone the absolute truth without getting herself into a great deal more trouble.

That said, she had lied under caution, so if anyone ever found out, she would be out on her arse faster than she could say Jack Robinson.

A mixture of resentment, bitterness and anger was building up inside her. A small but growing part of her was even considering jacking the whole thing in. She didn't need this kind of bollocks in her life, and she certainly didn't need to be treated like shit by the likes of Anderson and his bag men. All but ignored by her daughter in her private life, it was too much to find herself all but ignored by her boss. She felt she had hit rock-bottom.

The job had become so much more difficult in recent years and it depressed the hell out of her. Advances in forensics and computing, as well as an expansion of police powers, had been welcome additions to the crime-fighting armoury, but they had been neatly balanced by an ever increasing number of technicalities that allowed the guilty to walk free.

The more she thought about it, the more clear it became that the job was at the heart of virtually all her problems. The fact that she was never around for Sophie, the conflict of interest over her past dealings with Jack Stanley, her inability to hold down any steady relationship with a member of the opposite sex, even her increasingly cynical demeanour were all the result of eighteen years on the job.

But was jacking it in really an option? What else

could she possibly do? And could she really afford to give up on her generous police pension now that she was more than halfway there? Quitting would also give out the wrong signals, especially so soon after her DPS interview. And no way in hell did she want to give the likes of Anderson the idea that they had got to her.

She thought back over what Jessica Matthews had said about Anderson not being happy about working with women. A quick glance around the incident room seemed to confirm this. She was the only female DI on the team. All five Detective Sergeants were men, and of the fifteen Detective Constables only two were female. Of those, the most junior seemed to do little more than fetch Anderson's coffee and sandwiches. Only one in eight of the Met's CID officers was a woman, so statistically the numbers were spot on, but Collins couldn't help thinking that things had been weighted in such a way as to ensure the officers Anderson worked with most of the time were male.

Well, that was one game Collins wasn't prepared to play. Anderson was going to have to get used to her working on this case, whether he liked it or not. She looked over in the direction of his office and scowled. The phone on her desk started to ring and she was still scowling as she answered it.

'DI Collins.'

'Am I calling at a bad time? You sound a bit grumpy?'

'Sorry, Jessica,' said Collins, immediately recognizing the voice. 'I was in the middle of something. What can I do for you?'

'I hear you're on the sidelines for this one.'

'Who told you that?'

'I have my sources. The thing is, I think I have something that might help you out. A heads-up to get you back in the good books. But it will mean that dinner's on you when we meet up.'

'You don't have to – ?'

'I want to. Anderson needs to be brought down a peg or two, and us sisters need to stick together. The way he treats some of his officers, especially the female ones, it's not right. Some men – most men, really – need to be taught a lesson and he's one of them. At least hear me out.'

'I'm all ears.'

Danny Thompson was driving like a moron.

In the half an hour since he had left London he had gone through two red lights, turned left at a junction after indicating right, circled a large roundabout three times and cut across three lanes of traffic on the motorway to make a sudden exit, only to rejoin the same carriageway an instant later.

Thompson knew he was risking a ticket but there was method in his madness: it was the only way he could be one hundred per cent certain that he was not being followed by anybody.

Satisfied that he was safe, he left the M1 at Junc-

74

tion 6 and headed up the Old Watford Road towards Bricket Wood, parking on a side street at the edge of the common. He walked down to the end of the road, turned right and then turned right again and again, walking directly past the car he had just parked. Satisfied that no one was acting suspiciously around his car, he continued down the road and this time turned left into the entrance of the Tin Man public house.

He took off his sunglasses as he reached the entrance and peered around the room, allowing his eyes to adjust slowly to the light. In the far corner, in a booth against the back wall, he spotted a middle-aged man with glasses and a neatly trimmed full-face beard just starting to turn grey at the outer edges. Thompson got himself a pint at the bar, then strode towards the man and, without a word of introduction, sat himself down opposite him.

'You're late,' said the man in a soft Scottish accent.

'Yeah? Well, I'd rather be late and have my arse covered than get here on time and have the shit hit the fan when I get back.'

'So how goes the big manhunt?'

'Stanley knows there's a leak, but there's no way that he or anyone close to him is ever going to point the finger at me.'

'You're sure about that?'

'Trust me. I'm rock solid.'

DCI Warren Milton took a sip of his orange juice and stared at the man opposite him. Several weeks had passed since the SOCA officer had hinted to DI Collins that an operation against Stanley was under way. Today was his chance to find out if that information had indeed been passed on. 'Good. So what have you got for me?'

Thompson sipped his pint before speaking. 'I'm not gonna tell you . . . I'm not gonna name names or anything like that.'

'No?'

'Not right now.'

'Fair enough.'

'Are you taping this?'

'No, no.'

Thompson leaned forward so that he was staring directly into the eyes of the man opposite him. 'Are you sure?'

'I wouldn't do that without telling you. This is all just background. Off the record. You've got nothing to worry about. If you're that bothered, you can frisk me if you like.'

Thompson cocked his head to one side. 'Nah, you're all right.'

'What can you tell me about the size of Mark Dennings's operation? What sort of drugs was he dealing in?'

'Everything.'

'Cocaine?'

'Yeah.'

'Ecstasy?'

'Heroin, blow, everything, mate. Where there was money to be made, he did it.'

'Did he make a lot of money?'

'Yeah, not mega-money, but he was doing all right. You have to think about this whole business like a game of chess. Everyone wants to be the king but most people just end up as pawns. Someone like Dennings, he had moved up the ranks a couple of places, but he was nowhere near the top.'

'So who killed him? And why?'

Thompson shuffled in his seat. 'Drawn a blank there, I'm afraid. If Stanley was directly involved, he's keeping it pretty close to his chest. I can't get anything out of him myself. I can't even be sure that he was there.'

'But you think he ordered the hit?'

Thompson shrugged. 'Can't be sure of that either. There were rumours that Dennings was skimming stock, but that means that anyone in the organization might have wanted to have a pop at him, just to see if he had a load of gear stashed away.'

Thompson knew he was being convincing, but the truth was somewhat different. In fact Thompson knew all about the murder of Dennings, a small-time dealer from the Blenheim Estate who had worked for Stanley. After getting greedy and skimming off a portion of the drugs that he was smuggling in, Stanley had decided to make an example of him.

Dennings had been shot twice in the head while

getting out of a drug boat on the beach at Margate a few months earlier. Stanley had been there to see his own brand of justice done, but it was Danny Thompson who had pulled the trigger.

'What about Stacey Collins?'

'What about her?'

'Does she help Jack out much?'

'Does she fuck. Little prick tease. He went out with her for about a minute and a half when they were teenagers or something, and he's been stuck on her ever since. He always reckons he gets stuff from her but the truth is it's all one-way traffic. He gives her plenty of tips, but everything she comes back with is a load of shite. I think Jack just likes the kudos of being able to say he had a cop on his books. But I told you all this last time.'

'I know, I just wanted to see if the situation had changed since then.'

'He hasn't mention her name to me. Read into that what you will.'

'Has Jack said anything about an up-and-coming raid?'

'What, drugs squad?'

'No. SOCA.'

'You lot? I didn't think you had anything yet, otherwise why do you need me?'

'There's been some talk about it in certain circles. I just wanted to know if the whisper mill had reached you yet.'

'Not that I'm aware.'

'Okay. But if you hear anything, let me know.'

'He might not have had time to mention it. He's having woman trouble and then there's this aggro with the Albanian mob. That's keeping him pretty occupied.

'You need to keep a lid on that, Danny. I don't want our hand being forced.'

'It's under control.'

'The kind of control that leaves a lot of dead bodies on the street?'

'You're funny, you know that. Ever considered a career in stand-up?'

'I mean it, Thompson. You lot go to war and all bets are off. We'll have no choice but to bring you all in.'

'And we'll be back out again in a day.'

Milton leaned forward. 'Let me put this in language you can understand. You fuck up the arrangements from your end and I'll do the same from mine. If you find yourself in the shit, there will be no point in calling on me.'

DCI Milton watched as Thompson finished his drink, stood up and walked out of the pub. A split second later a man from a nearby table came and sat down next to him.

'You get it all?'

The man held up a miniature recording device.

'Clear as a bell. You think we can trust him?'

He looked back round to face the front. 'The thing you have to understand about grasses is that out of all the people in the world, they're the ones everyone despises. Criminals hate them and, even though a lot of police work relies on them, we don't like them much either. Sell their own grannies if they thought it would get them somewhere. So if you ask me do I trust Danny Thompson the answer is a definitive no. I wouldn't trust the fucking scumbag as far as I could throw him.'

Thompson's driving during the return journey was equally erratic.

Every roundabout was circled at least twice; he joined and rejoined the motorway three times and doubled back on himself every half an hour. Cocky and confident, he was certain that he had made himself impossible to follow. And he had, which is why the team keeping him under surveillance had opted to fit a small GPS device to his car instead.

His entire journey appeared on the screen of a laptop computer, and it was only when he stopped for more than a few minutes that one of the team of cars and motorcycles that were always a few miles behind was sent forward to investigate.

As the map showed Thompson pulling up to his home, the head of the team hit the redial button on his mobile and held it up to his ear. 'He's back now,' said the man in his strong South African accent. 'I don't think he'll be going anywhere else so I'm going to call it off for the day and send the rest of my boys home. The photographs will be with you by the morning. There will also be a couple of audio recordings, though the quality isn't great because we didn't want to risk getting too close. Is there anything else we can do for you, Mr Stanley?'

'No,' Jack replied softly. 'I'll call you when I get the prints. In the meantime, feel free to send me your invoice.'

6

The shelves in the incident room at Peckham were creaking under the weight of all the reports being written up by members of the team, but so far nothing seemed to have taken them even a single step closer to finding out who was behind the triple murder.

Rajid Khan, a geeky computer expert attached to the unit, had been brought in to examine Chadwick's home and laptop computers to see if they held any clue to his whereabouts in the weeks before he died. Khan used specialist software to scan the hard drives, looking for evidence of incriminating emails, letters or instant messages.

His investigation had produced hundreds of pages of data, all of which had to be read, recorded and cross-referenced. Yet, despite the huge number of man hours invested in this part of the inquiry, nothing of interest was found.

Leroy Banks, the lover of Sandra Miller, had been arrested, brought to the station and subjected to a lengthy interview under caution. He made no secret of the fact that he hated his love rival and that he had publicly expressed a desire to see him dead on numerous occasions. However, he had a cast-iron alibi for the night the bodies were dumped.

'He can't be totally in the clear because we don't know how many people we're talking about,' said Porter as the team discussed their findings that afternoon. 'There could be two or three killers all working together. Just because Banks wasn't actually driving the car on the night the bodies were dumped doesn't mean he's innocent.'

A murmur of agreement passed through the room. Collins looked across at Porter and found herself unable to resist the urge to cut him down to size. 'It's not Banks. That theory only works if there's some kind of connection between the victims,' she said. 'They'd have to all live in the same street or work for the same company. It's one thing having a lone killer working at random, quite another having group effort. If that kind of link existed, we'd already know.'

Now it was DI Hill's turn to speak. 'Maybe you just haven't found the link yet. Don't go knocking our end of the investigation while your own research is coming up short.'

Collins couldn't believe what she was being accused of. She could feel her chest tightening as anger rose up within her. She was just about to let loose a stream of vicious swearwords and put-downs when, out of the corner of her eye, she spotted DCI Anderson entering the room.

Collins had spent all morning psyching herself up for what she was about to do and knew that it was now or never. She had to make her move, and revenge on DI Hill would have to wait. Anderson had barely reached the halfway point across the room when Collins appeared beside him.

'Sir, I need to attend the post-mortems this afternoon.'

Anderson raised a cynical eyebrow. 'Myself and DI Hill are already attending,' he said, his voice calm and firm. 'I really don't see the need for anyone else to be there. And besides, you already have your assignment – '

'I need to know if there are any distinguishing marks on the unidentified body.'

'That will be in the report – '

'But that won't be ready for a couple of days. I've got a contact on *Crimewatch* but their deadline for the next show is the day after tomorrow. If anything useful comes out of the PMs, I need to know about it as soon as possible.'

Anderson reached one hand up to his chin and began scratching it slowly – a habitual gesture. Collins could see that he was deep in thought and held her breath.

'Let's talk about it in my office,' he said at last. 'Right now.'

Moments later Collins found herself standing in front of Anderson's large wooden desk while he seated himself and studied her cautiously.

'I don't think it's any secret that you do have something of a reputation as a loose cannon. I'd even heard about your exploits long before I arrived at MIT, and, I have to confess, some of what I've heard makes me very uneasy,' he said.

Collins blinked and shrugged her shoulders. 'I don't know what to say. I get results. Sometimes my methods may be a bit unorthodox but I get the job done.'

'But there's no point in getting the job done if it all falls apart when the case comes to trial. And with the kind of antics you get up to, that's just the situation we're likely to end up in. That's my big fear.'

'I know the law, sir,' snapped Collins. 'I'd never do anything to jeopardize a trial. Just because I'm determined doesn't mean I'm an idiot.'

'I never said you were.'

Anderson sat back and scratched his chin again as he ran through the options in his mind. He enjoyed the challenge of running a murder squad – so far as he was concerned it was what policing was all about – but he was unhappy about having inherited so many officers that would not have been his first choice had he been putting the team together himself.

He was equally unhappy about officers from the DPS coming to see him shortly after he had been appointed to inform him that one of his DIs was under investigation and that she should be kept away from any sensitive parts of the inquiry.

Collins had since been given the all-clear, but Anderson was in no hurry to make her part of his core team. He was all too well aware that he had gained a reputation for being something of a misogynist but knew that in reality it was entirely undeserved. Some of the female officers he had worked with in the past had been razor-sharp and excellent. Others, however, had been absolutely hopeless. But exactly the same could be said of the men he had worked with.

The simple truth was that good officers, regardless of gender, ethnicity or disability, were thin on the ground. He didn't plan to let anyone drop the ball on one of his cases, least of all Collins.

Anderson paused and steepled his fingers. 'I was having a chat with DCS Higgins the other day and your name came up.'

Collins said nothing. Instead she waited for Anderson to carry on.

'He rates you very highly,' he said at last. 'He told me to be sure to make the most of you, that you'd be a real asset. He was sorry to see you go.'

'I was sorry to leave,' Collins replied.

'It's clear you two had a pretty special relationship.'

'I wasn't sleeping with him if that's what you're getting at.'

'I wasn't. Not at all. I mean it's clear that he empathized with your way of doing things. It's also clear that I do things very differently. You're just going to have to get used to that.'

'So it would appear.'

'I run a tight ship, Collins,' he said. 'There isn't any room for mavericks in my team. If you take one step out of line, you're off the squad. Do I make myself clear?'

Collins leaned forward and placed both palms flat down on the desk. 'Listen, I want to get whoever is responsible for these murders every bit as much as you do. I'm going to do my job to the best of my ability. That's all I ever do. I'll always put the case first. You might surround yourself with yes men who'll take the fall for you if you mess up an investigation and maybe it pisses you off that I'm not like that, but, like I said, I put the case before my own career and I certainly put it before yours.'

Anderson was staring hard at Collins. 'You didn't answer my question, Collins. One wrong move from you and you won't just be off my team, you'll be out of MIT altogether. Do I make myself clear?'

Collins stepped back and folded her arms in front of her body. It was the most defiant gesture she could make under the circumstances.

'Yes, sir. Crystal.'

Collins stared silently out of the side window of the squad car taking her, Hill and Anderson to Guy's Hospital, where the post-mortem was due to take place. She sat in the back alongside Hill while the DCI was up in front next to the driver.

The first few minutes passed in silence but then Anderson folded up the newspaper he had been reading, turned to Collins and smiled. 'So, you're a tad sceptical about the chances of Leroy Banks being involved.'

Collins was taken aback by both the question and Anderson's friendly tone but rapidly regained her composure. 'I just don't think he's serial killer material. I know he has motive for wanting to attack Edward Miller, but I don't see him going as far as killing him, let alone the other two. You don't seriously think he's involved, do you?'

Anderson smiled again and Collins realized that this was probably the first time she had ever seen him do so. 'I don't like to leave any stone unturned,' he said, 'just in case it comes back and bites me on the arse, if you'll forgive my mixed metaphors.

'One of my first murder cases involved this teenage girl who had been stabbed to death in her own home. I got to the scene and it was a terrible mess. Blood everywhere, a real frenzied attack.

'There was no sign of a forced entry, and the only people in the house were the mother – she called it in – the stepfather and the girl's younger brother. When we went into the brother's room we all had a bit of a shock. He was one of those death-obsessed teenagers. Every square inch of the wall was covered in posters for slasher films, heavy-metal music and vampire memorabilia. There were skulls and cruci-fixes everywhere, as well as a load of marijuana and speed.

'Everyone on the team liked the kid for the killing,

and there was a suspicion that the stepfather might have helped. It looked like an open-and-shut case but my guv was less sure. Made us do a trawl of the neighbourhood. That was when we found a home-less guy, care-in-the-community case, wandering around in a drunken stupor. He had no blood on him and no weapon, and there would have been no way that he could have entered the house. The only things in his pockets were a couple of chocolate bars. I was all for letting him go but the guv said we had to bring him in anyway to cover all the bases.

'Cut a long story short, it was the homeless guy that did it. To this day we don't know how he managed to get into the house but what we do know is that he stabbed the girl while she was in her bed so her blood got soaked up by the duvet. We found a tiny spot on his sweatshirt but what had really nailed it was that the governor had noticed a little bowl full of chocolate bars by the side of the girl's bed. The guy had nicked a handful on his way out. Ever since, I like to bring in as many people as I can — isn't that right, Len?'

DI Hill nodded with a grin. 'Right pain in the arse it is too, but more often than not it pays dividends.'

Anderson still had a smile as he turned away from Collins but it slowly started to fade from his lips. 'Funny thinking back to that old case,' he said wistfully. 'Somehow I don't think this one is going to be anywhere near as easy to solve.'

*

Ten minutes later the three officers, all wearing their protective gowns and masks, were following Dr Matthews into the chilly hospital mortuary. Just before entering the room Collins placed a swimming peg on the end of her nose, forcing her to breathe through her mouth. It made her look and sound a bit ridiculous, but the smell of decay was one she had no desire to get used to.

All three bodies had been brought out of storage and each one was lying flat on a stainless-steel table covered by a green plastic sheet. Matthews headed to the nearest table and stood on one side of it, inviting the three officers to stand opposite her.

'We'll begin with Raymond Chadwick,' she said. 'Now, as I am sure you know, there are usually five stages to the autopsy process: the Y-incision, followed by the removal of the organs, examination of the stomach contents, collection of samples, and finally examination of the head and brain.'

Matthews reached out and pulled back the green plastic sheet with a flourish to reveal the body underneath. 'But, as you can see,' she said, 'most of that does not apply to the current cases.'

Chadwick had been straightened out from the foetal position and now lay flat on his back. He was completely naked and his skin had taken on a pale green-grey tinge. A brown, soupy fluid was seeping out from the base of his body. Collins noted with alarm that the tiny white maggots she had observed in his chest and neck at the crime scene seemed to have grown. 'Aren't they potentially destroying evidence?' Collins said, pointing at the mass of white worms.

Matthews followed her gaze. 'Potentially, but getting rid of them before I've carried out my examination would be far more damaging. It's too cold in storage for flies to lay eggs, but if a body comes in already infested there really isn't very much that we can do. In this case, the amount of raw flesh on the body has proved particularly attractive to the little blighters. We'll wash him down when I'm finished, but I can't do it now; otherwise I might wash away trace evidence.'

Collins frowned in confusion. 'But I thought the theory was that the bodies had been kept in cold storage, Miller's for at least two years. That doesn't tally with this kind of decomposition.'

Matthews nodded. 'Cold storage only slows down the process. It's like putting a piece of chicken in your fridge. If you don't eat it, it will still go off and start to smell after a few days. To stop the decomposition process completely you have to freeze the body. If you freeze a body, it will last more or less indefinitely. We only do that once we've carried out an autopsy. I can't do anything with a body that has been turned into a block of ice. I can't even get a tissue sample.'

Anderson coughed gently, a subtle way of asking Matthews to get on with it. She smiled politely.

'The first thing I want to do is to confirm what

might seem to be completely obvious but needs to be stated for the official record. In my opinion all three victims were murdered by the same person or persons. The tools used to sever the hands and head, as well as those used to open up the chest cavity and remove the internal organs, seem to be identical in each case.'

Matthews's gloved fingers began to move across each area of the body as she described it. 'The neck has been cut through the skin and deep tissues right down to the point of separation, which is between the fifth and sixth vertebrae. The sixth remains in situ and is deeply notched.'

Her fingers moved down to Chadwick's chest. 'The intercostals between the fourth, fifth and sixth ribs have been cut through, exposing the thorax. The pericardium is open, and the heart and lungs are missing. There is also an absence of thoraco-abdominal viscera.

'All the skin cuts, particularly those at the neck and edges of the chest cavity, show distinct ecchymosis. Now I want to – '

Anderson held up a hand. 'I'm sorry, you're talking about bruising, right?'

Matthews flashed another smile. 'Right.'

'But surely that would only happen if the cuts were made while the victim was alive.'

'That's correct. And I've found similar bruising patterns on all three bodies.'

'My God,' gasped Collins. 'You mean someone

did this to them while they were fully conscious?'

'Not necessarily. Alive doesn't mean conscious. We can't jump to any conclusions. We'll have to wait for a full toxicology report before we know which, if any, drugs were in their systems. It's possible they may have been sedated, but in any event they would probably have passed out from shock and loss of blood soon after the first incision?'

Anderson scratched his chin. 'When it comes to the removal of the head and the hands, do you have any idea what the killer used?'

Matthews picked up one of Chadwick's forearms and examined the bloody stump. 'We're going to do a further procedure after the main autopsy to remove the radius and ulna of each arm, along with the exposed cervical vertebrae, to make a better determination. My initial thoughts are that it looks like the work of a small saw. There are serrations visible and you wouldn't have those with a knife or an axe.'

Collins joined the conversation. 'Would that be something specifically medical? A specialist instrument of some kind?'

'Possibly, but to be honest there are a number of craft tools and kitchen implements that would do the job just as well. However, a straight-bladed knife was used to do this.'

She pointed to the mutilated genitals. Collins noticed that both Anderson and Hill winced visibly as they gazed at the remains of Chadwick's manhood.

'What we're trying to get at,' said Anderson,

looking away from the victim's crotch, 'is whether we're talking about someone with medical or surgical training.'

'I can't give you a definitive answer, I'm afraid, but my instinct would be to say yes. Surgeons tend to make very bold, clean incisions through tissue. Experience teaches them exactly how much pressure is needed and they will often go through the skin one layer at a time. An amateur cutting open a body for the first time is likely to either over- or underestimate the amount of pressure needed. That might lead to multiple-entry incisions – hesitation marks – or possibly to damage of the internal organs or ribs from pressing down too hard.

'I haven't found anything like that in this case, but that isn't totally conclusive. Surgeons are taught how to open up a body in a way that allows life to be preserved. If the intention is to kill, the level of skill needed drops away dramatically. Your average family butcher would know enough anatomy to accomplish what has been done here.'

Anderson had moved down towards Chadwick's feet. 'What are these marks here near the ankles?'

'I was just getting to those,' said Matthews as Hill and Collins moved down the table to get a better look. 'They're from ligatures. Identical marks appear on all three bodies.'

The marks were dark brown in colour and had a vivid plum-red band on either side. The skin had broken in parts, and yet more maggots could be seen slipping around in the wounds. 'The width of those marks – that's the width of the rope or cable used,' said Matthews. 'You'll notice they don't circle each ankle completely but are in fact confined to the outside part of the legs. This indicates that a single ligature was used to bind both ankles.'

'The marks are raised on the side nearest the ankles,' said Anderson. 'Does that mean the ligature was uneven? Is it something we can identify?'

'Actually, it means that at some point the victims were suspended upside down or dragged along the ground with their entire weight supported by their ankles.'

Matthews called over an assistant and together they raised Chadwick so that his back was visible. 'There are also marks across the top of the shoulders and on the buttocks; these seem to indicate that at some point the body was dragged along the ground, probably around the time it was placed into the car. Once again, the other two bodies have similar marks. I've taken samples of the grit embedded in the skin to help isolate a location.'

Once they had finished with Chadwick, Matthews showed the team the similarities on the bodies of Edward Miller and then the unknown third victim.

'You haven't said anything about cause of death yet,' asked Anderson.

'Without the heads I'm reluctant to make a firm statement, but it seems that all three died in the same fashion. From exsanguination.'

'They bled to death,' said Collins flatly.

'Exactly. There is very little blood left in any of the bodies and it must have gone somewhere. The severing of the neck would have opened up the carotid artery but there are also blood stains on the outside of the skin of the chest. Your crime scene, wherever it is, is going to be awash with blood.'

There was a pause while the members of the team took in the new information.

'Is it possible,' asked DI Hill, looking up from his notebook, 'that all this has been done deliberately in an attempt to make it impossible to carry out a proper autopsy?'

Matthews shook her head slowly. 'I really don't think so. Although it's going to make it almost impossible to determine a precise cause of death, there is no doubt that this is a murder we are looking at. That kind of subterfuge would only really be necessary if you were trying to fake a suicide or something like that.

'Besides, this kind of thing is more common than you think. Jack the Ripper took out his victims' organs; so did Jeffrey Dahmer, Richard Chase and several others. Having said that, however, none of what has happened goes any way towards making my job easier.'

Collins slowly walked around the table holding the body of the third victim, the first of the group to do so. 'What's this mark here?' The others gathered around and saw that Collins was pointing to what appeared to be a pale smudge on the outside of the man's thigh, though it was partly obscured by a patch of dried blood and the fluids leaking out of the body.

'Let's see.' Matthews gathered up a soft sponge and began gently wiping the area.

'Just an area of discoloration, mild scarring, possibly the result of childhood eczema.'

'Are you sure?' said Collins. 'The pattern seems a bit too regular.'

Matthews picked up a magnifying glass from a nearby desk and examined the area again. 'I think you're right. It looks like an incredibly faint tattoo. My guess is that this man underwent laser-removal treatment. It usually takes about five or six sessions to get rid of the tattoo completely so he must have had one or two procedures still to go. That's a good spot.'

Anderson looked from Matthews to Collins and back again. Collins could feel herself starting to blush as she spoke. 'It might be possible to reconstruct the tattoo. Even without knowing exactly what it is I can use it to eliminate hundreds of names from my list. Better still, if we get something we can put out to the media we might get lucky.'

Matthews nodded. 'I'll have the patch of skin removed. I'm sure we can get the pattern to show up more clearly under certain kinds of light. Bravo, Detective Inspector Collins.'

Anderson's face remained stern as he nodded in Collins's direction. 'Good work. Get a copy out to the press a.s.a.p. and let's see if we can give this poor bastard a name.'

Matthews explained that X-rays showed none of the bodies had any broken bones, other than those caused by the opening up of the chest cavities. External examination of the bodies had failed to reveal the presence of needle marks or puncture wounds, though it was possible that the relevant areas of skin had been removed.

As Matthews spoke, Collins looked at the three bodies around her, her eyes fixed on the marbled fat and muscle on the inside of the open ribcages. All three victims had been turned from men into carcasses. It was an image she was finding impossible to get out of her mind.

'How long did you say it would be for the toxicology reports?' asked Collins.

'I did an initial test with the equipment we have here,' explained Matthews, 'but nothing came up in large-enough concentrations to be detected. That makes me think it's unlikely we'll find anything but I want to be absolutely sure. The spectroscope at the FSS HQ is a lot more sensitive but it will be at least a week before they can run any of the samples through it. I'll let you know as soon as I hear.'

The examination over, the three officers made their way out of the mortuary, ready to head back to the incident room. Collins was the last to leave and looked back at the figure of Jessica Matthews through the glass window in the centre of the rubber-edged double doors. The pathologist's plan to help get Collins into her senior officers' good books by telling her about the faded tattoo, which Collins could then 'discover' during the autopsy, seemed to have worked like a charm.

Matthews glanced up and saw Collins looking over at her. She smiled and, raising a blood-smeared gloved hand, gave her a thumbs-up sign.

7

The three teenage boys emerged from the school gates half an hour after most of the other pupils had left. They had been held behind in detention but the time they had spent struggling over maths problems had done little to dampen the rowdy behaviour that had got them into trouble in the first place. The noisy trio jostled and teased one another as they lazily made their way home.

'They're not going to expel us,' said Nick, the tallest of the three, shaking his head slowly. 'And even if they do I don't give a fuck. The only reason I go to school at all is so I can hang out with you two. If we get kicked out, we'll just hang out somewhere else.'

'You can; I'll be dead,' said Chris, the youngest. 'My mum will fucking kill me if I get kicked out again. I'll be on the streets.'

'If that happens,' replied Nick, slapping the flat of his hand on the back of his friend, 'you can always come and live with me!'

'What, in your shithole of a house?' gasped Alex. 'No one in their right mind would ever want to live there.' The three boys burst into fits of giggles. They were a few streets away from the school and still giggling when they first spotted the girl.

She wore a pair of skinny jeans and a cream summer blouse. Her lips were bright red with lipstick and her eyes lightly painted with black mascara. Her hair was blonde, moving gently with the breeze.

'Here, look at that. She's well fit,' said Alex.

'No way, she's a tramp,' said Nick.

'And a brass,' added Chris.

'What, you think she's on the game?'

'Well what's she doing, then? Ain't no bus stop there.'

She was leaning back against a low wall, her elbows resting behind her, one leg folded up beneath. Two thin white wires led down from her ears and into an iPod fixed to a clip on the side of her belt. Her eyes were closed and her head bobbed gently in time with music none of the boys could hear. A soft smile was on her lips.

It was only as they got a little closer that Nick had a revelation.

'Shit, that's Sophie Collins.'

'She doesn't look like that when she's got her uniform on.'

'But she looks like a fucking brass!'

'Yeah, I know.'

Nick put his finger to his lips and his two friends stopped speaking as the three drew almost level with the girl. Her eyes were still closed as Nick reached out and tapped her on the shoulder.

Sophie smiled lazily and spoke with her eyes still shut. 'You took your time,' she said, stretching her arms up above her head. Then she opened her eyes and instantly realized her mistake. 'Oh, what the hell do you want?'

'Hey, Sophie, what you doing here?'

'None of your business.'

'Why you all dressed up? You meeting your boyfriend?'

'Piss off.'

'Who is it?' asked Chris. 'Mr Glover?'

The boys laughed. Glover was the physics teacher notorious for his bad teeth and powerful foot odour.

'I told you to piss off.'

'I bet she's waiting for a customer,' said Alex.

'Or her pimp,' snorted Nick.

'Yeah, how long you been on the game for, eh, Sophie? Not getting enough pocket money? How much for the three of us?'

'I ain't paying for it,' said Alex. 'You don't know where the slag's been.'

Sophie's eyes narrowed with anger. 'Who you calling a slag? What the fuck are you three talking about, you little shits? Why don't you fuck off before my friend arrives and kicks the living daylights out of you?'

'Check her bag,' shouted Chris. 'I bet it's full of condoms.'

Before she could protest Alex had darted forward and snatched the handbag from her shoulder. She moved towards him but he immediately threw it high over her head towards Chris, who caught it neatly.

Sophie turned and advanced on him but he threw the bag across to Nick. Sophie spun on her heels. 'Give it back, give it back, you bastards, give it back.' There were tears of frustration building up in the corners of her eyes.

'Oh, I'm sorry,' said Nick softly. 'Didn't mean to upset you.' He held out the bag towards her. Sophie hesitated, then stepped towards him, her arm outstretched. She was just inches away from her bag when Nick's face exploded into a mischievous grin and he tossed the bag back to Alex.

'Gotchya,' he hissed.

The impromptu game of piggy-in-the-middle continued for a few moments, Sophie getting increasingly upset as the boys teased her relentlessly. Then there was a sudden screech of tyres and the sound of a horn, long and loud, as a jet-black Ranger Rover mounted the kerb at speed, screeching to a halt just inches from Nick's knees.

The driver's door flew open and Jack Stanley leaped out, his face alive with rage.

'What the fuck are you little bastards playing at?'

The three boys stood frozen to the spot like rabbits caught in the glare of headlights. Stanley walked up to Nick and snatched back the handbag. The boy made no sound other than a faint whimper.

Stanley glanced over at Sophie. 'You all right, Princess?'

She was trying to tidy her hair, which had become dishevelled after all her running around. 'I'm fine.'

'Okay, get in the car. I'll sort this lot out.'

Sophie clambered into the passenger seat while Stanley grabbed Nick by the scruff of the neck and dragged him towards the other two boys, both of whom were stiff with fear.

Stanley's breathing was heavy and laboured, like a bull winding up ready for the charge. He stared at each of the boys in turn, moving his face so close that they could smell the mixture of stale coffee and tobacco on his breath. 'If any one of you three even so much as looks at Sophie again, I'll make sure that the very last fucking thing you see on this earth is my face. Do you understand?'

The three boys nodded meekly.

Minutes later Stanley and Sophie were driving through South London, safely hidden behind his tinted windows, grinning like a pair of Cheshire cats.

'The look on Nick's face. Honestly,' giggled Sophie. 'I thought he was going to wet himself.'

'Yeah. I get that a lot. So, how long have we got?'

'A good few hours. Mum thinks I'm heading to a friend's house so that we can do our homework together.'

'You know you are going to have to do your homework.'

'What? You're kidding me.'

'If this is going to work, you can't fall behind with your schoolwork.'

'Anyway, I've already done my homework.'

'Well, then, you won't mind me checking it.'

'You know much about simultaneous equations?'

Jack's face quivered slightly. 'I ... er ... so, you thought that kid was going to wet himself, eh?'

'Pathetic.'

Sophie rolled her eyes before leaning forward and plugging her iPod into the car's stereo system. For the rest of the journey the pair sang along to their favourite songs.

Sophie was so absorbed in the music that she hardly noticed the roundabout route Jack was taking or the numerous precautions he employed to ensure they were not being followed. He did it as a matter of course, whether his sources said he was being watched or not. Better safe than sorry was a philosophy that had served him well over the years and he saw no reason to change it now.

But even if Sophie had noticed she wouldn't have cared much. For the first time in her life, she felt complete. She was smiling inside and out. She had finally found exactly what had been missing during all the years with no father in her life. Someone to champion her, someone to look after her, someone to fight her corner. Someone with big strong arms that she could snuggle up in. Someone who made her feel completely and utterly safe and protected.

The door to DCI Anderson's office swung open and the senior officer leaned out and scanned the incident room. 'Hill,' he barked, 'can I borrow you for a mo?'

DI Hill put down the pile of papers he was sorting

and wove his way through the maze of desks and filing cabinets. By the time he pushed open the door of the office, Anderson was back behind his desk, hovering over a handful of photographs.

'I want you to go back and see Miller's widow,' he said without looking up. 'I know it's a rough time but we need to ask her a bunch of follow-up questions. I've managed to get hold of a few pictures of Chadwick, his car and some of the places he used to hang about. I want to see if she recognizes anything. It's a bit of a long shot, but we need to know for sure whether there's any connection between our victims. I'm sure you treated her with every sympathy the first time around, so she'll feel comfortable talking to you again.'

Hill nodded. 'No problem. But I can't do it until the morning – I'm seeing Miller's mother and sister in an hour or so . . . unless you want me to cancel.'

Anderson frowned momentarily. 'That's what I get for not checking the action logs. No, stick with your plan. I'll get copies of the snaps for you to show the relatives and put someone else on this job.'

Anderson followed Hill to the door of his office. He looked around the incident room until his eyes fixed on a dark-haired woman with a bored expression on her face as she tapped entries into her computer.

'Collins! Come into my office when you have a minute.'

*

Sandra Miller lived in a small three-storeyed terraced house that was on the edge of a trendy new development in Thamesmead. She opened the door and led the way into the compact ground-floor kitchen. Collins sat down at a breakfast table in the far corner and watched while the widow made tea for them both. Miller looked thoroughly exhausted and seemed to be moving in slow motion.

'Thanks for seeing me at such short notice,' Collins began when Miller finally joined her at the table. 'I don't think I'll need to take up much of your time. I can only imagine what you are going through right now, and I don't want to make things any more difficult for you than they already are.'

Miller smiled weakly. 'It's so weird. I just don't know how to feel. We were together for fourteen years. Those first couple of years, I used to say I was full of sunshine whenever I was with him. He was the love of my life back then. But those feelings never last, do they? People change. You end up wanting different things.'

She paused for a moment, lost in her thoughts, before continuing. 'When he went missing, I guess I always knew it was possible that he had died. I thought I had accepted that I'd never see him again. But now that I know he's dead for sure, it's come like a bolt out of the blue. I'm all over the place.'

Miller eyed Collins carefully while taking a noisy slurp of her tea. 'Am I a suspect?'

The question took Collins by surprise. 'Do you think you should be?'

'They questioned me when he went missing, of course. And then that whole business with Leroy. I thought maybe you'd found something that implicated me.'

Somewhere deep inside, Collins's senses were tingling. It was screamingly obvious that Sandra Miller was not being treated as a suspect and that this meeting was entirely informal. They were talking in her kitchen, not at a police station, she was not under caution, and Collins had come without any back-up. There was only one reason that Miller would have asked a question like that: she had something to hide. And from that moment on Stacey Collins was absolutely determined to find out exactly what it was.

'So far as we can tell, you were the last person to see Edward alive, so that means you're vital to the inquiry. The reason I'm here is to find out if you can recall something that might help us when it comes to tracking down your husband's killer.'

Collins spent the next ten minutes employing the softly, softly approach, trying to ease her way into the more sensitive questions by starting out with innocuous ones: how Sandra and her late husband had met, where they had worked, what hobbies they had and so on. Only once she felt sure her subject was sufficiently relaxed did she show her the photographs given to her by DCI Anderson.

'Do you recognize this man?'

Sandra took the picture and held it directly in front of her. It showed Raymond Chadwick wearing a dinner jacket and bow tie, holding up a glass of champagne and toasting the photographer. It had clearly been taken at some kind of upmarket social function.

'No. I've never seen him before.'

'There's another picture here,' said Collins, 'a little more formal. It's from his last passport.'

Miller took the second print. This one showed Chadwick stony-faced staring directly at the camera. It looked a little like a police mugshot.

'I really don't think I've ever seen him before. Should I have?'

'I need you to think very hard about it. It could be important.'

'Do you think he killed Edward?'

'Actually,' said Collins, 'he's another one of the victims. His body was found along with that of your husband.'

'Was he married?'

Again the question took Collins by surprise. 'Yes. Why do you ask?'

Miller's eyes flicked upwards and to the left before she spoke. Collins spotted it right away and knew that whatever was said next would be a lie. 'I just wonder how his wife is coping,' said Miller. 'I mean, this is something you never really think you'll have to go through. Losing someone like that. I don't know anyone else who it's happened to.'

Collins could sense that a part of Miller was desperate to open up, to get things off her chest. She moved towards her and placed a reassuring hand on her arm to encourage her to go on, hoping she would eventually reveal the truth.

'What I can't work out is how I'm supposed to feel,' Miller continued. 'What I'm supposed to feel. I don't know if I'm doing it right. I don't think I feel sad enough; I don't think I feel enough grief. To be honest, I just feel relieved.'

Collins nodded. 'Sometimes it takes a little while to sink in. It's the shock. You've been in limbo for a long time, and now that's over a kind of relief is quite natural. We have some very good family liaison officers and victim support can be – '

'No, it's not that,' she interrupted. 'It's that I don't feel any guilt, I don't feel any sadness.' She looked at Collins, her face deadly serious. 'I'm glad he's dead.'

Collins held her stare for a few moments, silently urging her to continue.

Miller nodded wearily. 'In the end I couldn't take it any more. The lack of intimacy. He wouldn't even so much as hold my hand, let alone kiss me or make love to me. Do you have any idea what it's like to have someone that you love lying just a few inches away from you in bed night after night and knowing that they don't have even the slightest interest in you?

'I'd actually been to see a couple of solicitors

about getting a divorce, but I don't think Edward would have consented. He wasn't interested in me as a wife, but it suited him socially to be able to say that he was married.'

Collins understood instantly. There were countless married men she had come across over the years who were habitually unfaithful but had no intention of ending their marriages. They went from one fling to another – usually with younger, easily manipulated women – but would never allow any relationship to get serious. The fact that they had a wife at home who would take them to the cleaners in the event of a divorce was always the perfect excuse. The affair would continue until the other woman finally accepted she was on a hiding to nothing and walked away. The man would then move on to his next victim. He would, in essence, have the best of both worlds.

'Was he seeing someone else?'

'He was always on the lookout. I wasn't his type any more.'

'You told my colleague that you thought he was trying to replace you with a younger model.'

Miller snorted with laughter. 'He was trying to. Bars, clubs, lonely hearts. Even those contact magazines.'

Collins sat back and took a good look at Sandra Miller. Although her hair was in need of a wash and she was dressed shabbily and seemed tired, her skin was like porcelain. Her hands were also flawless and wrinkle-free. She was slim, toned and petite. Scrubbed up, Collins reckoned she could easily pass for a student.

'You're not exactly old yourself.'

'Too old for him,' she said quietly.

'How old is that?'

'I'm thirty-two.'

Collins frowned as she did the calculation in her head. Miller guessed what she was up to and gave her the answer she was searching for. 'We got married just after my eighteenth birthday. He was thirty-two.' She smiled at the memory. 'My mother was horrified.'

'That's quite some age gap.'

Miller suddenly sat forward. 'When we first got married, we couldn't keep our hands off each other. We had some amazing times back then.'

'So you think Edward wanted to re-create those early days by finding himself a younger woman, someone who reminded him of the way you used to be when he first met you?'

Miller began shaking her head furiously. 'No, no, you don't understand. I always looked very young for my age. Always. Up until three years ago I still had to show ID before I could get served in the pub. People who didn't know us, they thought I was his daughter. That's how young I looked. And he loved it. He absolutely loved it. That was the point. The whole point. I was so naïve back then that I couldn't see it myself, not for years and years. You see, he never wanted to be with a woman. He wanted to be with a girl. A little girl.'

8

DCI Anderson felt as though his whole investigation had arrived at a fork in the road and that he had absolutely no idea which way to turn.

Within the Metropolitan Police there was always great reluctance to label any murder the work of a serial killer until it was absolutely necessary. Most serial killers went after a particular social group – prostitutes, the homeless and so on. In cases where there seemed to be no link between the victims, news of a potential killer on the loose would do nothing but spread panic.

There was also the issue of feeding the fantasy of the killer. Many such psychopaths were known to get a thrill from seeing details of their handiwork reported in the press or on television. The oxygen of publicity could easily encourage the murderer to strike again.

On the other hand, failing to warn the public of the potential threat could lead to complaints and even legal action. All it would take was for the family of one victim to claim that he or she would never have left their house on that fateful night had a proper warning been issued. Then there would be more than enough shit flying around to ensure some of it would stick to everyone involved in the case.

Anderson needed to know exactly what he was dealing with, and that meant talking to an expert. A profiler. Michelle Rivers, the usual first choice for many senior MIT officers, was on secondment in America, so instead he had asked Dr Jacques Bernard, a Canadian professor of forensic psychology who was teaching at King's College, to come in. The professor had been highly recommended by officers in both the UK and US who had used him in the past.

Rather than briefing the whole team, Anderson decided it would be better for him to first have a quiet word with Dr Bernard in order to help him decide on his next move. Tall and distinguished looking with dark brown hair flecked with grey at the temples and a heavy moustache, Dr Bernard looked more like a film star than a university professor. All female eyes in the room drank in his features as he made his way across the office floor. As the guest made himself comfortable in the corner of the DCI's office, Anderson gave strict instructions that he was not to be disturbed for the foreseeable future.

'Well,' said Anderson as he sat behind his desk opposite Dr Bernard. 'What do you think?'

'I can honestly say I have never seen anything like this before in my life,' he said, his accent a perfect blend of Canadian French and English. He reached into his briefcase and pulled out the copies of the files that Anderson had sent him earlier in the day. 'There have been cases before where several mutilated bodies have turned up at one time, particularly when it comes to battles between rival gangs of bikers back home. But this, this is different. What you have here is not just someone who wants recognition for their work, but someone who wants to be identified as a leading serial killer right from the word go. As I'm sure you already know, the classic FBI definition of a serial killer is a person who kills at least three times with a cooling-off period in between murders.

'The reality is that most of the time serial killers can get away with what they do because we don't even know they are out there. You have three bodies from three different time periods. Had the killer not dumped them in plain view, it's unlikely that anyone would ever have known for sure that they had been killed.'

Dr Bernard paused as Anderson shifted some papers to one side of his desk to make way for a ruled pad on which he began making notes. 'Please, continue.'

'There are many elements in this case that I find particularly disturbing. The victimology is one. Every serial killer is different but the thing they all usually have in common is that their victims tend to be similar. They all go after people who are short and slight. The reasons are obvious – such people are easier to attack, move around or dispose of. Small men, slight women and children. That's why female serial killers tend to go after babies or the elderly. But even male serial killers tend to choose victims who are smaller than themselves. They don't want to risk someone being able to get the better of them.'

Bernard sorted through the pages in front of him, searching for details from the initial autopsy reports. 'But look here, Raymond Chadwick was a big man. Six feet two inches and more than seventeen stone. Miller was smaller – only five ten – but still fit and strong. Your unknown was somewhere in between the two. They are not typical serial killer victims.'

'What does that tell us?'

Bernard shrugged. 'I think it's too early to tell. Could be you have more than one person involved in the murders.'

'Great.'

'There's also the fact that two of your victims appeared to be successful businessmen. Serial killers tend to go after runaways, prostitutes or drug addicts – the kind of people who are easier to target because they live on the edge of society. The sort of people who, when they disappear, nobody even misses.'

'Makes sense.'

'What that says to me is that there is a specific reason why these people are being targeted, but as of yet there is no clue about what that might be.'

Bernard rotated one of the photographs from the autopsy through a full three hundred and sixty degrees before placing it back in his file.

'I also have grave concerns about the MO.'

'Why?'

'Because it's identical in each case.'

'I don't understand. Surely the fact it's identical proves we're looking for a serial killer.'

'To some degree, but not as much as you'd think. If you look at crimes other than murder, criminals tend to be fairly consistent. If you burgle houses and you like to break in through the back door, you'll probably do that every time. But burglars go out to work several times a week. Serial killers murder only once in a blue moon. There might be years in between. When they become ready to kill again, they often try to fix or change anything that failed to work properly last time around. Or they might have found a way to get much more of a thrill.

'I know a case in which a serial killer switched from stabbing to strangling because he cut himself while carving up his last victim and got covered in blood. Another who didn't tie up his first victim and got kicked in the balls. You can be sure he tied up every victim after that. I know other cases in which killers have switched from murdering their victim right away to torturing them to death over a period of days because the first time it was all over too soon and they wanted to have more time to enjoy themselves.

'Using MO to link crimes can be problematic. An MO could change from one killing to the next; you don't know what other factors might be in play. Someone who always stabs his victims five times may stab one twenty times because they somehow insulted him. Someone who always rapes his victims may have been disturbed by someone walking their dog or forgotten to pack his condoms or simply changed his mind.'

Bernard spread the autopsy photographs of each victim across the front of Anderson's desk. 'But in this case the modus operandi is absolutely identical. This to me speaks of someone who has already perfected their methods and techniques. Even though one of your bodies is two years old, I think you're looking for someone with a record of crime and violence that stretches back far, far further. There are going to be other bodies and they will be even older than these.'

Anderson stopped his scribbling and looked up for a moment, his face grim. 'I'm very grateful for all of this, but, at the same time, if you're correct, this opens our investigation even further.'

Dr Bernard nodded in agreement. It was clear he too wished he had better news to deliver. 'The MO is worrying for other reasons too. There are dozens of serial killers out there that nobody gets to hear about because, to be perfectly honest, they just aren't interesting enough. If you want to be a famous serial killer, you have to stand out from the crowd. You kill more than a dozen victims, send taunting letters to the police or do bizarre things to the bodies.

'What you have here is someone who is not only ensuring that they are counted as a serial killer but who, thanks to the mutilation of the bodies, is ensuring that as soon as the details are released to the public they'll join the ranks of serial killer royalty.

'Most killers would have to work their way up to something like this. They would have to practise again and again, refining what they do. As I said before, what you have here is the work of someone who has already passed that stage.'

Anderson put down his pen, then reached up and rubbed his palm against his chin. 'I don't know what I was expecting. To be honest, all you're doing is making me realize that we're up against someone who is even more steps ahead than I'd imagined they were in the first place.'

Dr Bernard shrugged his shoulders. 'I'm sorry.'

'Don't worry. Working a murder case is all about playing catch-up. I just didn't realize quite how much catching up we had to do.'

'Do you still want me to speak to your team?'

'Yes and no. They're pretty motivated out there and I think something like this could really take the wind out of their sails. It's one thing looking for a killer who has committed three random murders, quite another to think that we're part of some bigger, sicker game. I think I'd like to wait until we identify the third victim before you give them a full briefing; that way we'll know for sure if there's a connection between them. What I would like in the meantime, however, is just a general sense of the way the mind of a serial killer works.'

'But nothing specific?'

'No, that's not necessary. I think it would be good for them to know what we're up against. To have an idea of the kind of clues that might be cropping up – the areas they should be concentrating on.'

'I'll do what I can.'

'How long are you over here for, by the way?'

'Officially just until the end of the academic year, but this is my sixth attachment in London in the past ten years. I really love it here. It's pretty much my second home. I'll almost certainly be staying on.'

Anderson opened the door to his office to find DI Collins pacing up and down outside.

She had returned from interviewing Sandra Miller soon after Anderson had shut himself away in his office with the psychologist and given orders that he was not to be disturbed. She had spent the time since making phone calls and collating information. What had started out as an interesting development in the murder case had now evolved fully into a potential lead.

She barged her way into the office, pausing only briefly as the handsome face of Dr Jacques Bernard smiled over at her from the corner of the room. Flustered for a split second, she regained her composure and turned to Anderson.

'Sir, I think I might have something here,' she gasped, her voice breathless with excitement.

The brief report she handed over made grim reading. At least four separate complaints from under-aged girls who claimed Edward Miller had molested them had been looked into. Each of the cases had been handled by a separate team of social workers working in a different local authority. Focusing their attention on the victims, rather than on the person behind the attacks, they never realized they were dealing with a repeat offender. The police were brought in each time but there was never enough evidence for them to be able to make any charges stick.

'How come none of this showed up on the PNC search?' asked Anderson.

'The cases were in Humberside,' Collins said simply.

'Oh, for fuck's sake.'

No further explanation was needed. Every officer in the country knew that, up until the mid-2000s, Humberside Police had a policy of destroying all computerized intelligence files. Senior staff at the force had misinterpreted the Data Protection Act and decided they would be in breach of regulations if they kept information about those who were arrested or questioned but never actually charged. No other force in the country made the same error.

Humberside's actions only came to light when it emerged that Ian Huntley, the Soham murderer, was able to get a job in a school despite numerous complaints that he had raped or sexually assaulted under-aged girls. Computerized background checks run by Cambridgeshire Police failed to throw any light on his past because the information had been erased.

'What about the wife? Why didn't she say anything before?'

'I think she was ashamed. She saw he had an interest in much younger women, but, so far as she knew, he never did anything to pursue it, at least where under-aged girls were concerned. She hoped it was just a phase he was going through and that, over time, he would fall in love with her as she was, not just yearn for the early days of their relationship when she was little more than a schoolgirl.

'She hinted at what was going on when DI Hill interviewed her, saying her husband was looking to replace her with someone younger, but he never pursued it.'

Anderson hit the speaker button on the front of his phone, then dialled a number. After two rings the gruff voice of DI Hill filled the room. There was a rushing sound in the background and Collins guessed that he was in his car.

'Hello?'

'Hill, you're a fucking idiot.'

'You what?'

'Just get yourself back here a.s.a.p.'

Hill's voice spluttered as he tried to work out why on earth his boss was delivering such a bollocking. He had barely begun to string a sentence together when Anderson hit the button again and cut him off, turning his attention back to the people in his office.

'Good job, Collins. I guess DCS Higgins was right. Let me introduce you to someone. This is Dr Jacques Bernard. He's a criminal psychologist with King's College. I brought him in to help us work up some kind of profile of the person we're looking for. Dr Bernard, this is Detective Inspector Stacey Collins, one of the lead officers on the murder team.'

Dr Bernard stood up, moved towards Collins and held out his hand. 'It's a pleasure to meet you,' he said. His voice was beautifully mellow. Their palms touched. His hands were large and powerful yet neatly manicured. When Collins went to pull hers away, he held on just a fraction too long.

'Nice to meet you too,' she said softly.

Anderson handed the report that Collins had given him to the psychologist. 'Do you think this could be relevant?'

Dr Bernard frowned in concentration. 'It's very hard to say. At the moment, so far as I'm aware, there is nothing to link the other two victims to this kind of activity. It could be nothing more than a coincidence, but I think it is undoubtedly a lead worth pursuing.

'There have been cases where killers have targeted, say, prostitutes in a belief that they are cleaning up the streets, ridding the world of its filth. Going after sex offenders could be part of a similar mission.'

Anderson nodded. 'But, as you say, it could be nothing more than a coincidence. I remember talking to a friend about the Soham inquiry. You know the night those girls went missing, a convicted paedophile from Devon who had previously abducted a couple of girls around the same age happened to be in town. Turned out his granny lived there. He had nothing to do with the crime, just a pure coincidence. These things happen. Collins, let's keep this material out of the briefing for now – I don't want anyone's thinking blinkered as a result – but I want you and Woods to follow this up in the morning. Top priority.'

It took half an hour or so before DI Hill and the remaining members of the inquiry team who were out and about returned to the office and arranged themselves in a semicircle to await the promised presentation.

Dr Jacques Bernard moved to the front of the room until he was standing directly underneath the board showing the names of the victims. He took in the faces of those around him, his eyes seeming to linger for a moment when they met those of Stacey Collins, who was sitting on a desk towards the back. Dr Bernard cleared his throat and began to speak.

'I can tell from the expectant expressions on your faces that you assume I'm about to perform some kind of minor miracle, that I'm going to tell you exactly what sort of person you're looking for, where they live, how many kids they have, how long they've been married and what they do for a living.

'But sadly this isn't some slick American television

show and I can't give you anything of the sort. What I can do is tell you everything that I know about serial killers. And you may be surprised to find that much of what you think you already know is likely to be wrong.'

Collins shifted in her seat and glanced over at Woods, who rolled his eyes up at the ceiling. She didn't like profilers at the best of times and felt that this one, though more pleasant on the eyes than most, was already starting to get on her nerves. It was as if she was back at school with some know-it-all teacher lording it up at the front of the class. She hadn't liked school much either.

'Statistically, the typical serial killer is a white male from a lower-to-middle-class background, usually in his twenties or thirties,' Dr Bernard continued. 'He is not a lunatic. He is far more likely to be a charming, impeccably dressed, polite individual than an out-and-out oddball. Like the best predators, serial killers stalk their prey by gaining their trust. Don't go out there looking for someone who stands out from the crowd: the person you're after will be able to blend in perfectly.

'He will be absolutely fascinated with the police and with authority in general. He probably spends a lot of time reading about police procedures, taking courses or watching detective shows. He may have attempted to become a police officer himself but probably got rejected and ended up working as a security guard or serving in the army. He may even have found a job that brings him into regular contact with the authorities. One thing that is particular to this case: the offender is going to be extremely physically strong, capable of lifting a full-grown man.

'It's likely that he also spends a lot of time reading books about psychology and sociology. He will use that knowledge to manipulate situations to help generate sympathy in those around him. This, of course, is the perfect way to get people to lower their defences.'

Collins folded her arms and shifted back on the desk in an effort to get comfortable. This might have been new to some of the others on the team but for her it was old hat.

Dr Bernard continued. 'In terms of actual background, you're looking for someone who may have been physically or emotionally abused by their parents. Some serial killers claim that exposure to violent images or events was the catalyst that sent them down the path of destruction, but the fact is that there are many children and adults who have witnessed such events and gone on to become perfectly normal, productive members of society.

'Although the popular image of a serial killer involves someone who takes a trophy from his victim or tortures and mutilates them, the reality is that this happens only in a tiny proportion of cases. Most of the time killers hit victims over the head, rape them or strangle them, and leave them wherever they drop. It usually happens very quickly. You're looking for someone who has the ability to put a lot of time and effort into what they do.

'He will have been extremely careful when it comes to covering his tracks, so it's perfectly possible that he does not have a criminal record for any kind of violent offence. Instead look out for incidents of arson or cruelty to animals. The small proportion of killers who torture their victims have often practised their brutality on their pets. Pyromania is another key indicator. Serial killers see their victims as objects rather than as human beings. To them, destroying a piece of property and destroying a person amounts to much the same thing.

'Finally, you're looking for someone who can remain extraordinarily cool under pressure. Research has shown that psychopaths and serial killers have a greater fear threshold, and are less likely to respond to fear-inducing stimuli or sudden shocks. Some researchers think they are virtually immune to those kinds of emotions.'

Dr Bernard turned around and took a long, slow look at the board that held the victims' details. 'Are there any questions?'

'What's your view on why the bodies were dumped?' asked Anderson.

'It's impossible to say for sure without having more information about a potential suspect but what I can say for certain is this. In many cases, serial killers who have got away with a number of murders over a period of many years can actually feel put out that no one has recognized what they see as their achievements. This is particularly true in cases where more than one murder has taken place but police have failed to identify a link between the victims.

'In such cases, it has been known for the killers to begin playing games with the police or the press, writing letters, sending them tapes or using some other way to communicate, all with an intention of steering them on to the right track so that they eventually realize a multiple murderer is on the loose. In such cases, the killers actually want to be caught.'

Anderson nodded. 'And you think that might apply here?'

'It is one possible scenario.'

'If that's the case,' said Collins, a mischievous smile spreading over her lips, 'it will make our job one hell of a lot easier.' A chuckle of laughter rippled throughout the room. Even Anderson couldn't help but giggle.

The briefing over, Collins was back at her desk, probing deeper into Miller's background, when she felt a sudden presence close by. She looked up to see Dr Jacques Bernard smiling down at her.

'Detective Inspector Collins.'

'Yes?'

'Excuse me for saying this, but I couldn't help feeling that you were, shall we say, a little bit sceptical about some of the information I was providing.'

'I'm sorry, I didn't mean to be. It's just that ...

well, I think that criminal profilers are a bit like psychics and mediums.'

'I don't understand.'

'When they talk, people remember the few accurate predictions they've made and forget all the stuff that they've got wrong. The trick is to use a whole load of ambiguous, vague stuff that can be seen to apply to anything. Smoke and mirrors.'

'You think that's what I've been doing?'

'I'm talking in general terms here. I wasn't trying to be specific to what you had said.'

'Well, I agree with you to some extent. You know a team at the University of Liverpool has just done a study and found that most serial killers don't fit into the behavioural patterns and distinctions that the FBI uses to catch them, so maybe you're right.'

'Maybe.'

'But, on the other hand, I don't always follow those patterns either. I can assure you that everything I've been talking about is extremely valid and very useful to someone such as yourself. Perhaps we could discuss it in more detail some day.' He hesitated then flashed that smile again. 'Perhaps over dinner? With a spot of PG?'

'Tea?'

The smile grew wider, more infectious. 'Pinot Grigio. It's my favourite wine.'

'Ah.'

Collins tried hard not to return the smile but felt it creeping across her face all the same. 'Perhaps.'

9

It was the middle of the next morning before the full reality of the situation began to dawn on her. And, once it did, it left Collins feeling thoroughly miserable.

When she had first come across the information about Edward Miller's background, it had seemed like an exciting development. Now she was far less sure. Ever since the investigation had begun everyone on the team had wondered what kind of animal they were dealing with. If the lead Collins had found was correct, it threw up all sorts of emotional conflicts that she had no idea how to deal with.

If the killer was truly targeting paedophiles and, in the words of Dr Bernard, cleaning up the streets, then there would be an awful lot of people out there who would believe he was doing a public service. As a mother, she had lived with the fear of her child being abducted on an almost daily basis. Did she really want to stop someone who was fighting back against those responsible?

Collins always became particularly emotional when it came to this sort of offender. More than once in the past she had bent the rules of evidence to the point that they almost snapped in order to secure a conviction. She wasn't proud of herself for having acted that way, but it was the only way to ensure the man was unable to go after any more children. As far as she was concerned they were all scum, and if they vanished from the face of the earth, so much the better.

All of which made her current assignment all the more difficult to swallow. She and DS Woods were sitting in the reception area of the South London officers of ViSOR, the Violent and Sexual Offenders Register. Anderson – on Dr Bernard's recommendation – had sent them there on the chance that, if there was some kind of paedophile link to the crimes, anyone who had gone missing from the register in recent years might be a possible victim.

ViSOR held details of everyone convicted, cautioned or released from prison for a sexual offence against children or adults. Those on the register had to report to their local police station at regular intervals, so Collins and Woods were hoping to trawl through lists of those who had failed to comply.

It was a long shot, for sure, but other leads had so far come to nothing. *Crimewatch* had passed on featuring the tattoo from the unknown victim on their last edition on the grounds that, without being able to use the words 'serial killer' as part of the appeal, it simply wasn't interesting enough to pass muster. Instead the reconstructed image had been circulated to local newspaper and magazine programmes across the south-east.

Hill and Porter had not made much progress either. Further checks into the background of Raymond Chadwick had failed to throw any light on how or why he had become the killer's most recent victim, while further interrogation of Leroy Banks had all but eliminated him as a potential suspect.

As Woods flicked through a copy of that morning's *Independent*, Collins bounced the heels of her shoes on the carpet and stared directly into space. It was obvious that she was far from happy about the situation.

Woods folded his newspaper and turned to her. 'You've got a real problem with this, haven't you?'

Collins nodded. 'Let's say it does turn out that all the victims are nonces. I'm just not happy about the idea of trying to track down someone who's killing off people who have no right to live in the first place. I don't want to sound like some kind of half-mad *Daily Mail* reader, but why not just let them get on with it?

'We might find that this person is being careful about who he chooses, that he's picking his targets well. It could be that he's going after people who have done wrong but have somehow managed to slip through the net, just the way Miller did. I say let him be. I don't know if I'm going to be able to do my best work when it comes to tracking him down.'

'For all we know, one of these dead blokes might have abused the killer's own kid. I know that I'd finish anyone who tried something like that with Sophie.'

Woods massaged the back of his neck with his hand. His dark eyes stared hard at Collins, looking right through her. He finally spoke. 'I can't say I don't have some sympathy with you, but you know it's not our choice, it's not our call. Our job is to catch whoever is responsible for these killings and then put them in front of a jury. If they decide this person is a hero, deserves a medal or a massive payout from public funds, then that's up to them, not us.

'You're assuming that Miller was guilty. Those allegations could have been false for all we know. And there's still nothing to suggest that Chadwick or the other guy had any link to sex crimes.

'Anyway, regardless of how we feel about this person's victims, the fact remains that people are not allowed to take the law into their own hands. There lies anarchy. Remember David Copeland, the London nail bomber? The first week he targeted the black community, then the Asian community. After that he bombed a gay pub and was planning to bomb a Jewish area when he was caught. So he's going after paedophiles at the moment but what will happen when he gets through with them? Suppose he moves on to rapists, then murderers, then adulterers, then liars? Where will it all stop?'

Collins shrugged. 'But you can't tell me that you seriously think that all people like that deserve to live, can you?'

'You're saying you want to bring back capital punishment?'

'For some offences, yes, I think I would.'

'But people make mistakes, people make false accusations, some people even have false memories. Once you've executed someone, murdered them in the name of the state, you can't take it back. I could never live with that on my conscience if I ever found out I'd got it wrong. It would be as bad as if I'd killed them myself.'

'I don't know, Tony. I know there's an argument that these people are sick and they can't help themselves, but you could say that about anyone involved in crime. Anyway, you don't understand the emotions that are involved because you don't have children.'

Woods snorted with disapproval. 'That's rubbish. You don't have to have direct experience of anything to be able to empathize. And, while I may not have children myself, I have been a child. I know what it's like to be that innocent and to place all your trust and love in a parent or carer. I know how vulnerable that can make someone and how easy it would be for someone to abuse that.'

'Remember too that most abusers have been abused themselves as children, and a significant proportion of those that they abuse will go on to abuse others. It's not black and white. Even the ones who start out as innocent victims might go on to become offenders in years to come.

'At the end of the day, the law is the law and it

exists for a reason. You can't go around making exceptions from the rule every time it suits you. It's only a short step before you start bringing in other crimes with a death penalty. Every case is judged on its merits. That's what the whole jury trial system is about. If there are extenuating circumstances, they can be explored and adjustments made if necessary. You can't get rid of principles like that, not in my mind.'

Collins could not think of a strong enough reply. Woods had a point and he had made it well. If anything it made her even less happy with the situation. 'Whatever,' she mumbled.

She paused for a moment and stared at the floor in front of her. 'What do you think of that Dr Bernard?'

Woods made an indistinct noise in reply. Not so much a word, more of a grunt.

'What's that supposed to mean?'

'I dunno. Something about the guy. Gives me the creeps.'

'Really?'

'Yeah, anyone who's that obsessed with the workings of the mind of a serial killer, anyone who's that encyclopaedic about the different things different deranged people have done to their victims – well, it's not exactly normal, is it?'

'You just don't like anyone who knows more about psychology than you do.'

'As if such a person exists. Why do you ask anyway? What did you think of him?'

'A lot of what he said was the usual crap, but some of it seemed to make sense. I thought he was all right. Quite nice, really.'

Woods eyed her cautiously. 'I think Yvonne and that civvy data clerk were planning to form a fan club. Perhaps you could be club secretary. I've got a mate who could do you a good deal on starting up a blog . . .'

Collins didn't have time to tell Woods to piss off. At that moment the door to the office opened and a secretary looked over at them. 'Mr Johnson will see you now,' she said softly.

Brian Johnson was the short, bespectacled head of operations for ViSOR. With his slightly flared suit, his full-face beard and weak, ineffectual handshake, he looked, Collins thought, like the sort of stereotypical bloke who should actually be on the register rather than running it.

His voice had a slightly nasal sing-song quality to it, and Collins could feel herself taking an instant dislike to the man. It was probably, she told herself, more to do with the situation she had been forced into than the man himself, but even at the best of times Johnson was not the kind of person she would have been able to warm to.

He led them into his comfortable office, sat them on the small dark leather corner suite and offered them coffee or water. When they refused both, he too sat down and clasped his hands.

'I understand the basics of your case but it's

probably best if you go from the beginning so I can work out how best to assist you.'

Collins leaned forward. 'We're currently investigating a triple murder case. The three bodies were found at one location but the indicators are that they were killed months, possibly even years apart.

'One of the victims had been accused on numerous occasions of sexual assault on a minor. There was a degree of genital mutilation in all three victims, and we're exploring the possibility that the killings may have been some kind of revenge attack.'

'Are the two other victims believed to be sex offenders?'

'There is no evidence that we have been able to uncover in the case of the most recent victim, Raymond Chadwick. As for the other one, we have yet to identify him at all. We didn't get a match for his DNA on the database, but that doesn't necessarily mean anything.'

Johnson was listening intently to her words. 'Are you thinking that this might be some sort of vigilante action? The parent of an abused child perhaps?'

'That's clearly a possibility. At this point in time, however, we're more interested in learning if there are any more potential victims out there. We were hoping you could provide us with a list of sex offenders who have gone missing in recent years so that we can see if any of them match the person we have yet to identify.'

'It's a bit of a long shot, isn't it? Surely if they were

convicted, you'd already have a DNA sample on file.'

'The point is, Mr Johnson,' said Collins, her jaw tightening with impatience, 'our boss doesn't like to leave any stone unturned. The three bodies we found were deliberately left out in a public place. This was an intentional act. We have every reason to believe that there may be far more bodies out there, including those of convicted paedophiles. What we're here to do is attempt to narrow down just who some of those victims might actually be.'

'Of course. I understand.'

'Well, then, now that you know all about our case, why don't you tell us about the system, so we don't waste too much of your time? Or ours. How many names are on the register?'

Johnson nodded and smiled warmly. 'Just over forty thousand.'

'What's the compliance rate?' asked Woods.

'It's good,' replied Johnson, shuffling in his seat. 'Very good.'

The two officers looked at him expectantly but he said nothing.

'An actual figure would be good,' said Collins drily.

Johnson nodded. 'Just over ninety-seven per cent.'

'You what?' gasped Collins.

Johnson swallowed hard. 'Ninety-seven per cent.'

'Oh, for fuck's sake,' spat Collins. 'This is a fucking waste of time.'

'It's . . . it's really quite good,' stuttered Johnson.

'For you maybe,' replied Collins. 'It's a great statistic to be able to quote to people but the reality is a bit different. You've got forty thousand nonces on the books and three per cent of them are missing. That equates to what? More than a thousand people.'

'Nine hundred and twenty-two at the moment, to be precise. We prefer the term sex offender,' mumbled Johnson. 'We know that some people deliberately pursue an itinerant lifestyle in order to avoid registration, but it's a relatively small proportion.'

Collins and Woods exchanged glances. Going to ViSOR had always been something of a stab in the dark. Now it was as though they were having their hands tied behind their backs. The list they would come away with would be almost endless.

'Are you planning to track down the people on the list who've gone missing so you can eliminate them from your inquiries?'

'That was part of the idea.'

'Hmmm.'

'What's that supposed to mean?' snapped Collins.

'I just don't really see how that's going to be possible. I mean, these cases are considered a high priority. Every police force in the country is on the lookout for these missing offenders. They are already deep underground. The chances of finding them yourselves are almost zero.'

'You let us worry about that.'

'Okay.' Johnson paused for a moment. 'There's probably something else you should know too,' he said, his voice now so low it was only barely audible. 'Something else you may not be aware of.'

'Go on, pour salt on my wounds.'

'Well, there's a sliding scale that dictates just how long people's names stay on the register. Those given a jail sentence of more than thirty months stay there indefinitely. Those imprisoned for between six and thirty months remain on the register for ten years. Those sentenced for six months or less are placed on the register for seven years. If they only get a caution, they only stay on the register for two years. And all those times are halved if the person is under eighteen.'

Woods rocked forward in his chair and placed his head in his hands. 'So what you're saying is that hundreds of names come off the register every year and that if any of those people had subsequently gone missing, you'd have no way of knowing.'

'That's correct, I'm afraid.'

'Is there any way of getting access to those deleted records?'

'They're all removed from the computer, but the hard copies are kept in storage. You'd be welcome to look through them.'

'You've got to be kidding me. We have to do it all by hand?'

'I'm afraid so. The rest of the records I can run through the computer. I can try different permutations but there are dozens so it's going to take a good few days.'

Collins was quietly shaking her head while listening but finally spoke up. 'I have another question. Say we're looking for a vigilante; who, apart from the police, has access to the information on this database?'

'More people than you'd think,' replied Johnson, 'though they receive the information on a highly confidential basis. The main list includes' – he counted them off on his fingers – 'head teachers, doctors, youth leaders, sports club managers and pub landlords. There might be a few other categories but it's quite a wide spread.'

Collins turned to Woods. 'Some of the pub landlords I know, they wouldn't think twice about passing on details of local paedophiles to their bouncers or some of their more unsavoury customers.'

'There is another possibility, of course,' said Johnson.

All eyes turned to him.

'And what might that be?' asked Collins.

'Well, I remember a case of a paedophile ring from a few years ago that ended with a murder. It was a bog-standard ring of blokes who were getting together to abuse children and share pics and videos. One member of the ring, the only one on our list, was murdered in his home. At first the investigating team suspected a local vigilante but it turned out it was actually another member of the ring that had killed him. I guess he wanted to make sure there was no way he was going to be able to point the finger at him.'

'So what you're saying,' said Woods, 'is that the possibilities are endless.'

'Yes. That's exactly what I'm saying.'

'Great,' said Collins, standing up. Her face easily betrayed the fact that she didn't think it was great at all but rather far, far from it. 'Where do we start?'

10

Sophie Collins and Jack Stanley walked side by side along the narrow garden path towards the gleaming red front door.

'What do you mean you don't like surprises?' gasped Jack. 'Everyone likes surprises.'

'Not necessarily. There are good surprises and bad surprises. You haven't told me which type this is yet.'

'Isn't it obvious?'

'If it was I wouldn't be so nervous.'

'Trust me. There are no bad surprises.'

'Of course there are. The good ones include surprise birthday parties and finding money in the street. The bad ones are being told you've got six months to live or finding out your house has been burgled.'

'They're not surprises, they're disasters. It's totally different. But let's not argue. This is a good surprise. Trust me.'

He took her hand and squeezed it gently as they continued along the path. 'Okay, Dad.' She snorted. 'Still sounds weird to hear myself saying that.'

They were only a few steps from the door when it swung open and a short, slightly plump woman with a mass of dark curls piled high on her head appeared.

She smiled, showing rows of crooked, nicotine-stained teeth, but projected so much warmth and gentleness that Sophie couldn't help but smile back. The family resemblance between all three of them was obvious and Sophie knew immediately who she was about to meet.

She looked up at Jack, the smile on her face having grown into a huge grin. 'Of course,' she gasped. 'I never thought about it. That's your mum. My gran! I've got another gran!' Sophie beamed with excitement as Ella Stanley held out her arms and gave her long-lost granddaughter a huge hug.

'I've heard so much about you, my dear,' she said with a voice that could have been straight out of an East End market stall. 'Jack's told me everything, of course, but it's so wonderful to meet you in the flesh at last.'

Ella stepped to one side and led Sophie into the house, making her way towards the living room.

'Cool. Is there a grandpa too?'

Ella's face flickered with emotion. 'Sorry, dear, no. Mr Stanley passed away some years ago.'

'I'm sorry, I really am.'

'Thanks, dear. You really are a sweetie. Now what can I get you to drink? A nice cup of tea?'

'Erm. I don't really like tea. It's too bitter.'

Ella paused for a moment. 'Well, I suppose you're still a bit young. I'll see what I can find in the kitchen. Make yourself comfortable, won't you?' She looked up at Jack. 'You're right, she is a little angel, isn't she?'

Sophie blushed and Jack smiled as he sat down beside her on the floral-print sofa that filled one side of the room.

'It's a bit weird thinking of you having a mum.'

'What, you think I was dropped off by a stork or something? I think I might have to have a word with the teachers at your school, you're obviously not learning anything.'

Sophie gave Jack a playful dig in the ribs. 'I just mean that you don't talk about her much, and she's so different to mum's mum. She's so ... well, she's just very different.'

'She means the world to me,' said Jack. His face became serious for a moment. 'She means as much to me as you do.'

Ella shuffled back into the room carrying a large wooden tray laden high with orange squash, fresh fruit, pieces of cake, sticky buns and chocolate. Sophie's eyes lit up in delight.

'Tuck in dear,' she said. 'You young people always look so skinny. I think you need to be fed properly. Would you like anything else?'

'No, this is brilliant. Thanks.'

Ella sat in a cosy-looking armchair that had been positioned opposite the electric fire and looked on lovingly as her granddaughter began to tuck into the feast in front of her.

'So tell me about yourself,' said Ella. 'What kinds of things do you like doing in your spare time? And how do you find school?'

'School's okay,' replied Sophie in between mouthfuls and sips. 'Some of the teachers are a bit annoying I like English and drama but I'm not keen on maths. Spare time? Just the usual, hanging out with friends, going to the cinema.' She looked across at her father for a moment. 'You know, the usual. Nothing special.'

The pair carried on shooting the breeze for a good half an hour and it was as if they had known each other their whole lives. Sophie particularly like it when Ella fetched down a photo album stuffed full of pictures of herself as a young child along with snaps of Jack as a baby and a teenager.

Sophie roared with laughter at the pictures of young Jack in flared trousers and tank tops.

'You have to understand,' he said defensively once the humiliation had drawn to a close, 'that it wasn't just me. Everyone dressed like that those days. In fact, it was the people who didn't follow fashion who looked silly. Trust me, thirty years from now you'll be looking back at pictures of what you wear today with kids of your own and they'll be splitting their sides.'

Ella sat back in her chair, enjoying the dynamic between her child and grandchild. Then her soft happy face suddenly hardened. 'Jack, I think you should go out of the room for a few minutes.'

'Why's that?'

'Don't answer back. Just do as I say.'

'Yes, Mum.'

Jack winked at Sophie, then made his way out of the room, closing the door behind him.

Ella moved from her armchair on to the sofa beside Sophie. Her smile had returned and was bigger than ever.

'Now, dear, the really wonderful thing about grandmothers is that you can tell them things that you don't want anyone else to know and still be sure that your secrets are completely safe.'

'Okay.'

'What we're about to talk about, none of it goes any further than this room. Most of all, him out there will never hear about it.'

'Sounds good.'

'So let's get started. Do you have a boyfriend?

Sophie giggled. 'Not really?'

'But there's someone you like, am I right?'

'Maybe.'

'What's his name?'

Sophie could feel herself blushing more and more deeply. 'Simon.'

'Go on.'

'He's lovely. Tall, and he's got this gorgeous curly hair and such a sweet smile.'

'Do you think he likes you too? What am I saying, look at you, you're beautiful, he must like you, otherwise he's crazy.'

'I think so; he's a bit shy. I don't know. We can talk when there are lots of people around, but whenever it's just him and me together, he clams up.'

'Well, listen to me, dear, whenever you feel the need to talk to someone about anything like this . . . I know you won't want to talk to your mother because girls never do, and there's no point in talking to Jack because he doesn't know anything about boys. Or girls for that matter. But if you ever need any kind of . . . let's just say I'm always here for you.'

'I don't know what to say.'

Ella Stanley tapped the end of her nose twice with her finger. 'Let's just keep it all between the two of us.'

'Sure.'

'Do you smoke?'

'Sorry?'

'Do you smoke, you know, cigarettes?'

'Oh. No. Not really.'

'Seriously? I certainly did by the time I was your age.'

'Well . . .'

'Waste of time. They make your breath stink. And no boy will want to kiss you. That's what I think. It's just not worth it, no matter what anyone else says.'

'Okay, I'll try to remember that.'

Just then there was a knock at the door and Jack poked his head around. 'Sorry, Mum, we're going to have to get going soon, if I'm going to have her back home before Stacey suspects anything.'

Ella looked down at the floor for a moment. 'It's been so wonderful to meet you, dear. I must say, I'm not sure I'm ever going to be able to forgive your mum for keeping you away from Jack. And from me.'

Sophie shifted awkwardly in her seat. 'She had her reasons, I guess.'

'I should hope so. But dads and their daughters, that's a special bond. No one should ever try to break it. The fact that you go to all this effort in order to see your dad shows just how important it is.' She turned to Jack. 'But honestly, all this cloak and dagger stuff, it's so ridiculous. I want to be able to call my granddaughter up on the phone, I want to be able to give my granddaughter presents.'

'I tried talking to Stacey,' said Jack. 'She won't see sense.'

'I never liked that girl. First time you brought her round I could tell she was ... I was so happy when you stopped seeing her. Sorry, dear, I know it's your mum I'm talking about but – '

Sophie stood up suddenly. 'I should go. I don't really need to hear this.'

'Leave it, Mum ... you're upsetting Sophie.'

'And now this. Just goes to prove it. Doesn't think he's good enough to be a father to his own daughter so she keeps her quiet for God knows how long.'

'Mum, please, leave it.'

Ella let out a long sigh, then turned to her grand-daughter once more. 'I'm sorry, it's just that I feel like I've missed out on so much of your life and it makes me so sad to think about how we could have been.

You're my only grandchild and I want to be a proper grandparent.'

'That would be great. I'd love it, but right now . . .'

'Don't worry, dear.' Ella reached across and took Sophie's hand between both of hers. 'I'm sure things will work out just fine.'

'So what do you think?' asked Jack as they drove back.

'I think she's quite a character. Certainly speaks her mind. But . . .'

'But what?'

'Well, it's just interesting.'

'What's interesting? You're not making any sense.'

'Well, it's just . . . you're not quite so tough around her, are you?'

'Listen, Sophie, my mother is a strong, bloody-minded woman,' Jack said softly. 'I don't mind telling you, even now, the thought of being on the wrong side of her still scares me shitless.' He turned and fixed his daughter with a steady gaze.

I I

By the third day the routine had become well established. Collins and Woods would stop off at the incident room for morning prayers and a general catch-up with other members of the team. From there they would make their way over to the ViSOR offices to continue ploughing through the files of sex offenders and compiling a list of all those who had gone 'missing' in the hope that one might turn out to be their unidentified third victim.

It had taken only a few hours of sifting for Collins to become thoroughly pissed off and disillusioned with the task at hand. Soon the names and faces of countless paedophiles and rapists seemed to be swimming through her head day and night. No matter how hard she tried to put them out of her mind, they seemed to have become a permanent fixture. They even haunted her dreams, along with the gruesome details of the crimes they had committed and the terrified screams of their victims.

More than once she found herself secretly hoping that some of the men who had been listed as missing had indeed been tracked down by the killer, decapitated and emptied of all their internal organs. She knew the victims had been put through untold agony, but scum like this had caused great suffering themselves. She felt sympathy for Edward Miller's widow, but none for the man himself. Men like him did not deserve to live. And they certainly did not deserve the undivided attention of good officers like herself and Woods.

She was supposed to be hot on the trail of a psychopathic killer who had committed the most horrific acts of violence, but the more Collins learned about the group he appeared to be targeting, the more she felt herself feeling a measure of sympathy for his cause. If he did turn out to be, say, the father of one of the victims, she knew she would find it almost impossible to remain entirely objective.

Johnson was focusing his attention on the computer system, working with technicians to find ways to isolate cases that fitted the criteria the murder detectives were looking for. Collins and Woods, in the meantime, were having to laboriously work their way through the paper files holding details of the cases that had been deleted from the computer system.

They sat at opposite ends of a long wooden table in a spare office a few doors along the corridor from Johnson. Each had a large pile of files on the floor beside them and a thick notepad by their writing hand. They would take one file at a time and examine its contents: a photograph of the accused, details of the crimes they had committed, and information about where they lived and worked before and after conviction. The files also contained details of the last-known sighting of each offender.

Files that held no promise were placed on the floor on the other side of the chair; those that were possibly of interest were kept in a new pile in the middle of the table. These would be taken to the incident room so that DC Natalie Cooper could add the relevant details to the case database.

The number of files on the table, and therefore the list of missing men, was growing by the day, but they were no closer to finding their killer or identifying the third victim. Johnson had been right. When Collins started making inquiries to try to trace the whereabouts of one missing man who might have been a likely target, she ran into brick wall after brick wall. The missing men were already deep underground and desperate to hide away from the authorities, but their files held a great deal of information that gave clues to their likely whereabouts. Many were creatures of habit and had gone back to old haunts in the hope of starting their lives over. Others had clearly changed their details in a bid to continue their sexual offending away from the watchful eye of the authorities.

Some of the men on the list had managed to stay missing for years. Unless their bodies turned up, it was unlikely they would ever be found.

'Do you ever wonder about what we're doing here, Tony?' asked Collins as the two of them sat in the beer garden of a riverside pub, washing down scampi, chips and peas with a couple of Diet Cokes.

Woods chewed thoughtfully and swallowed before he replied. 'You mean here in this pub, here on this assignment or here in this universe? I'm not entirely clear on just how philosophical you're trying to be.'

'Ahh, now I get it.'

'Get what?'

'Why you're still single.'

Woods smiled, pushed another forkful of scampi into his mouth and then pushed it into the side of his cheek so he could speak. 'You're still really struggling with all this, aren't you?'

'Not as much as I'm struggling with your table manners.'

Woods waved his fork so that the prongs were pointing towards his colleague. 'I think we should have a rule. Once a week or so you should temporarily give up your rank, just so I get a chance to tell you what I really think of you without risking being hauled in front of the commander on a discipline charge.'

Collins cocked her head to one side and placed a finger on the corner of her mouth in a mock gesture of deep thought before screwing up her nose. 'Nah, I don't think so.'

'Joking aside, boss,' said Woods 'at this stage we don't even know if the other two bodies are linked to any kind of sex crime. Everything we're doing here could be a complete waste of time. This might not have anything to do with it. There's no point in letting your feelings get in the way of doing the job before we know the whole truth about what the job actually involves.'

Collins's mobile began to ring before Woods had finished speaking, and while she fished it out of her bag he quickly stuffed the remaining pieces of scampi into his mouth.

He watched as Collins listened intently and then got out her pad and frantically scribbled notes, her face stern with concentration.

'What's happened?' he asked as she ended the call.

'Looks like the mystery is about to be solved. That was Anderson. We've had a hit on the tattoo.'

Brazilian-born Roberto Medina first fell in love with the trendy North London district of Crouch End when his wife suggested they go there for a drink one summer's evening. Medina had been bowled over by the vast number of bars and restaurants seemingly representing the four corners of the globe, but he had also been struck by something else.

Despite a thriving high street scene and thousands of young, hip residents, there was not a single tattoo parlour anywhere to be found. Medina had first become interested in the body-art business as a teenage graphic-design student in his home town of Rio de Janeiro. After graduation, he had spent five years working as an apprentice at a parlour on the Ipanema beach front before feeling confident enough to set up on his own.

He had arrived in the UK a decade earlier to study English but, like so many others before him, had met a girl, fallen in love and decided to get married and stay put. The tattoo parlour in Crouch End, the most recent of his many business ventures, had been running for a little less than three years and was thriving.

'Man,' said Medina as Collins and Anderson arrived at his tiny workshop. 'I always check the papers and watch the news – it's like there's usually some tattoo they want to know about; it's much more common than you'd suppose. But never in a million years did I ever think that I'd actually recognize one of them. To be honest, it's a little spooky.'

Collins was finding it a little spooky too. Every few years she toyed with the idea of getting a tattoo herself – something small and discrete, perhaps one of those inspirational messages in Chinese characters – but she always managed to talk herself out of it. She didn't like the idea of doing anything to her body that she might later regret.

The patrons of this tattoo parlour clearly had no such reservations. Every inch of wall space around them was filled with a host of weird and wonderful images. Some were original drawings of designs; others were photographs taken of works performed on satisfied customers, stretching and flexing their body parts in order to show off the results to best effect.

She could not deny that some of the tattoos

appealed to her: tiny multicoloured butterflies on hips, bunny rabbits on ankles, hearts on shoulder blades. They were simple, understated, almost cute. Others made her want to shake her head with disbelief: a lime-green iguana stretching from the small of a young woman's back all the way up to the base of her neck; a fire-breathing dragon emerging from a cave that covered an entire arm.

A large board close to the door listed the prices for having tattoos applied on various body parts. The thought of some made her wince in horror while there were others that made her brow wrinkle in confusion. She had no idea which parts of the anatomy some of the terms referred to, and she had no wish to know.

Collins turned back to Medina. He drew nervously on a cigarette as he explained in his soft South American tones how he had been watching the early-evening news on a small television in the corner of the workshop during a quiet spell when he spotted his handiwork.

'I said, "Oh my God!" I recognized it right away. I called my wife, Maria, and said you're never going to believe this. I've just seen one of my tattoos on the telly. I was in complete shock. Especially when they said the guy was dead and no one knew who he was.'

Collins waited until Medina put the cigarette back in his mouth before asking her question. 'How can you be sure it was one of yours?' She waved a hand at the walls surrounding them. 'You've obviously done so many.'

'You're right,' he said, a stream of wispy smoke emerging from his thin lips. 'But this particular one stands out. That's what's so weird about it. Before I opened up this place I had a parlour down in Brixton. That's where I was living when I first came to England. There's a big Brazilian community there. We're talking nine, maybe ten years ago.

'The guy I did the work for, he seemed well enough when he first came in, but, looking back, I guess I must have missed the warning signs somewhere along the way. I remember I could smell beer or something like it on his breath, but a lot of people have a drink or two in order to dull some of the pain so I thought nothing of it. And it's not like he was really drunk or anything like that.

'He looked through a few samples, then said he wanted me to combine a couple of my own original designs to create something unique – that's another reason it stands out. So anyway I did the job and then a few days later, just when the first scabs were starting to form, the guy comes back into the store with his girlfriend and starts having a go at me while I'm trying to work with another customer. He started ranting and raving, complaining that I tricked him into getting it done.

'I'd never had a complaint like it before so I really didn't know what to do. He was saying he was going to sue me and that he would shut my business down.

The guy was going crazy. At one point I thought he was going to start to trash the place. And his girlfriend, she wasn't saying anything, but it was like she was urging him on. I think she was just as upset about the tattoo as he was, maybe more so.

'I told the guy there was nothing I could do about it. He'd signed the consent form and that was that. But I ended up giving him details of a place where you could undergo laser treatment to have tattoos removed. I don't know if he ever followed it up. I spent the next few months living on tenterhooks, waiting for a solicitor's letter in the post. But it never came and eventually I managed to put the whole thing out of my mind. Well, until now.'

'I don't suppose,' said Anderson, seemingly bracing himself for a potential disappointment, 'you kept a record of the man's name or address, did you?' Medina nodded. 'Of course! In the old days anyone could walk in and out and you'd have no idea who they were. But ever since AIDS we have to keep records of everyone, partly because of the risk of infection but also to prove consent and that the client is over eighteen. I dug out his old form for you already.'

Medina picked up a sheet of paper from the table beside him and handed it to Anderson. He scanned the contents before passing it on to Collins. The top of the form was taken up with a medical-history checklist, asking if the customer had a history of heart disease, low blood-pressure and a range of allergies. Below this was a section taken up with the customer's name and address, their date of birth and the location of the place where they wanted the tattoo to go. Collins focused immediately on the spidery handwriting that gave the name: James Gilbert. It seemed that at long last, they had a name for their third victim.

Back at the incident room, Collins, Anderson, Hill, Porter and Woods crowded around a computer terminal as DC Cooper entered Gilbert's details into the missing persons database.

It took only a few moments for the system to come back with a match. The screen was suddenly filled with the image of a clean-cut young man. He had a boxer's nose and dark, intense eyes. His wavy, bushy, black hair was piled untidily on top of his head and a wispy beard and moustache covered his chin and upper lip. He wore an open-neck shirt and a tiny silver crucifix was visible at the base of his neck. He was half smiling and one eyebrow was raised in a quizzical manner as if he wasn't a hundred per cent comfortable with having his photograph taken.

'That's our man. James Gilbert,' announced Cooper. 'Unmarried. No siblings. No kids, both parents dead. Lived alone. Reported missing by his boss, a Mr Roger Wincup, just under eight years ago.'

Anderson sighed as he read through the on-screen details to the right of the picture. 'Not much to go on there. No grieving widow, no heartbroken mother, no brother or sister wondering what happened to him. Looks like it's going to be something of a dead end so far as our investigation is concerned.'

'Not necessarily,' said Collins. She reached forward and touched the bottom-left corner of the screen with the nail of her little finger, distorting the image slightly. 'Look at where he used to work.'

Anderson peered forward. 'The Penvsey Private School in Dorset,' he read out loud. 'Sorry, I don't see the relevance.'

'That's because you haven't spent the last three days going through shed-loads of records from ViSOR the way that Woods and I have. It's been driving me absolutely barmy having all this stuff going through my head all the time.'

As Woods and Anderson looked on with confused expressions on their faces, Collins made her way back to her desk and began sorting through the large pile of files that she had brought back from ViSOR. She smiled triumphantly as she located the set of records she had been looking for, then quickly made her way back over to the others.

'Here you are,' she said, holding open the relevant pages. 'I came across this case yesterday. Five years ago, they uncovered a paedophile ring based at the Penvsey School made up of staff and outsiders who worked together to procure children to be abused. The whole thing was thought to have been run by one of the senior teachers, a certain Roger Wincup, who, it turns out, had prior convictions for possession of child pornography.'

She pointed at the picture of Wincup in the file. His face was far more youthful than would have been expected for a man in his late fifties. He was looking off to one side, the light reflected in his round silver glasses. His neatly trimmed hair was greying a little at the sideburns and his face had a few dimples and liver spots towards his chin, but he looked to all intents and purposes just the way a teacher should. Strict but fair. Trustworthy.

'He resigned in disgrace and was charged a few weeks later. He served three years and was placed on the register after he was released but vanished into thin air a few weeks later. No one has seen hide nor hair of him since. Now, take another look at the missing person record DC Cooper has up on her screen. James Gilbert worked at that same school before the scandal broke and was there when he went missing. It has to be more than a simple coincidence, don't you think? I really think we've found our connection.'

Anderson shook his head. 'It's not exactly rock solid, is it? There's no evidence at all that Gilbert was involved in any kind of abuse.'

'But I don't think there would be any evidence,' said Collins. 'If whoever is behind these murders is doing what I think they are, they're going after people who have managed to get away with their crimes. The ones who perhaps should have been convicted but got off due to a lack of evidence or the fact that their victims were too scared to come forward. That was what happened with Miller. Maybe it's what happened with Gilbert too. We're not going to find any hard evidence of involvement because it's unlikely to exist.

'The way these rings operate, they're so far underground they're almost impossible to locate. It's the *CSI* effect. These guys watch TV, they read books, and they follow other court cases. They know what we're capable of and the methods we use to try to track them down. And that means they know how to avoid coming up on our radar. Miller, Chadwick and Gilbert could all have been working together and we'd never have any way of proving it.'

Anderson reached up to stroke his chin. Collins fought the urge to reach across and slap his hand away.

'If what you're saying turns out to be correct, then it takes us right back to one of our original theories,' he said. 'The one that supposes this is the work of one of the abuse victims, taking revenge against those who wronged him, or a member of the ring itself who wants to silence the others. Here's what's going to happen. We're going to dig out all of the Penvsey School case files and go to see each and every victim and each and every offender. We're looking for anyone with the motive, the opportunity and the capability to carry out this crime. We're looking for anyone who fits the profile that has been drawn up for us. We look at everyone and then eliminate them from our inquiries one by one. If what Dr Bernard says is true, then there are a lot more bodies to be found, and someone who was connected to that school is responsible.'

The paedophile ring that had been operating at the Penvsey School for more than two decades was uncovered not as the result of diligent police work or high-level intelligence, but rather through the stupidest of mistakes. A peripheral member of the gang had taken his home computer to a local workshop in order to repair a fault with its USB connectors. Carefully following the advice from colleagues within the ring who were far more technically savvy than he, the man had, of course, diligently erased the thousands of pornographic images and videos from the machine's hard drive. As an added precaution, he then used special 'shredding' software to ensure even the most skilled technicians would not be able to find any trace of the illegal files on the machine. Rather than lose the precious pictures he had worked so hard to collect and that gave him so much pleasure, he copied them to a dozen DVDs. These he kept stored in a safe concealed beneath floorboards in the spare bedroom of the home he shared with his wife and young child. He had been astonished at just how many images there had been – it had taken many, many hours and a total of fifteen blank DVDs to store them all.

The day after he took the machine to be repaired, another member of the ring asked him to supply copies of a particular photo set that had become hugely popular among the Penvsey devotees. It was while he was searching through his copied DVDs to find the correct one that he made a horrifying discovery: there was one missing.

He had taken every possible precaution when it came to wiping information from the machine itself, only to leave one DVD full of images inside the drive of the machine.

Any hope that the repair man might not have noticed was utterly shattered just two days later when a dozen police officers arrived at his front door early one morning and arrested him for possession of child pornography.

From there the investigation grew swiftly, extending to his colleagues from work, his friends and his contacts worldwide via the internet. Before too long victims of the ring, emboldened by the fact that those responsible for the abuse were finally being brought to justice, were coming out of the woodwork from all directions.

Many of those pictured or filmed by the gang had been pupils at the school. They told members of the inquiry team how they would be summoned one at a time out of extra-curricular lessons and taken to specially set-up offices where they would be subjected to one horror after another. Threats of severe punishment and even death were made to ensure the young victims never breathed a word of what had happened to them.

At first the members of the Penvsey board of governors played down the scale of the problem, hoping all the blame could be attached to one or two errant members of staff. But it was not to be. With increasing numbers of teachers and associates being drawn into the police inquiry, it soon became clear that this was no storm in a teacup. Midway through the summer term, the school announced it would be closing its doors for ever and that the few remaining pupils – most had been extracted by their parents in the days after the scandal first broke – would have to find somewhere else to go.

The raw details of what had transpired over the years at the school made harrowing reading, but, for the first time in weeks, the members of the inquiry team felt they were finally getting somewhere. The fact that they had identified the third victim, combined with the emergence of their first credible lead about where whoever was responsible for the murders might be found, had acted like a shot of adrenalin.

In the days that followed the incident room was a hive of constant activity as phone calls were made, files studied and meetings arranged with officers from the original inquiry. While Anderson oversaw operations, tracking down the whereabouts of the victims and the remaining perpetrators was split between the two main teams: Collins and Woods, along with Hill and Porter.

A key task was to compare the profiles of both the abused and their abusers to see if any of them fitted into the patterns of behaviour identified by Dr Bernard. It did not take long for a shortlist of potential suspects to emerge and the officers set out to conduct their first interviews.

'You seem pretty fired up by all this,' said Woods as they made their way down to their car one afternoon on their way to see a former teacher at the school. 'Does that mean you've changed your views on what we're doing?'

'Not at all,' replied Collins flatly. 'I just want to get it over with. I want to be done with it all as quickly as possible. If we don't nail this case soon, we're going to be working on it for the next three months at least. I can't handle that. It's doing my head in. I want to get a result because, once we do, we can get back to some proper police work.

'If there's an arrest to be made, I would rather let Hill and Porter take the lead on it. I'm sure they'll be more than eager anyway. I don't want to have to deal with this shit for a moment longer than is necessary.'

'I know what you mean,' said Woods. 'Give me a dead drug dealer or Yardie gangster any day over this lot.'

First on their list was a 47-year-old former

geography teacher named Albert Davidson who had been on the edge of the ring and served an eighteen-month suspended sentence for possession of indecent images. He had been accused by several pupils of being actively involved in the actual abuse, but insufficient evidence had meant he had managed to escape being charged.

Banned from working with children, Davidson had switched professions and now sold life insurance. Collins hated being with him. He seemed every bit as clammy and slimy as she expected a sex offender to be. He appeared completely unrepentant about anything he had done, claiming he had only started looking at the pictures out of curiosity, not out of a genuine sexual interest.

'You had almost two thousand images on your computer. You must have been very curious indeed,' snapped Collins.

Davidson shrugged. 'I never counted them. I never realized there were so many.'

Short and skinny with a history of lower-back problems, Davidson was obviously not someone capable of overpowering those bigger and stronger than himself. After forty-five minutes of uncomfortable conversation, Collins was ready to dismiss him from the inquiry.

'I feel like I need a shower after talking to him,' she told Woods as they made their way back to the station.

'You're not the only one.'

'You do realize, don't you,' said Collins thought-fully, 'that if we're right about what this killer is up to, someone like Davidson could easily be the next victim?'

'I try not to think about it too much,' said Woods.

The interviews continued in a similar fashion for the whole of the next day. Some were incredibly disturbing; others just downright sad. Although the abuse was long over, it was clear that some of the victims would carry the emotional scars for the rest of their lives. Each afternoon the pair returned to the incident room to write up their statements and enter the results of their investigations into the computer database.

Comparing notes with Hill and Porter, they found their experiences were broadly similar. Although the mood was still overwhelmingly positive, the fact that the expected result was yet to emerge was starting to be of concern. Word of the inquiry was starting to get around, and there were fears that whoever was responsible for the murders might get wind of the investigation and go to ground. The pressure was on to get through the lists as quickly as possible.

As the middle of the week arrived, Collins and Woods found themselves on their way to Charing Cross Hospital to interview Billy Moorwood, a former pupil of the school who now worked as a porter.

The two detectives arrived at the ward where he had been assigned to work and made their way to the nurses' station to find out where they could locate him. The heavy-set black woman in the dark blue, scarlet-trimmed uniform of a head nurse looked around and could not see him so offered to page him instead. A few seconds later a shambling figure emerged from the other end of the long corridor of the ward. Moorwood was young but powerfully built, with a square jaw and slightly crooked nose.

One of the ring's earliest victims, he looked far younger than his twenty-five years. His auburn hair looked an unfortunate shade of red under the bright fluorescent lights. Even from a distance his green eyes shone out like emeralds. He wore a long-sleeved pale grey top with navy blue trousers and black trainers. A red ribbon around his neck held his identity card. He had both hands thrust deeply into his pockets and whistled jauntily as he made his way towards them. Collins and Woods turned to face him, and Moorwood suddenly hesitated.

The announcement over the public address system had made no mention of anyone wanting to speak to him; it had simply asked him to come to the main nurses' station. But the closer he got the more obvious it became that the request had nothing to do with hospital business. Moorwood's pace slowed down more and more, until he was almost standing still, staring intently at the two officers.

He was still more than sixty feet away when Collins took a step towards him. And then it happened. The look of concern on his face suddenly turned to full-blown panic. Moorwood spun on his heels and ran.

'Shit!' Collins looked helplessly at Woods before taking off after the fugitive. 'Come on,' she called back to Woods as he started to follow her.

Moorwood had a good head start and his footwear was far better suited to the slick, tiled floor than the low heels Collins had chosen to wear that day. He dodged his way past oncoming doctors and patients, and suddenly took a sharp left. By the time Woods and Collins had reached the turn, he was nowhere to be seen.

Like all hospitals, this was a rabbit warren of inter-connecting corridors and wards and private rooms. Moorwood undoubtedly knew the place like the back of his hand. There was no way in the world the two of them were going to be able to catch him.

'Fuck,' spat Collins, instantly regretting making the outburst in a public place. She was breathing hard, not out of exhaustion but out of sheer frustration. She looked over at Woods, who was slamming his hand against the wall in disbelief. He caught her gaze and managed a tight grimace. 'We could call security, get them to seal the exits,' he said.

'It would take too long to organize. There's only one thing to do now. Call Anderson.'

Billy Moorwood lived in the centre of a run-down estate of low-rise housing on the edge of Stockwell. The road leading to the main square was littered with rusting bicycles, discarded mattresses, abandoned car parts and huge piles of rubbish.

It had taken Woods and Collins less than twenty minutes to make their way there through the lunchtime traffic in the back of a speeding patrol car, blues and twos going like the clappers. It had taken a few more minutes for a van-load of uniformed back-up to appear on the scene. Anderson was on his way over too, but Collins had no intention of waiting any longer.

If Moorwood was their man, he would likely be trying to destroy any evidence linking him to the crimes. Time was precious. Every second they wasted would be another hurdle they would have to get over to make the case stick.

Ideally Collins had wanted Hill and Porter to make any key arrest, but with Moorwood she seemed to have drawn the short straw. The whole case still bothered her to some degree, but she had also been pissed off that Moorwood had done a runner and managed to get away from her. She didn't like to let anyone get the upper hand.

Curtains had begun to twitch the moment the first police car arrived, and as the band of officers made their way through the debris and up the short path leading to Moorwood's front door a small crowd gathered to observe them.

'So much for the element of surprise,' said Collins as they reached the door.

None of the officers had thought to bring an

enforcer — the hand-held piston used to smash through hinges — so instead two bigger uniformed men jointly kicked just below the position of the lock. On their second attempt there was a splintering of wood and the door flew open.

With the uniformed team leading the way, Collins stepped into the hallway. 'Police. Come out and show yourself,' she shouted. There was no reply. She turned left into a small lounge, which held only a few items of scruffy furniture. Woods moved past her. 'Kitchen's clear,' he shouted back.

Collins moved back into the main hallway. The two officers who had led the raid reached the door at the end and discovered it was locked, or more likely blocked from the inside. Collins stepped forward and slapped the flat of her hand against the wood several times. She heard movement.

'Billy Moorwood? My name is Detective Inspector Stacey Collins. I need you to come out of there right now. If you don't we're going to break the door down. You have only a few seconds.'

'Fuck off.'

'I'm warning you. Either open the door yourself or we're coming in. There's no reason to make this any more difficult than it already is.'

'Just fuck off and leave me alone. Just leave me alone.'

Collins turned to Woods. They had worked together long enough for him to know what she was thinking without her having to utter a single word.

He headed back out through the front door and, with two more uniformed officers as back-up, moved around to cover the rear entrance.

'This is your last chance, Billy,' said Collins. This time there was no reply and she nodded at the two burly men, who once more kicked the door open.

Billy Moorwood was standing flat against the back wall of the room. A small, single bed was pushed up against the corner to the right. On the left was a narrow metal desk with a cumbersome-looking computer sitting on top of it. A small door glazed with semi-frosted glass led out to the small garden area.

In between the door and the bed was Moorwood. His skin was pallid and shiny as if he had become sweaty from running all the way there. His hair had fallen out of place and was totally unkempt. His face was the very picture of panic. He was still wearing his hospital porter's uniform but the sleeve on the right-hand side had been rolled up. Moorwood held a Stanley knife, the blade fully extended, against the side of his wrist.

'I'll fucking do it,' he gasped. 'I'll fucking do it, I will. You come one step closer and I'll fucking do it.'

Collins's eyes were drawn to the blade as it glinted in the light. She held up a hand to prevent any more officers from coming into the room.

'Billy, you've got to listen to me. Don't do this. Put the knife down and let's talk about this.' She took a step towards him.

'One more fucking step.' His voice was louder, more panic-stricken. 'I'll kill myself. I'll fucking end it all right here, right now.'

Moorwood had his back right up against the wall. He was so far back that he couldn't see the distinctive form of Tony Woods looming large in the frosted glass of the back door. Collins knew that if Woods tried the handle or if Moorwood spotted him, it might be enough to push the desperate man over the edge.

She looked down again. Moorwood was holding the blade at a right angle to his wrist, which was the way they always show it happening on television. Collins knew only too well that slit wrists are rarely fatal – to make it effective you have to cut lengthways to expose the artery and then cut across it – but she didn't want to give Moorwood the chance to hurt himself at all.

She held out both her arms so that her hands were just level with the bottom of her hips and took another step forward. Her palms were facing towards Moorwood, a classic non-threatening pose. She was going to have to call his bluff. And she was going to have to do it fast.

'No one wants to see you get hurt, Billy,' she said softly.

'Back off. Stop right there. Back off.' Moorwood raised the wrist with the blade next to it, an attempt to show just how serious he was. 'I'm gonna do it, I'll fucking do it.'

Collins kept moving forward. She was now over

an arm's length away – just out of reach, just far enough away for Moorwood to believe he was still in control.

'Please, Billy, I only want to talk to you. I only want to –'

Her right foot flicked out with all the grace and style of a ballerina's, her toes connecting perfectly with Moorwood's scrotum, and the young man groaned and sank to the floor like a sack of potatoes.

At that moment Woods burst in through the back door and the two officers with him rushed forward, kicked the knife out of the way and began to clip Moorwood into a pair of handcuffs.

His hands safely clipped behind him, Moorwood was laid back down on the floor and curled up into the foetal position, still moaning softly. She looked down at him and all her mixed feelings about the case came flooding back to her. She hadn't wanted any of this. She still didn't.

'Hey,' said Woods. 'Have you seen this?'

Collins turned and saw that Woods was examining the rear wall of the bedroom. Every square inch of space was taken up with newspaper clippings and magazine articles about the abuse that had taken place at the Penvsey School.

To the right of the clippings were three laser-copy photographs. Each had been savagely mutilated – sliced with razors, covered in an illegible scrawl, repeatedly stabbed with the point of a knife. Yet each one was still recognizable to all the members of the inquiry team. Woods recited their names out loud as he pointed to each one: 'James Gilbert, Roger Wincup, Albert Davidson.'

Below each photograph a scrap of lined paper had been used to record possible sightings, addresses, telephone numbers and places of work. It was, to all intents and purposes, a hit list. The sheets of paper below the pictures of Gilbert and Wincup were almost full, while it appeared that Moorwood's hunt for Davidson had only just begun.

Her eyes glanced over some of the newspaper clippings. Although Moorwood was never actually named, it was clear that the boy seen in some of the photographs and videos that formed the heart of the court case was him.

Collins looked back from the wall and down at Moorwood, who seemed to be recovering well from the low blow. He looked up at her, his eyes red with a mixture of pain and anger. A wave of guilt washed over her, and she had to turn and walk away.

A few hours later a more thorough search of Moorwood's home had generated a wealth of material. There was no smoking gun – no blood stains, no body parts, no DNA material and no property belonging to any of the victims, at least not in plain sight. But there was ample evidence that Moorwood had been doing his best to track down some of those responsible for abusing him.

He had befriended several pub landlords and

social workers and managed to trick them into giving him details of sex offenders registered in their area. In the case of Davidson he had recently sent a series of anonymous threatening letters promising that the man would suffer a long and painful death.

Anderson arrived soon after the search started, and he and Collins stood in the kitchen discussing their findings. 'We know there's a connection to at least one of the victims and there is also strong evidence of both motive and intent,' he said. 'I think our next move is an obvious one.'

Collins nodded solemnly. With Anderson following close behind, she made her way back into the bedroom, where Moorwood was now sitting up on the edge of the bed, flanked on either side by uniformed officers.

He looked up and met her gaze. 'William Moorwood. I'm arresting you on suspicion of murder. You do not have to say anything but it may harm your defence if you do not mention when questioned something which you later rely on in court. Anything you do say may be given in evidence. Do you understand?'

Moorwood's face remained impassive as he replied, 'Do you know what they did to me?' He nodded towards the photographs on the wall. 'Do you have any idea what those men put me through? You can't treat people like that. You can't do the things they did. They were all so smug. They all thought they were going to get away with it. But I was going to make them pay. I wanted to make them pay. That's the only way to make it right. Don't you see? For fuck's sake, lady, just whose side are you on anyway?'

Collins could see the tears welling up in the corners of his eyes and hear the heartbreak in his voice. She pushed a lump rising in her throat back into her stomach so that she could speak again.

'Take him away.'

12

They had arranged to meet at 4 p.m. and it was now well past five. He had been there the whole time, anxiously watching and waiting for her to turn up. He would, he decided, wait just fifteen more minutes before giving up. Fifteen minutes and no more. He had already wasted so much time. He really didn't want to look like an idiot.

Half an hour later he was still there, drumming his fingers on the table and biting his lip to relieve the tension. He was rooted to the spot, too scared even to go to the toilet just in case he missed her. To pass the time he began playing solitaire and, during his third game, his patience was at long last rewarded when a high-pitched chiming sound from his computer's speakers told him she was finally online.

He reached for the mouse and cleared the cards from the screen to reveal the dialogue box for the chatroom. He felt a ball of excitement rising in his stomach as he read her words. His fingers flashed across the keyboard as he typed his reply.

shygirl351: hello
shygirl351: um . . . hello
shygirl351: anybody there?

sportsfan52: hi – sorry, didn't have the right screen up

shygirl351: ahh, thought you were ignoring me

shygirl351: lol

sportsfan52: no – I thought you weren't coming

shygirl351: I got held up, couldn't get away early

shygirl351: you been waiting long?

sportsfan52: yeah, but not a problem, I had plenty of stuff to do

shygirl351: maybe I can find a way to make it up to you?

He paused and allowed a smile to creep across his lips. He had been worrying about nothing. It was all going according to plan.

Jason Bevan had first struck up a conversation with shygirl351 four months earlier, pretending he was a fourteen-year-old from Morden named Sally. During that first chat, the pair had bonded over their mutual love of Justin Timberlake, swimming and Girls Aloud. Sally wrote that she felt particularly drawn to shygirl351 because, like her, she was obviously far more mature than most girls of their age.

The conversation soon turned to more personal matters. Sally confessed that she had a boyfriend who was much older than her whom she had met online. Sally explained that she had now had sex more than fifteen times and enjoyed it enormously. shygirl351 coyly admitted that she herself was a virgin, but it was clear from her subsequent responses that she had been intrigued and hugely impressed by Sally's sex life.

A few chats later, after the pair had swapped pictures of one another (Bevan had simply downloaded a slightly blurred headshot from someone else's internet profile), Sally emailed shygirl351 a picture titled 'Youth and Experience'.

'He's like sooooo, soooooooo old,' Sally wrote in a note accompanying the image, 'but she's about your age, isn't she? I'll tell you what, I get really hot and bothered looking at them together. It must be how I look with my boyfriend. I think it's so amazing when it's someone like that with girls our age, don't you? The thing is, you don't want someone from school, they're still kids. You need someone more experienced, someone who knows what they are doing. That way, you know the first time is going to be incredible. And every time after that too. And they have money so they can buy you anything you want.'

The following week Sally said she had met an older man online who seemed really nice. She wasn't interested herself because she already had a boyfriend, but she had told him all about shygirl351 and he was extremely keen to chat to her.

That same afternoon, Bevan created a new character for himself – that of sportsfan52 – and knew that his pursuit of shygirl351 could finally begin in earnest.

Bevan knew exactly what he was doing. The techniques he utilized to 'groom' shygirl351 had been tried and tested by thousands of other online predators like himself and were almost guaranteed to lead to success. Like others of his kind, he felt a certain kind of pride in understanding the intricacies of the grooming process, and believed his particular skills raised it up a good few levels to the point where it was almost an art form.

Since that first day as sportsfan52, Bevan had been steadily working his way through the five stages of grooming. The first, friendship, had been easy. Sally had done all the groundwork and it took no time at all for shygirl351 to agree to meet in a private chatroom and email over a picture of herself in her school uniform.

From there Bevan moved on to developing the relationship, urging shygirl351 to talk to him about whatever problems she was having in life in order to create greater trust between them.

sportsfan52: how are you today?

shygirl351: bit down. Anniversary of gran's death

sportsfan52: Oh I'm so sorry. My wife died a couple of years ago so I know how much it hurts

shygirl351: how awful for you

sportsfan52: It was very sudden. No pain. Sadly these things happen to us all at some time or other but we must not dwell on it

shygirl351: why not?

sportsfan52: You have to let them live on in your heart. Remember the good times, not the pain of the loss

shygirl351: k

shygirl351: did you have kids?

sportsfan52: no. glad because it would have been hard on them

shygirl351: let's change the subject. Too depressing

sportsfan52: No problem. But if you ever need to talk, I'm always here

With trust established, Bevan then set about finding subtle ways to assess the level of risk involved in pursuing his latest target. shygirl351 didn't have a webcam, so he was unable to confirm what she said (making the issue of trust all the more important), but she explained that her computer was in her bedroom and that her parents rarely came in. She had an older brother but he had a computer of his own. The chances of anyone else using the machine apart from her were virtually nil.

It was all good. For any online predator the worst-case scenario is a computer in a living room or family room where anyone can walk by at any time and witness the conversation. With an element of privacy in place, Bevan knew he was able to talk to shygirl351 about whatever topic he wanted to with total freedom. And if his target ever showed signs of nervousness or hesitation, good old Sally was always on hand to provide encouragement and reassurance.

As the days went by, Bevan endeavoured to bury himself deeper and deeper into her psyche. Whenever she spoke of a minor insecurity, he would trade one of his own in order to bring them closer. When shygirl351 said she might have to wear glasses, Bevan lied and said he already did. When she worried about her acne, he wrote back that he had been known as pepperoni pizza face at school but that it had soon cleared up. When she admitted — unprompted — that she was worried her breasts were not growing as quickly as those of her classmates, he felt a frisson of excitement wash over him as he replied that he preferred them on the small side.

It was a landmark moment. Bevan knew that he was the only person in the world shygirl351 felt comfortable discussing such things with. Whatever happened between them, he felt certain she would not tell anyone else about it.

From there Bevan gently began to challenge her, seeing how far he could push things. He would make occasional assertive statements to show that he was firmly in charge of the relationship.

shygirl351: so what made you choose me to talk to?
sportsfan52: Sally said you sounded nice
sportsfan52: and you sounded a bit more mature than most girls of your age
sportsfan52: But you must have lots of friends online. Why did you want to talk to me?
shygirl351: I have my mates, but there are a lot of time-wasters though
sportsfan52: there are plenty of them about
shygirl351: yeah

shygirl351: the way you say that makes it sound like you're not one of them?

shygirl351: I mean, I don't want to waste your time

sportsfan52: I have for many years now, I have come across timewasters from people just getting kicks to those who chicken out at the first sign of any action

shygirl351: tell me about it

sportsfan52: It sounds like you are not one of them

shygirl351: by the way, I like the sound of 'many years'

sportsfan52: I take it you know my age

shygirl351: not exactly no

shygirl351: I guess you're a little older than me lol

shygirl351: but that's why I'm interested

sportsfan52: you're 13, right?

shygirl351: yup

sportsfan52: that's a lovely age to be

sportsfan52: I'm 42 in 4 weeks

shygirl351: ok

shygirl351: thinking about that

shygirl351: yeh I've thought

shygirl351: it's cool with me

sportsfan52: good

shygirl351: wanna know why?

sportsfan52: yes, if you would like to tell me

shygirl351: because you've got lots of experience

shygirl351: and you're funny too

shygirl351: are you smiling right now?

sportsfan52: yes pmsl

shygirl351: me too

shygirl351: lmao
sportsfan52: sounds like we are on the same wavelength . . .
shygirl351: could be

He hadn't always been like this. Far from it. He wasn't some man in a dirty mac that hung around school playgrounds. He was a successful business-man, a man with the world at his feet. The web, he told himself, had led him astray. It was just too easy. There was no way he would ever try talking to girls of this age in real life, but in cyberspace, behind the anonymity of a made-up username or a false identity, he feared no one and nothing. The numerous social networking sites were a veritable hunting ground for curious young girls. There were hundreds of shygirl35rs out there. All you had to do was log on.

It was time to move on to the next stage.

sportsfan52: The thing is, I don't like cyber, in fact I hate it. I'm asking you real questions about your experiences, cyber is when you make it up and pretend to have sex and stupid crap like that. It's childish and doesn't make you feel good cos it's all fake
shygirl351: so what do you want?
sportsfan52: I'm interested in the real thing. One on one
shygirl351: wow
sportsfan52: I have been thinking about you a lot. What it would be like to be with you in person.
shygirl351: really
shygirl351: I worried in case I was being too forward

sportsfan52: not at all. Well it depends . . .

sportsfan52: how far do you wanna go?

shygirl351: dunno, what do you think?

sportsfan52: well, how much do you wanna learn about SEX and everything?

shygirl351: I don't want to get into trouble.

sportsfan52: You won't. It's me that gets into trouble and goes to jail if anyone finds out . . . it's your body and you can do whatever you want, when you want. You don't have anything to worry about. I'll be gentle and considerate.

sportsfan52: I'd like to give you some homework

shygirl351: what kind of homework?

sportsfan52: sexual homework

shygirl351: lmao you'll have to explain.

shygirl351: hello?

shygirl351: are you still there.

sportsfan52: sorry, phone ringing. brb

shygirl351: k

The phone wasn't ringing, of course. Instead Jason Bevan had heard the sound of footsteps heading up the stairs towards the attic room where he had set up his office.

His hands swiftly moved the mouse to the task bar at the bottom of the page, replacing the open page of the chatroom with that of iTunes.

'How's it going, darling?'

Cynthia Bevan was wearing well for her age by most people's standards but all her husband of fourteen years could see were the lines on her forehead, the crow's feet beside her eyes and rolls of sagging flesh around her belly. He forced a smile.

'Just sorting out our music collection. I found a few more old CDs that I'm loading into the computer. Once that's done we may as well take them down the charity shop.'

'But I might want to listen to them again.'

Bevan's smile grew wider. His wife had never got to grips with modern technology and probably never would. 'You'll still be able to, Cyn. They will be right here on the computer.'

'But that means if I want to hear an album, I'll have to come up and sit in front of the computer. But supposing you're working? Why can't I just stick with the CDs?'

'They're old-fashioned. And besides CDs take up loads of room. The great thing about a computer is that it stays the same size no matter how many albums you load into it.'

'I'd still rather have my CDs.'

'Well, if you really want some songs to play downstairs, I can burn off a few tracks for you.'

'You what?'

'I can make another CD for you, using the music that I've stored on the computer.'

'Then why don't I just keep the original CD in the first place?'

Bevan sighed. He was getting impatient and this conversation was going nowhere. 'Did you want something?'

'The girls want to show you their homework. The pictures are lovely, really adorable.'

'Okay, I'll just finish off here and I'll be down in a minute or two.'

'Okay. Love you.'

'Love you too.'

Bevan watched as his wife's head disappeared down the trapdoor in the attic floor and vanished out of view. When he was absolutely sure that she had gone, he flicked the cursor over the task bar again until the chatroom returned. He saw with enormous relief that shygirl351 was still there.

He had to work fast. He had been interrupted at a crucial point and now needed to regain the momentum. He typed as fast as his fingers allowed.

sportsfan52: back
shygirl351: hi
shygirl351: I need the loo
shygirl351: you ok for a minute?
sportsfan52: yes
shygirl351: brb

Bevan watched the minutes ticking by on the clock in the bottom-right-hand corner of his computer screen. Any minute now his wife would begin calling him, wondering why he had not yet seen to his children. 'Come on, come on,' he hissed under his breath. 'Hurry it up for fuck's sake.'

shygirl351: back. All peed out.

sportsfan52: lol

shygirl351: so who were you talking to just now?

An ice-cold shiver raced down Bevan's spine. His fingers were trembling above the keyboard. His head was filled with thoughts about his whole world crashing down. He could manage only a single character.

sportsfan52: ?

shygirl351: on the phone, dummy

Bevan's relief was palpable.

sportsfan52: just the office, checking on the schedules for tomorrow's meetings.

shygirl351: sounds dull

sportsfan52: like you would not believe

sportsfan52: listen, I have to go soon. have you given any more thought to us meeting – where & when

shygirl351: um

shygirl351: dunno

shygirl351: if it's day, it's hard during the week

shygirl351: Saturdays any good?

sportsfan52: sometimes – not this weekend – going away

shygirl351: um

shygirl351: so, when?

sportsfan52: I am reasonably free later this week and next week at the mo

shygirl351: wow

shygirl351: u want me to get my diary?

sportsfan52: how about Monday for Lunch

shygirl351: can't

shygirl351: Friday maybe

shygirl351: or Thursday maybe

sportsfan52: Yes that could be good

shygirl351: which?

sportsfan52: thurs

shygirl351: ok

sportsfan52: next Thursday

shygirl351: tomorrow silly

sportsfan52: ok

shygirl351: wow, I've got butterflies in my stomach now

shygirl351: say we meet, yeh

shygirl351: tomorrow

sportsfan52: yes

shygirl351: what happens then?

sportsfan52: let's wait and see – you may not like me!

shygirl351: but supposing I do?

sportsfan52: well let's just take it as it comes . . .

shygirl351: fine by me

sportsfan52: tomorrow it is then

sportsfan52: hello?

sportsfan52: you still there?

A neatly manicured hand reached out and lifted the chilled glass of Pinot Grigio Blush that sat on the side of the computer monitor. There followed a long, slow sip, savouring the flavours and cooling sensation against the tongue, before the glass was lowered and placed down directly on top of the ring of condensation it had already left behind.

Finally he's on the hook. I love it when a plan comes together. Sportsfan52 has been well and truly fooled and is now ripe for the picking. The sick perverted bastard doesn't suspect a thing. How delicious is that?

Fingers flexed before they began to type a reply to sportsfan52's last message.

shygirl351: still here.
shygirl351: I can't wait to meet you.
shygirl351: We really do have so much in common.
shygirl351: I know I'm going to like you
shygirl351: I feel you could be my soulmate.

13

'So, ladies, are you ready to order?' The chisel-jawed waiter with the Hollywood smile and faintest trace of an Italian accent looked eagerly from one to the other in anticipation.

'I know what I want; how about you, Stacey?'

'You go ahead, I'll make up my mind while you're ordering.'

Jessica Matthews's eyes flicked up and down the menu, coming to rest in the centre. 'I'll have the filet steak, French cut. Rare.'

'Excellent choice.' He turned to Stacey and smiled. 'And you, madam?'

She bit her lip nervously. 'Umm ... sorry about this ... um ... I'll have the chicken.'

'Fabulous. Any starters?'

'I'm happy with bread and olives,' said Jessica. Stacey nodded in agreement. The waiter refilled their wine glasses, then made his way to the kitchen. Jessica watched closely as Stacey turned to the waiter's attractive physique as he walked away.

Stacey turned back to her dinner companion and broke a guilty, embarrassed smile. She took a sip of her red wine. 'Rare? I don't know how you can eat something like that, what with your job and everything.'

'Oh, the rarer the better as far as I'm concerned. That way it just melts in the mouth. Have you ever had steak tartare?'

Stacey shook her head. 'No. Doesn't appeal to me at all.'

'You don't know what you're missing. The first time I had it was when I got taken to dinner at Coq d'Argent in the City by an uncouth stockbroker. Why I agreed to go to dinner with him is a story we don't have time for tonight. Anyhow, he was desperately trying to impress. First he orders this really expensive wine and then for his main course he orders steak tartare. I guess he must have thought it was steak served with tartare sauce. Anyway, his meal comes out of the kitchen and it's literally just a big pile of raw minced steak with a raw egg on top.'

'Jesus Christ. What did he do?'

'He was all for sending it back but I really wanted to try it.'

'You're kidding me. Why?'

'It was on the menu as one of their specialities so I thought it must be good. And to tell you the truth it was. It was divine . . .'

The two women smiled at each other again.

'This is nice. I'm really glad we did this.'

'Me too,' said Stacey. 'Long overdue.'

'Now, look, I know the whole idea of meeting up away from the morgue was so that we could not talk shop, but I know what you're like and I know what I'm like. The job is always going to be at the back of our minds. So why don't we agree to spend, say, ten minutes talking about the case and then drop it for the rest of the evening?'

'Sounds like a plan.'

'Great. I don't have anything new for you, I'm afraid. The toxicology results came back but they're pretty inconclusive. It's possible the victims were given something to keep them quiet, maybe barbiturates, but we're talking trace elements, not enough for the lab boys to give you anything you could use in court. I'll send over a copy but honestly there's nothing in it. That's it really. Bit of a dead end. How about you? Any closer to finding the killer?'

'Well, we got him to the station last afternoon so we've got a day and a half before we have to apply to the magistrates for our first extension. All we have to do now is come up with the goods.'

'Him?'

'Billy Moorwood. A hospital porter.'

'Has he confessed or something?'

'Not exactly. There's a lot of circumstantial evidence but nothing concrete yet. It's not like he's going to be going home any time soon. He'll be charged with something – we've got drugs and offensive weapons coming out of our ears – but we still need to find a more direct link to the victims to put him in the frame for the murders.'

'No pressure, then. I'm surprised you didn't cancel tonight.'

'I thought about it, but there's not much I can do right now. The SOCOs are going to spend all night gathering what they can at his flat. I'll go through their reports first thing. I don't expect to do a first interview until at least midday tomorrow.'

'But you're sure it's him, right?'

'Well, it's clear that he had actively tracked down one of the victims and was stalking another. He's got motive and opportunity. But he's not going down quietly. He's so paranoid, convinced that we're trying to frame him. I guess part of the problem is that he's still more of a victim than anything else. Some of the things those teachers put those pupils through, just too awful for words.'

'You make it sound like you almost think he'd have been justified.'

'I think a part of me does think that. I'd kill anyone who tried that on with Sophie. In a heartbeat. People like that, they want shooting.'

Jessica gripped the base of her chair in both hands and lifted it forward, shrinking the gap between the two women. 'I couldn't agree more. You say you don't know how I can eat rare steak; I don't know how you can do your job in a case like this. No one really gives a shit about these people, do they? I know I don't. I mean, are you really giving it your best shot?'

'I like to think so, but in my heart of hearts I know

I'm playing a different game. On the Daniel Eliot case, I put my heart and soul into finding the killer. But you're right, this is different. Daniel got to me, I couldn't help it. This case is just a job. It doesn't haunt me when I get home from work. Back then, I was desperate to make an arrest before someone else got killed. This time around, if there had been another victim, I honestly don't think I would have lost much sleep over it.'

'That's an interesting attitude,' said Jessica. 'It's quite rare to find someone in this world who – ' She was interrupted by the return of the waiter, who placed a basket of bread and a bowl of olives in the centre of the table. They both smiled at him.

'Not bad,' said Jessica as he headed back to the kitchen. 'Not bad at all. You seeing anyone right now?'

'Not really. There's may be someone on the horizon but it's early days yet. We're going out over the weekend.'

Jessica nodded towards the waiter. 'You want me to put in a good word for you?'

'God, I'd like to think I can do better than a waiter. How about you? Seeing anyone?'

Jessica gazed around the restaurant, settling her eyes on two well-dressed middle-aged men sitting to her left, one of whom gave her a quick smile. 'I was seeing someone who I really liked. He was a biologist. Good-looking too. He was keen, but he had this terrible surname. I just knew if it ever got too serious and he proposed, I could never marry him.'

'Just because of his name?'

'It was Rabit. One b.'

'Rabit?'

'He was half Algerian and when he said it with an accent it didn't sound too bad, but most people, when they see it written down, rabbit. I had to end it. Otherwise I would have become – '

'Oh my God! Jessica Rabbit!' Stacey burst into a fit of chuckles and after a moment's hesitation Jessica did too. The sound of their laughter echoed around the room, prompting other diners to wonder what was going on.

'Actually, I'm surprised you had a problem with it,' said Stacey once they had calmed down. 'I had you down as the more progressive type. You could have married him and kept your own name. Or just lived in sin.'

'I'm an old-fashioned girl at heart. And I don't feel particularly attached to Matthews. I'll happily trade, just so long as it's something sensible. How about your parents?'

'Still alive, still together, thank God. They went through some rough patches – for a while they were more like brother and sister than husband and wife – but they've managed to tough it out. They live just around the corner from me so I get to see them a lot.'

'That's great, that they live so close and that they're still together. I think we're part of a generation that demands instant satisfaction. If something isn't working out we just end it and move on. Our parents, they always tried to work through problems. Society has definitely changed, and not for the better in my opinion.'

'I couldn't agree more.'

'Talking of change, how are you getting on with Anderson?'

'Much better. He's treating me like I'm part of the team now rather than as some sort of outcast. And I know I have you to thank for that. That tattoo really moved things on.'

'You're welcome. And remember dinner's on you!'

'My pleasure.'

It took only a few minutes more before their main courses arrived. Stacey watched Jessica cut into the meat, releasing a trickle of pale red liquid that slowly spread out towards the edge of the plate.

'So is that one of your beauty secrets? Rare steak?'

'Along with bathing in the blood of virgins.'

'Really, those must be some pretty shallow baths. Especially if you live where I do.'

'It's certainly not easy.'

'They grow up so fast. Sophie knows far more about sex than I did when I was ... actually, come to think about it, I think she knows far more than I do now.'

'It must be amazing being a mother. I don't know if it's ever going to happen to me now.'

'You're not that old!'

'No, but I don't want to rush into it. I don't really fancy the single mother thing. No offence, I just don't think I could handle it.'

'I can't pretend that it's easy. Sometimes it feels almost impossible to keep it together, especially doing this job.'

'I imagine it's hard not having other people to talk to. You can't exactly burden a teenager with what it's like at a murder scene and some of the stuff you see.'

'Same goes for you. Who helps you to unwind and get it off your chest?'

'I've got a group of close friends that I've known for a while, mostly from university, mostly doctors. They're all very good listeners. Does your daughter see much of her father?'

Stacey shook her head. 'No. He's ... not a very good influence. I made a real mistake there. That's why we didn't stick together.'

'Pretty tough having to grow up without a dad at all, though. That can really mess you up.'

'She's a tough kid. She'll be okay. I guess you have to strike a balance. Is it better to have no dad or a crap dad? To be honest, I'm still trying to decide.'

'But she knows who he is and everything?'

'Actually she just met him for the first time recently but ... I had to stop her seeing him. It's pretty complicated. It was starting to get in the way ...'

Stacey's voice drifted off. Jessica reached across the table and placed her hand on top of her friend's. 'Sorry. Let's talk about something else. I apologize for sticking my nose in where it's not wanted. I take after my own mother in that respect.'

'Are your parents still together?'

Jessica's eyes flicked across to the man sitting on her left once more as she answered. 'Yeah. I don't see them much. I find them hard work.'

'Who doesn't?'

Jessica smiled. 'I remember being really, blissfully happy when I was young and then when I got to about seven everything in my life changed. I changed, my parents changed, we moved house. It was tough.'

'You seem to have done okay for yourself.'

'You have to make the best of the hand that you're given, don't you?'

The conversation continued to flow easily, and Stacey found herself feeling increasingly relaxed. She spent so much time in the male-dominated environment of the police, or looking after her daughter, or on her own, that she sometimes forgot how good it was to just go out and have a good time. She resolved to try to do it more often.

'So, Stacey, I've always wanted to ask: what made you join the police?'

'Long story.'

'So? I'm in no hurry. Let's order another bottle of vino. Especially as you're paying.'

Stacey laughed. 'Okay, if you insist, I'll give you the quick version.'

She went on to talk about her childhood growing up on the Blenheim Estate and the gangs of kids that used to hang out in the passageways causing trouble. She then moved on to the events of the day when she, her mum and her dad had been walking through the estate back from the local supermarket, all of them carrying heavy bags of shopping. The lifts were out of order, as they almost always were, so the trio had no choice but to struggle up the stairs to the fifth floor of Block E where their flat was. As they rounded the third flight of stairs, three young men emerged from a corner and blocked their way. Though many years had passed since, Stacey could still remember their faces, the casual smirks they wore as her father asked them to please step out of the way.

The boys demanded money but Stacey's father refused to pay, berating the boys for bringing the area into disrepute.

After that everything seemed to happen so fast. As one boy walked past, his hand flashed out and grabbed the straps of her mother's handbag, which was hanging from her shoulder. Her mother screamed in shock and surprise, and the boy tugged harder, jerking her body roughly away from the wall.

Then everything went into slow motion. Stacey remembered seeing her father's mouth wide open in a fierce scream of disapproval as he tore down the few steps that separated him from the boy. His right arm stretched out and clamped around the boy's neck. The two other boys turned and began making their way up the stairs to help their friend.

The boy tried to punch and claw and scratch the man's hands off of him but Stacey's father was too strong. The boy's two friends grabbed his shoulders and pulled him down. Stacey's father somehow lost his footing and began falling towards them. The boys swerved to avoid him and he crashed head first into the top stair, cartwheeling over and over down the flight of steps, landing with his body twisted and broken in a way that even a child could tell was simply not natural.

The boys ran off. Stacey and her mother tried to help her dad to his feet, but as soon as they moved him he started coughing up blood. So they called an ambulance. The rest of that night was a blur of flashing blue lights, hospital rooms and polite but grim-faced doctors. His spine had been badly damaged. He was going to be okay, they were told, but they should prepare themselves for the fact that he'd probably never walk again.

When the police turned up at the hospital bed, Stacey's father refused to tell on those who had attacked them for fear of reprisals against his family – a family he felt he could no longer protect. A shortage of available housing stock meant there was no chance of the family moving any further from the Blenheim Estate than the ground floor of Block E – the only level that was even vaguely wheelchair accessible and just five floors away from their old home.

From that moment on everything in Stacey's life changed. Until that point her father had always been fiercely independent – he wouldn't even let his wife iron his shirts for him. The adjustment to being completely and utterly reliant on others was not one he was able to deal with. He hated his wheelchair, hated the way his life had become and most of all hated for anyone to believe he couldn't still manage on his own.

'And that's where they've been ever since.'

She finished the story and the two women sat in silence as the full gravity of the life-changing experience washed over them.

'Did they ever catch the people who attacked your father?'

'They got caught for something else. My father refused to cooperate with the police because he didn't want to make me and my mum vulnerable. I guess I joined the force because I wanted to be able to stand up for people who couldn't do it for themselves. To bring the bad guys to justice.'

'Cool.'

Jessica refilled their glasses from the last of the second bottle of wine as they continued their conversation.

'How about you? What made you want to become a pathologist?'

'Oh God, why would anyone want to become a pathologist, eh? Certainly not by choice.'

'What, then?'

'Pushy parents. Seriously pushy parents. They sent me to private school and when I was about to head off to university they made it clear that I had only two choices about what I was going to do with my life, if I wanted any support from them. I was going to be either a doctor or a lawyer. Nothing else would do.

'I'd always enjoyed *Quincy* as a kid, you know, that American TV show about the forensic examiner who lives on a houseboat, turns detective and solves murders by the dozen. The more I looked into it, the more it intrigued me. And it still does. The workings of the human body, dead or alive, absolutely fascinate me.'

Stacey could see Jessica's pride and passion for her work written all over her face. She raised her glass in admiration. 'I still don't know how you cope with it all. The bodies and all that.'

'Humour. I know it sounds crazy and I'm always respectful to the dead, but humour plays an important part. And, talking of that, if there's ever anything I can do for you to help a case go more smoothly – swapping bodies around, planting evidence, faking lab tests – you just let me know.'

'Thank, Jessica. And, likewise, if you ever need a couple of extra corpses, just let me know. I've got friends in high places.'

They both chuckled.

Jessica cocked her head to one side. 'It's funny, back in the old days, back in the seventies say, the pathologist and the senior police officers would all head down the pub right after the post-mortem and get totally pissed. It was a bit of a tradition. Doesn't happen any more because everyone's supposed to be more professional and we have to appear impartial.'

'You think we shouldn't be doing this, then, talking about Moorwood?'

'Nah. We've been working together for years. Besides, how truly impartial can either of us be when we both want to see the guilty get punished and the innocent go free?'

'I'll drink to that.'

Each woman moved her glass towards the other's, ready for the toast. At that moment the chisel-jawed waiter, who was making his way towards a table on the other side of the restaurant, tripped on a carelessly placed handbag and sent a tray piled high with empty glasses flying through the air. It landed with a devastating crash.

Stacey jumped at the sudden noise, the jolt spilling a little of her drink. She spun her head round to see what was happening and joined the other diners in giving the mortified waiter a cheer of commiseration. When she turned back to her dinner companion, her wine was still sloshing back and forth in the glass.

Jessica still had her hand out ready for the toast. Her wine was as calm as a mill pond. 'Happens every time I'm here,' she said. 'That's man's all thumbs.' She smiled gently.

'To justice,' said Stacey.

'To justice,' said Jessica.

14

Not only was Billy Moorwood refusing to speak, he was also refusing to make eye contact. He slumped forward across the table of the interview room, staring at the wall in front of him with a dumb, vacant expression. He couldn't even be bothered to say no comment.

It was fast approaching midday. Woods and Collins were having their third interview with Moorwood that day but were getting less and less out of him each time. They were really starting to feel the pressure.

At the end of the first day of interrogation DCI Anderson had applied to the Magistrates Court for an extension allowing a further thirty-six hours after the first thirty-six hours had expired. He had successfully argued that further detention was necessary in order to secure evidence relating to the murder investigation.

When no such evidence emerged, Anderson made the decision to charge Moorwood with drugs and weapons offences in order to ensure he would be remanded in custody. But the charges were minor, and his solicitor had indicated his intention to apply for a bail hearing. Anderson knew there was every chance that Moorwood would be released and every chance that he would instantly vanish so far underground that they would never find him again.

It meant everyone on the team was working double-time to try to find the evidence to link him to the murders. Forensic officers were going through his shabby flat with a fine-tooth comb, collecting samples of everything from hair and fibres to fingerprints and body fluids.

Other officers were busy interviewing friends and family, checking out alibis and tracking down his movements at the time each of the dead men went missing and at the time that the bodies were being driven across South London.

And meanwhile Collins and Woods were desperately trying to get something out of him. It was frustrating work. There were so many gaps in their knowledge. It could easily have been the case that Moorwood was the man they were looking for. But at the same time they had managed to uncover almost no hard evidence that brought them any closer to proving he was guilty.

'Listen, Billy,' said Collins, desperately trying to make one last-ditch attempt to get him to open up. 'I shouldn't be saying this, but I have a lot of sympathy for you. A lot of people here do. The world isn't black and white. Right and wrong aren't always at opposite ends of the scale. Sometimes things get blurry in the middle. We want to help you, but we can't do anything unless you speak to us.'

There was a long silence. Collins waited as long as she could bear before beginning her closing statement. 'Interview terminated at – '

'What's the point?' snorted Moorwood. 'Whatever I say you're going to twist it around and make me out to be the bad guy. That's what you people do. I've seen it before. You've made up your mind about me, you don't care about the truth, you just want to lock me up.'

'That's not true, Billy. I want to know the truth. I want to know what happened. This is your chance to tell us, your chance to put your side of the story across.'

Moorwood slowly moved back in his chair until he was fully upright, though his gaze remained on the wall behind the officers. 'You don't understand. You couldn't possibly understand.' He suddenly turned his gaze on Collins. 'I just wanted to scare them.'

'You did a little more than that. Didn't you?'

'No. I'm not saying any more.'

'Then we must presume you're guilty.'

'Good. I want to go to court.'

'What do you mean?'

'I want to tell people what happened to me. I want everyone to know what those bastards did. There's gonna be reporters and all sorts there. The story will be everywhere. That's why I was going to top myself. I knew it would make the papers. I knew they would be called to account. There's enough evidence there to put them away. That's all I wanted. To see them brought to justice. Nothing more. Killing's too good for those bastards. It would be over too quickly. I want them to suffer. I want to ruin their lives the way they've ruined mine. I wanted to be the last thing they thought about every night before they went to bed. I'm not saying any more, not until the press are right in front of me.'

Collins sighed. 'But, Billy, the press won't come unless they know what the story is going to be about. You have to give me a taster. Something I can interest them with.'

'What sort of thing?'

'Tell me when you started following them.'

Moorwood dragged the back of his hand across his nose and sniffed. 'It was after the case. Half of those bastards managed to get away with it. They lied and used the fact that people were still scared of them. It was like they had planned it out from the start. They were teachers, they were respected members of the community. We trusted them. They can't treat kids that way. They thought they were above the law. They're not. I had to make them pay.'

'So you killed them.'

Moorwood's eyes widened. 'Killing's too good for them. I told you that. I just followed them. I just wanted to scare them. That's all. I don't know anything about anyone ending up dead. But I'll tell you one thing: I'm not sorry to hear it. Not sorry at all.'

*

Jason Bevan's fingers trembled with excitement as he turned on his computer.

After what had seemed like a lifetime of waiting, the day when he was going to meet up with his latest conquest had finally arrived.

The machine seemed to take ages to boot up, and when the usual musical notes played to say it was ready he felt a new rush passing through him. Bevan didn't want to come across as being overeager. He had fought hard to stay cool. He glanced at the clock in the bottom-right-hand corner of the screen: eleven thirty. Time to make the final arrangements for their lunch. He double-clicked on the messenger program, moistening his lips with his tongue as it loaded.

sportsfan52: hi – how are u

shygirl351: nervous

shygirl351: and excited

sportsfan52: good – neither is a bad thing

shygirl351: lol

shygirl351: that must mean we're still on then

sportsfan52: correct – ready to go

sportsfan52: have u told anyone about our meeting

shygirl351: nope

shygirl351: not a soul

shygirl351: have you?

sportsfan52: no

shygirl351: wow

shygirl351: where shall we meet then

sportsfan52: not sure. Would normally say pub but guess that is out of the question

shygirl351: lol

shygirl351: have been in more than you think – make up works wonders

sportsfan52: shall we do a pub then

shygirl351: rather not. hate being in pubs on my own. What if you were late

sportsfan52: I'll be early

sportsfan52: If you like – just ring my phone when you arrive and I will come outside

shygirl351: have a better idea

shygirl351: do you know Gladstone park

sportsfan52: yes, what about it

shygirl351: there's a bench by the rotunda, opposite the pond

shygirl351: me and my mates used to hang out there. Could meet there

sportsfan52: would be private. Sounds good. Let's do it. Four thirty?

shygirl351: great

shygirl351: can't wait

shygirl351: bye

He had arranged it all perfectly. His wife was away for the night visiting her parents and the children were over at friends' for a sleepover. Despite having had less than twenty-four hours' notice, he now had the place to himself. He would be able to do whatever he liked knowing he would not be disturbed.

Shygirl had been by far the best of the bunch and his favourite from the start. There had been others that he had chatted to over the preceding months but this was to be his first actual meeting.

Another young girl had seemed interested at first but she had gone a little cold. She didn't respond in the flirtatious way that this girl did. He struggled for a moment to think of her screen name. DreamGirl99, that had been it. If she had been a bit more forthcoming he would have arranged a meeting with her as well. Instead he had put her on the back burner a couple of days earlier to pursue Shygirl instead. If things went well, he could always return to her at a later date. He was on a roll.

The hours seemed to drag by until it was time to leave. He checked his appearance in the mirror. Teeth clean, clean shaven, hair washed and neatly styled. He looked younger than his forty-two years, which was good, though he had been open and honest about his age right from the start and the girl didn't seem to mind at all. In fact, if anything, she had been increasingly excited by the prospect of meeting up with him.

In the circles that he moved in, such girls were highly sought after and they generated a great deal of excitement. He would be able to teach her everything. She would be able to give him the ultimate pleasure. She would, for a few years at least, be everything he could ever want her to be. Better still, he would be able to use her to draw in others, perhaps to enhance his standing among his community, sharing her out and swapping her with his peers.

He tried not to get ahead of himself. He couldn't blow it at this stage. He had put too much time and too much effort into the girl so far. He had to be so slow, so cunning. Above all he had to be careful. It's easy to avoid giving the game away when every response can be carefully thought out. It's a very different matter when you are in the midst of a free-flowing conversation. shygirl351 still did not know that Sally, the girl that had introduced them, had actually been him all along and he had to ensure he said nothing that would give it away.

And he had to think about the future. None of this was going to last for ever. All good things, he knew only too well, would have to come to an end. He could have his fun for now but ultimately there would come a time when he would have to replace her with a younger model.

It was a beautifully sunny afternoon, the pale blue sky dotted with thin wisps of pure white cloud and the odd snaking white jet stream left by high-flying aircraft. He sucked in a deep breath of air, then turned and headed down his front path towards his garden gate.

Somewhere at the back of his subconscious mind he registered the fact that the street seemed to be a little quieter than usual. Several of his neighbours were retired or elderly and could usually be found in their front gardens. No one was walking their dog.

A few curtains twitched on the opposite side of the street.

He was still pondering this when the sound of heavy footfalls from behind snapped him out of his daydream. He turned just in time to see a large man, his mop of blond hair flying up in the wind, his tie flapping behind his neck, bearing down on him at high speed.

Before he could say a word the man had launched himself towards him in a vicious rugby tackle that knocked Bevan down to the ground and forced all the wind out of him. As he lay gasping for breath, clutching at his sore ribs and trying to rub his bruised shoulder, the rest of them appeared.

They came from all directions. Men in suits, men and women in police uniforms. So many of them that he quickly lost count. They emerged from behind cars; they vaulted over hedges; they appeared from around corners – and all of them were rushing towards him.

The blond man was now on top of him, forcing his shoulders down and squeezing at one of the pressure points close to his neck. He had yet to say a word.

'Jason Andrew Bevan?' asked the blond man, an unmistakable snort of satisfaction in his voice. Bevan nodded weakly, still wondering what on earth was going on.

'I am Detective Inspector Michael Carter of the Metropolitan Police's Child Exploitation and Online

Protection Unit. I am arresting you on suspicion of using a computer to groom a child. You do not have to say anything but anything you do say may be given in evidence against you.'

'But I haven't done anything,' blurted Bevan. 'I haven't even touched her.'

Other officers helped Carter drag Bevan up to his feet, where he was immediately handcuffed. Carter plunged his hands into Bevan's pockets and extracted his house keys, then gave the signal for the prisoner to be led to a waiting van.

Using the keys to gain entry, Carter led a group of officers into his house to examine his computer. The team had spent the last three months posing as a young girl online using the name DreamGirl99 and hoping to catch Carter in the act of grooming. When he ignored their most recent communications, they suspected he had found a genuine victim and knew they had to move fast.

Unable to intercept his communications, they had put him under surveillance and watched out for the warning signs, key among them being the departure of his wife and children.

In the attic room that served as Bevan's office it took only a few minutes for one of the tech guys to call up that day's internet activity.

'Guv, he's supposed to be meeting her this after-noon. We've got a record of the IR chats. Supposed to be there in half an hour. Gladstone Park. The bench by the rotunda.'

'Okay, who can we spare?'

'Got a whole bunch of uniforms to choose from.'

'Nah, that'll just scare her off. We need to send someone in plain clothes. Whoever she is, she's obviously very vulnerable and delicate. I want this handled with care.'

'All the plain clothes people are men. DC Lyons has been off this week. I could call the station and get them to send someone along.'

'There's no time. Send O'Neill. He's got a kind face. That will have to do.'

15

It had taken Detective Sergeant Patrick O'Neill quite a while to find the right bench, the one where the girl who had been due to meet with Jason Bevan was supposed to be. It had been close to the car park, in the midst of a fenced-off area of flower beds, well shielded from the main road by trees and a pain in the arse to get to.

When he finally located it there was no one to be seen. For a while the young officer worried that he had got there too late, but then, off in the distance, he saw a young girl who seemed to be heading his way and tried his best to look as relaxed as possible. It was, he decided, important to get the balance right, If he looked too much like a pervert, she might be put off, but then again if he didn't look like enough of one, she might not come over at all. But O'Neill needed to talk to her. Urgently. The inquiry team needed to ensure she was safe and understood the danger she had potentially placed herself in every bit as much as they needed to ensure that Bevan was out of circulation.

His heart began to beat a little faster as the girl came closer and closer, through the centre of the main tree-lined path that led to the gate. She was looking directly at him now, he was sure of it. Was she the one? It was too soon to tell. She looked a little older than a teenager, but he knew only too well that clever make-up could work wonders. He turned away for a few moments so as not to intimidate her. When he looked back she had turned off on to a smaller side track and was rapidly heading away from him. He didn't know what to feel. Disappointment, relief? Was it her? Should he go after her or wait just in case it was someone else?

O'Neill was still weighing up his many options when he felt a sudden sharp pinch in the back of his shoulder.

'Hey! What the . . .'

O'Neill spun around as quickly as he could, just in time to see light glinting off a syringe. He couldn't take his eyes off it, the cloudy liquid in the chamber, the streaks of blood glistening at the end of the long silver needle. What the hell do you think you're . . .' He never managed to finished the sentence. After those first few words everything started to spin and his breathing began to get laboured. He could feel his eyes travelling up into the top of his head and knew he was going to pass out.

He came round some time later and found himself sitting in what appeared to be the passenger seat of a car. It was hard to tell for sure. He was looking straight ahead and slightly downwards, and could see his legs in the footwell, part of the seat and the bottom part of the glovebox. On the edge of his field of vision he could see that the door to his left was wide open.

When he tried to turn his head to look around, nothing happened. For some reason his body seemed to have stopped working. His legs, his arms, his hands, even his lips and tongue had all become useless. He couldn't swing his legs out to escape. He couldn't even blink. All he could do was sit there.

From somewhere behind came the sound of footsteps. Solid shoes on a tiled floor. A steady clip, clip, clip, coming closer and closer. Then the sound of heavy machinery, a grinding of gears, a squeal of metal on metal. Then footsteps again coming closer still. O'Neill watched helplessly as something that looked a bit like a steel cable passed between his legs and tightened around both of his ankles. Pressure started to build up, as if the bones were being crushed. And then, almost inexplicably, he began to move.

He fell to the right first, his arm smashing into the gear lever, his head against the edge of the steering wheel. He felt both blows but any noises he made sounded only inside his head. He continued to move. It was as if his feet were being pulled out from underneath him, out through the door of the car with his body following, the motion completely unnatural. Within a few seconds his legs were high in the air and he was being hauled upwards, swinging upside down with the weight of his entire body supported by his ankles.

The pain was like nothing he had ever known. And he couldn't even scream. He couldn't even cry.

Once he reached some ten feet off the ground he stopped rising and instead began to move sideways. He looked around as much as the swinging motion of the cable would let him. He was in a cavernous warehouse building. He could feel cold air rushing past him, burning his cheeks and nose. The floor was tiled, and the walls were painted a dull grey and lined with shelves and bookcases.

A sudden slapping sound on the ground below was followed by a halt in his movements as the machinery controlling his journey was switched off. O'Neill knew at once what had happened. His warrant card had fallen out from his back pocket. The footsteps approached once more. O'Neill was still gently swinging and could see nothing. He didn't need to. It was obvious what was happening. Whoever had attacked him had walked over to retrieve the wallet and was now opening and inspecting it.

It would, he felt certain, change everything. The card clearly identified him as a serving police office. Whoever had taken him, surely they had to let him go. Whatever sick game they were playing would, he assured himself, now come to an end.

There was a pause. A long pause during which time seemed to stand still. The room became very silent and O'Neill became acutely aware of his own racing heartbeat. Then another slapping sound, softer than before, and the machinery started up once more. O'Neill began to move again.

He felt a sick wave of horror pass through him when he realized in one bigger than usual swing that he was heading towards a large stainless-steel table in the centre of the room. Not only that: he also realized what the soft slapping sound had been – the sound of his warrant card being casually tossed aside. Whoever had taken him cared nothing for the fact that he was a police officer.

Sure enough, he continued moving until he was directly above the table and then was slowly lowered down until he was lying on it, flat on his back.

The dazzling overhead lights were painful to look at, like staring directly into the sun, but there was nothing he could do about it. He felt his clothes being removed from his body. Occasionally he saw the top of a head covered in a mop of brown hair at the bottom of his field of vision.

'Don't worry. Everything is going to be all right. You're going to be just fine. There is nothing to worry about, Patrick. You're going to be just fine.'

The voice had a beautifully mellow, almost hypnotic tone to it. But O'Neill didn't trust it at all. He desperately wanted to stand up and fight his way out. Whatever was about to happen to him, he wanted no part of it. But he was rooted to the spot. He might just as well have been made of stone.

A clatter of metal against metal was followed by the return of the head and a warm sensation on

O'Neill's chest as a soft palm pressed down on to the space between his nipples.

Again he tried to speak, to scream, to shout, to pull away, anything, but it was no good. A face, half hidden by a surgical mask and cap, appeared above his. Only the eyes were visible. And they were as cold as ice. The pressure from the fingers increased. O'Neill felt something – most likely a thumb – sliding back and forth across his chest, seemingly searching for something.

Suddenly the hand pushed him down hard, the weight of an entire body behind it. He felt his shoulder blades push into the metal beneath him, his spine straighten out and the breath hiss out of his lungs.

Then a new pain, a terrible pain. A hot burning sensation in the middle of his chest that grew wider and deeper in an instant. He caught a glint of metal, of something red. For a moment he thought he had been stuck with the syringe again, but this was far deeper, far more deadly than any needle.

He could feel blood rising up inside his mouth, cold air sweeping over the inside of his body. He could feel the life force seeping out of him. By the time he felt hands pulling the two sides of his ribcage apart, he knew he had only a few moments left.

The voice that had once gently called his name was now breathless with excitement.

It sounded as though she was laughing. Laughing at him and his pain but in his dying moments he realized the truth was far, far worse. The voice was not laughing, it was not even speaking. It was moaning. Writhing, rocking backwards and forwards in ecstasy.

The sound of euphoric laughter was still ringing in O'Neill's ears as the life seeped out of him and the bright lights slowly faded into absolute, eternal darkness.

He didn't look like a paedophile – but then again they never do. There was something about the way he carried himself that screamed out 'I don't belong here'. Not for the delights of under-age sex anyway.

But then you can't argue with the facts. He was at the bench – and that one's a bugger to find. Nobody goes there by accident. He was in the right place at the right time, and there was only one way he could have known about the meeting. So he had to pay the price.

It took me quite a while to get him into the car – all that dead weight – but once he was inside it was plain sailing. I tied the cables round his ankles the way I always do and used the jig to lift him up into the air. It's poetry in motion to watch and never gives any trouble. A machine that's designed for lifting dead cows isn't going to struggle with a full-grown man, no matter how overweight he might be.

It was while he was upside down, swinging his merry way along to the killing room, that the wallet fell out of his back pocket. It gave me quite a shock at first. A police warrant card. Had they been watching me? Were they going to burst through the door at any moment? I got a bit paranoid, I don't mind admitting, but it didn't last long. It was so unlikely anything was going to happen. He had been alone. He had been off his guard. If this had been some kind of major operation to find the killer, they would have jumped me there and then.

But if they weren't after me, they must have been after Bevan. It didn't take me too long to learn that he had been taken into custody.

I know that in reality the police don't have a clue about me. They're chasing the likes of Billy Moorwood. They're wasting their time. I've been too clever. Too careful. The clues all point somewhere else. That made it all the more deliciously ironic. I love the attention.

Anyway, just because Patrick O'Neill is a police officer doesn't mean he doesn't deserve to die. And I must admit I am becoming incredibly excited at the prospect of my first killing of an innocent and I plan to make the most of it.

This will be even better than when I killed Chadwick. Not a lot of people knew about the fetish clubs he visited on a weekly basis, and even fewer knew about the awful things he did to some of the women he encountered there. Vulnerable women. Some of them little more than girls. Broken girls from broken homes. Lives shattered by abuse from an early age. He thought he could buy their silence and it worked to a degree. But then the smug bastard made the mistake of attacking the wrong person. A friend of mine. A good friend. She came round for a coffee and was trying to hold it together, then burst into tears and told me all about it, blurting out every sick, perverted and despicable thing he did to her. She was covered in bruises and whip marks from where he had beaten her to within an inch of her life for his sexual gratification. There had to be revenge.

I knew I was taking a risk when I dumped the bodies, but it had to be done. Chadwick's victims had a right to know what had happened to him. They would know that he'd paid the ultimate price. I've now been doing this for so long without any recognition of all the effort I've put into clearing the streets. Until I dumped the bodies of the three stooges, not a word of my work had made it into the press. Chadwick had been a good kill. The others too. Righteous kills. I enjoyed every minute. I enjoyed all of them.

It took far longer to identify the other two than I thought it would have. The police can be so useless at times. You have to give them everything on a plate if you want to get anything done.

O'Neill had opened up easily enough, which is always the way when the body is warm, but there had been a surprising amount of fat around the internal organs. More than usual, and that was going to be difficult to dispose of. But the organs themselves, with the exception of the liver, turned out to be in remarkably healthy condition.

I continued the 'work' along the usual patterns with few variations. I am, however, particularly pleased with the level of mutilation I managed to achieve around the genital area. I was using a new combination of instruments that has proved highly effective. I will continue to do so.

I can't deny it any more. It's not about clearing the streets. It's all about the killing. That was the real high. The sensations as the life force slipped out of him were more intense than any I have known. And I know why.

Killing the scum of the earth, doing the world a favour, has been fine up until now, but crossing that moral line has generated a massive new rush. I found myself masturbating once again. I have always been aroused by my work but having an innocent body has taken it to new ecstatic heights.

The risks are going to be greater, of course. O'Neill's death is going to give the police a real bee in their bonnet about trying to track me down. I obliterated the trail to the others but this new one will be almost impossible to destroy completely. The net is going to close in. It's only a matter of time.

Killing O'Neill has been by far the most satisfying piece of 'work' to date in so many ways and has left me with a deep craving, a passionate longing, in its wake. Who would have thought that innocence could be such an aphrodisiac?

I can't fight the urges any longer. What's the point? I've started planning the next one already. It's going to be the ultimate rush, it really will. Because at long last I've discovered the truth about what I do: the less deserving the target of my brutality, the better.

The excitement in the CEOP office following the arrest of Jason Bevan was so intense that it took several hours before anyone realized that Detective Sergeant Patrick O'Neill had failed to report in.

DI Carter had just emerged from the interview room after his first session with Bevan when he asked his DS to find out how Carter had got on with the girl he had been sent to look after.

'Don't know,' the officer replied. 'He hasn't got back here yet and he hasn't been in touch.'

DI Carter glanced at his watch and frowned

deeply. 'He's been gone four hours. What the hell does he think he's playing at? I've got to get back in with Bevan in a few minutes. Call him on his mobile. Find out what's going on for me and report back later.'

It took only minutes to establish that O'Neill's mobile had been switched off, that he was not answering his home phone and he hadn't spoken to anyone else on the team since the arrest had been made.

He was a popular and solidly reliable officer who was in a long-term relationship with one of the team's civilian support staff, so the fact that his girlfriend had not heard from him either quickly ensured the attitude of the officers searching for their missing colleague rapidly moved from bemusement to serious concern.

A trawl round O'Neill's friends and family showed no signs of depression, no dissatisfaction with any aspect of his life, no clue whatsoever that he was planning to run away and leave it all behind. It became increasingly clear that, if O'Neill was missing, it was not by his own choice. Clues were thin on the ground, but, leaving the members of the inquiry team aside, the obvious place to start seemed to be with the person who had seen him last.

By the time DI Carter sat down opposite his interviewee for the third time that evening, the case he had spent so long working on had moved to the back burner.

Jason Bevan bit his nails nervously as DI Carter entered the room. He knew he was in trouble. He knew the police had all the evidence they needed not just to put him away for a very long time but also to change his life for ever. His darkest secret was about to be exposed. His marriage, his relationships with his children, with his friends and with his work colleagues – it was all about to come to an end.

He had been caught red-handed, so to speak, and strategies like refusing to speak, lying through his teeth or trying to put the blame on the girl were all pointless. He was in it up to his neck and there was no way out. No way out of it at all. Or at least that's what he thought, right until the moment that DI Carter sat down and offered him the possibility of a deal.

Carter pushed a copy of the transcripts of his last internet conversation as sportsfan52 across the desk towards him. 'One of my men is missing. I think they may have met up with the person you were communicating with. I need you to tell me everything you know about shygirl351. And I mean absolutely everything.'

The two sessions of morning prayers that followed the arrest of Moorwood had been glum affairs, with everyone on the team staring at their shoes and worried about being singled out because they simply had nothing new to add. No one wanted to be blamed for stalling the operation, and Anderson's mood had become darker and darker; he barely seemed to leave his office at all. A second 36-hour extension on the custody time limit had been obtained and Anderson was preparing the paperwork for another, acutely aware that, unless hard evidence of a link to the murders could be found, Moorwood was unlikely to be their man.

Difficult as it was to believe, Moorwood's story appeared to be true. His connection to the case and the fact he had been stalking one of the victims shortly before he had been murdered were nothing more than coincidence.

Charged with drugs offences, various breaches of the peace and weapons violations, Moorwood had been remanded in custody to await his day in court and the team at MIT had gone back to the drawing board.

Just before lunch on Friday a sandy-haired man arrived and was shown into Anderson's office. The pair remained there for almost an hour before emerging side by side, causing a hush to sweep across the incident room.

'Okay, gather around everyone,' said Anderson, pointing his open hand towards the man on his left. 'We've had a development. A major development that, I'm afraid, may well prove that we've been chasing our own tails for the last few days. Now I know you've all been working extremely hard and I don't want to take that away from you, but when you hear what I'm about to say you're going to feel as if we've been sent back to square one.

'This is Detective Inspector Michael Carter from the CEOP – Child Exploitation and Online Protection. I'm going to let him tell you what he's just told me.'

Anderson perched on the edge of a nearby desk as Carter stepped forward. He slowly scanned the room, taking in the faces of the officers before he began to speak.

'My unit has been involved in a series of long-term operations against paedophiles using the internet to groom victims. Our main tool is to use officers who hang around in online chatrooms using false identities that have been specially created with a view to attracting those involved in this kind of behaviour.

'We recently moved in to arrest a man known as Jason Bevan who had been online using the alias sportsfan52. He engaged in conversation with one of our officers, who was pretending to be a fourteen-year-old girl. Bevan began to groom our officer and tried to arrange to meet but we quickly became aware that Bevan was also in touch with other youngsters on the net and that there was a huge danger he would attempt to meet up with one of them before he met up with our team.

'We tried to bring forward our own meeting by making our responses to his messages more eager and offering him a mobile telephone number so that he would be able to send text messages or even call; however, this had the effect of making him extremely nervous and cautious. We feared that our operation may have been compromised.

'Bevan was arrested yesterday and immediate examination of his computer showed that he had been in touch with a fourteen-year-old girl using the screen name shygirl351. A meeting had been arranged that very afternoon, so I sent one of my men along to meet with the potential victim and ensure that she was safe.

'Detective Sergeant O'Neill never reported in after meeting up with shygirl351. He has now been missing for almost twenty hours and we're all gravely concerned about his welfare. A more thorough analysis of Bevan's computer, along with interviews with Bevan himself, has led me to believe that, far from being a genuine fourteen-year-old girl, shygirl351 is in fact an alias created by an adult male with a view to luring paedophiles out into the open.'

Woods cocked his head to one side. 'Like a vigilante operation?'

'Something along those lines.' A murmur of nervous chatter spread throughout the members of the team. 'When we looked back through the chat logs,' Carter continued, 'we realized the person was using the same techniques and methods that we do when our officers go undercover in order to make the potential paedophiles feel safe and comfortable. The irony is, whoever was behind this character managed to do a far better job than we did ourselves, and we're supposed to be the experts.

'That was when we started getting extremely worried. Our initial concern was that if O'Neill had been snatched by members of a vigilante gang, they may have acted before they realized he was a police officer, and not a paedophile. Or they may have discovered he was a police officer and realized that they couldn't release him without exposing themselves.

'But then when we entered details of what little intelligence we had into the HOLMES system, we became even more concerned. I'm aware that one of your lines of inquiry is following the notion that your triple killer has been targeting unconvicted sex offenders.

'Although we have no hard evidence at this stage, our concern is that the person who snatched O'Neill, the person who engaged in conversation with Jason Bevan, may in fact be the person that your team are looking for.'

Collins felt a twitch in her stomach. Crimes involving fellow officers as victims were always hard to deal with. It was, for the most part, the random nature of the crimes that made them so difficult to handle. The beat bobby on a bicycle who knocks at a door to voice complaints from neighbours about the noise, only to be shot dead by a group of drug-crazed Yardies – there but for the grace of God they all went. It could have happened to any of them.

Carter reached into his briefcase and pulled out some sheaves of paper. 'I have here copies of transcripts of all the conversations that we've been able to retrieve between Bevan and shygirl351. I'll be passing them on to your profiler with a view to getting some more insights into our man's mindset.

'In the meantime I can tell you what I have learned – this person is extremely accomplished at what they are doing. During the time they were online with Bevan they were totally convincing, able to use slang and teenage language with ease. They also seem very comfortable with assuming the role of a female.

'This person has an extremely advanced level of knowledge when it comes to computing. Our attempts to track down the computer shygirl351 has been using have got us nowhere. The results say the computer is based somewhere in Kazakhstan. We know from the conversations and the arrangements to meet that they are based in London, but the signals we receive are being bounced around and diverted. I have spoken to our computer experts and this is extremely difficult to do.'

The volume of the chatter intensified. Carter looked across at Anderson, who silenced the room with a wave of his hand and stepped forward.

'Now I can see that some of you are a little sceptical,' said Anderson. 'An hour ago I was too, but DI Carter and I have spent the morning comparing notes and I'm afraid to say that the more we look into this, the stronger the links seem to get. What really sold it for me is that, if you take away the fact that Bevan has a couple of kids, his profile is almost identical to Miller's.

'Although we have yet to find the link in the case of Chadwick, it seems pretty certain that our killer has been actively targeting paedophiles. At the time someone like Miller was killed, the internet was still in a relative state of infancy and people with those kinds of interests had a limited number of ways to meet up and swap information. We know that Miller made use of contact magazines and lonely hearts, which were a precursor to the modern-day chatroom. It makes perfect sense that if someone was targeting paedophiles today, they would do it online.

'There is, of course, a whole separate team looking into O'Neill's disappearance and trying to track him down. It's a multi-level operation, attacking from all sides, and we are now a key part of it. What we plan to do, along with DI Carter's help, is see if we can set up some kind of a sting operation, draw shygirl351 out into the open. In order to do this, instead of posing as a vulnerable young girl, we are going to pose as an online predator.'

Collins shook her head. 'There is another possibility with all this, isn't there?'

All eyes turned to Collins and she half shrugged her shoulders before continuing. 'Sorry if I'm speaking out of turn, I don't believe in holding back.'

'No. I appreciate you speaking your mind, Collins. It's always good to get another perspective on a case. What have you got?'

'Well, I don't know O'Neill at all, but we have to

accept the possibility that the reason he may have been targeted is that he too is an unconvicted paedophile. It certainly wouldn't be the first time an officer with those duties was found to have that kind of weakness.'

Around the room all the officers nodded gently to themselves. It was an uncomfortable truth that, in more cases than any of them cared to recall, officers with paedophile tendencies had worked their way into child pornography units. That way they could spend their days viewing thousands of images without fear of prosecution. Psychological screening was supposed to weed out the worst cases – the same way it was supposed to weed out gun fanatics from the armed response teams – but a few always managed to slip through.

Carter and Anderson looked at one another before Carter spoke. 'That is something I've considered but I believe the chances of that being the case are pretty negligible. O'Neill was one of four DCs on the job that day. I picked him at random to go and meet this contact. The chances of him turning out to be a paedophile and our killer knowing about it are just too high to be taken wholly seriously. I know Patrick. I've known him for a while. You can never say never, but I'm sure he's clean.'

Collins nodded in agreement but after only a few seconds began shaking her head again. 'Then what are we wasting time for? It's going to take days, maybe even weeks to build up a relationship with shygirl351. There's no way this guy doesn't know that O'Neill is a copper. Either O'Neill would have told him or the killer would have found his warrant card or something. The idea that he's going to be up for an online conversation is just ludicrous. He'll be on his guard. Dr Bernard talked about the fact that these people often have an intimate knowledge of police procedure. You said he's already displayed knowledge of the techniques used by undercover officers working online. Surely he'll be expecting something like this.' She looked across at Woods and her fellow officers for moral support.

'That's a chance we have to take,' said Anderson. 'It could go either way. Now that a policeman has become directly involved it could send him underground but he may also be thinking that he has nothing to lose. Dr Bernard also talked about some of these people being on some kind of mission. Our man may now think he's running out of time. Or he may be planning to use O'Neill as some kind of bargaining chip, but wondering how to get in touch with us. The only way to find out is go online. That's our best hope of tracking this person down.'

16

The heavy-set man in a bomber jacket, blue jeans and army boots leaned casually against the fence post smoking a cigarette. He stepped into the middle of the dirt track as the car carrying Jack Stanley and Danny Thompson rounded the corner and began heading towards him.

Stanley stopped a few yards short of the gateway and rolled down his window. 'We're here for the party,' he said.

The man stared hard at Stanley, then shifted his gaze to do the same to Thompson. Finally he cupped one hand against the rear window and peered into the back of the vehicle.

'No cameras allowed,' he said at last. His Northern Irish accent was as thick as treacle. 'And that includes camera phones. Anything like that will have to stay in the car. We'll be checking. Follow the path round to the right until you can't go any further. Park up next to the stables. The party's in the building opposite.'

The man returned to the fence post as Stanley rolled up the window, shifted the car into gear and drove on.

'So that's one of them, eh?'

'Has to be,' said Stanley. 'The accent's a dead give-away.'

'He doesn't seem so tough.'

Stanley turned to his friend. 'He doesn't have to be, does he? I hear they've even got a bird on their team.'

'Fucking hell! She'll probably end up in tears before the end of the night.'

They wove their way through the farm complex until they found the stables. Dozens of other cars had got there before them and seemingly taken up every inch of available space. Stanley managed to squeeze his car in at an awkward angle at the far end, dangerously close to what appeared to be a huge pile of manure. He and Thompson clambered out, noses held against the stench, and started to make their way over to a dilapidated out-building with a rusty, corrugated-tin roof.

It was nearly nine and the sun had almost completely vanished below the horizon. The door to the out-building was slightly ajar, revealing a strip of bright light; the sounds of chatter came from within.

It had been more than three months since Stanley had last visited the barn, back when he was searching for a venue for tonight's event. On that occasion it had been filled with old farm equipment and had no artificial lighting, but the owners assured him they would be able to transform it. As he and Thompson stepped inside, he could see immediately that they had kept their word.

Four mobile arc lights had been placed in each corner, the farm equipment had all been cleared away, and the centre of the barn was now dominated by a fifteen-by-fifteen-foot roped-off ring. At floor level, the boundary was marked off by a low breeze-block wall.

A large crowd had already gathered inside, and Thompson and Stanley made their way over to the ring, acknowledging several friends along the way, jostling among the other spectators until they found a good viewing spot.

Chilled cans of beer, joints and even a few pills were being passed around and both men soon indulged. During the next fifteen minutes the barn became even more crowded as further spectators arrived. The atmosphere was electric.

Finally, a bald-headed man with an enormous beer belly and sweat stains in the small of his back and under his armpits climbed into the ring. He was carrying two buckets of water, each with a sponge floating inside, and placed one in each corner. He then moved to the middle of the ring and turned three hundred and sixty degrees, taking in the faces of all those who were there before raising his voice to speak.

'From this moment on, the only people who are allowed to speak before the fight starts will be the handlers. If anyone else makes a sound, their bets will be null and void as they will be deemed to be cheating.'

Silence fell among the crowd. A few seconds later the first handler appeared. He was in his late twenties, Asian, with baggy black jeans and several gold chains hanging from his neck. Tucked under his right arm was a jet-black American pit bull terrier.

Thompson leaned over towards Stanley and whispered in his ear, 'Those Southall boys love this shit, don't they?'

The dog was raring to go, a black ball of fury and aggression. The man put it down in the corner of the ring and removed its muzzle but was having trouble keeping the animal in place.

Just then the opponent arrived. The handler was the man who had been guarding the entrance when Stanley and Thompson had arrived. His dog seemed much smaller and quieter and was pale grey with white and brown patches. As soon as they got sight of the other dog, the men gathered around the ring began betting furiously. Huge wads of cash, thousands of pounds at a time, were being passed back and forth to the bookkeepers, who had based themselves at a small folding table at the side of the room.

The referee entered the ring and all betting stopped. The two handlers turned their dogs to face each other. Both animals were shaking with excitement but hardly making a noise. The referee then gave the command everyone had been waiting for: release the dogs.

The two animals raced towards each other and

slammed together with a sickening thud of bone smashing into bone. They clashed so hard that the momentum sent both dogs spinning over, kicking up dust from the floor of the ring as they went. It took only seconds for them to turn and set on each other again. By now they were using their mouths, each ripping chunks of flesh out of the other, both twisting and turning, trying to get a better hold. Blood began to spatter on to the ground around the two dogs as they fought.

The crowd watched and whistled and cheered on their chosen dog. To a man the looks on their faces showed just how much they were enjoying the spectacle. A life or death struggle was going on right before their very eyes. It was the ultimate buzz.

Despite being smaller, the Irishman's dog soon proved itself to be the more capable of the two. Fit and agile, it repeatedly outmanoeuvred its opponent in order to inflict far greater damage that anything it received. At one point it spun quickly and sank its teeth deep into the bigger dog's neck. When it let go several minutes later, a huge spray of blood shot out from where the bite had been.

There was a hushed gasp in the crowd. Everyone knew what it meant, and sure enough within thirty seconds the larger dog began to slow down, the energy draining out of him as the blood left his body. When the dog collapsed completely, the referee stepped in and ended the fight. The Irishman raised his own animal high in the air as the crowd went wild.

The injuries to the other dog were so severe that there was no hope of recovery. Despite having fought bravely, he would be destined for the bath – a barrel of water outside the arena where losing and badly injured dogs could be held under until they drowned.

Stanley bit his lip in frustration. The festivities had been organized at the behest of a group called the Farmer's Boys, one of the largest dog-fighting gangs in the UK. Based in a small town in County Armagh called Tandragee, the group had been involved in the scene for years and were rumoured to have links to the IRA and other paramilitary gangs.

Known for the viciousness of their dogs, they had agreed to bring a selection of animals over to the mainland to take on the best that the English had to offer. Stanley, a relative newcomer to the sport, was determined not to lose but this had been a bad start. The dogs he sponsored were due to fight next but if all the opponents were the quality of the one they had just seen, the Farmer's Boys would be leaving victorious.

Fresh sawdust was swept over the centre of the ring to soak up the blood and the next two dogs were brought out. Shaft, as black as coal with white scars covering his muzzle and body as a testament of past battles, was being handled by a slender red-haired woman wearing tight jeans and a loose-fitting t-shirt. Thompson nudged Stanley in the ribs and smiled as their dog Brutus was brought out.

Brutus, a relative newcomer to the scene, was the colour of wet sand with a strip of white at the base of his neck. Stanley had purchased the dog from a specialist supplier in Helsinki and had him shipped over three months earlier. Since that time the dog had been kept at a specially converted terraced house in East London that had been converted into a training school.

Wary of attracting police attention to the operation, Stanley had visited only once – two weeks earlier following a scare in which one of the nine dogs being kept at the house had escaped and begun running wild in the local park, harassing other dogs.

Stanley arrived at the house the following day. The whole place had been cleared of furniture and the centre of the living room was dominated by a large treadmill that had been specially adapted so that a dog's collar could be attached. Each of the animals was forced to run at least five miles each day in order to maintain them in peak condition. Their diet was also supplemented by muscle-building powders and tablets.

'How the fuck did it get out?' asked Stanley after inspecting the back room where the cages storing the dogs were kept.

'Chewed at the bars until they buckled and the lock broke,' admitted Paul, the skinny youth in charge of training the dogs. 'Took some doing. Lost a couple of teeth in the process but carried on. Shame he's dead. That dog had real heart. He would have been a killer in the ring. But Brutus is still around and he's top.'

'Hasn't been traced back to you, though,' said Stanley.

'Nah, there's no evidence. I kept them quiet so that no one knows they're here. People know I've got dogs but they don't know how many or what breed. When I have to take them out I load them up in the van and go out of the garage. It's the perfect set-up.'

'Not that perfect if one of the little fuckers escaped, is it?'

Paul hung his head with shame. 'I messed up. It won't happen again.'

'Whatever,' snorted Stanley. 'Just so long as my dogs win on the night; otherwise you're really going to be fucked.'

It was Paul himself who was carrying Brutus into the ring, pausing to wink at Stanley on the way.

At a signal the dogs exploded into action. Like two missiles on a collision course, the dogs flew at each other, exploding in a mass of flesh and fangs. Within minutes the dogs had locked together as one. Blood and spittle and chunks of torn fur covered their bodies as they tumbled around in the stained sawdust. Brutus caught his opponent round the neck and the dog's jaws gripped so hard that Shaft's eyes bulged from their sockets.

The crowd screamed and whistled. This is what they had all come to see. Stanley was jumping up and down with excitement, cheering Brutus on. Though blood gushed from a gaping wound in his neck and one of his ears was hanging by a tiny flap of skin, the rest of it having been torn off, Shaft did not understand the concept of surrender.

The dog's natural instincts had been trained and beaten out of him by his owner. All that remained was pure adrenalin, pure aggression. With each twist that Shaft made in his frantic efforts to dislodge Brutus, the wound in his neck grew deeper. Brutus's jaws were removing his opponent's face, exposing teeth, bone and tissue.

The audience hungered for the kill, and the cheers and shouts grew more frenzied. For Shaft it was all over. As the life left his exhausted body, the crowd scrambled to place bets on the next bout, and Stanley and Thompson made their way to the table to collect their winnings.

The next fight involved two ten-month-old pups who tore into each other like they'd been fighting for years. Without any hesitation they pulled and ripped at each other, squealing with pain. After fifteen minutes they were replaced with fresh dogs, which grew older and bigger as the night progressed.

The final fight involved two huge dogs, weighing in at more than fifty pounds each.

They clashed like two bowling balls – an instant shower of teeth shot into the air followed by the noise: the ripping, popping, slashing and grinding. They fought for more than an hour until one dog was so exhausted it could no longer move out of its corner. The loser was taken outside and given a bath.

The evening ended with the best possible result: Stanley's dog had won while the Farmer's Boys had been held to a draw.

'Good night all round,' said Thompson as the crowd began to drift away.

'It's not over yet,' said Stanley as a group of the Farmer's Boys headed over in his direction. Like the man who had been guarding the gate, they were all stocky, well-built lads, some of them even towering over Thompson and Stanley.

They shook hands and talked about which fights they had enjoyed most. Spirits were high and jokes and smiles filled the air. Then Brendan, leader of the Farmer's Boys, nodded in Thompson's direction.

'So is this him,' he said softly. 'Is this the grass?'

'That's him,' said Stanley.

The smiles quickly faded as all the Irishmen stared intently at Thompson.

'What the fuck are you talking about?' he said to them. Then he looked at Stanley. 'You're all off your fucking heads.'

'Cut the crap,' said Stanley flatly. 'You were seen going up to your mates at SOCA. I've known for months, Danny, I've known what you were doing but I couldn't do anything about it because I didn't know exactly what you had planned.

'Truth be told, I still don't know exactly what it is that you're up to. Are you planning to give me up to the cops or to the competition? Are you planning a new life on the Witness Protection Programme or have you met some new bird you want to shack up with? Or is it just that you want to be the top man for a change and you know the only way you're ever going to get there is over my dead body?

'I can't work it out and to be honest I don't really care. Right now you've become too dangerous, too much of a liability, and that means you have to be dealt with. And these boys here have very kindly offered to help me out.'

Thompson said nothing. There was nothing he could say. He had been caught out and now he was going to die. He stood up straight, determined to take it like a man. He fought the urge to close his eyes, keeping them open and fixed on Stanley as one of the Irishmen handed him a heavy automatic revolver.

Two of the Farmer's Boys manhandled Thompson into the centre of the blood-stained fighting ring and Stanley moved directly in front of him. Thompson looked him right in the eye. If his friend was going to kill him, he wanted to make it as difficult as possible. Stanley stared right back. 'You got anything to say for yourself, you fucking scumbag?'

Thompson said nothing.

'You were like a fucking brother to me. I would have done anything for you. We were going places. We could have ruled the world together, but you had to get greedy. You had to get stupid. Fucking stupid. And now you bring it to this. You think this is what I want? But what choice do I have? All the times we spent together, all the things we've done together in the past, they don't mean fuck all now because of you.

'One more thing: all that shit you've been feeding your SOCA friends, it's all been bollocks. I knew you were talking to them so I've been keeping you out of the loop. How does it feel to know you've been played for a fool?'

Thompson puffed out his chest, the rush of fear and adrenalin filling him with bravado. 'You gonna fucking talk me to death, you wanker?'

He saw Jack's face flash with even greater anger and his hand tense on the trigger.

There was a flash of light and a pop. Not a crack, not a bang, but a pop. Thompson shut his eyes briefly, bracing himself for the impact. But it never came. The sound was one they all knew well. One they all dreaded. The cartridge had been a dud. The gun had misfired.

Thompson could feel his heart beating at a million beats per second. He was still high on adrenalin. If he was going to have a chance, he would have to take it now. He spun round and forced a heavy fist into the man behind him. He began running towards the edge of the fighting circle, body checking men to the left and the right like some deranged American footballer.

The situation had taken everyone by surprise and he made the most of the confusion. He had almost reached the edge of the circle when a dozen hands grabbed at his arms and legs and pulled him back down to the ground. Fists and boots rained down on him, leaving his face a bloody pulp. He felt one of his ribs crack, his jaw come out of joint, the bone in his nose twist out of place. He felt warm trickles of blood all over the back of his head.

Then he heard Jack Stanley's voice calmly calling for everyone to stop, for Thompson to be lifted back up to a standing position.

Blood leaked into his right eye and Thompson had to blink repeatedly to make sense of what he saw ahead of him. Jack Stanley was advancing slowly. The gun was gone and in its place was a large, shiny steak knife.

'Hold him,' said Stanley.

Two burly men grabbed Thompson's arms and held him upright while another held his legs from behind. He was completely immobilized.

Stanley came closer, his face sneering as he pushed into Thompson's personal space, so close he could smell the blood and the sweat on his face.

'You brought this on yourself,' he sneered.

Thompson sucked in some air and suddenly spat a wad of blood-streaked saliva into Stanley's face. Stanley reeled back in disgust and Thompson smiled at his handiwork, pleased with what he had done. 'You're a dead man, Stanley. They know where you live, they know where you go. They know everything about you. You're a fucking dead man.'

Stanley wiped the spit off his face, leaving a long glistening blood-stained streak across the corner of his forehead. 'Who, the Albanians? You've set the fucking Albanians on me?'

Thompson only grinned in reply. 'You're bluffing, you're fucking bluffing. You haven't got the balls for it.'

Stanley stepped forward again and, as Thompson struggled against the men who were holding him, he placed the tip of the knife against Thompson's chest, working it so that just the tip began to pierce the surface of his skin.

Thompson grunted with pain. Stanley carefully positioned the knife so that it fitted into the space between two of his ribs and directly in front of his heart. Then he placed the palm of one hand on the hilt of the knife and looked up into Thompson's eyes.

The men stared at each other for what seemed like an age.

'Do it,' hissed Thompson. 'Do it, do it, do it, you fucking wan – '

Stanley shoved forward hard and plunged the knife forward, driving it all the way up to the hilt. The tip of the blade emerged out of Thompson's back and he cried out in agony, a long piercing menacing scream that made even the men holding him wince. Then Stanley held the end of the knife in both hands and twisted it violently to the left. The sound of bones cracking, tendons tearing and flesh parting could be heard around the arena.

Blood shot out from Thompson's wound and more seeped out from the corners of his mouth. He started to breathe more quickly, more noisily, a horrible death rattle, then it went silent. Dead.

Stanley pulled out the knife and let it fall to the floor. 'Get rid of him,' he said.

Jack Stanley remained still for a few moments and watched as the body of his former best friend was manhandled out of the fighting ring and towards the car park, where a specially prepared truck was waiting.

From there the body would be decapitated and have its hands removed; the remainder would be fed to pigs owned by the farmer who ran the complex – another reason why the fight had been staged there.

Stanley had used pigs to dispose of bodies in the past, having got the idea from the Mafia wars in Sicily in the 1980s when more than four hundred corpses were believed to have been disposed of in this way. The Mafia favoured the use of pigs because of their huge, omnivorous appetites and the fact that they leave little of a body behind other than dentures, which could easily be buried. With the pigs on the job, Thompson's body would be completely consumed within the space of twenty-four hours.

Stanley nodded at a couple of men to begin sweeping fresh sawdust over the centre of the ring to cover up the blood stains. He looked down at his own hands, which were also covered in blood. He made his way to the men's room in the next building and began to wash them, watching his reflection in the mirror. He had ordered the deaths of many men in his criminal career, but he had taken the lives of only four personally.

He felt surprisingly little. No remorse. Like a soldier in a war, he justified his actions in the sense that it was him or Thompson. He could not hesitate, he could not show mercy. Thompson had been aware of the rules. If you live by the sword you die by the sword. His conscience was clear; he had nothing to worry about.

His phone began ringing. There was still blood on the back of his hands as he reached for a paper towel to dry them. His lips curled into a thin smile as he saw the name on the display screen and quickly put the phone up to his ear.

'Hello, my little Princess, how are you?'

17

The moment they entered through the huge dark wooden doors, Stacey felt as though she had walked in on the set of the popular eighties sitcom *Cheers*. Delicious smells wafted towards her as she looked out over the New York-style bar-cum-dining room, its walls covered in posters from theatrical productions from around the West End.

'So, what do you think?'

Stacey turned to Dr Jacques Bernard and smiled sweetly. 'It's amazing. You'd never have guessed that something like this was around here. I'll admit it, I'm impressed.'

They had met an hour earlier in a wine bar close to the Embankment, where they had enjoyed a swift glass of chilled Chablis before making their way to the restaurant that Jacques had booked. They had walked through Covent Garden and then into a side road devoid of pedestrians and traffic. For a moment Stacey wondered where the good doctor was taking her, when, suddenly, he stopped outside a seemingly abandoned building and pointed up to a tiny brass plaque on the wall.

'We're here,' he said with a grin.

'And where is here?'

He pointed towards the plaque. 'The coolest restaurant in London.'

Collins leaned forward and read the name engraved on the plaque, which was about the size of a paperback book: JOE ALLEN.

'The food's a little dated, as if the place is somewhat stuck in the eighties,' Jacques continued. 'And the jukebox hasn't worked for years – which is probably something of a blessing. But the atmosphere is fantastic and you can do some serious star spotting here. One time, Gwyneth Paltrow was on the table next to me. The great thing about having all these old posters around is that you can be pretending to look at them when in fact you're checking out who else is here. It's the perfect excuse.'

They were escorted through to a table in the middle of the main dining area. As soon as she sat down Collins reached into her bag and pulled out her mobile phone. She checked the signal strength and then placed it face up on the table beside her before beginning to study the menu.

'Sorry,' she said as Jacques's eyes looked pointedly at the phone. 'If anything happens I need to know about it right away.'

'I understand, of course,' he replied, returning his eyes to his menu, where they remained until the waitress came to take their orders.

He surprised her by ordering the cheeseburger. Her eyes scanned the menu once more before the waitress held out her hand to take it back.

'I didn't see any burgers on the menu. Are they just humouring you?'

'Ah, it's one of their trademarks. They serve them but they are not on the menu. It makes people who are in the know feel a bit special.'

'You mean it makes them feel a bit smug.'

'Sorry, did you want a burger yourself? It's probably not too late.'

'No, it's fine, I'll stick with the chicken. Christ, I've lived in London all my life and I've never heard of this place. How come you do?'

'Well, it's not my first time here, in London, I mean. I've lost count of how many times now. I was here a couple of years ago for almost six months, a couple of years before that and a couple of years before that too. I'd like to think I know the city pretty well.'

'I guess that helps when it comes to impressing attractive young students.'

'Oh, they're all putty in my hands by the time I've finished telling them my name. Is that what you want to hear? Is that the sort of person you think I am?'

'This is the first time we've spent any real time together. I have no idea what kind of man you really are.'

Jacques smiled warmly. Stacey was aware that several women in the restaurant were having sneaky glances in her direction, wondering if her handsome companion was some new hot film star.

'I'm very glad you agreed to come out with me,' said Jacques. 'I was worried that I was being too forward when I asked you to have dinner on the same day that we met.'

'Well, for someone who works as a psychologist, you must be pretty poor at reading signs.'

'I specialize in the minds of criminals. I could tell if you were planning to rob a bank, or molest a child, but have dinner with me? I am clueless.'

The conversation flowed easily throughout the rest of the evening, as did the wine. They polished off the first bottle before they had made it through their main courses and Stacey hesitated only slightly before agreeing that they should order a second.

'Some of us have work in the morning,' she scoffed.

'I have to work too,' protested Jacques. 'But not until Monday. I have to give a lecture at two thirty in the afternoon and my students will be most upset if I'm not there by at least two forty-five.'

'Honestly, you academics. You don't know you're born.'

'It's a quiet start to the week, I admit it,' he said sheepishly. 'But there's a lot that happens outside of lectures. There are one-on-one sessions with students, tutorial groups to monitor, essays and papers to be marked. It's a full life.'

'Yeah,' replied Stacey. 'Full of leisure. I picked the wrong job, didn't I?'

'But you love your job. How is the case going?'

'I didn't think you had taken me out to dinner in order to talk shop. Anyway, part of the reason I came out with you is because I need to take my mind off of it all. It's pretty full on at the moment.'

'I can imagine. Any sign of Pat?'

'Who?

'Patrick O'Neill, your missing officer. The one working with CEOP.'

'Do you know him?'

'Not really, but our paths crossed once upon a time, a while back.'

'Right. No, not a peep. Poor guy. My heart really goes out to him. It's like half the force is looking for him. But no one has a clue where he might be. You've read the transcripts?'

'Oh, yes. Impressive stuff. We're dealing with someone with a high level of intelligence, very slick. First class in fact. I have no doubt it's the same person that your team are looking for. I'm so glad I'm involved in the case. So much more exciting when you've got access to the inside info. Especially when you're facing someone in the psychopathic equivalent of the premier league.'

'Steady on. You sound like you're verging on admiration.'

'Maybe I am. Let's face it: the vast majority of criminals out there are stupid. Really stupid. That's why they get caught. They don't plan, they overlook the obvious, they get overly confident. You get a case like this, where someone has been active for years and never so much as shown up on the radar, I can't help but feel a certain sense of awe.'

'So I see.'

'Sorry. It's just that I live for this stuff, I really do. The whole cat-and-mouse thing, it's such a buzz. This is like a chess game. You don't want to play against someone who is useless – it's over much too quickly. You want someone who challenges you, makes you think. I've actually written my own computer program that compares and contrasts types of activity. It's fascinating, especially when you look at the guys at the top. If I were going to be a criminal, that's the sort of criminal I'd want to be. An artist, not a hack. There's a lot of scum out there, Stacey, a lot of losers; some people don't even deserve to live at all, let alone prosper. The thing about your job is that most of the time you're scooping up the stuff that floats to the top; the real geniuses always keep their heads down. A lion attacks the sick and weak from the herd and what is left is stronger, more efficient; in the same way every two-bit killer you arrest leaves a more sophisticated, slicker pool of criminals behind.'

'I hadn't thought about it like that. You saying I should give it up? Leave it to the vigilantes?'

'Why not? You'll never eliminate crime completely. All you can do is try to keep a lid on it. And for your own sanity, try to work only on the cases where your opponent's skills are a match for your own. You have many great skills, Stacey. I can tell. You may be closer to cracking this case than you know.'

They smiled at each other again as they lifted their glasses in unison and took deep sips of their wine. There was something tangible in the air between them. You could almost feel the electricity.

Stacey looked directly into Jacques's eyes and smiled again, toying with her wine glass.

'I think I need to say something. If we decide to take this any further, it has to be on my terms.'

'And what terms are those?'

'I'm not looking for anything serious. My life is complicated enough. I don't need someone to come along and fuck things up for me; I can do that myself.'

'Carrying a little baggage, are we?'

'Don't even go there, Mr Bigshot Psychologist. We take this one night at a time.'

Jacques nodded thoughtfully. 'Okay, then that leaves only one question for me to ask.'

'What?'

'Do we go to your place or mine?'

Home for Dr Jacques Bernard during his stay in the UK was an executive apartment just off the Strand in a plush block reserved exclusively for professors and wealthy postgraduate students of the university.

Stacey's heart had sunk when he first mentioned that he had been assigned student accommodation, but it quickly turned out that the place was more than pleasant enough. It was a comfortable studio flat decorated in a modest but cosy manner.

A slightly smaller-than-average double bed was up against one wall. Across from that there was a tiled area with a sink and tiny cooking unit. A small area in the centre served as the living room, complete with a two-seater sofa and a folding wooden table with a couple of chairs.

Two of the four walls were lined floor to ceiling with more books than Stacey had ever seen in her entire life. She stood, awestruck, casting her eye along row after row of volumes. There were dozens of books on psychology and forensics, of course, but also dozens more on the law, computing, history, chemistry, mathematics and philosophy. A whole curriculum's worth of knowledge. 'Have you read all these?' she asked, almost absent-mindedly.

'What's the point in having shelves full of books that you've read?' replied Jacques with a grin. 'I hope to read them all one day. In the meantime, they are just there to make the shelves look good.'

He began inching closer to her. She stood in the centre of the room, facing him as his eyes bored into her. In an instant his arm was round her waist and he was pulling her towards him. His other hand moved to the side of her face, smoothing down her hair. She buried her head in the side of his neck, enjoying the tickling sensation of his moustache against her cheek. She could feel his heart beating against hers. She gave a soft moan and then used both her hands to draw his face towards hers. They kissed. It was a long, passionate kiss, and when they broke apart she had to gasp for breath.

He sank to his knees, pressing his face into her chest, into her belly. She looked down to see his delicate mop of brown hair moving across her torso. A sense of ease slowly washed over her.

He deftly removed her top and his mouth moved up to caress the space between her nipples. His fingers spread wide and felt good against the cold skin of her back. A thumb slid back and forth slowly across one of her shoulder blades.

He pushed her back against the edge of the small bed and they fell on to it as one, sinking slowly into glorious oblivion.

She awoke in the morning alone in the bed. A delicious smell was hanging in the air – a mixture of coffee and something sweet. She pushed herself up on her elbows and saw Jacques sitting at the small desk at the end of the bed. He was completely naked apart from a pair of boxer shorts, his legs crossed, staring intently at the screen of his laptop.

'Good morning,' she said softly.

In one seamless movement Jacques turned to face her and eased down the lid of the computer, switching off the screen but keeping the machine itself running. In that split second Stacey had caught a glimpse of what had been on the display – a series of windows with dozens of short lines of writing on the left-hand side of the largest box. Her brow curled into a frown as she looked across.

'Just catching up on work emails,' he said with a grin as he stood up and walked towards her. 'I've made coffee and I'm warming some croissants. How many would you like?'

'I thought you'd be having a lie-in.'

'Didn't seem fair when you have to get up. Besides, I wanted to make you breakfast.'

Up until then there had been no awkwardness, nothing uncomfortable. But all of a sudden Stacey felt incredibly vulnerable. Sex, especially with the best part of a bottle of wine inside her, was one thing, but sitting and having a cosy breakfast, that was true intimacy. She didn't feel ready for that. She knew she had to get away.

'Thanks, but it's getting late. I'd better get going. I'll grab something on the way.'

She wrapped the duvet around herself, picked up her clothes from the side of the bed and headed for the bathroom. When she returned, having showered and dressed, Jacques was still in his boxers. He was sitting at the tiny table unit, chewing a croissant and sipping from a steaming cup of coffee. A second croissant sat on a plate opposite him. She instantly became ravenous.

'I guess it makes more sense for me to have this here,' she said sitting down and reaching for the pastry. Jacques smiled, reached for a second coffee cup and filled it for her.

'Suppose I want to see more of you,' said Jacques.

'I think last night you saw pretty much all there is to see.'

Stacey laughed at her own joke but stopped when she realized Jacques was being serious.

'I know everything you said last night about wanting this to be on your own terms,' he continued, 'and I respect that. I totally respect that. But suppose it's not enough for me. Suppose I want something more.'

'We'll just have to wait and see.'

'Come on, Stacey, stop kidding yourself. There was a connection there the first time we met. We both felt it. Now, I don't want to hear about what's happened to you in the past. I know enough police officers to understand what a male-dominated world you work in and how tough it must be to get along on your merits rather than because of the old boys' network, but that doesn't mean you have to shut yourself off from everything else.'

Stacey held up a hand. 'Stop. I don't want to hear any of this. You don't know me. Don't try to fit me into some box. I don't want to listen.'

'Because the truth hurts. Because I'm getting to the truth, aren't I?' said Jacques, leaning forward. He was almost shouting now, shocking Stacey with his sudden outburst. 'You think you can stop yourself from ever getting hurt by never opening up, by keeping all your emotions and feelings locked up tight inside you. But what you don't realize is that by doing that, you're only hurting yourself in the long run anyway. You're fucking up your ability to feel anything at all. And if you don't start to let go and trust someone soon, if you don't sort your fucking head out, it will be too late for you.'

Stacey stood up abruptly and took a step back. 'I don't know who the hell you think you are. You might be great when it comes to analysing crime in theory, but when you start to talk about real people and real emotions you're just full of shit.

'We had a bit of fun, but that's as far as it goes. You can theorize as much as you like about what you think might be going on inside my head, but only I know the truth.

'It's not that fucking complicated. I'm a single mum, I've got elderly parents who I sometimes need to look after, and I've got a demanding job that plays havoc with my social life at the best of times.

'We had a nice evening. Don't make me regret it.'

Stacey picked up her handbag and grabbed the last of her croissant. 'I've got to go to work. I'll see you around.'

Jacques rolled his eyes. 'Don't let the door hit your planet-sized ego on the way out, will you?'

18

Morning prayers had only just begun as Collins bustled her way into the office wearing the same clothes as the day before and hoping to high heaven that no one noticed.

Anderson raised an eyebrow in her direction but she guessed it was more of a comment on her arrival time than on her clothing. She moved quickly into a back corner of the room alongside Tony Woods, who gave her a nod of acknowledgement. The two officers then turned their full attention to the DCI.

'As you know, we've to focus attention on the abduction of Detective Sergeant O'Neill. We suspect the person who took him is the same person that Bevan had been speaking to on the internet, who in turn we believe is the person behind the killings we are investigating. CEOP have been working around the clock on the case, and they've managed to strike up a conversation with shygirl351.

'They've arranged to meet in a chatroom later this morning,' Anderson continued. 'I've arranged with CEOP to relay whatever is being said to one of our computers here so we can monitor the conversation. The hope is that we can draw this person out into another meeting.

'According to Carter, it's going to be a slow process. They estimate usually it takes between two and six weeks to get to the point where they are willing to arrange a meeting. Coming so soon after a potential murder, it may take a little longer. But I think it would be good for us to look in on the first couple of conversations, as it might give us more of a clue about the sort of person we are looking for.

'There's a little bit of politics going on here and it's not yet clear who's going to take the lead on the job. In theory we're all working together but you know what they say about too many cooks spoiling the broth. I'm hoping that won't be the case here.'

The briefing over, Collins and the other officers returned to their desks, an air of uncertainty hanging over them. The officers were increasingly split about the best way forward with the case. Although Patrick O'Neill had been missing for almost four days, they had no absolute proof that he had been killed, or that he had fallen victim to the killer, or even that their killer was using the internet to find potential victims.

A new search of Chadwick's computer and his laptop had failed to find any link to this kind of activity. No one on the team wanted to admit it, but they were blundering around in the dark.

As if the pressure of work wasn't bad enough, Stacey was finding it difficult to concentrate for other reasons too. Jacques Bernard's words were playing heavily on her mind. There had been plenty of men over the years but always on her terms. That was the way she had always wanted it. The job, Sophie, it was all too much to deal with on its own, let alone with a man in tow. In her experience men were not to be trusted, they were after only one thing and once they had it they turned into complete bastards. They would do or say whatever it took to get inside your head and once they were there, they would fuck around just for the sake of it.

Stacey had done her best to prevent this from ever happening. The kind of men she liked, the ones she found herself drawn to, tended to live for the thrill of the chase. She made it relatively easy for them, she knew that, but nine times out of ten she would end the relationship at that point. The men had got what they were after, for sure, but so had Stacey. And they would get nothing more.

But Stacey was getting older. She couldn't keep on behaving like a horny teenager. In a few short years' time her parents would be dead and Sophie would have left home. And then she would be all alone. Is that what she wanted?

Was Jacques really different or was he as full of shit as all the others? There was something about him that made her a little uncomfortable, though she found it hard to put her finger on exactly what that was. Woods had sensed it too and made no secret of his hostility towards the man. But they had slept together now, and it had been good. And Jacques clearly wanted more. Perhaps it was time to soften her attitude, to let down a few of the barriers she had built up over the years. Time would tell. She would have to tread carefully. She would give it a few days, and then she would agree to meet with him again.

'Are you okay? You look like you're a million miles away.'

Collins looked up to see Tony Woods smiling at her. 'Sorry, Tony, deep in thought. What's up?'

'Shygirl's online. They're about to hook up with the feed.'

The computer had been set up in a side office on the far side of the incident room. On the way Collins and Woods passed the board in the centre of the incident room that carried the pictures of the victims and many of their details. Collins suddenly felt drawn towards the images and stood directly in front of them, looking up at each face in turn. Woods was soon beside her.

'Come on, we don't want to miss this,' he said.

'This is weird.'

'What?'

'Well, I never noticed before how much our three victims look alike. I mean, it's not like anyone would be able to mistake one for the other, they're very different, but they are very much all of the same type. Dark hair, intense eyes. Strange, really.'

'Not necessarily. Killers often have a particular type of victim they're looking for. It's quite common for men who go after prostitutes to kill all blondes or all brunettes. A lot of the gay male killers will go after men who look very similar to one another because that is what they find attractive. Even if it's not sexual, as in the case of one man killing another, there may still be a distinct type. An ideal victim.'

'Sounds like you've been reading up on this.'

Woods allowed a smile to creep along the corner of his mouth. 'Just keeping it real. Come on.'

Collins and Woods joined Anderson and the rest of the team, who formed a semicircle around the large computer monitor where Rajid was sitting.

Anderson folded his arms as he waited for the chatroom conversation to begin. His face was taut with concentration and it was clear that the strain was starting to get to him, as it was the rest of them. Collins caught his eye as he looked around the office.

'I have no idea how this is going to go,' he said. 'It may be a complete waste of time. The only thing we know for sure is that whoever is behind shygirl351, they're not what they appear to be. And I for one am anxious to find out exactly who they are.'

Rajid hit a few buttons and a large window appeared on the screen in front of him. 'Here we go,' he said. The group shuffled forward, waiting for the first words to appear.

'Is that an email programme?' asked Collins.

'Nah,' replied Rajid. 'It's a chatroom site, pretty big with teenagers. Why?'

'No reason. Just looks familiar.'

'You don't let Sophie go online, do you?' asked Woods.

'She's a teenager with an iPod Touch. I couldn't stop her even if I wanted to.'

A hushed silence fell over the room as the screen name of the undercover officer from CEOP appeared.

dangermouse37: hi

shygirl351: hey, nice to see you here again

dangermouse37: well I really enjoyed chatting to you yesterday

dangermouse37: I know you're young, but you seem really mature

dangermouse37: much more so than most girls of your age

shygirl351: thx

shygirl351: flattery will get you everywhere!

dangermouse37: where might that be?

shygirl351: lol

shygirl351: depends on where you want to be

dangermouse37: I quite like the idea of being wherever you are

shygirl351: whoa, slow down there stud

shygirl351: this won't be any fun if you try to rush things

shygirl351: lol

shygirl351: I'm guessing you must be new to this

dangermouse37: kinda. Sorry, didn't mean to upset you

shygirl351: not upset. No harm done

shygirl351: so are you a friend of Patty?

dangermouse37: Who is she?

shygirl351: Not she, a he, silly. Patty's my nickname for him. You probably know him as Patrick

A cold chill passed through the members of the team gathered around the screen. 'Oh shit,' breathed Anderson. There was an uncomfortable delay before the next words appeared.

dangermouse37: sorry, who are you talking about

shygirl351: oh come on, don't play games. I'm not in the mood

shygirl351: you guys are all one big happy family aren't you

shygirl351: CEOP and MIT, all working in perfect harmony

'Oh fuck,' gasped Collins.

'How the hell does he know about CEOP?' said Anderson.

'O'Neill must have said something,' Collins replied. 'This is bad.'

dangermouse37: Where is Patrick now?

shygirl351: That's more like it. Now you're asking the right question.

dangermouse37: please, tell us where he is

shygirl351: He's right here with me. I'm looking at him right now

dangermouse37: Is he all right

shygirl351: Depends on what you mean. He looks fine to me

dangermouse37: Can we speak to him.

shygirl351: Of course, I'm only looking at him from the neck up.

dangermouse37: You need to stop this right now

shygirl351: Stop now? But it's so much fun

shygirl351: I'm just getting warmed up

dangermouse37: If you stop now, it might make a difference

shygirl351: You must be kidding

shygirl351: The only way you could believe that crap

shygirl351: is if you have no idea how many there have been

A wave of despair washed over the members of the team.

dangermouse37: Let us help you

shygirl351: I think I'm doing just fine on my own. Have to go now.

shygirl351: Things to do

shygirl351: People to kill

shygirl351: Bye

There could no longer be any doubt. Whoever was online masquerading as shygirl351 was also the killer of Chadwick, Miller, Gilbert and, it seemed, several others. It was also time to accept that Detective Sergeant Patrick O'Neill was almost certainly dead too.

In many ways it was a huge step forward for the investigation: at long last they had a definite suspect. But at the same time the development was a huge step backwards. It was clear that the killer was incredibly sophisticated and unafraid of being caught. They had long known they were dealing with someone extremely dangerous. Now that was looking like the understatement of the century.

Watching the online conversation had taken the wind out of everyone's sails and the officers that made their way from the side office back into the main incident room did so with their heads bowed low.

Anderson followed them back, then called for their attention. 'Okay, people, we need to focus. I know this is a hell of a lot to take in. This is the worst-possible scenario, but we still need to do our jobs – for O'Neill's sake, and for the sake of any other victims that there might be out there. We need to find this bastard. I need you all to be on the case here.'

Anderson announced that there would be a briefing in thirty minutes' time, after he'd had a chance to speak to DI Carter over at CEOP and plan a strategy. Collins and Woods headed back to their desks to wait.

Collins's mind was filled with images of the earlier victims. Had the same fate awaited O'Neill? Were his excavated remains rotting in the back of some car waiting to be discovered? There but for the grace of God, she thought again.

But there were other thoughts in her mind too. She couldn't get rid of the feeling that she had seen the chatroom page somewhere before and that it was important. She struggled to place it but came up blank time and time again. But then it came to her. She knew exactly where she had seen that pattern of windows before. She had seen them briefly that very morning, in the split second it took Dr Jacques Bernard to close the screen of his laptop computer.

'Shit,' she gasped.

'What is it?' asked Woods. 'What have you got?'

Collins opened her mouth to speak but caught herself just in time. It sounded ridiculous. Beyond ridiculous. But then again . . .

'It's funny, isn't it, Tony?' she said slowly. 'All those things Dr Bernard was saying about the guy we're looking for, about how he'd be fascinated by the workings of the police and would try to get a job that had close links to them, about how he'd be intelligent and methodical, good with computers.'

'Yeah, what about it?'

'Well, that could all apply to him, couldn't it?'

'Right, him and every other member of the civilian support staff, apart from the good with computers bit,' said Woods with a grin. But Collins did not return the smile. 'Are you serious?'

'I went out with him last night. He told me he'd written his own programs. He's strong too. It all fits.'

'Jesus. You are serious.'

'I don't know. I need to do some research. I need to cross-reference the times he was in the country with the times the murders took place. Can you help me?'

Woods exhaled loudly. 'I dunno, Stacey. I don't like the guy but putting him in the frame for this is something else. Was your night out with him that bad?'

'He fits the profile.'

'For God's sake, Stacey. Even if he does, even if he's killing paedophiles, why would he go after O'Neill?'

'Because he would have recognized him. He told me that he knew him. You should have heard him last night. He was practically grilling me for information about the case.'

Woods snorted with laughter. 'So let me get this right. This guy is so smart that no one can catch him, that he can operate under the radar for years, but one night out with you and he's spilling the beans and putting himself in the frame? No way. And of course he asked you about the case. He's a consultant. He's supposed to do that.'

'You said he gave you the creeps.'

'For crying out loud, Stacey, he's a player. It's written all over his face. I could tell you were interested in him. I was trying to protect you.'

'Forget it.' She spun to face her computer and began typing frantically. 'I'll do it. Just let me get on with it.'

'With pleasure,' said Woods, getting up to leave.

Ten minutes later Collins had found nothing to dissuade her from the idea she was on to something. Far from it. The dates that Dr Bernard had been in the country matched the times of the murders, though that alone was far from conclusive. Bernard had been in the country for months or years at a time. It could easily be nothing more than coincidence. Then again, if he had been out of the country during

278

the time of one killing, it would have been incontrovertible proof that it could not have been him.

Collins rushed up from her desk and made her way over to Anderson's office. She burst in just as he was picking up the phone to dial a number.

'Sir . . .'

'What is it, Collins? I need to speak to Carter. Can't this wait?'

'Sir, how well do you know Dr Bernard?'

'What?'

'Dr Bernard, the psychologist – how well did you know him before you hired him for this case?'

'Collins! Well enough. He's done a lot of this kind of work, has done for years. Why? Look, this is no time to be thinking about your private life.'

Collins frowned. 'He fits the profile.'

'What on earth are you talking about?'

'Dr Bernard fits the profile of the man we're looking for. The killer. Not only that, he knew O'Neill, and he has a level of skill with computers. He uses the same chatroom site as shygirl351 . . .'

'Are you trying to tell me that the man we're looking for is right under our nose?'

'I've got no proof, I haven't got anything. I just want to make sure we can eliminate him from the inquiries.'

'He's one of the most highly respected psychologists in the world.'

'I know it sounds crazy.'

'No. It is crazy. I think the pressure must be

getting to you. Why else would you be trying to put him in the frame?'

She thrust two sheets of paper across the desk towards Anderson. 'Look, I've checked the dates. He was in the UK when the other murders occurred. It's got to be worth following up. Just give me a day on this.'

'No. You won't get even a minute. It's a waste of time. It's the most ridiculous line of inquiry I have ever heard in my entire life.'

'But, sir – '

'Leave it.'

'But, sir – '

'Jesus, Collins, do you know where Bernard was the night that O'Neill went missing?'

Collins paused. 'No, sir.'

'He was having dinner with me and my wife. So unless you think the three of us were in on it together, I suggest you get out of my sight and get on with some real police work.'

By the time Collins got back to her desk Woods had also returned. She sat down sheepishly. 'Sorry,' she said softly. 'It was a non-starter. Maybe I am losing it after all.'

'Don't be stupid,' said Woods. 'You're just up against it. We all are. We all want to see this thing solved, catch the guy. He's playing us for fools at the moment. It's enough to drive anyone a bit gaga.'

They sat in silence for a few moments before

Stacey spoke again. 'You think the killer knew O'Neill was a policeman when he took him?'

Woods shrugged. 'There's no way of knowing.'

'It's important, though, isn't it? It goes back to what you were saying about the killer spreading his net wider. If he knew and just didn't care, that's because he's moved on beyond paedophiles to members of the wider population.'

'For all we know,' said Woods, 'that might have started with Chadwick. We still have no evidence to link him to any kind of a sex crime.'

Collins held up a single finger in the air. 'Except for the fact that the killer thought he was meeting up with Bevan. Three weeks after Chadwick, he was still targeting a paedophile, a sex offender. If it was a case of mistaken identity, there doesn't seem to be any remorse or regret. Quite the opposite. I think we missed something with Chadwick. Not every crime gets reported, not everyone ends up on one of our databases. I think we missed something and now I think it's too late.'

'Why do you say that?'

'Because the killer has clearly moved on. I truly think we're dealing with a monster here, Tony, I really do. Up until O'Neill we at least had an idea of what sort of person was being targeted. But it's open season now. Anyone in the world could be next. Our chances of catching this evil bastard just tumbled a good few notches.'

DC Natalie Cooper walked over from the far

end of the office and greeted them both. 'You've got a visitor downstairs. She arrived while you were watching the feed and said she wanted to wait.'

'I'm not expecting anyone. Who is it?'

'She wouldn't say. But she told the desk sergeant that it was important and that you'd be keen to speak to her.'

Collins nodded slowly. 'I'm guessing it will be Miller's widow. Maybe she's remembered something new.

'Do you want me to come down with you?' asked Woods.

'I'll be fine. No sense in intimidating her. If there's something on her mind, I want her to feel free to tell me all about it.'

Collins opted for the stairs rather than the lift. She descended the flights swiftly, rounding the last and pushing her way through the double doors that led to the foyer. From there she made her way through another set of doors that led to the waiting room adjacent to the main entrance. But instead of Sandra Miller, she found herself face to face with a woman she had not seen for many, many years and had no desire to spend any time with.

'What the hell are you doing here?'

Ella Stanley stood up and stepped towards Stacey. Her face was taut with anger.

'I need to talk to you, right now.'

Stacey shook her head. 'I'm too busy. I'm in the middle of a murder investigation, for Christ's sake.'

Ella moved forward until she was toe to toe with Stacey. 'Either you talk to me right now or everyone in this place is going to hear what I have to say. The choice is yours.'

Stacey looked into Ella's eyes and knew at once that she was deadly serious.

'All right,' she said at last. 'But not here. Let's go for a walk.'

The moment they were out of earshot of the station Ella Stanley let rip. 'You've got some bloody cheek.'

'What?'

'You heard me. I said you've got some cheek. What the hell do you think you're doing, playing around with people's lives? Who do you think you are? God? You think you have the power to give and take way. Why the hell did you tell my Jack he had a daughter, only to then say he can't see her any more? What was the point of that?'

'It's none of your business.'

'None of my business? I'm making it my business. You come here with your fancy job and your big-head attitude and think you can push people around. Well, you can't push me around. You were always a spoilt little brat when you were growing up and time has only made you worse.

'You might look down your nose at me but I'm telling you, in my eyes you were never good enough for my Jack. I was as happy as Larry when he got shot of you, best thing he ever did if you ask me. You like to pretend it was what you wanted but I know how upset you were. I used to see the way you looked at him, the way you went after him. You were like a fucking Rottweiler, you were. Once you got your teeth into him, you were never going to let him go. He was just your type, wasn't he? Everything you ever wanted. Thought you had the world at your feet. And then he dumped you and you thought you'd get your own back. Keep your little secret to yourself.

'You can mess up your own life just as much as you want but Sophie, she's something different. She's his daughter. And daughters need their dads. That's not something you can replace, no matter how special you think you might be. You've got no right messing him around like this. Messing her around like this. You're totally out of order. Just because you spend your whole time acting like a man for your job doesn't mean you're any kind of substitute for a real father.'

'Are you quite finished?'

'I'm just getting started.'

'I've heard enough of your crap. It's you who thinks you're God. You think you can waltz in here and tell me how to live my life, tell me what is best for my daughter? Who the hell do you think you are? You don't know anything about her. You don't know anything about me and my life right now.'

Ella longed to tell her that she had met her daughter but knew she had to keep it secret. She took a deep breath. 'I'm the woman who's trying to put right all the things you've made wrong. I'm the woman who has to come along and clean up the godforsaken mess you're making of other people's lives.'

'Nah, you're just some busybody who's sticking her nose in where it's not wanted. You always were.'

'Oh grow up, Stacey. You had both your parents around all the time and you're still fucked up. You wouldn't go around treating people this badly if you weren't. What the hell do you think is going to happen to Sophie if you continue to mess her around like this?'

'She understands the situation. She knows the reasons why.'

'That's what she tells you. Jesus Christ, woman, how many times did you ever lie to your mother? You think Sophie is so perfect that she won't tell you the odd lie if she needs to?'

Stacey thought back to the summer, when Sophie had gone missing for several hours. She had told her she was going to spend the evening with a friend but had ended up at a wild party. Although they had never spoken about it in detail, Stacey was certain that Sophie had taken drugs that evening too.

It was all too much for Stacey to handle. She had just learned that the brutal serial killer they were after had managed to make everyone on the team look like an idiot. On top of that the murderer was now taunting them with the fact that he had taken another body from right under their noses. A serving police officer, no less. Then she'd gone and made herself look like a total idiot by going to her boss and insisting the killer was someone it simply could not be.

All this was going through her head and she wanted nothing more than the chance to sit down and think through it all, to work out a way to go forward. Instead she had Jack Stanley's idiot of a mother shouting at her. It was more than she could bear. It felt as if her whole life was collapsing around her.

'You want to talk about being a good mother? You think I have anything to learn from you, you fat bitch? Where were you when little Jack was growing up, going out mugging people and selling drugs and killing and all of that? Is that what you brought him up to do? What on earth qualifies you as an expert when it comes to parenting?'

Ella Stanley hit back immediately. 'Because I've seen the damage that can be done when there is no father around. It might be more obvious for boys but that doesn't mean it's any less damaging when it comes to girls. It's more subtle but it doesn't mean there is no effect. I just want what is best for your daughter. She's a little angel and – '

'Best for my daughter. You don't even know my daughter.' Stacey stared at her hard as the realization dawned. 'Jesus Christ, you've met her, haven't you? You've actually bloody met her. When did this happen?'

'It's not important – '

'It's important if I say it is. I want to know what the hell is going on. Have you met her or not?'

'No. I haven't met her. I've seen pictures. Jack has told me all about her. He adores her. I want to meet her, is all. I'm her grandmother and she deserves to have the love that I have to give her as well as the love that comes from your parents.'

'She gets more than enough love already.

'You can't get too much love. You're just being silly now. You don't know anything about kids, just like you don't know anything about men. If you didn't want Sophie to grow up like this, if you didn't want her to be surrounded by people that love and care for her, if you didn't want her true father to be a part of her life, then you should never have told him about her. You should have given her up for adoption the day she was born. But you didn't and that means you have to face the consequences.'

'What are you talking about?'

'I don't want to do this but you're giving me no choice. I know that no one back there' – she flicked her head in the direction of the police station they had just emerged from – 'I know that none of them know about the situation. And I know that the fact that my Jack hasn't always been a good little boy is going to reflect very badly on you. So here's the ultimatum. I don't want to have to do this but you don't give me any choice. You haven't seen the damage you've been doing, you don't see the way it's tearing my boy apart.

'Either you let Jack start seeing his daughter again or I'm going to make sure everyone in that building and all of your bosses and supervisors know exactly who Sophie's father is.'

Stacey said nothing for a few moments, turning over her thoughts in her mind. The two women stood on the side of the street staring at one another intently. When Stacey spoke it was not out of anger. Her voice was calm, controlled and utterly menacing.

'What you need to understand is this: the only reason that Jack Stanley is still out and about, the only reason you get to see him without a glass partition in the way, the only reason he isn't eating prison food and panicking about what to do every time he drops the soap in the shower, is because of me.

'I made one terrible mistake fourteen years ago. I slept with Jack and I got pregnant. And I've paid back that mistake a thousand times ever since. If you don't back off, and I mean right off, I can take it all away. I'll put Jack behind bars and I'll make sure he has so many charges against him that he'll never see daylight again.

'If that's want you want, Ella, then just keep on talking. Just keep on doing what you're doing right now. If you want things to remain the way they are, then what you need to do is shut your big mouth, turn around and make sure I don't ever have to look at your face again.'

Ella Stanley hesitated for a moment or two. Her lips were moving together as if she were grinding her teeth in frustration. For a moment Stacey expected her to take a step towards her, for things to get really ugly.

But then, suddenly, Ella Stanley turned on her heels and stormed off.

19

Stacey Collins pushed open the door of her house and stepped inside. She cursed under her breath as she stood on a pile of letters and leaflets and almost lost her footing.

It had been one hell of a day at the office and she was glad that Sophie would be spending yet another night at her grandparents'. Although she loved her daughter dearly and knew that they desperately needed to spend more time together, the only way she could deal with the workload and maintain her position in the force was to have regular nights when she was able to work as late as she needed to.

It was now nearly ten in the evening and she had been far from the last one to leave. She would get to the office early the following morning. There was still so much work to be done. She had reread the case files and the autopsy reports and the background profiles of the murder victims so many times that she knew many of the details off by heart. But she was still convinced she must be missing something.

There was something else playing on her mind too. The row with Ella. The woman's words kept bouncing around inside her head. The image of her twisted, rage-ridden face refused to fade away.

You spend your whole time acting like a man.

Why did it bother her so much that Ella had said that? She had certainly heard worse insults, and besides, it just wasn't true. She had got as far as she had in the force because she was dedicated and effective. Hadn't she? She needed a distraction to take her mind off it all.

She reached down and picked up the pile of post, sorting through it slowly as she made her way through the house into the kitchen, where she pulled a half-bottle of white wine out of the fridge and fetched a glass from the shelf. There were two bills, one from her credit card and another from the gas company. There were two leaflets from pizza delivery companies and a mailshot from a replacement window agency. The remaining letters were addressed to 'the householder' and received only a cursory glance before taking a trip to the bin. But, as she reached the last of the junk pile, she paused.

Stacey usually had little time for junk mail but something about the thin white envelope caught her eye. The lettering in the top-left-hand corner was thick and black: HELP THE INNOCENT VICTIMS OF CRIME. Underneath the wording was a picture of a man in a wheelchair. Instantly Stacey was reminded of her father. The look on the man's face was the same. He was trying to cope with the inconvenience and the shame of it all, but at the same time he refused to lose his dignity. The man was a good few years older than her father and was being pushed along the street by a young woman, someone like her. This was the reality of how her own life would be in the years to come if the unthinkable happened – if her mother died first.

It was something she thought about often, the possibilities for the future and what it might hold. For the most part she tried to put it out of her mind but every now and then it all came flooding back to her.

She opened the envelope swiftly and took out the sheets of glossy folded paper inside. It was a mailshot for a charity that helped support the victims of crime. Stacey herself was no stranger to the inadequacies of the criminal compensations scheme. A few hundred pounds for losing an eye, a couple of thousand for losing a leg. She had seen it time and time again with the victims of attacks that she dealt with on a daily basis. Most of all she had seen it with her own father, who had got only a few hundred pounds for having to spend the rest of his life in a wheelchair.

She read quickly through the details of the charity, the work they had done and the people they had supported. 'We understand that as a professional person, you get deluged with requests for help from charities all the time. Unlike most organizations we do not ask you to commit to a long-term standing order. Instead a small one-time donation is all it will take in order to help the lives of thousands.'

Stacey was sitting down at the table and reading as she was sipping a glass of wine. By the end tears were welling up in the corners of her eyes, not from the charity's appeal but from her thoughts about her father. By the time she had reached the end she was reaching for her cheque book and writing out a one-time donation of twenty pounds. She placed it in the return envelope and on top of her pile for posting the next day.

She then picked up the phone and dialled a number. After a few rings the line was answered. There was a cough, followed by a slightly shaky voice repeating the last four digits of the phone number – an old-fashioned habit that he had been unable to shake, which Stacey always found charming.

'Hi, Dad.'

'Hello, darling,' John Collins replied. 'Sophie's gone to bed already. It's quite late.'

'I know. I didn't call to talk to her. I wanted to speak to you.'

'Oh? Anything wrong?'

'Not at all. Just thought it would be nice to have a chat.'

With an early start planned for the following morning, Stacey stayed up just long enough to finish a second glass of wine before turning in for the night.

It was only then that she noticed a flashing light from the corner of her eye. The answering machine. She clicked the play button and a smooth French-Canadian accent drifted up to her ears.

'Hope you don't mind my calling you at home. I

know you won't be there till you finish and I really don't want to bother you while you're busy. Just wanted to wish you good night and find out how the case is going.'

Stacey smiled. A few hours earlier she had been convinced that Jacques himself had been the killer. It all seemed to fit. Now, in the cold light of day, it seemed absurd that she had ever entertained the notion.

Sleep refused to come to her. Instead Stacey lay awake thinking about what Ella had said. It was so unfair and made her so angry.

Acting like a man.

That stupid woman had no idea how hard it had been bringing up Sophie on her own. Ella had even gone so far as to suggest Stacey should have given her up for adoption, not knowing how painful a topic that was for her.

Giving her up for adoption had appeared like the easy option in the beginning. She had gone as far as filling out the forms and signing up with an agency. It seemed to be the right decision. Stacey still had her whole career ahead of her and had no desire to become a parent and be consumed by the responsibility.

It would have been hard enough at that age with a steady, reliable boyfriend, but with no one else on the scene to share the burden it was just going to prove impossible. Adoption would be far better for the baby. That was what Stacey had told herself time and time again, and that was what she truly believed as she was wheeled into the delivery room.

But the moment she had given her final push and then had that tiny sticky, noisy bundle of life thrust into her arms, she knew she could never be parted from her. She smiled at the memory, and then at the irony of just how much things had changed in the past thirteen years. If the woman from the adoption agency were to turn up during one of their full-on mother–daughter arguments, she would not hesitate for a second.

She lay on her back with her eyes closed, Ella Stanley's angry face still imprinted on her mind, still bugging the hell out of her. She realized she was also angry about the old woman's razor-sharp insight into her relationship with the young Jack. He had been the bad guy all the girls wanted and she had gone after him with every ounce of her being. When they finally ended up together, it was as if all her Christmases had come at once. And when it ended, she felt as if there would be no more summer, no more spring, no more anything. Life seemed to lose all meaning. Until she learned of the new life growing inside her.

Ella had been spot on. Jack Stanley had been just her type. And, although she had no desire to rekindle any aspect of their relationship, in many ways he still was. She had spent the years since finding herself attracted only to men who shared his traits. That swaggering arrogance and powerful presence that men like Dr Jacques Bernard had by the bucket-load. A fatal flaw that had seemingly made it impossible for her to find anyone to settle down with.

Acting like a man.

Yes, the police force was a male-dominated world, but Stacey truly believed she had made it to Detective Inspector because of her hard work, dedication and ability to close cases. Acting like a man had nothing to do with it. Nothing at all.

So why did it bother her so much? *Acting like a man.* The words rebounded around her brain again and again, coming in a steady rhythm, like the beat of a drum. Then something stirred deep within her, a tingling of a sixth sense honed by years of police work, an increasingly powerful feeling that something was very, very wrong.

She sat up, paused for a few moments, then made her way across the room to her briefcase and pulled out the copies of the chatroom transcripts CEOP had provided to all the officers on the case.

It was the same tingling sensation she felt whenever she got a hunch about a case. Who was guilty, where the money was hidden, where the bodies were buried and so on. That sense that someone had not told all they knew, that they were holding back, that they were lying.

There was no magic or smoke and mirrors about it. Like most sixth senses, it was based on experience, on intuition and on good police work. As unlikely as it seemed, Ella's words had been the spark that had ignited the flame. And now the flames were growing rapidly. A forest fire raging out of control.

She flicked through the pages of conversation, running her index finger along the columns of text, Ella's words still echoing in her head, driving her forward. She started with the exchanges between Jason Bevan and DreamGirl, the undercover officer from CEOP.

Bevan, posing as a teenage girl called Sally, had tried to sound the part. Mostly he had succeeded but then he gave himself away. It was nothing overtly obvious – it was simply that as the mother of a thirteen-year-old girl, Stacey could see that some of what was being said simply didn't ring true.

She had heard Sophie chatting on the phone to her friends, occasionally stumbled across the odd text message and more than once peeked sneakily over her daughter's shoulder as she composed emails or exchanged instant messages over the internet. Teen-age girls just didn't talk that way, not even when they thought their parents were far away.

The differences were small and subtle, and it was only now that she began to study them intently that they came ever more apparent

She hadn't spotted it right away – and neither had her fellow officers – because they all knew right from the start that they were dealing with an adult male pretending to be a teenage girl. They read his words with that in the back of their minds and thought nothing more of it.

But shygirl351 was different. When whoever was using that screen name wrote about the trials and tribulations of being a teenage girl, they nailed it every single time. Right down to the last detail. And that could mean only one thing.

But it was so absurd, so ridiculous that Stacey could barely bring herself to think about it. Perhaps Anderson was right. Maybe the case was driving her crazy after all. In truth she felt more tired now than she had for years. She desperately needed a break. But something compelled her to go on.

She sat staring at the lines of text, rereading the conversations again and again. And the more she thought about it, the larger the question loomed in her mind. All the victims had been male – some of them strong, powerful men – and that fact had made them jump to conclusions. But was it possible that they had made a terrible error? Was it possible they had all been deceived?

Could shygirl351 be a woman?

Stacey checked the bedside clock – just after midnight – picked up the phone, dialled a number and then thought better of it, putting the phone down before it could connect. This was stupid. This was insane. There were a million and one reasons why it simply didn't stack up. She couldn't possibly be right. Someone, somewhere, must have made a mistake and it was probably her. But then again, could it be true? There was only one way to find out.

She picked up the phone again and dialled. The

voice that answered was fuddled by sleep. A part of Stacey could not help but smile. She was glad this was not a video phone so no one could see her cheeks turning red.

'Jacques, it's Stacey. I'm really sorry to call so – '

She never finished the sentence. She had still been speaking when she had heard the faint but unmistakable sound of a woman's voice close to Jacques ask, 'Who is it?' She sounded young, student young. Stacey reacted not so much out of shock but out of instinct.

'Is there someone there?'

Jacques's voice became flustered; she heard him pace rapidly to another part of the room. 'No, no. I have the television on.'

'You're sleeping with the television on?'

'I must have fallen asleep with it on. I've turned it off now.'

There was now a slight echo in the background as Jacques spoke and she guessed that he had moved into the bathroom. She knew he was lying to her about being alone, and she now knew that everything he had said to her over the preceding week had also been part of a cool, calculating ploy to get her to lower her defences. She knew the type only too well. It wasn't enough for him to have seduced her, to have got her into bed; he wanted to win over her mind as well as her body. He wanted her to fall for him, to be pining for him. And then he could toss her aside like an old pair of shoes.

But she didn't have time to dwell on any of that now.

'Whatever,' she said sharply. 'Look, Jacques, I don't give a fuck who you're fucking right now, I called because I need your help on the case. I need to know if it could be a woman.'

'If who could be a woman?'

'The killer. shygirl351. Could a woman be behind all this?'

It seemed to take forever before he began to speak again.

'It is possible,' said Jacques, quickly pulling himself together, glad for the chance to talk about anything other than his immediate situation. 'Anything is possible. I hadn't considered it before because all the evidence seemed to point towards a male perpetrator. As you know, the vast, vast majority of serial killers are men. Not only that, but female killers tend to focus on elderly victims or children. They kill with poison or by smothering. More often than not, they have been involved in some kind of intimate relationship with those that they kill.

'Furthermore, they carry out the killings in places where they feel comfortable, relaxed. Homes or the places where they work. Beverley Allitt, the so-called Angel of Death, was a classic example, killing children at the hospital where she was employed. But Aileen Wuornos has rewritten the rules on female serials because she broke every one of them. She killed men because she liked it, attacked total strangers and used a gun instead of poison. Before she came along I would have said no, but, thinking about it again, yes, it is possible. Wuornos is going to inspire a whole generation of psychotic women to go out and commit multiple murders. It's already happening in the States; it's only a matter of time before we see it happening here too. What makes you ask?'

'It's the transcripts of conversations between Shygirl and Bevan. You can tell he's a man pretending to be a girl, but she doesn't make any of the same errors. I think she's the real thing.'

Ten more minutes of conversation with Jacques left Stacey more convinced than ever that she was on to something and had several new avenues of inquiry to pursue. Although no useful forensic evidence had been recovered from any of the bodies, Jacques suggested she review the autopsy reports to see if any aspects of the killings supported the existence of a female suspect.

Another tiny smile crept across Stacey's lips. She could feel that rising ball of excitement that manifested itself whenever she came close to solving a case, and she was certain that she was now on the final straight for this one. She picked the phone up once more and immediately dialled a number from memory, a number she had called dozens of times before over the years.

Not only would this call give her the chance to qualify her theory further, it would also be an opportunity to share what could be a key development with one of the few people she considered to be a friend. After half a dozen rings the call connected and a familiar voice sounded through the earpiece.

'This is Dr Jessica Matthews. Sorry I'm not here at the moment . . .'

Oh God.

Stacey was sitting down but that didn't stop her feeling her knees buckle. The moment she heard the voice of Jessica Matthews, her stomach seemed to rise up inside her, making her gag, and she could hear a rushing sound pounding away inside her head. She felt as though she were going to faint. A jigsaw puzzle of scraps of information instantly came together in her mind and formed a crystal-clear picture of the face of her friend.

Stacey held the phone at arm's length and stared at it, mouth wide with astonishment, as though it were some alien piece of technology she had never seen before. Fragments from the profile of the killer flooded into her mind.

Intelligent. Methodical. Close links to the police. Possible medical background. Able to blend in perfectly.

It couldn't be. Could it?

The bodies had been dumped in the area Jessica covered. She had been oh so pleased that Stacey had been assigned to the case and had helped her identify one of the victims – was it all part of a desire to play games? Scenes and snippets of conversations the two had shared in recent weeks replayed inside her head.

'No one really gives a shit about people like that, do they? I know I don't.'

'I've always been fascinated by the workings of the human body.'

'It's nice to have someone on the team that I trust.'

'Some men need to be taught a lesson.'

Could this really be happening? She had known Jessica for years; they had eaten dinner together less than a week earlier. They had shared jokes about men and work and other girly topics. They had worked together on dozens of cases. Could she have been hiding such a ghastly secret all this time?

Stacey thought back to the moment at the end of their last meal together when the waiter had dropped a tray. Everyone in the restaurant had jumped at the shock. Everyone except Jessica.

Now she heard Jacques's voice in her head once more: 'Research has shown that psychopaths and serial killers have a greater fear threshold, and are less likely to respond to fear-inducing stimuli or sudden shocks. Some researchers think they are virtually immune to those kinds of emotions.'

And that moment there was a heavy click on the line and a real voice sounded in her ear. Jessica Matthews had switched off the answering machine and answered the call.

'Hello, is anyone there?'

Stacey said nothing. The seconds ticked by slowly before Jessica Matthews spoke again, first with a small giggle and then with a few softly spoken words. 'I know you're there. I can hear you breathing.'

Stacey was taken aback by the friendly tone. This just couldn't be right. She had to be crazy. It couldn't possibly be right.

'Hi, Jessica. It's Stacey.'

'Stacey. How lovely. I was just thinking about you. What can I do for you at this late hour?'

Stacey did her best to think on her feet but too many things were happening at once, events were moving too fast for her to keep on top of them all. She was listening hard, trying to detect signs of – what? What exactly did psychotic serial killers sound like?

'Oh, I was wondering if we could meet up in the morning. Maybe I could pop round. We could do that coffee we were going to do the other day.'

'Sure, why don't you come along to the hospital? I've got a meeting just before lunch but you can join me for elevenses. Hey, there's a great new café near here called the Stone Bridge. The guy behind the counter is gorgeous.'

'Really?'

'Oh, yes. The moment I saw him I thought to myself, wow, who do I have to kill to get to go out with him? You know what I mean.'

'Uh huh. Right.'

There was a pause before Jessica spoke again. 'You and me, we're the same, aren't we, Stacey?'

'Are we?'

'Yeah. That's why we get on so well. That's why I've always tried to help you out. You remind me of me.'

'Jessica . . . I . . .'

'I have to go now, Stacey. Way past my bedtime. I'll see you soon.'

The line went dead. Stacey shuddered, then dialled a new number, an extension at the office where she knew the night team would be staffing the incident room.

'DC Cooper speaking.'

'Natalie. It's Stacey. Do you have the toxicology reports from the case?'

'I don't think so.'

'Why the hell not?'

'They never arrived. We never got them.'

'But you're supposed to chase them up. That kind of thing should get flagged up. That's what HOLMES is all about.'

'They did get flagged up, and I made a manual adjustment to the file. I knew they weren't going to contain any pertinent information so I cancelled the alert. I was just trying to save time.'

'Who the hell told you? Who said they weren't worth looking at?'

'I . . . I . . .'

'Was it Jessica Matthews?'

'No.'

'Are you sure?'

'It wasn't.'

'Then who?'

'It was you. You told me. Last week.'

Stacey again thought back to her dinner with Jessica Matthews, the one when she had casually mentioned that the reports were not worth looking at, a fact Stacey had happily and trustingly passed on.'

'Get hold of them now. And not from the pathologist's office. Don't even call them. Go direct to the lab. I want the originals. Nothing else. And I want them as soon as possible. I'll call you later and let you know where to send them.'

There was one more call to make. Edward Larcombe was a veteran forensic pathologist whom Stacey had known for almost as long as she had been in the force. He could have retired years ago, but his skills and experience were in such demand that he felt almost obliged to continue working.

He answered the phone with all the world-weariness of a man who had become accustomed to having his sleep interrupted.

'Hello?'

'Edward. It's Stacey Collins. Sorry to wake you up.'

'Not a problem, my dear. If I wanted to only work nine to five, I should have become a filing clerk. What can I do for you?'

'I need your help on a case. But this has to be off the record, strictly between the two of us.'

'That sounds highly irregular.'

'I know I'm asking a lot. I can't explain right now,

but you're the only person I can trust. You're the only person I can turn to.'

Stacey waited while Larcombe coughed noisily away from the phone. 'What do you need?'

'I need you to meet me at the mortuary at Guy's as soon as you can. But you can't tell anyone where you're going or why you're going there. Can you do that?'

'Well, frankly I think I'm getting a little too old for all this cloak-and-dagger stuff, but, as it's you, I should be able to be there in thirty minutes.'

By the time Edward Larcombe arrived at the hospital, Collins had made all the preparations. She led him through the entrance and past several bemused security guards to the mortuary, which was entirely deserted.

They made their way through the double doors and into the main room, where Collins pulled open one of the storage drawers on the far wall where the bodies were kept. Inside was the chilled corpse of Raymond Chadwick.

Larcombe looked at her intently, then peered down at the body in the drawer.

'You're a bit late, Stacey,' he said softly. 'Someone's already done an autopsy on this body. Twice by the look of things.'

'I know this is highly unusual,' said Collins, 'but I need you to look at this body and tell me as much as you can about how this person died.'

'You don't trust the opinion of the first doctor?'

'Let's just say I'd be very interested to hear what you have to say.'

'Then I suggest you don't tell me anything more until I've finished my own examination. When I've finished it would be good to see the original reports for comparison.'

'I'm having them sent over. They should be here soon.'

'Then I suggest you make yourself comfortable. This could take quite a while.'

Collins sat in a corner while Larcombe went to work with gloved hands, probing and prodding at the body, a look of intense concentration on his face. Half an hour later the reports arrived by courier and he asked for them to be placed on a desk close to the examination table so that he could read them after his examination. It hadn't taken long for Larcombe to finish. He snapped off his gloves and tossed them in the nearest bin while making his way over towards Collins.

'It hasn't been easy. There wasn't a lot to work with in the first place,' explained Larcombe, 'and there has been more decomposition since the first post-mortems were carried out. That said, two things stand out. First, the incision to the chest cavity was made by someone not only with medical training but also with a great deal of experience. There are no hesitation cuts, and the amount of pressure used was correctly varied from the top of the thorax to the top of the pelvis to avoid damaging any internal organs. I know student doctors two years into the job who still can't manage to get that right.

'Second, the victim was given intravenous medication while they were being cut open. I'm going to assume it was some kind of anaesthesia or paralytic, most likely a combination of the two. That's the kind of procedure you only ever get in a medical environment. I've never seen it in a crime victim. What was particularly interesting is that the entry point for the IV needle was at the base of the neck. A very unusual site, though a highly effective one. I found the mark quite easily but it seemed that it had recently been covered up. By make-up. Fresh make-up, applied since the body has been in the morgue. I have no idea why anyone would want to do that. So tell me, Stacey, what exactly is going on?'

Collins nodded towards the desk on the other side of the room. 'I think it's time for you to read the reports.'

Larcombe nodded and glanced at the large clock above the desk. 'I hope I'm going to be able to get overtime for this.'

'Edward, if you help me crack this case, I'll make sure you get a medal.'

Larcombe read the report in absolute silence with Collins looking on intently. When he had finished he removed his reading glasses and folded them neatly on the desk beside the tightly bound sheets of paper that made up the report. He pinched at the bridge of his nose with his fingers before he spoke. 'Well, Stacey, I'd have to say that ninety-five per cent of what has been put in the autopsy report is absolutely accurate. Dr Matthews did her job very competently. Very competently indeed.'

'Ninety five per cent, you say. So what was she keeping back?'

'Well, there's no mention at all of the IV puncture mark – which is either a sign of enormous incompetence or a deliberate omission.'

'Anything else?'

'The toxicology reports are rather fascinating.'

'I was told they held no relevant information.'

'That couldn't be further from the truth. They've come back positive for an analogue of rocuronium.'

'Which is?'

'In a nutshell, it's a muscle relaxant and is used in surgery as part of the general anaesthesia when patients need to be intubated.'

'You'll have to spell this one out for me.'

'Of course. If a patient has trouble breathing, we do what's called an endotracheal intubation. You see it all the time on hospital dramas on TV. They use a metal pole with a curved stick a little like a sword on one end and slip it into the throat to hold the airways open, while a plastic tube is inserted down into the lungs.'

'I've seen that. I know what you mean. But I don't understand the relevance. Are you saying the killer has been intubating the victims?'

'Not at all. The difficulty with trying to intubate a patient who is still conscious is that the gag reflex is still active. Anything inserted into the throat makes the patient cough violently. The throat tightens up and it's impossible to get a breathing tube down there. It's a huge problem.

'Rocuronium is one of a family of drugs that instantly make the muscles relax. Within seconds of receiving the drug, the patient will be as limp as a ragdoll and their gag reflex will be disabled. They can be intubated without difficulty.'

'So it's like a tranquilizer.'

'Not exactly. It doesn't make people unconscious. It doesn't prevent pain. It just prevents people from moving. It would render them totally and utterly paralysed. Any decent hospital would only ever administer it alongside other drugs so the patient would be asleep during the procedure. By all accounts, being given the drug on its own is a pretty scary experience. Because it paralyses all the muscles including those of the chest, those who are on it can feel like they are suffocating to death. It's said to be akin to having a severe heart attack, only you can't tell anyone about it; you can't even scream.'

'Did the tests find the presence of any kind of anaesthesia?'

'This was the only drug present in all three victims. Nothing else was being used. Nothing at all.'

'Are you telling me,' said Collins, stuttering as she tried to get the words out, 'that our victims would have known they were being cut open, operated on?'

There was a pause before Larcombe replied. 'You have to understand, Stacey, that after a minute or two these people would have been in so much pain that their brains would not have been able to handle it. They would have blacked out to prevent them dying of shock. But up until that time they would have felt every single incision.'

20

DCI Anderson ignored the phone for the first few rings, convinced that he must be dreaming. It was only after his long-suffering wife leaned across and elbowed him in the ribs that he reached across and lifted the handset from the cradle.

'Hello?'

Collins was determined to extract every ounce of pleasure out of being able to phone Anderson at 2 a.m.

'I'm not waking you up, am I, sir?'

'What the hell do you think, Collins? What do you want?'

She couldn't help but smile at the grumpy, hoarse tone of his voice.

'It's Jessica Matthews,' she said firmly. 'She's our killer.'

'What are you talking about?'

'This case. Chadwick and the others. I believe Matthews is responsible.'

She could almost hear Anderson blinking furiously in disbelief at what he had just heard.

'Did you say Jessica Matthews?'

'Yes, sir.'

'Dr Jessica Matthews.'

'Yes.'

'The forensic pathologist?'

'Yes.'

'Your friend.'

'Well, yes.'

'Are you out of your mind?'

'Sir, I've gathered a lot of information. I know it sounds unlikely at first but all the evidence points towards her.'

'It better do for you to have woken me up at this time. Tell me what you've got.'

'I can do better than that, sir. I can show you.'

'Where are you?'

'Outside your front door.'

Collins heard Anderson emit a noise that was halfway between a grunt and a roar. She knew he wasn't going to be happy to see her, but for once she didn't care.

'Give me a few minutes,' muttered Anderson, before putting the phone down.

Ten minutes later Anderson opened the front door of his home and ushered Collins inside. They sat on opposite sides of his dining-room table, and Collins pushed a sheaf of papers across at him.

'Let me get this straight,' he said, leaning forward intently. 'You've come here to tell me that Jessica Matthews' – Anderson said the name slowly, each syllable heavy with sarcasm – 'is a serial killer? Have you lost your mind?

'Yesterday you were convinced the killer was Dr Bernard, one of the leading forensic psychologists in the world. Today it's a top Home Office pathologist. Are you doing any actual police work or are you just working your way through *Who's Who*?'

Collins moved a hand up to her hair and, realizing how unkempt it was, tried to smooth it down. 'Okay, I know I sound crazy. I know I probably look crazy . . .'

'You got that right. You're seeing guilt everywhere. Are you sure you're not just trying to find a suspect to fit the facts, instead of the other way around? You've got too many years in the job to make an error like that, surely.'

Collins shook her head. 'But I also thought I was crazy when this idea first came to me. But it all fits. She has the right kind of background and the right level of knowledge. She fits the profile.'

Anderson tossed the papers back on the table. 'Dozens of people fit the profile. That's the way they're put together. Deliberately vague. It doesn't mean anything. Pretty much everyone on the team fits the profile. For crying out loud, I fit the profile! You're going to need a lot more than that.'

'There are errors in the autopsy, major omissions.'

Now it was Anderson's turn to shake his head. 'That's the best you have? You might have misheard her. It could be nothing more than a simple mistake. She's a highly respected doctor. She's virtually part of the inquiry. She's a close friend of half the senior staff down at Scotland Yard. Oh, and in case it's somehow slipped your attention, she's also female.' He threw his hands high in the air in frustration. 'Female serial killers are pretty much non-existent.'

'They're rare but not unheard of. Look at Rosemary West – ten murders over a period of sixteen years – or Myra Hindley – five murders. You're making the classic mistake of dismissing her because she's female.'

'Yes, but in both those cases the women had male accomplices . . .'

'And who's to say that's not the case with Matthews? There are things that she has said to me, things that have happened when we've been together.'

Anderson sat back and put his hands in his lap. 'It's all theory. Nothing concrete.'

'There's reasonable doubt.'

'Not enough to make me want to touch this with a barge pole. It's all very well when we're dealing with the likes of a Billy-no-mates, of whom Billy Moorwood is a prime example. Spending a couple of days in a police cell makes precious little difference to his shitty life. For all we know it's probably the highlight of his year.

'But someone like Jessica Matthews. We can't go around arresting people like that just because you've got some kind of stupid hunch about them.' Anderson sat back in his chair and put the palms of his hands together, touching the tip of his nose with the tips of his fingers. 'What I want are facts, not speculations. I can't do anything based on theories pulled out of the air. You have to take into consideration all of the potential consequences of what you're saying. Dr Jessica Matthews is one of the best pathologists there is. She's been the lead examiner on literally hundreds of high-profile cases over the past few years. If we're not a hundred per cent sure about this, the shit will really hit the fan.

'Even if she's cleared of any involvement in the murders after we've arrested her, the mud will stick to her name for years to come. Not only will she not be able to get any work but anyone who has ever been convicted on the basis of her evidence, anyone whose case file she's even simply looked at, will have instant grounds for an appeal. We're talking major, major disruption to the entire criminal justice system here. This needs to be entirely watertight. We can't afford to fuck up, not even for a second.'

'You're right,' snorted Collins. 'You're absolutely right. It's much too big a risk. God knows what damage we might do to our careers if we carry on down this route. I'm sure Mrs Anderson would rather be the wife of a superintendent who played it safe than someone who actually cared about doing his job properly.'

A horrible silence hung in the air and Anderson narrowed his eyes for a moment. Then he snatched the papers out of Collins's hand. He studied them carefully, his brow furled in concentration, while she stood up and paced impatiently back and forth in front of the dining table. At long last he looked up at her. 'This part here, I don't understand what I'm reading.'

Collins walked over to Anderson and he pointed at the paragraph he was reading.

'It means she's been giving us false information,' said Collins. 'I had Edward Larcombe take a look at one of the bodies. There are significant differences between the actual condition of the bodies when they arrived at the morgue and what she told me about them at the scene and during the autopsy.

'Matthews told me it was possible the bodies had been frozen, that temperature readings were far below ambient. It's true that the bodies must have been kept in cold storage – it's the only way to explain the lack of decomposition – but by the time the bodies arrived at the morgue they had all thawed out. They were at room temperature and must have been for some time. There's no way the bodies could have warmed up that fast.

'And that's just the start. There are dozens of other omissions. Needle sites not documented, toxicology results not passed on, details about the incisions not properly recorded. The only reason anyone would miss out that level of detail is to stop the finger of suspicion pointing back at them.'

'Could just be mistakes, innocent mistakes,' said Anderson.

'She's not that incompetent.'

'So why lie? What was the point?'

'She was playing games. Giving us a head start. You have to remember what Dr Bernard said about the personality types who get involved in this type of crime. They are desperate to prove that they can outsmart the police. They want that level of confrontation. They want to be right there in the middle of the investigation. To some extent, they want to be suspects because they believe they're clever enough to get away with it. That's Jessica Matthews to a T.'

'I don't know, Collins. It's a bit of a jump. We all take short cuts, we all makes mistakes with paperwork. If that alone were grounds for suspicion, half of MIT would be banged up by now.'

'Even if you think that, we should at least talk to her, ask her about the anomalies in the autopsy reports.'

Anderson looked down at his watch. 'Okay, let's talk to her. There's no harm in that. But let me do the talking. I don't want to accuse her of anything just yet.'

'And we should get Edward Larcombe to re-examine the bodies officially.'

'Let's not run before we can walk. One step at a time.'

Matthews did not answer the phone at her office; nor did she answer her mobile or the landline at her home. It took only a few more calls to establish that, despite having both an autopsy and a meeting scheduled for later that morning, Matthews had not been seen since the night before.

A check with security staff at the hospital showed that Matthews had entered the building shortly after Collins and Larcombe had made their way inside to carry out a second examination of the victims. Suddenly it all fell into place. Matthews had seen the pair together, guessed what they were doing and fled.

Collins was using the phone in Anderson's study on speaker setting. He had been pacing back and forth as she made one call after another in an attempt to track Matthews down but stopped and stared intently at her as news of the pathologist's sudden flight emerged. Collins did not meet his gaze; she did not want to be blamed for tipping off the main suspect but knew there was no way she could possibly avoid it.

'I spoke to her last night, sir,' she said sheepishly. 'I said nothing about the case or my suspicions, but she must have sensed something in the tone of my voice. I think that's partly why she's taken off.'

It took a few minutes more to establish that Matthews had left the hospital by the rear security gate and that her vehicle was no longer in the car park.

Much to Anderson's frustration, details of the vehicle itself were not available. Matthews had changed it a couple of weeks earlier and, despite requests from the head of security, had yet to submit the form giving details of the new make and model. There was nothing on file with the DVLA either.

Collins was not surprised that they had nothing. She had got over the shock of having tipped Matthews off. That wasn't important. They seemed to have found their killer – why else would she go on the run? Now all they had to do was bring her in.

Anderson had been barking orders into his mobile phone. He finally finished and turned to Collins. 'We're all set. Let's get to the main entrance. The Territorial Support Group are going to pick us up there.'

'Where are we going?'

'No more softly, softly. We're going to make a house call on Dr Matthews.'

The driver killed the flashing lights as they approached their final destination: a small row of terraced houses in an affluent part of West London, just as the sun was breaking over the tops of the trees and the first rays of light fell across the road like spindly fingers.

Two teams of heavily armed officers from CO19 – sixteen in all, representing the entire Armed Response capability Anderson could muster in such a short space of time – were crammed into two vans that drew to a halt at the far end of the street, engines idling and waiting for the go-ahead.

No one had any idea what they were going to find

inside Matthews's house and no one was willing to take any chances.

The car carrying Collins and Anderson pulled up behind the van at the rear. The unit commander emerged from the side and came over to talk to Anderson.

'We're not expecting any kind of armed resistance but we're going in fully prepared just in case,' said the unit commander. 'Whoever is in there, we'll have them subdued for you in no time at all. We're just waiting for your signal.'

'Go ahead when you're ready,' he said.

Within minutes the house was surrounded; all the armed officers were pumped full of adrenalin, awaiting the final order. Each member of the team carried a Heckler & Koch MP5 carbine as their main weapon, along with a Glock 17 9mm automatic pistol, more than a match for anything the crooks might have. A few yards from the entrance the team split into two, half moving around to cover the windows and rear entrance.

Then to the cries of 'attack, attack, attack', the men and women of Blue Company, dressed in black combat trousers and bullet-proof vests, moved in with such ferocity that no one would have stood a chance.

Collins watched in awe, butterflies rising in her stomach as members of the first entry team took up positions on either side of the door and cleared the way for a man carrying an enforcer, which reduced the door to splinters.

Now the team were moving inside using skills they had perfected hundreds of times before. With the door gone, one officer flung himself down on a heavily padded knee and raised his gun to his eye, activating the flashlight slung just below the barrel.

There were muffled shouts of 'armed police, don't move' and 'put your hands out in front of you, on the floor now' mixed with the sounds of screaming, breaking glass and the dull pop of stun grenades. Flashes of light could be seen through the windows on each floor as the team made their way through.

At last there was silence and then, after a few minutes when nothing at all happened, one of the junior members of the team came out of the house. He was somewhat unsteady on his feet, gulping down lungfuls of air. He moved to one side of the garden path, bracing himself against the wall; then, swinging his gun out of the way just in time, threw up violently again and again.

'What the hell have they found in there?' breathed Anderson, as the commander of the entry team, his face pale with shock, emerged through the doorway and approached the two officers.

'We're ready for you now sir. The building is secure.'

'Any trouble?' asked Anderson.

'I think you'd better come and see for yourselves,' came the sombre reply.

Collins knew they were going to be dealing with a dead body the moment she entered the narrow hallway. The familiar stench that she had come across time and time again during her career was hanging heavy in the air.

She and Anderson followed the firearms team leader as he made his way to the back of the house into the kitchen. The stench grew stronger with each step.

Collins saw the far side of the dinner table first. An empty bottle of Bordeaux was standing next to a white china plate that held the remains of a meal – a few small bones, dried-up sauce and a few scraps of green vegetable matter. A silver knife and fork were neatly placed in the centre of the plate and an empty wine glass still had drops of condensation clinging to it.

It was only when Collins took a few steps further forward that she knew what had made the young officer react so violently. At the opposite end of the table sat a man whom she instantly recognized to be Detective Sergeant Patrick O'Neill, or at least what remained of him.

He was naked and had been propped up in the chair so that the palms of his hands were lying flat on the table in front of him. His head was still attached to his body despite a massive gaping slit like a thin-lipped second mouth that smiled out across the width of his neck. His chest had been split wide open all the way down to his belly button and beyond, and inside Collins could see the now familiar marbled fat on the inside of his ribs, all too reminiscent of the hanging carcasses she saw in the trucks that pulled up outside the butchers' shops to make their deliveries.

O'Neill still had his face. His eyes were wide open, seemingly in shock, his mouth was twisted into what seemed to be a horrific silent scream. The skin around his cheeks was as thin as tissue paper and had started to tear and peel as decomposition settled in.

A second plate of food and glass of wine had been placed in front of him as some kind of grotesque joke. It was clear that Matthews had eaten her own meal while staring at this macabre sideshow.

It took a team of twenty specialist officers the rest of the day to complete a search that ultimately yielded scores of items that needed to be followed up.

Then there were boxes and boxes of books, research papers, dissertations, newspaper and magazine clippings in the top-floor room that Matthews used as a makeshift home office.

Every item would have to be tagged, read and reported on to see if it could shed new light on the case.

In the past, days like these filled Collins with adrenalin and she would feel strong enough to keep going and never ever have to stop. Today was different.

Today she felt completely and utterly exhausted. She knew deep down that nothing would have been left behind that was of even the slightest significance. Matthews had been too clever, right from the start. It was almost as if she had been planning all of this, right down to the dumping of the bodies in an area that would ensure the case was taken on by MIT South for at least six months, perhaps even longer.

On top of that, she had day-to-day access to police records, reports and living breathing officers whom she could use as sounding boards to ensure she had covered all the bases. And that was exactly what she had done. Collins herself had played right into her hands. She wondered how many other officers she had pretended to give a helping hand to, knowing it would make them far more willing to spill the beans about future cases.

Late in the afternoon there was a flurry of excitement from within the house when one of the search team found a laptop computer tucked away behind the bed in Matthews's spare bedroom. Collins knew better than to attach any importance to the item. If it had been left behind, it was either completely worthless or it was a deliberate red herring, a ploy to send them off on yet another wild-goose chase.

An excited Rajid arrived at the house half an hour later and was set up in a corner of the kitchen to see if the laptop contained any useful information. It took only a few minutes for him to uncover logs showing that Matthews was indeed shygirl351, but

Collins couldn't help but feel that they had already known that anyway.

Rajid found little else of interest – certainly nothing pointing to an alternative address or a place where Matthews might have been taking her victims to slaughter them. They were all still in the dark.

By ten in the evening Collins was fighting a losing battle against exhaustion and Anderson could tell.

'I think we can call off the search for the day. There's nothing useful to be gained here and I don't think there's any point in being too exhausted for work tomorrow. I want you to head off home and get a good night's sleep. I'll get the team to tag and bag everything they find here and get it over to forensics. We can start going through it all tomorrow from the comfort of the office.

'There are two questions we need to answer. Who the hell is Jessica Matthews? And where the hell is Jessica Matthews? If you can have both the answers on my desk tomorrow, you'll make me a very happy man.'

Collins managed a weak smile. She felt certain that if she told Anderson that it was her fault Matthews had gone on the run, he would be forgiving and understanding. But she was too exhausted to take the chance.

'What about Rajid?'

They looked down the hallway and into the kitchen, where Rajid's face was illuminated by the light from the computer screen. He was staring intently and typing furiously as a stream of letters and symbols whizzed past his eyes.

'He's young,' said Anderson. 'When I was that age I didn't even wake up until it was dark. If anyone can work through the night without suffering any ill effects, he can. There will be someone to take him home when he's done. Go on, you get off, otherwise you won't make it home at all.'

Thirty seconds later a thoroughly exhausted Stacey Collins finally climbed into the back of the un-marked patrol car that had brought her to the house that morning. She collapsed across the seat, curling up like a baby.

'Wake me up when we get to my house.'

'Yes, ma'am.'

The big Vauxhall pulled away from the kerb and off into the night. A few seconds later a second car pulled away from the kerb five hundred yards along the road.

With her hair dyed a different colour and cut into a different style, Jessica Matthews was totally unrecognizable. She smiled as she eased her foot off the accelerator to keep an even distance between herself and the car she was following.

Collins should not have gone to her house but she had done so anyway. The least she could do now would be to return the favour.

The full details of Jessica Matthews's true background and traumatic childhood emerged slowly as the result of painstaking research by every member of the murder team.

At an emergency morning prayers session in the hours that followed her disappearance, assignments had been handed out to ensure every aspect of her life was uncovered and explored.

All were shocked by what they found but few more so than Collins herself, who felt like a fool for allowing herself to be thoroughly manipulated by a dangerous and psychopathic woman who had clearly had an agenda right from the start.

Although she tried her best to stay focused on the task at hand, it was impossible to stop her thoughts from returning time and again to the lunches and dinners and coffees that she and Jessica Matthews had shared over the years. She was beating herself up about having failed to spot any of the clues about the woman's behaviour and actions that now, with the benefit of hindsight, seemed oh so obvious. Woods, Anderson and the rest of her colleagues did their best to be supportive and told her not to be too hard on herself – after all Matthews had managed to fool many others besides – but Stacey couldn't help but feel she had let them all down.

Interviews with friends and colleagues shed little light on Matthews's character – no one had a bad word to say about her, professionally at least. It was only when Collins and Woods met up with the pathologist's parents that they truly began to understand just what a troubled individual they were dealing with.

As they travelled to Matthews's home town Collins and Woods hoped they might finally gain some kind of insight into the making of the monster.

The house where Jessica Matthews had grown up was a nondescript semi-detached in the heart of suburban Enfield. It was only a few doors away from a large, partly forested park that had a sizeable play area complete with swings, slides and roundabouts as well as a paddling pool that operated during the summer months.

With dozens of other families living nearby, shops and other amenities all within easy reach, the area seemed to provide the perfect setting for an idyllic middle-class childhood.

Each house on the street had an immaculately kept front garden – to allow even a single blade of grass to be out of place was to risk being accused of lowering the tone by the head of the residents' committee. Rear gardens, though hidden from public view, were a matter of equal pride, with the local MP

– a Tory of course – being chief judge of the annual contest in which prizes were awarded for the best-kept plot.

For those who had chosen to make this part of North London their home, the only cause for concern came in the form of three enormous tower blocks from a local housing estate that rose up over the horizon like angry weeds. Much to the dismay of the parents outside the estate, it was here that many of their children found most of their fun and recreation, travelling up to the top floors in the lifts, running in and out of the underground garages and hanging out with gangs of kids hell bent on vandalism and mischief. These were exactly the kinds of children the parents had warned their offspring to avoid at all costs, and fear that their influence might spread had resulted in constant vigilance throughout the area.

This was the reason that, although the car that Collins and Woods arrived in was unmarked, curtains twitched on both sides of the road as they emerged and made their way up the front path towards Number 230.

'You think they already know?' asked Woods, glancing around.

'Doubt it,' said Collins. 'I think it's just that kind of area. Everyone is into everyone else's business. Try to make a mental note of where the biggest busybodies are – the houses where the most noses are poking through the curtains. Might be worth having a word with them later on. We'll get a different take on the home life of young Miss Matthews.'

The door was opened by WPC Louise Mitchell, who, earlier that morning, had been appointed family liaison officer to Jessica's parents. It was her job to fend off the unwanted attention of the press, remain with the family at all times and provide a direct link to the highest levels of the investigation. It was a service performed not just for victims but also for families of the accused, who, in many cases, became victims in their own right. Although some parts of the press were likely to end up calling Matthews a hero for killing off paedophiles, they could never be sure exactly how people would react.

'They're in the sitting room,' said WPC Mitchell. 'I'll show you the way.'

The living room was like something out of a catalogue. Beautiful but entirely sterile. It was the kind of room that existed more for display purposes than anything else. Only on special occasions would anyone actually be allowed to sit there. The carpet was deep and luxurious, the shelves filled with figurines and trinkets far too delicate to touch. For Woods it was the sign of a house ruled with an iron fist. The kind of house where discipline was a constant companion. The kind of house that any young girl would be dying to run away from.

'Mr and Mrs Matthews, I presume,' said Collins, extending one hand in greeting.

The man and the woman were sitting close

together on the larger of the two sofas in the room. Their hands were tightly clasped together between them. The woman was slim, her hair cut just below the line of her chin in a kind of carved bob. She looked tired and strained but smiled up at him. The man wore a full beard that was starting to show patches of grey. He had a muscular build, his broad shoulders pressing tightly against his shirt. His eyes twinkled with a fierce intensity. He wore a cream and brown Pringle-pattern knitted vest over a thin-striped shirt and tie.

'Actually it's Robertson,' said the man, extending his own hand to meet that of Collins. 'Larry Robertson. I'm Jessica's stepfather and this is my wife, Lucy. Jessica's birth parents died when she was young. Matthews was their name. She was Robertson for a while during the time she was with us but changed back to Matthews almost as soon as she left home.

'During her time here we did our best to make her comfortable but she could be incredibly difficult, very mischievous and at times, to be perfectly honest, a little bit frightening.'

'I understand,' said Collins.

Mrs Robertson spoke up for the first time, her voice cracking with emotion at the end of each word. 'Is there any news? Have you found her? We're worried sick. Do you think she might have done something to herself? We've been looking in the papers. All those terrible things she is supposed to have done. I can't believe it would really be her. And that's why I think she might do herself in.

'It's just awful, so awful. And then this ... this killing. How on earth could that little girl be involved in something so horrible ...'

Her sentence trailed off into a stream of sobs, and Larry edged towards her on the sofa, putting his arm around her shoulder and pulling him towards her. 'Come on, love,' he said gently. 'They're here to help. We need to help them so that they can help us.'

Collins and Woods watched them closely. Larry pulled the woman's sobbing face into his shoulder before speaking once more.

Larry Robertson was speaking again. 'I don't want to believe it's true, I really don't, but the more I think about it, the more some of the clues have been there all the time. We used to have a small holding up in Bedfordshire. That's where we were when Jessica first came to live with us. We thought it was the perfect environment for any small child – lots of fresh air and dozens of animals to play with – but she was never that happy there.

'And then one year we had a spate of attacks on the animals. A couple of horses got slashed, one of the rabbits was killed. At the time it was all blamed on gangs of local lads looking for kicks, but now I'm not so sure. The finger of suspicion never turned to Jessica – well, it wouldn't, would it – but the following year we had to sell up and leave. New health and safety regulations and all that. Made it impossible for us to continue. We shut the whole thing down and that's how we ended up here.

'Jessica seemed to like living near London – a lot more for teenagers to do – but when I think back ... well, you just wonder, don't you? We always feared there would be some backlash, considering what had happened to her before. But we never imagined it would be anything like this.'

Collins and Woods looked at each other, silently confirming that neither knew exactly what it was that Mr Robertson was talking about.

'I'm sorry,' said Collins. 'When you say what happened to her before ... I think you need to explain.'

22

Thirty Years Earlier

She had relaxed in a nice warm bath, brushed her teeth thoroughly and spent twenty minutes reading from her favourite story book, but she was still far too excited to get to sleep.

'Please, please, please, Mum, can't I just stay up a bit longer? I really don't feel tired at all.'

Joanne Matthews looked down at the pleading face of her young daughter and smiled. 'Now then, Jessica, we talked about this. If you don't get to bed soon you're going to be too tired to enjoy your party tomorrow. And all your friends who come and give you presents will end up being very disappointed. And we don't want that, do we?'

Jessica shook her head slowly. The seven-year-old had been ready to burst with excitement over her birthday for the best part of the past month, and now that the day had almost arrived, she was ready to go into overdrive.

Joanne Matthews kissed and cuddled her daughter, pulled the blankets up so that her little shoulders were covered, switched on the nightlight and then shut the door.

'Sleep tight, my little angel. I'll see you in the morning. Love you.' Jessica shut her eyes tight, certain that if she closed them tightly enough and for long enough, the next time they opened it would be morning.

She was somewhere in the in-between twilight world of sleep and wakefulness when she heard the doorbell ring. She turned over and lifted the thumb of her right hand up to her mouth. It was an old habit she had repeatedly fought but failed to kick. Despite knowing it made her look incredibly childish, nothing else gave her quite so much comfort. Sleep did not always come easily and the fact that the following day was her birthday was making it more difficult than ever for the little girl to drift off.

The sound of footsteps, the creek of the front door opening, followed by her father's voice, deep, low, serene. A voice like a warm blanket. A voice you could wrap yourself up in. A voice as smooth as warm chocolate. It was a voice that for years had been at the heart of a massive dilemma. Each night she would have to choose which of her parents she wanted to read her a bedtime story. Her father's voice was so thick and dreamy that it would send her to sleep within minutes and she would get to hear only a few pages of whatever story they were reading. By contrast, her mother's voice was delicate and expressive and displayed a talented mimicry that made a story's characters seem to truly come alive. But her mother often stuttered and stumbled over her words and lost her place, which meant they would often have to go over the same parts of the story time and time again in order to make sense of it all.

There were days when she wanted her father to read to her and days when she wanted her mother to have a chance. Even at the tender age of five she had been mindful of the fact that favouring one more than the other might lead to the one who was left out being upset. If she could, little Jessica was determined to please everybody.

Lying in bed on the eve of her birthday, she listened hard to her father's voice, hoping it would soothe her. But for the first time ever it did the complete opposite. At first he had sounded the way he always did – calm and serene. The voice of whoever was at the door was nothing like it. Far more excited, far more agitated. Far more angry.

In response her father's voice began to rise in both volume and tempo until he was sounding so unlike his usual self that it was almost as if he had been taken over by another person.

She had heard her parents argue only a handful of times and it had always been a shock to her. She hated the ugly, brutish tones they used on one another. But now her father was using that tone once more, not to her mother but to whoever it was at the door. Much of the sound was being muffled or distorted and she couldn't work out exactly what was being said. He was shouting at the top of his voice and Jessica was sure she could hear flashes of the words her mother had told her never to speak, the naughty words that she and her schoolfriends giggled about in the corners of the playground. The one that rhymed with cluck, the one that rhymed with knit.

Her eyes were open now. She pulled her thumb from her mouth and tucked her knees up so that they were touching her chest. The voices were continuing to get louder and more violent, and now her mother's voice seemed to have joined in, pleading, crying, screaming.

And the sound of movement. Feet shuffled back and forth on the wood floor of the hallway. The door slamming hard, the slim telephone table at the side of the stairs being overturned. The slaps and thuds of punches and kicks being landed with force. Her mother's desperate, warning scream. 'Look out, he's got a ...' Her father's voice, a grunt followed by hollow, gasping, choking, coughing, spluttering sounds as the very air he needed to breathe spilled out of his chest.

More screams from her mother, footsteps running up the stairs. Footsteps following close behind. Then the voice of the man, the intruder, screaming, cursing, as if he had been tripped up. More kicks, more punches, more impact sounds Jessica simply didn't understand. Cries of agonized pain from her father. The sound of her name, her mother's name, her name again, on his lips. Again and again.

Her mother burst into the room, her silhouette illuminated by the lights from the hallway. She scooped Jessica out of her bed and carried her over to the wardrobe. Jessica had never seen her mother look so frightened, so completely and utterly terrified. She had never seen any human being look so terrified. She was speechless with shock.

Her mother opened the door and shoved her daughter into the base at the back. 'For God's sake don't make a sound,' she pleaded, then slammed the door shut.

Tiny shafts of light slipped in through the door's wooden slats. Through them Jessica could see her mother quickly, frantically smoothing out the sheets on the bed before picking up the portable cassette player from Jessica's bedside table and returning to the hall.

By now her father had fallen silent. The footsteps that started making their way up the stairs were slow, deliberate. There was no need to hurry. There was no escape.

The man appeared at the top of the stairs, directly opposite the open door of Jessica's room, slightly to the right of where her mother stood. The man's hair was wild and matted, his clothes were filthy and threadbare. He looked like the homeless men they often saw sleeping in shop doorways late at night. In his right hand he held a long, thin knife, the tip of which sparkled in the light like a tiny star.

Jessica's mother was holding the cassette player high, waiting for her moment. When the man reached the top of the stairs she threw it towards his head with all her might. He ducked easily and moved quickly towards her, knocking her down to the ground with a punch to the side of the head. For a moment it seemed he was going to advance on her with the knife but then he paused, turned and walked right into Jessica's room.

He looked around slowly, his eyes taking in every detail.

'Is there a kid here?'

Jessica could see her mother crawling slowly along the corridor floor. She shook her head but he did not see her. 'Hey, bitch, I asked you a fucking question. Is there a fucking kid here?'

Jessica heard her mother speak through her swollen jaw and loose teeth. 'She's having a sleep-over,' she lied. 'She's not here.'

The man looked around the room again. The bed seemed unmade; everything else seemed to be in order. 'Shame,' he hissed, before turning his attention back to Jessica's mother, who was now slowly pulling herself to her feet.

The man placed the knife on a bedside table, moved out into the corridor, grabbed Joanne by her hair and dragged her into the little girl's bedroom. What he did next would stay with little Jessica for the rest of her life.

He threw her down on the floor in front of the bed. She held up her hands, palms outward, in a gesture of helplessness, of powerlessness. He flew at her, knocking her back down. Then he was on top of her, his left hand clasped over her nose and mouth, pushing her head down hard into the carpet, his knees pinning her elbows, his right fist pounding down again and again. As her resistance started to fade, he reached down with his right hand, tugged up her skirt and ripped away her knickers. He then began to undo the waistband of his jeans.

So far as she could remember, little Jessica Matthews had twice walked into her parents' bedroom when they were making love. Not that she knew what they were actually doing. It was only later, during talks with friends at school, that she learned other children too had seen the strange positions, heard the curious grunting noises and the angry shouts. She had watched that special embrace transfixed for several seconds, unnoticed by either parent, until a change of position brought her face to face with her mother.

What the man was doing to her mother was nothing like what she had seen. Her mother wasn't moving, wasn't making any noise. The man was doing everything. He was facing one side, directly towards the door of the wardrobe, as if he were staring directly at her.

Suddenly he stopped thrusting, moved his left hand from Joanne's face and looked down at her. He slapped her cheek a couple of times, hissed a stream of swear words and then moved off towards the bedroom door. As he did so Joanne's head rolled to one side so that she too was facing the wardrobe door. Her lips and nose were a mass of blood; there were deep lacerations on her forehead; tufts of hair were missing from her fringe. Her eyes were wide open but utterly lifeless.

Jessica couldn't help it. She gasped in horror.

The man was in the doorway and spun round in an instant. His trousers were around his ankles but that didn't seem to slow him down as he flew towards the wardrobe, ripping open the door and pulling Jessica out by her hair.

She screamed. He slapped her face. She screamed again and he slapped her even harder, picking her up and throwing her across the room so forcefully that her head smacked against the wall as she landed on her bed. Now she could only whimper and sob. He was on her in an instant. She could smell cigarettes on his breath mixed with the sweat from his skin. His rough hands were everywhere, pulling up her nightdress, holding her down, shaking her this way and that. Poking, probing, prodding. His black eyes were shiny with excitement.

She punched and bit and tore with her own small hands but it was useless. He was too strong, he was too powerful. There was no way to stop him. All she could feel was pain, a burning sensation between her legs that grew and grew. The vision of her mother's face a few moments earlier flooded into her mind along with one single thought: she would not let it happen to her.

Her hands were flailing about uselessly, trying to

pull herself away. One landed on the bedside table. On the knife. She grabbed it. His eyes were closed now, he was smiling, pulling himself towards her, hurting her more and more with every thrust. She swung the knife as hard as she could. The blade sank into his neck, just below his ear. His eyes opened wide in shock and horror. He tried to scream but could only gurgle, blood spattering out of his mouth and his wound at the same time.

He fell hard to one side. She fell too, landing on top of him, feeling the beat of his heart slow, watching the pool of blood behind his head grow, weeping softly as the light in his eyes slowly faded away to nothing.

The four days that followed passed by like shadows on the curtains. Little Jessica Matthews managed to crawl off her attacker and into the corner of the room but was too terrified to go any further. She stayed there, without food or water or sleep, looking across at his body and that of her dead mother.

On the third night she could have sworn she heard her mother call out her name and shift towards her. She stared hard into her mother's cold glassy eyes, willing her to say something else, willing her to move and wrap her up in her loving arms. It would only be years later, after she had trained in pathology, that she would learn the sound was simply the result of built-up gases escaping from her mother's body as a result of decomposition.

Lighting streaming through the curtains on the fourth morning showed that her mother's skin had begun to develop dark, bruise-like patches all over and had started to swell up significantly. Fluids began to seep out of every orifice and there was a strong smell of decay in the air. A smell that would stay with her for the rest of her life.

That same afternoon, alerted by concerned neighbours and work colleagues, police broke into the house. They found her father dead from multiple stab wounds at the foot of the stairs. It seemed he had used the last of his strength to try to reach his wife and child upstairs but had been unable to make it.

Jessica herself was close to death. She was badly dehydrated and malnourished and had painful sores on her legs and buttocks from barely having moved since seeing her mother murdered before her very eyes. Rushed to hospital, she spent the next two weeks in intensive care.

It was clear what had happened and what she had witnessed, but child psychologists cautioned against asking her to relive any part of her ordeal. Her mind, they said, was far too fragile and still in deep shock. There would, they insisted, come a time when she would be able to deal with what had happened, but it might be many years away.

Two months later Jessica left hospital and was taken into the care of a foster family. With the help of extensive trauma counselling, she slowly began to rebuild her life. Much to everyone's surprise, there seemed to be little long-term damage as a result of what had happened to her. She enrolled at a new school, made friends easily and quickly began to warm to her new mother and father who did their best to make her feel welcome in their home. Two years later, they adopted her, changing her name to Robertson.

No one ever brought up what had happened to her parents or what she had done to defend herself, and Jessica never showed any inclination to speak about it. She became a normal, somewhat shy, happy-go-lucky and occasionally troublesome teenager before knuckling down to study for her exams.

She had dreamed of becoming a doctor since the age of twelve and worked hard to make it into medical school. It was only while she was there that the seemingly long-forgotten trauma of what had happened to her as a child finally returned with a vengeance.

It was towards the end of her first year as a medical student, during an anatomy class, that she saw a dead body close up for the first time since witnessing her mother's murder. The class involved learning about the position of the organs of the body by dissecting a corpse.

Matthews did not react when the white sheet was drawn back to reveal the freshly chilled body. She did not react when the tutor pointed out the first signs of putrefaction on the skin, indicating bruise-like marks similar to those that had appeared on the body of her mother in the days following her death.

Nothing untoward occurred until Matthews was invited to make the first incision into the corpse. As the scalpel pierced into the skin, something happened. Something utterly unexpected. At first she attributed the tingling sensation to something to do with nerves, but it grew and grew. Then for a moment it felt as though time had stood completely still.

Her breathing went from being fully relaxed to little more than a series of short, desperate gasps. An electric tingling sensation began to spread out from between her thighs. The feelings grew and grew until she felt as though she were going to explode. Muscles all over her body started to go into contraction; her hands began to tighten up. Her back started to arch against her will. Her legs began to tremble, her toes started to curl under, and from somewhere deep within her belly she heard herself let out a low, guttural moan.

Desperate to hide what was happening from the other students in the class, Matthews faked a fainting fit, collapsing to the ground in dramatic fashion. It seemed to work. Students were always fainting during the early years of medical training, especially when it came to the less savoury parts of medicine, so her classmates were none the wiser.

Only Matthews herself knew the truth of what had happened. It had not by any means been her first orgasm, but it had been by far the best.

Her initial shock soon turned to concern. She knew what had happened to her parents and, although she could remember almost nothing about the night her mother died and the days that followed, she was also vaguely aware that she had been the victim of something brutal and violent. But none of that answered the question that was now ringing throughout her mind: what on earth was wrong with her if she reacted in that way to death?

It did not take long for her to discover that she was not alone. The links between death and sexual arousal were everywhere, and her position as a medical student gave her access to vast amounts of information on the condition. Both the legendary seducer Casanova and the controversial physician Magnus Hirschfeld wrote about women who masturbated while viewing public executions. Casanova personally witnessed the execution of a French criminal who had attempted to kill the king. He was tortured first with red-hot pincers; then the hand he had used in the attempted assassination was burned down to the bone using sulphur, molten wax, lead and boiling oil. Horses were then harnessed to his arms and legs and made to run in different directions with the intention of pulling him apart. Despite being in absolute agony, the man's limbs refused to separate and he did not die. Finally the executioner used a sharp knife to cut into the man's joints and the body was successfully torn apart. And all the while at least two couples in the middle of the crowd had frantic, passionate sex while they were watching the spectacle.

Matthews read on, flushed with excitement at the images flooding through her head. She learned that, so common was the notion of arousal by the sight of death during these times, it was said the best way for an Englishman to break down a woman's resistance or scruples was simply to get her to attend a public execution. It was rated even more highly than wine.

She discovered that similar scenes were witnessed during Roman times. Their mass games, which included battles to the death between noble gladiators and desperate slaves, also included all manner of sexual shenanigans, followed by the mutilation and murder of those involved. The Empresses Messalina and Theodora routinely masturbated and had sex in the stands while watching these events.

From there Matthews read up on sexual deviation and decided she had developed necrosadism, a powerful fetish in which corpses led to sexual arousal. Her fetish was unusual, that was for sure, but, having discovered it, she realized that she had found the perfect way to service it at no risk to others. So long as she remained in the medical professional and had regular access to corpses, her needs would be satisfied and she would want for nothing more. Or so she thought.

It was around this same time that Matthews started seeing her first serious boyfriend, James Gilbert. Ten years her senior and working as a teacher, Gilbert had a reputation as a bit of a ladies' man and liked to treat his women roughly. He and Matthews experimented with a vast range of fetishes and perversions; she desperately wanted to find something that gave her the same level of satisfaction that she had felt when she cut into that first body. Nothing even came close and after less than a year together the couple split.

As time went by, the thrill of cutting into a long dead, cold body faded more quickly that she could ever have imagined. Like a drug addict, she realized that she needed a more powerful high, a more intense hit, if she was ever going to re-create that first beautiful moment. She would need to witness the moment of death itself.

She began seeking out snuff movies – an extreme form of pornographic film in which the performers are allegedly killed on camera. Matthews soon learned that such films were little more than an urban legend and, a few poorly made fakes aside, did not exist. The closest she came to true snuff were dozens of so-called 'crush' videos in which small animals were tortured and killed on film.

Her favourite began with a close-up of a guinea pig lying spread-eagled on the floor, each of its tiny legs fastened in place by sticky tape. The camera slowly pulled back to show a woman, seen only from the knees down, pacing around the stricken creature in bright red stilettos. Her voice was soft and low: 'You are my victim. Are you frightened, little man? You know that your destiny is under my heels . . .' Squeals of pain rang out as the sharp point of one stiletto was brought down on each leg in turn, shattering the bones. Next, the creature's back was crushed under a toe, cigarettes were stubbed out on its fur, and hip and shoulder bones were systematically trampled and broken, until, finally, the woman killed it by driving her heel through its skull. The torture lasted almost thirty minutes.

For Matthews the film was an interesting diversion, but she knew that she needed something involving real people, not just animals.

Once more, she discovered she was not alone. Her research soon threw up the fact that several murderers had recorded their acts on video, and she sought out the results. In the early 1980s Charles Ng and Leonard Lake videotaped their torture of the women they would later kill. Serial killers Paul Bernardo and Karla Homolka had videotaped some of their sex crimes in the early 1990s. Time and time again she was led to believe she had finally tracked down the footage, only to be disappointed.

The rise of the internet, combined with the war in Iraq, proved to be her saviour. Again and again she watched gruesome videos depicting actual murders and deaths, but still felt removed from the activity. Before too long, she realized she would have to get more involved herself.

Then she came across the case of Alexander Pichushkin, an unassuming supermarket worker from Russia. He would offer passers-by in a southern

Moscow park a shot of vodka or beer. Sometimes he offered to show them his dog's grave. Or he would invite them to a game of chess. Then, without any warning, he would bludgeon them to death with a hammer. He would record each murder by marking each one on the square of a chessboard. He had been caught after one of his intended victims escaped. Arrested, he instantly confessed to what he had done and claimed to have murdered at least forty-eight people.

In a televised confession after his arrest Pichushkin told his interviewer: 'For me, a life without murder is like a life without food for you. I felt like the father of all these people, since it was I who opened the door for them to another world. I never would have stopped, never. They saved a lot of lives by catching me. For me, the act of killing was a perpetual orgasm.'

There was little doubt about what Matthews had to do. Becoming a serial killer opened up a whole new world of sensation and pleasure. She learned that spontaneous orgasms at the moment of death were common among serial killers. Matthews desperately wanted to experience that for herself.

But how to choose her victims, how to avoid being caught? One obvious answer was to pursue pathology as her speciality. That would bring her into regular contact with police and other law enforcement authorities and keep her one step ahead of them and their techniques.

Having studied the work of others in the field, Matthews also decided that her victims had to be people that no one would care that much about, people no one would look too hard to find if they vanished. Deciding what to do with the bodies would be the most important part of her work. Without a body, it was unlikely that a murder case would ever begin and there would be nothing to point the finger of suspicion at her.

It was around this time that she bumped into her old boyfriend, James Gilbert, once more. He was depressed and contemplating a move abroad. He had threatened to expose a paedophile ring at the school where he had been teaching. He told Matthews — far too insistently, she thought — that he himself had not been involved in the abuse but that several of the guilty men had said they would name him if they were themselves exposed.

The couple briefly reconciled. But this did little to lift Gilbert out of his increasingly deep depression at the prospect of having to come forward and testify against the paedophile ring. And that's when Matthews realized he would be her perfect first victim.

Unable to provide her with sexual satisfaction in life, he would make amends in death.

Matthews planned the crime carefully. With access to corpses and cadavers all day long at work, she had perfected her technique long before she came to kill for the first time. And she instantly knew that her first time would not be her last.

In the space of thirty-six hours – the time that had elapsed since she had gone on the run to avoid being arrested – Jessica Matthews had seen it all. She had watched Collins rise first thing in the morning and then go out jogging. Collins had returned home half an hour later, via the paper shop, and cooked breakfast. At around eight fifteen she had climbed into her car to take her daughter to school. From there she had driven directly to the incident room. The routine had differed slightly the day before.

Since Matthews had disappeared, Collins had spent increasing amounts of her time interviewing family members, friends and colleagues in order to build up a picture of what the pathologist was really like, in an attempt to discover her hiding place.

Matthews wasn't at all concerned by any of this. She knew that there was no one out there who would be able to do anything to lead them to her. She was as safe as safe could be. And in the meantime she was free to continue stalking her prey. Eager to know every little thing about the woman who was pursuing her, she logged her daily movements, her clothes and even went as far as to learn what she ate for lunch.

Once she was convinced that Collins had seen her but it turned out to be a false alarm. The disguise that she had chosen was extremely effective. So much so that Collins could almost have run into her with a supermarket trolley and been none the wiser.

Matthews hadn't quite decided how she felt about Stacey Collins. She was by far the cleverest of the officers on the murder squad. She had seen her work her magic in previous cases and known what a thrill and challenge it would be to go up against her head to head.

She had to admit she was surprised when she got the early morning call when Collins had clearly begun to suspect her. She knew she had been taking an enormous chance when it came to meeting up with Collins for dinner and slipping little clues into the conversation. She knew too she had been taking an enormous chance when it came to helping Collins along, giving her the information about the possibility of the bodies being frozen and about the tattoo. But it had been worth it. The thrills she had felt as a result had been so completely and utterly delicious.

She already knew a great deal about Collins from the time they had spent working together and she had gathered a great deal of information since then, but she wanted to know much, much more. She wanted to know absolutely everything.

Two weeks earlier, long before Collins had had any suspicions about her, Matthews had applied for a birth certificate in Collins's own name. The document had arrived in the post after a few days and had made fascinating reading.

Matthews made her way to the branch of Mail Boxes Etc. where her post was being forwarded.

There were several envelopes there but the one that caught her eye was thin and white and had no stamp. She picked it up with a huge smile on her face. She ripped it open and pulled out a cheque from Stacey Collins for twenty pounds. Collins had responded to the fake charity mailing that Matthews had set up, just as she knew she would. Once she found out all about her father being confined to a wheelchair during their last dinner together, she knew exactly how to pluck at the woman's heartstrings. The cheque was a godsend. She now had Stacey's bank details, and her signature. It was time to move on to the next phase of her operation.

She picked up the phone and dialled a number.

'Hello, I just wanted to check the balance on my account.'

'Certainly. What's the account number?'

Matthews reeled it off from memory, followed by the branch sort code.

'Okay,' said the woman at the other end of the line, 'and for security I just need your date of birth, your full name and your mother's maiden name.'

'Of course. My date of birth is 15 August 1972. My full name is Stacey Elizabeth Collins and my mother's maiden name is Mason.'

Three more phone calls and thirty minutes on the internet later, Jessica Matthews had all the information on Detective Inspector Stacey Collins she would ever need. She already knew her home address but through a combination of knowing where to look, a few shady sources, social engineering and an awful lot of front she had managed to get the lot.

There was something extremely odd about watching Collins closely, intensely. There was a certain humour in knowing that Collins was working so hard to find someone who was so close to her the whole time.

She had not yet decided what she wanted to do. One thing was certain, however: the urge to kill was building up inside her once again. She knew only too well the depression that followed a murder. It was part of a cycle of extreme emotions that she had been through more times than she could count. There was only one way for her to feel completely normal again. She would have to find another victim, commit another murder.

23

On a bench in a quiet corner of Gladstone Park, Sophie Collins looked at the display on her mobile phone briefly before tucking it back into her bag.

'Who is it?' asked Jack.

'Mum.'

'Shouldn't you take it, just in case she gets suspicious?'

'I don't want to talk to her.'

'Are you sure?'

Sophie nodded. 'I've got nothing to say to her.'

'She is your mother, you know.'

'That's what everyone says. But that's not the point. You can't force your children to love you; you have to earn it. If you break the contract, if you don't do a good-enough job, then you risk losing that love. And that's what she's doing. And the worst part is she doesn't even seem to care.'

Sophie's face was screwed up tightly as she fought against the tears that were welling up in the corners of her eyes. But it was a battle she was always going to lose and within a few seconds she had begun sobbing uncontrollably.

'Come here.'

Jack held out his arms and Sophie melted into him.

It felt good to be wrapped up in his strong embrace. Once more she felt protected, as if nothing bad could ever happen to her when Jack was around.

'You know what I wish,' she said softly, still sobbing, 'I wish I could live with you. I wish I could stay with you all the time.'

'So do I, love, so do I.'

From her vantage point in the bushes a few yards back from the bench, Jessica Matthews saw the embrace too. Only to her it looked like anything but the loving and caring embrace it actually was. The man with the young girl was no better than the other perverts she had spent so long tracking down.

When she peered into the soul of the man in the park, she saw nothing but evil. She saw nothing but the face of a man who deserved to die. His body language spoke volumes, as did his choice of location. His kind always wanted to get together in secluded areas of parks, away from prying eyes, away from anyone who might go for help.

His posture and position said that he was concerned that they might be being watched, that he was not relaxed, that he was constantly on the lookout for trouble. It would not help him. Matthews had learned her art from the best. She could walk across a tiled floor in stilettos and still not make a sound.

She knew exactly the sort of man who preyed on those kinds of emotions: the sort who could spot girls with that sort of vulnerability a mile off and home in on them like a missile; the sort who knew the right words and phrases to use to get them to open up; the sort who would seem to be everything the girl was looking for, only to vanish and then leave them hurt and embittered.

And she knew exactly what she had to do in order to stop it.

It took a few more minutes for the sobbing to subside before Jack Stanley lifted one of his arms in order to look at his watch.

'Oh God, not yet, please not yet,' moaned Sophie.

'I'm sorry, love. If we don't leave now she's going to be suspicious. And that might mean the end of all these meetings. You don't want that. I certainly don't want that.'

Sophie was reluctant to let go. She held on to her father more tightly than ever for a few moments and then relaxed and leaned back. The pair smiled at each other, then Jack stood up, took her small hand in his and started walking towards the gate on the edge of the park.

'So when am I going to see you again?'

'Won't be until next week now.'

'Next week? How come?'

'Oh come on, Sophie, don't make me feel bad about it. For one thing I have to make a living. For another if we keep doing this too often someone is bound to spot us or get suspicious. I mean, suppose all those rumours flying around the school about you having an older boyfriend get back to your mum?'

'They won't. And even if they do she'd never

believe it. She knows I'm not interested in boys.'

'And long may it stay that way.'

'Well, there is this one boy at school.'

'Tell me his name so I can kill him.'

'He's really cool. He's in a band.'

'No way, absolutely no way. Just forget it. No musicians. Not now, not ever.'

'What's wrong with musicians?'

'You'll find out. And don't think you're going to be bringing anyone back to my house. Not unless you want them leaving in a wooden box.'

'What about bringing back some of my girl-friends?'

'Oh, I'd have no problem with that.'

'I bet you wouldn't, you dirty old man. That's what you are you know, a dirty old man.'

Sophie smiled and snuggled into the hook of Jack's shoulder as they reached the gate. He pulled her towards him and gave her a little squeeze before leaving her to open it. Then, all of a sudden, he made a quick movement and let out a cry of alarm.

'Dad, what is it?'

As Sophie watched in horror, Jack collapsed to one knee, his hand clutching at his chest.

'Oh my God, Dad, Dad, are you all right?'

Sophie was convinced Jack was having a heart attack or maybe a stroke. She had studied first aid at school and knew she had only minutes to react. She racked her brain to try to remember what she knew. She had to raise his legs, but nothing seemed to happen. There was nothing to put them on, no way of getting them above his chest.

She closed her eyes, forcing back the tears. What else? There was no need to check his breathing: she could hear him gasping.

Sophie was still wondering what to do when she saw movement for the first time just behind where Jack was lying. Until then her entire focus had been on her father, but now she realized that there was someone else there too.

Any thoughts that someone might be there to help were dashed instantly when she saw the deranged face of Jessica Matthews bearing down on her. In her hands she held a syringe and a taser gun.

Matthew's mind was racing. This wasn't some pervert; this was Sophie's father. The man she thought was no longer around. Collins had lied to her and she had not realized it.

The woman stepped over Jack's convulsing body and advanced on her. Sophie Collins opened her mouth and screamed.

24

Stacey Collins was totally lost in the world of Jessica Matthews. She was rereading every statement and interview with anyone who had ever known Matthews in an effort to get inside her mind, to understand her better than anyone in the hope of finding the clue that would assist in tracking her down.

Dr Jacques Bernard had been very clear about criminals, and psychopaths in particular, using established patterns of behaviour. They would do everything for a reason. There would be conscious decisions behind every seemingly minor detail. Nothing would be a coincidence, nothing would be without thought. Dumping a body down a quiet country lane said more than wanting to hide it for a while; it would speak of a place known as a child or in the past. More often than not there would be strong and powerful associations of time and place.

Collins scanned the pages again and again. There had to be something she was missing, something she was not picking up on. There had to be a clue to exactly where Matthews might be hiding, where she might have carried out the killings. Matthews needed somewhere where she could work in absolute privacy, somewhere the smell and sight of blood would not cause alarm, somewhere with access to a cold-storage facility.

Then there was the question of the heads. They had not been found and it was all too likely that Matthews had kept them as trophies. She needed to know where they were.

Her eyes danced across the pages as she flicked through them. She was concentrating so hard that at first she did not even notice that the phone on her desk was ringing. It was only when one of the DCs on night duty called out her name and said he was putting a call through that she picked it up immediately.

It was after seven and the rest of the day team had already left for the evening, leaving only Collins and a couple of DCs on night duty to man the office.

The voice on the other end of the line was slurred and quiet. At first she thought there was some kind of fault on the phone but then all at once something in the voice became eerily familiar.

'Jack?'

The sound he made in reply was somewhere between a gurgle and a splutter. She felt her hackles rising immediately. She turned her face away from her colleagues and whispered into the receiver, her voice taut with anger.

'You're drunk. You fucking idiot, I can't believe you're calling me at work, let alone doing it when you're pissed up. Is this some kind of a joke?'

'Sophie . . .' he gasped.

'Just forget about her, Jack, just forget you ever had a daughter. It's over. It was a mistake to ever introduce her to you.'

'You don't understand . . . not drunk. Sophie . . . gone.'

This time his voice was a little clearer, a little louder. His breathing was hard and laboured. And now Stacey wasn't quite so sure that he was drunk after all.

'What the hell's going on?'

She could hear him gulping in great big breaths, trying to steady himself.

In the call box on the edge of the park, Jack braced himself against the side of the booth. He had to make her understand, but he was so tired. So much had happened and his mind was still spinning with the effort of it all.

That woman, that mad crazy woman, whoever she was, had appeared out of nowhere and jumped towards him. She had caught him by surprise but it had taken only a few seconds for him to compose himself. His rule about not hitting women did not apply to those who were in the process of attacking him. This in particular was a special case. As soon as he saw her, he knew she was there to kill him. She had clearly been sent by the Albanian gang to assassinate him. He had heard rumours about such gangs using women for these tasks and now he was going to experience it first-hand.

He could not hesitate, he could not delay. The natural reluctance to fight with a member of the opposite sex had to be overcome if he was going to survive this. There was another reason to fight too. Experience had taught him that gangs from this part of the world had none of the usual reluctance when it came to killing women and children. Their philosophy was one of leaving no eyewitnesses. If he did not survive this encounter, then Sophie too would be dead.

He had drawn back his right arm, ready to deliver a blow to her head, when he suddenly felt like a balloon with a leak. It was as if all the air, all the energy, was seeping out of him.

There had been a flash in her hands and all too late Stanley realized that she was holding a stun gun. The voltage shot through his body and felt like ... his body froze and his mind went numb. He started to fall to the ground. He realized he had been tasered. As he lay there, eyes open and unable to move, the woman advanced on him. He felt a pin prick of pain in the side of his arm. Sophie's screams were in the background. She had injected him.

He saw the woman, her mad eyes flashing with excitement. Sophie started screaming, but it seemed as though time had slowed down. Her scream was of a much lower and deeper pitch than usual. It was like a record being played at the wrong speed. Time seemed to be dragging.

The woman was saying something, but he couldn't

really hear her words properly at all. All the strength was seeping out of him. As he started to lose consciousness he saw for the first time the syringe in the woman's hand. He knew he had been injected with something but he had no idea what. And then everything faded to black . . .

When Stanley came round he had no idea how much time had passed. He was certain his eyes were open but he could not see anything. It was as if he was in the dark. Then, slowly, his eyes began to adjust. Sophie and the woman were nowhere to be seen. His mobile phone had been taken along with his wallet. All he had left were just a few coins in his pocket.

When he tried to stand up his legs collapsed as though they were made of rubber. He felt around him and soon realized he was still in the park, behind a bench. He held on to the back of it and tried to drag himself to his feet. The effort made him sweat. Whatever had been injected into him was still affecting him deeply. But none of that mattered. He knew what he had to do. He had to find Sophie. And fast.

Who had the woman been, what had she wanted? At first he was certain that she had been after him. He assumed that she was an assassin hired by the Albanian gang. He had been wrong.

He had expected to wake up in the back of some van, blindfolded and off to meet his death. Instead Sophie had been taken away.

What was it the woman had called him? A pervert?

Then Sophie had started screaming over and over: Dad, Dad, Dad. In the past he had always enjoyed hearing her use that word. It had meant so much to him, it had been so moving, but this time the anguish in her voice made it painful to hear.

He made his way, limping, staggering, towards the gate of the park and the nearest exit.

His body felt as if it did not belong to him; he could feel his legs wobbling beneath him. It was like being completely drunk, only his mind was fully functioning – it was just his body that would not respond in the way he wanted it to.

He tried to flag down a car. When he spoke his mouth and lips were numb, like having had an injection at the dentist. His arms flailed around uselessly. A couple of cars slowed down, but as soon as they heard him speak and saw his jerky, uncoordinated movements, they decided he was a drunk and wouldn't risk opening their doors to him.

Jack was close to giving up when he spotted the phone box on the other side of the street. He staggered across, narrowly avoiding being struck by a speeding vehicle, to reach it.

Without his mobile he had no idea of Stacey's mobile number and could not call her on that. Like most people of his age, he had lost the ability to remember numbers long ago. Most of the time he could not even remember his own number without writing it down.

His first call to directory inquiries got the number

of the main police station in her area. He hoped to be able to leave an urgent message for her but was surprised to get through directly.

Now he was having trouble speaking but somehow he had to force her to understand the urgency of the situation.

'It's Sophie,' he said, his voice becoming clear at last. 'Someone's taken her.'

Less than three minutes later Stacey Collins and two other officers were in a patrol car, blues and twos blazing, as they made their way to the park. Other uniformed teams were already on their way.

She knew exactly what had happened. She asked Jack for a description of his attacker and knew immediately that Jessica Matthews was behind the abduction – but what on earth did she want with Sophie?

By the time she arrived at the park Jack had almost fully recovered from his drug ordeal; he was now suffering from the guilt that had descended on him for failing to protect Sophie.

She instructed him to say nothing. As far as the officers at the scene were concerned, Stanley was merely an eyewitness. He had seen the girl being taken away and was able to describe the woman. No one knew it was his daughter. He was just a man in the wrong place at the wrong time. The girl had clearly been taken against her will.

'What the hell's going on, Stacey? Who was that woman?'

Jack Stanley's face was twisted with pain and distress.

'She's the killer we've been looking for.'

'Why did she take Sophie?'

'To get to me.'

'Jesus.'

The irony of the situation did not escape her. She had wanted Sophie to stop seeing Jack because of the problems it would cause for her at work, but also because it was too dangerous, because she was worried about him being attacked while Sophie was around. She did not want her daughter to get hurt because of something Jack had done. Rival gangs might try to kidnap or snatch Sophie in order to extract leverage from Jack.

But here they were, and the fact was it was her fault that Sophie had been taken; it was her actions that had led to her daughter's being put into jeopardy.

She called Anderson. 'She's taken Sophie, my daughter.'

'Who has?'

'Jessica Matthews. She's taken my daughter. I don't know where.'

'Why? Why would she do that? It doesn't make any sense. It doesn't follow any of the patterns of behaviour that we've experienced so far.'

'For fuck's sake, sir. We're talking about a woman who kills people by taking out their organs while they're still awake, who gets off on dead bodies big time, who pretends to be normal during her daily working life. What the hell makes you think she's going to be rational? She's a fucking lunatic. Nothing she does makes any sense. Why would it? All I know is that she's got my daughter and I have to get her back. She just likes killing people. It makes her happy. There's nothing more to it than that.

'Of course it doesn't make sense. It isn't supposed to make sense. She had bodies safely hidden away for years and no one knew anything about what she had been getting up to. And then she exposes herself by dumping them in a car in the middle of town, inviting all the police and public attention that would never have existed if she hadn't done so. She keeps their heads and does God knows what to their internal organs. And all the time she's playing at being the competent professional with the very people who are trying to track her down. Why? Because she's a fucking nutter. No matter how much fancy psycho babble you want to attach to it, that's what it comes down to. The woman is insane, so why should anything she does make any sense?'

'Why would she go after your daughter?'

'I don't know. I don't care why. That's not important. We just need to do something. I need to get my little girl back.'

'Come on, Collins. I need you to focus. I need you to do your job. That's the only way we're going to get anywhere with this.'

Collins bit her lip and counted to five. 'I guess she

sees this as personal. She blames me for exposing her. I guess I was the one who realized she was behind the killings. Now that the net is closing in, she's trying to get revenge.'

Anderson's face became deadly serious. 'Stacey, I don't know if I can allow you to work this case. I mean, you must know what the possibilities are. Protocol demands that you be taken off all duties. This is a very difficult situation.'

'For fuck's sake, this is my daughter we're talking about. You don't really expect me to sit around on my arse all day and do nothing. And if you don't let me work this case officially, you know that I'll just go off and continue on my own. I have plenty of friends in the department who'll pass information on.'

Anderson shook his head. 'It doesn't work like that.'

'What the fuck are you talking about?' said Collins, exploding in fury. 'You told me that no one was better placed to handle this case than me. You said that my special relationship with Matthews was the reason that this case was going to get solved. And now you're telling me that none of that matters – that I should just abandon the case.'

'This changes everything,' said Anderson. 'When I said those things you weren't personally involved the way you are now. It's your own daughter that's been taken. How can anyone else on your team trust you to get their back, to look out for them, if you're looking out for her all the time?'

'Look, sir, we know the timescale here. We know it isn't very long. If this follows the same pattern as that of the police officer she snatched, we only have a matter of hours to track her down.'

'But, Collins, we don't know if her intentions are the same. Sophie doesn't fit in with her usual pattern at all. For one thing she's a child and for another she's female.'

'But nothing fits in with the pattern any more. The pattern has completely changed. Chadwick wasn't a paedophile; he was probably someone who just pissed her off. Detective Sergeant O'Neill wasn't a paedophile, he was a serving police officer, and we know she would have checked his wallet and papers before she killed him, but that didn't put her off either.'

Collins shut her eyes. Immediately the ghastly pictures – of the bodies in the back of the car, the open ribcages, the marbled flesh, the tiny white maggots gathered around the neck where the head had been severed – came into her mind. Would that be how she would find Sophie?

'I think we've reached the point where she's so unstable that we can't rely on her to do anything that she has in the past. I think we have to assume the worst.'

Anderson sighed. He could see he wasn't going to win this argument. 'Is there anyone else you need to contact – Sophie's father for instance?'

'Don't worry,' she said softly. 'He already knows.'

'Are you sure you don't need some time to deal with this?'

'What I need is the chance to get out there as soon as possible. Just before I found out about all of this I had a lead I was working on. I think it might be something worth checking out.'

'Do you have any idea where she might have taken her? Are we any closer to knowing where the killings took place?'

'Right now we don't have squat.'

Rajid Khan felt as though his eyes were going to pop out of his head. He had been staring at his screen intently for the past four hours without a break and felt almost as though he and his screen had become one.

He was working a puzzle, a puzzle that he had no idea how to solve. How on earth was Jessica Matthews able to hook up to an instant message system but leave no trace of the ISP address she was using?

It was important work. An ISP could lead them to a computer, which in turn could lead them to the actual, physical, real-world address she had been using for her communications. This, the team had surmised, would likely be the same address that she had been using to murder her victims.

Rajid had tried a variety of techniques using similar versions of her screen name to try to re-create the same set of data he received whenever he attempted to run a trace on Matthews. If he could produce a similar result, he figured, it was likely he had stumbled upon a similar method of disguising the signal's origin. So far none of them had been successful.

He was working on a 24-inch widescreen monitor that gave him plenty of space in which to operate. The main box was to his right. In the lower-left-hand corner was a document file with a list of protocols that he had yet to try. Above that was a screen from the online role-playing game he was trying to keep an eye on. His character was mining rare ore from a distant planet in a dangerous Level 2 star system – a long and laborious process. He had set up a series of bots – automated programmes – which meant he could mine even while he was sleeping, but he had to watch out for pirates.

Rajid blinked twice when the message first appeared on his computer screen. Surely there had to be some kind of mistake? He checked his network protocols and the source of the connection. Both seemed legitimate.

His next thought was that one of his old hacker friends was playing a trick on him, getting him all wound up and trying to make him look like a bit of an idiot among the top brass at the police. They knew he had begun working there only because he had been caught vandalizing the local police website and, though he enjoyed the chance to crack codes, he couldn't shake the feeling of shock at finding himself sleeping with the enemy.

His fingers hovered over the keyboard as he worked out how to respond. He hit the return button on the instant message screen and his online identity – Geekking – appeared. He paused for a moment or two, trying to work out what to do next. He quickly decided that the direct approach would be best.

Somehow – he couldn't work out exactly how – they had managed to learn the screen name that he had been using during the last exchange he had been working on. Very clever, but not something he could appreciate at a time like this.

Geekking100: Fuck off, Ben, I'm busy

shygirl351: I'm disappointed in you, Rajid. I was always hearing how smart you were.

Geekking100: Mate, this isn't funny. All sorts of shit going on here.

shygirl351: I know, it can't be easy trying to work out how she blocked your trace on her lms.

Geekking100: How do you know about that?

shygirl351: Come on, Rajid, put two and two together. And when you do, you might want to run and get someone else. I'll give you exactly 45 seconds. Starting now.

Rajid sat staring at the words on the screen for a few more seconds before bolting up from his seat and rushing across the incident room towards the office of DCI Anderson. He pushed open the door without bothering to knock.

'Sir,' she's on my computer.'

'Doesn't anyone in this station know how to knock on a door?'

'She's on my computer, right now.'

'Who is?'

'Matthews.'

The two men arrived back at the screen just as the first sentence popped into view. Anderson immediately glanced through the conversation up until that point and decided on the next move. There was no time for specialist help. There was no time for anything. He sat Rajid back down and instructed him to type what he told him to in reply.

shygirl351: Time's up. Has the penny dropped?

Geekking100: Who is this?

shygirl351: Don't play the idiot, Rajid. It doesn't suit you.

Geekking100: What do you want?

shygirl351: To trade.

Geekking100: I don't understand

shygirl351: I've got the girl. What will you give me for her?

Geekking100: What do you want?

shygirl351: It's not fun if I make it too easy for you.

Geekking100: I don't follow.

shygirl351: You have to guess. And you get only one shot at it. Or Sophie Collins is dead. You have exactly twenty-four hours. Starting right now.

Anderson and Rajid looked at one another. Time was running out and the pressure was building. No one

377

seemed to have a clue where Matthews might have taken the child. And unless they found one soon, Collins would never see her daughter again.

25

Sophie Collins stared blankly out of the window of the fast moving car with dry eyes that she could not close even if she wanted to.

She was as still as a china doll. She couldn't even feel herself breathing. She was absolutely terrified. Deep down, part of her knew she had to remain calm if she was going to survive, but it was impossible. She was only thirteen. She couldn't deal with any of this.

She knew nothing about this woman who had attacked her and could think of only one reason why she had been taken. It had to be something to do with her father. It had to be something to do with his past. They were taking her to get to him.

Jack Stanley had been dying. That's how it had seemed. He had been on the ground, struggling to breathe. After that everything had gone so fast.

The woman seemed to react strangely when she realized that Jack was her father.

What on earth had she been thinking before? That he was her boyfriend? She had moved away from Jack and then come towards her. Sophie had tried to run but something sharp pierced the back of her leg and she fell to the ground. The woman picked her up, carried her to the car and then set off.

The more she thought about it, the more convinced she was that she was correct. The woman had taken her to get to Jack. Far better to kidnap his daughter to get him to bend to their will. She was determined to be as brave as she possibly could. She knew that her father would never let anything bad happen to her. He would be there to rescue her. He would make everything all right.

The drive seemed to last for ever. Eventually the car turned off the main road and travelled through a series of small villages before finally heading up a narrow wooded path to what looked like a farm complex and finally drawing to a halt.

Her body was frozen rigid in an unnatural position and she was starting to ache all over. She comforted herself with the thought that her suffering would not last much longer. Her dad would soon be there.

There was no need to use the winch.

For once Jessica Matthews had selected a victim who was small enough for her to carry to the make-shift operating theatre on her own. But for every plus there was always a minus.

Sophie Collins was by far the smallest person she had ever used her paralysing drug on. Matthews had only been able to estimate the correct dose for a child.

Sophie was still fully immobilized and Matthews worked quickly, laying her down on the stainless-steel table and fixing a series of stick-on monitors to her heart and head in order to check her vital signs. The drugs were dangerous in large doses and could easily stop the heart or prevent the lungs from filling up with air. It would be tragic if that were to happen with Sophie, she thought. Where would the fun be in that?

Sophie watched the woman move about in the room, examining various pieces of equipment, occasionally glancing at her. The woman had no idea that she was starting to get feeling back in her legs and arms. She had even been blinking. She waited until the woman had turned her back and was in the furthest part of the room before she slipped off the table, pulling the monitors from her body, and bolted for the door.

She had managed only a few steps when she felt something tighten around her throat. To her shock, she realized she was being choked. She twisted around and saw the woman with a piece of yellow nylon rope in her hand. The rope was knotted; she was tightening it to cut off Sophie's air supply. The woman's eyes were penetrating, cold-blooded steel.

Sophie struggled to breathe, pulling at the rope and asking the woman what she was doing. The woman was apparently determined to finish the job: she pulled Sophie down to her knees and increased the pressure against her neck, getting better leverage so the rope could not slip from her grasp. She was strong, but Sophie was fighting for her life; this knowledge gave her a shot of adrenalin that helped her to resist being placed in a more vulnerable position.

Determined to try anything that might help, Sophie kicked her attacker and attempted to ease the pressure of the rope, but this woman seemed to know what she was doing. In addition, she was strong, despite her size. She managed to avoid being thrown off and regained her advantage, never letting go of the rope. Using her full weight, she pulled and pulled.

Sophie did not give up easily. She dragged them both across the floor, trying to find something with which to hit out against this woman, but the rope was doing its work; everything around her started to go black. She passed out.

The girl had proved far more feisty and resourceful than she had imagined. She was truly her mother's daughter. But Matthews had still managed to prevail. She had never been concerned that the girl might actually escape but she had not been fully prepared for the attempt. However, if anything, the little escapade had added to the general excitement of what was going on that evening. Sophie's death would be an event like no other. It could eclipse everything that she had done up until now. Even Gilbert, her first. Even O'Neill.

Killing O'Neill had brought her a thrill like nothing she had ever known. She realized it was his very innocence that had proved such a boost to the sensations – the fact that he did not deserve to die.

And what could be more innocent than a child, a little child? Untouched, unsullied by the world. The thrill of taking the life of a child would, she imagined, be the greatest thrill of all. Killing without justification, without reason, without a care in the world. What could be better than that?

26

They knew who the killer was. They knew who her next victim was going to be. They knew in terrible detail exactly how she was going to die. A newly installed countdown clock on the wall of the incident room meant they knew exactly when she was going to die. The one thing they did not yet know was where on earth Jessica Matthews had taken Sophie Collins and just where she was planning to carry out her next murder.

Collins was feeling sick with worry and guilt and grief. The prophetic words of Tony Woods were now ringing in her ears. So far as Matthews was concerned, her campaign of violence had started out for noble reasons, but now, now that she had begun to run out of legitimate targets, she had widened her net. Now, in her eyes, everyone and anyone was guilty of something. No one was safe. Even little Sophie.

At some point in the past Collins and Matthews might have occupied the same moral high ground, but Matthews had since fallen from grace. The simple truth was that she liked killing for the sake of it. There was nothing more to it than that. And now that she had a real taste for it, nothing in the world was going to stop her. The only hope Collins had of getting her daughter back alive was to track her down. And fast. The clock was ticking and Sophie would be dead in less than sixteen hours.

The background research Collins had done showed that at the age of twenty-one Matthews had gained access to a sizeable trust fund, which was now all but depleted. As Matthews had always lived a relatively modest existence, the betting was that she had spent it on property. But where? They were back to looking for a needle in a haystack.

All around her the incident room was buzzing with activity as every last officer attached to the case followed up leads and reviewed case papers in a desperate effort to find a fresh lead.

Part of Collins felt it was wrong to be stuck inside – that she should be out and about, searching for her daughter. But where to start? The truth was, as awkward as it felt, the incident room was the best place for her to be. It was the best place to start looking for her daughter.

She shut her eyes against the increasing level of background noise in the room but immediately opened them again. The image that had burned itself into her mind at the beginning of the inquiry, the first time she had seen Chadwick's body, had returned with a vengeance.

But the headless, handless body, the gaping hole in its chest, its internal organs ripped out, the marbled flesh clinging to the ribs – now it all belonged to

Sophie. Knowing the fate that awaited her and not being there to help was the worst part of it. Her sweet darling little girl was going to be brutalized, reduced to something less than human. Turned from an adorable creature into a shocking carcass.

And then the same thought she had experienced when she first saw the bodies came flooding back to her: that they all looked so much like animal carcasses. And that's when it hit her.

She opened up a web browser on her computer and typed a few words into a search engine. It took several more attempts, with various combinations of words, before she finally found what she had been looking for.

The video was small and grainy but it took only a few minutes of viewing for Collins to begin to feel that her theory might have some validity. Everything was starting to fall into place; a possibility was slowly beginning to reveal itself.

'Tony, come here for a minute,' she called out. 'I need you to look at something.'

When Woods appeared and perched on the edge of her desk, she ran the video again.

'What is this?' asked Woods.

'Just watch it and tell me if it reminds you of anything.'

The first few seconds were completely black. Then a logo for a well-known animal rights group appeared on the screen. Woods raised a questioning eyebrow. 'Guv . . .'

'Just wait, Tony. I really need you to see this.'

The logo faded and the screen was filled with the image of a man, wearing bright yellow dungarees, white Wellington boots, a long white apron and a white hat, walking towards the back of a large, brightly lit room. There was no sound.

The tiles were the colour of sand and the walls seemed to be made of stainless steel. At the back of the room stood a huge metal contraption. The camera followed the man as he moved to one side of this contraption, where the head of a cow stuck out through a hole. He reached to one side and picked up a device that resembled a gun but for the fact it was connected by a flexible metal pipe to a machine on the wall. The man held the barrel of the gun against the forehead of the cow and pulled the trigger. The cow shook visibly.

'Ah Jesus! Why are we watching this?' gasped Woods.

'Please, Tony. Just bear with me.'

More men wearing similar costumes appeared and pressed buttons on the side of the contraption, which made it fall sideways, spilling the body of the cow on to a platform directly in front of it. Immediately, one of the men stepped forward and, using a long sharp knife, made a clean incision across the throat of the animal.

A torrent of blood poured out from the wound and the animal began twitching wildly. Every man on the team seemed to know his job off by heart. The blood washed over their shoes, and splashed on to their aprons and trousers, but none of them seemed to mind. It was clear that they had gone through this exact procedure many, many times.

While the man with the knife continued cutting his way through the neck, one of his colleagues moved to the rear of the animal, cut off the rear hooves and then attached two metal clamps to the rear legs. Another man removed the front hooves, while the remaining worker held up the head to make it easier for the first man to remove it completely.

As the head came away from the body, one of the workers reached up and grasped a bright blue box that was hanging down from the ceiling on a thick wire. There were buttons at the top and bottom of the device, and he pressed the uppermost one. Immediately the metal clamps began to rise up into the air, taking the cow with them. It rose higher and higher, until the remains of its rear legs were well above head height and the blood stump of its neck was swinging a foot or so above the ground.

The flow of blood had completely stopped; the blood that had spilled out over the tiles seemed to have drained away. Even the aprons and clothes the men were wearing showed little sign of what had happened just moments earlier.

The man who had been operating the clamp and crane now produced a knife of his own and made a deep slit from the centre of the cow's belly all the way down to the top of its ribcage. A cloud of steam seemed to hiss out from the wound, which the man, assisted by two of his co-workers, quickly pulled apart to make even wider. What appeared to be a shiny grey sack began to emerge from the wound, followed by masses of pink and grey coils. One of the men reached inside the animal's belly right up to his elbow and pulled out its internal organs, using a knife to cut away whatever parts remained. The animal's guts were lowered into a wheelbarrow and immediately taken away.

Collins paused the video. The frame showed one of the yellow-costumed men directly to one side of what remained of the cow. It was hanging upside down, legs splayed, empty inside but for the marbled flesh of the inside of its ribcage.

When Collins looked over at Woods, his mouth was open in shock.

'Before they cut them open,' said Collins, 'they use a special gun to stun the animals. It doesn't kill them. It's supposed to render the animal completely senseless so that when they cut its throat, it doesn't feel anything. The heart has to still be pumping when they cut the throat to prevent clots building up inside the animal's body. Death is from – '

Woods was ahead of her. 'Exsanguination.'

'Clearly a place like this is used to dealing with huge amounts of blood. Just look at how quickly it's all drained away. Now take a look at the device attached to the back legs. It's called a yoke. Sometimes they use clamps; sometimes they push metal hooks through the flesh of the calves. The yoke is the wrong shape to work on a human body, but it wouldn't take much to, say, hook a strong piece of wire around it and use that to raise it up. It would also explain how a woman of slightly less than average height and weight could manipulate full-grown men into the positions she needed in order to do this to them.'

'It would also explain the marks around the ankles,' said Woods.

Collins pointed at the computer screen. 'Then we have the removal of the internal organs. Yet another very strong parallel. Now the next stages are clearly different to anything that we've seen with our victims. From here the video goes on to show the animal being skinned and then being completely sawn in two to create two sides of beef. But do you know what happens after that has been done?'

Woods shrugged his shoulders. He was still taking in the details of what he had just seen. The similarities between the end result on the screen and the bodies they had found were remarkable. Truly terrifying.

'They place the sides of beef in cold storage,' said Collins flatly. 'Every slaughterhouse has a huge room just for that purpose. It all fits. It has to be what she's doing.'

'But there's no way anyone could carry out a murder in an abattoir. Too many witnesses, too many people around.'

Collins tapped the screen with her knuckles. 'Everything about the way the killings has been carried out suggests that she's been using a very similar set-up. Besides, the other alternative is that she could be operating absolutely anywhere in the country. At least this gives us somewhere to start. It's got to be better than nothing.'

'Well, you've convinced me, but I don't count. It's Anderson you're going to need to get on side.'

'Then let's get him over here to watch this video.'

Moments later, the video having played through once more, DCI Anderson's face twitched with confusion.

'I know it sounds crazy,' said Collins, 'but it really fits in with the evidence that we have so far. We know that Matthews needs a place that gives her the freedom to kill at her own pace. It would have to be somewhere where large quantities of blood would not cause suspicion and finally somewhere with access to cold-storage facilities. And right now it's the only possible lead that we've got.' Collins leaned forward and placed her palms flat on the desk. 'You yourself said that the killer was just as likely to be a butcher as they were to be someone with medical training. I think you were more right than any of us realized at the time.'

Anderson was nodding. 'You're right, it does fit. But it's unlikely to be anywhere that's being used on a regular basis. It would be too difficult to hide this kind of thing.

See if there's some kind of trade association. Get a list of all the slaughterhouses within a hundred-mile radius. Find out which ones are closest to the place where the bodies were dumped and let's pay them some surprise visits. Time is short and if anyone from this industry is involved, I don't want them having a head start.'

It turned out to be a far less daunting task than anyone on the team had expected. With the vast majority of Britain's farming community located well outside the capital, there were only a handful of slaughterhouses to be found unless you travelled deep into the Home Counties. Of those some dealt only with chickens, while others operated under religious guidelines and had little or no automated machinery. That left three premises: Anderson and Porter would visit one, Cooper and Hill another and Collins and Woods the third.

They drove in silence, Collins deep in thought and Woods unable to say anything useful.

They arrived at the abattoir on the edge of an industrial estate in Crawley just after 2 p.m. Collins glanced at her watch. They had only fourteen hours to find Sophie. She hoped to God they were not on a wild-goose chase.

The slaughterhouse was a large windowless building that sat on the edge of a field adjacent to a corrugated-metal structure where the animals were kept prior to being taken inside. Large gates to the left of the main entrance led to the loading bay, while a small door at the front led to a neatly furnished reception area.

'I don't know what I was expecting,' said Woods. 'But this wasn't it.'

'I know what you mean.'

But as soon as she stepped out of the car, Collins was immediately hit by a combination of sounds and smells that made her feel queasy.

Both officers heard the sounds of cattle coming from behind the building. Not the usual gentle mooing that you hear strolling down a country lane but a frantic, rapid kind. Collins had heard it once before, as a child, when she and her parents had gone to the country for the weekend and stopped off at a farm for some fresh produce. Right before the eyes of the horrified nine-year-old, one of the cows was attacked by some stray dogs. The sound the animal made at that moment was almost identical to what Collins was hearing right now. It was the sound of panic. The sound of terror.

All of a sudden Collins felt herself go slightly weak at the knees. It had been one thing watching the silent video and thinking about how it related to the case; it was quite another being in the midst of it all. Actually experiencing the screams and the smell of the blood and the flesh and the guts made it all too real. If she and the others didn't manage to find Sophie in time, the horrors that were taking place in the building in front of her would be almost identical to what her daughter would be going through. Seeing it up close and personal might be too much for Collins to bear.

'You all right, guv?' said Woods, placing a steadying hand on her shoulder. 'You're looking a little pale.'

Collins sucked in a silent breath. She needed to be strong. This visit to an abattoir might well provide the missing piece of the puzzle and lead them to Jessica Matthews. It might lead them to Sophie. And as long as there was a chance, she could not back down.

'I'm fine, Tony. Let's go.'

The manager of the plant, Ronald Hale, was a tall, affable man with the kind of rounded belly that showed he liked his food and his red meat in particular. To say he was taken aback to be visited by two detectives on a murder inquiry would have been the understatement of the year.

'I really think you're barking up the wrong tree if you're looking for anything like that here. We're at the upper end of the market. We supply the likes of Tesco and McDonald's. I don't think you'll find so much as a single wellington boot out of place, let alone some psychopathic serial killer on the loose.'

Collins looked around at the pens full of animals on their way to be slaughtered. All she could see was Sophie's face.

'This place is guarded round the clock,' continued Hale. 'The killing floor has to be washed clean at the end of each session, and that's a job that takes at least five men to do. There can't be any blood there first thing in the morning, there just can't. We're subject to random inspections every couple of days and the animals are inspected almost constantly. Believe me, if there was any way this place could be used to commit the perfect murder, I'd be a widow by now.'

'What about cold storage?'

'We're in the business of selling meat, not storing it. The longer we keep it here, the more the price goes down. The freezers we have are emptied out at the end of every day. There isn't room to keep anything here, and nowhere to keep anything where it wouldn't be seen. This isn't some Victorian mansion full of hidey holes and secret passages; everything is out in the open. This place is purely functional. Every slaughterhouse in the country is. But how far back do these killings go?'

'Maybe ten years.'

'And you think we've got a corner of our cold-storage room where no one has been for the best part of a decade? Do me a favour, love. You're barking mad if you think anything sticks around here for that long.'

Collins could feel the panic starting to rise up within her. Her phone had been in her pocket the whole time, set to maximum volume. If any of the other teams had discovered something at one of the other abattoirs, they would have called her by now.

This had been the strongest lead that they'd had and now it seemed to be coming to nothing. Time was running out, Collins had nowhere to turn. Her little girl was going to die and she was never, ever going to be able to forgive herself.

But, at the same time, the environment she was in just felt so right. The video and now the sights and sounds around her seemed to fit so well with what Matthews had been up to. There had to be some kind of a link, there had to be.

She turned to Hale. 'If not here, where else? Where else can you similar facilities?'

Hale shrugged. 'Nowhere. Not within a hundred miles of here anyway. Not any more.'

'What do you mean not any more?'

'Well, you're saying these killings go back at least ten years, right?'

'Yes, that's what we believe.'

'Ten, twenty years ago, there were a hell of a lot more abattoirs operating in the UK than there are today. The whole foot and mouth crisis and Mad Cow scare put paid to all that. There used to be loads of little premises all over the place, but they didn't have the money or the space for all the upgrades necessary to stay in business. They had to shut down.'

'How many places are we talking about?'

'Don't know off the top of my head, but I remember reading an article about it the other day that said there had been 2,500 slaughterhouses in operation at the start of the eighties and today there are fewer than 300 still around, with most of the big ones consolidations of the smaller ones.

'In fact, half the staff I've got here came from smaller places in the area that shut down in the past couple of decades. It's a skilled job, you see, but not one that many people want to train up for. It means if you're involved, you've pretty much got a job for life.'

Collins felt a rush of excitement, of hope, rushing through her. 'And do you think some of these places, the ones that have shut down, might still have their equipment in place?'

'I guess so,' said Hale. 'I don't think any of them will still be operating, but it's possible that all the stuff is still there. If you ask me, it would be a lot easier to commit a murder in a place like that than it would be in a place like this.'

Suddenly Collins realized something that had been staring her in the face all along. She headed for the door dialling a number on her phone at the same time.

'Mr Robertson? It's Detective Inspector Stacey Collins; I came to see you with my colleague yesterday.'

'Of course. Do you have any news of Jessica? Have you found her?'

'Not yet I'm afraid. But you may be able to help. You said something about a small holding you used to own. Can you tell me more about it?'

'That was years ago. We had to shut it all down. It's just a set of abandoned buildings now.'

'What kind of holding was it?'

'It was a small dairy farm. With an abattoir on the side.'

27

It was just starting to get dark as Woods and Collins pulled up on the outskirts of the farm complex, the buildings that the Robertsons had abandoned years ago and that, it now seemed, Jessica Matthews had bought and refurbished with the money she had inherited at the age of twenty-one.

The rest of the team were scattered around the country but Anderson had promised to get them to the location as quickly as possible, along with an armed team. He warned Collins in no uncertain terms not to make a move until he got there.

Woods switched off his lights the moment he turned up the main path and drove carefully and gingerly, navigating cautiously, until he parked the car close to a clump of trees. Keeping to the shadows, the two officers then made their way towards the main set of buildings on foot.

'You sure she's in here?'

'I'm certain of it. We need to get an idea of the lie of the land.'

'We're gonna need that,' said Woods. 'CO19 won't go into a building at this sort of time unless they know exactly what they're letting themselves in for. They'll do a raid at dawn if they have the element of surprise but something like this, they'd want to wait a couple of hours at least to scope out the lay of the land. They don't want to find themselves walking into a UK version of Waco.'

Collins nodded furiously. 'Then there's no time to wait for them. We can't leave it that long. Sophie might be dead way before that. We might have to go in ourselves and get this sorted.'

Woods grabbed Collins around the arm and gripped her tightly. 'Guv, you know I can't let you do that. We've got to wait. I'm every bit as concerned about Sophie as you are, but we have to do this right.'

At that same moment the ground around them was suddenly lit up. Another car was approaching, its headlights seemingly on full beam. They ducked behind a tree and watched in horror as the vehicle drew to a halt alongside their own.

'Shit,' breathed Collins. 'That could be her.'

'If it is, she's going to come out guns blazing. We'd better stay out of sight.'

The headlights died and the car's engine spluttered to a stop. Collins and Woods skulked back into the shadows of a small barn and tried to make themselves as small as possible. They heard the door of the car open and the crunch of boots on the path. The footsteps started to come towards them.

Then came the sound of a voice, whispering her name. A voice that was far too familiar.

'Stacey? Stacey, where are you?'

'Jack?'

Stacey stood up and saw Jack Stanley walking cautiously towards the complex of buildings. She motioned for him to move quickly towards her and stay out of sight. He reached her in a few moments.

'What the hell are you doing here?'

'I followed you. I've been following you for the last hour.'

'Why the fuck have you been doing that?'

'Why do you think? Because of Sophie of course. I really let her down earlier today. I need to make it up to her.'

Woods was shaking his head. He was about to say something when Collins put her finger to her lip and sent him out of earshot. Once he was gone, she let rip into Jack.

'You fucking idiot. That stunt just now, pulling up with your lights on and engine roaring – you've probably woken up ever fucker in a ten-mile radius, all because you want to play Rambo. You're a fucking idiot.

'This is what I do, Jack. This is my job. For once in your life you need to take a back seat and let me get on with things.'

'What, you and him?' He jerked a thumb in the general direction of Woods. 'Neither of you would last more than ten minutes in my firm and you know it. You've got the law on your side and all that bollocks, but I'm staying put because Sophie needs me and this is where I have to be.'

Collins shook her head again. 'Are you going to make me arrest you?'

'With what army? You don't have any cuffs on you. You never do. And I'm sure pretty boy doesn't have any either. Besides, I could flatten him with one hand behind my back. I know you haven't got any back-up coming. I know there isn't time. So just make the most of it – let's go and rescue our daughter as soon as we can. Which building do you think she's in?'

Collins sighed deeply, then lifted a finger and pointed towards a solid brick building at the far end of the complex.

Jessica Matthews was almost breathless with excitement as she moved out of the cold-storage area into the main room of the disused abattoir.

She had killed so many times, but this was going to be completely different. Completely new. Here was someone who had committed no sin, who had no evil inside them. This was the very definition of innocence. This death would be the most exquisite of all. The thrill would last a lifetime.

She moved towards the stainless-steel table where the body of the girl lay, her heels click-clacking against the tiles. Sophie Collins's eyes were wide open and her face was frozen in a grimace of terror. Matthews knew she could see her; she knew by now exactly where to stand in order to ensure her victims could see her perfectly, and she moved to that position now.

'Hello, Sophie. I must say, it's very nice to meet you at last. Your mum has told me so much about you. You're not quite what I expected. I thought you'd be a little taller, and for some reason in my mind's eye you were a bit chunky, you know, puppy fat. I don't know why. I was a little bit like that when I was your age so maybe I imagine all other girls are.'

Matthews walked slowly around the table, taking in every inch of Sophie's form, almost the way she did when she was carrying out an autopsy. 'It might not seem important, but it is to me. I want to be able to picture you in my mind in the future, so I need to see you as you really are.'

She moved to a side table, where the shiny silver instruments she would be using were waiting on a tray lined with dark green paper. There was an entero-tome, a skull chisel, rib cutters and a set of toothed forceps. She picked up a scalpel, then moved back to the table. She held it up level with her head, and, for a brief moment, thought she saw Sophie shudder. She moved back to the table and checked the flow of the paralysing agent. It was fine. Occasional muscle tremors were a known side effect. There was nothing to worry about.

She moved back to where Sophie lay and stood over her, desperately trying to control her breathing. 'My God,' she gasped. 'I'm so excited. I'd better calm down. This next part is a bit delicate and, believe me, you really don't want me to mess it up. Not at all.'

She lowered the scalpel and, starting just below the base of Sophie's neck, began to cut away the material of her t-shirt, exposing her naked flesh.

'You've got lovely skin, Sophie,' she said admiringly. 'It's so frustrating, no matter what you do to try to look after it, it wrinkles up like a prune. All the elasticity goes. It's tragic really. Of course, that's not something you're going to have to worry about. You lucky thing. You lucky, lucky thing.'

Deep inside her head, Sophie Collins was screaming as loudly as she could. It was almost deafening. She knew that no sound was coming out but she was convinced that if she could just scream loud enough that perhaps something would give.

It was all she could do; it was her only option. Every other chance of escape had gone. It was as if she were trapped underwater or frozen in a block of ice. She was completely immobilized and this crazy woman was going to do whatever she wanted to her.

When the woman had lowered the scalpel, Sophie had felt the pressure on her chest and was convinced that she was about to be cut open. It was only when she felt the cold air on her tummy that she knew it was her clothes that had been cut. Her relief was short lived. What was about to happen was inevitable.

All she could think about was ... not her mother, not her grandparents, but her father. Seeing him collapse on the grass, hand clutched to his chest in agony ... all she could think about was that he was somehow being taken away from her. She had felt as though her whole world was collapsing around her. Now, more than anything, she wanted him to be here. She wanted to know that he was all right. She wanted to see him one last time.

Jessica Matthews finished lining up the last of the instruments she planned to use for the living autopsy, an antique bone saw that held real sentimental value. It was the saw she had used on James Gilbert and on every killing she had committed since.

Almost no one used hand saws any more. They were considered slow and cumbersome. A vibrating saw was much faster and far more efficient, but Jessica liked the tactile sensation of knowing whether she was cutting through bone or flesh or sinew. The vibrating saw made them all feel the same. The hand saw let her experience each different texture in a way that was simply without comparison.

She turned back to Sophie, who was still immobilized. She was ready to begin but something was nagging at the back of her neck. Something was missing. Then it suddenly came to her. This was such a special occasion, such a once in a lifetime event, that the others really should be allowed to share it.

She moved back to Sophie, leaning low over her body and smiling down into her frozen face. 'I have a special treat for you. One that nobody else in here has ever had. I really hope you like it. I have some people here that I want you to meet. Don't go away. Wait right there.'

Sophie had nowhere to look but up, right into the lights in the ceiling. She had seen Jessica Matthews smile at her own joke – don't go away – before vanishing from view. She could only wait and wonder who else was there, who else was about to witness her demise.

She heard footsteps approaching, but this time they were accompanied by the sound of scraping and squeaking, as if some kind of metal pole was being dragged along the ground. The sound got closer and closer and was accompanied by a gurgling, bubbling noise that Sophie could not place.

The sound got so close that Sophie was certain that, if she had been able to move, she would have been able to reach out with her right hand and touch whatever it was that had been dragged into the room.

Jessica's face reappeared above her own. It was still smiling but this time was sweaty with exertion. She was breathing hard. A tiny bead of sweat dripped into Sophie's open right eye. It stung like crazy but there was nothing she could do about it.

Matthews was taking deep breaths, clearly excited about something. Eventually she calmed down. 'Are you ready?' she said at last. Matthews put one hand on either side of Sophie's face and gently tilted her head to one side, so she was looking across the room rather than directly up at the ceiling. 'Here you are, Sophie: these are my friends.'

If Sophie could have screamed she would have. A metal shelving unit had been dragged within a couple of feet of the edge of the bed. She was looking directly at it. On each of the three shelves were several large glass jars. Each contained a human head that gently bounced and twisted in clear fluid.

'This is James; he's been a bit down lately, I think he's been feeling left out. Haven't you, James? Well, don't worry, I'll be spending some more time with you soon. I promise. This one is Raymond. He really wasn't very nice. He has been apologizing ever since, but he knows I'm still angry with him.' Matthews was standing by the shelf, lovingly stroking each jar in turn as she spoke about the remains inside.

'Now this one, this is Ed. He's got a really black heart.' She giggled. 'Somewhere!'

It took ten minutes for Matthews to finish her conversation with James and Raymond and Ed. When she was done she had a very satisfied look on her face. She moved the shelf back a little to give herself room to manoeuvre and then moved the table with the instruments closer so that she could have them within reaching distance.

'It's show time,' she said to no one in particular. Then, turning back to where the heads were: 'Now, I want everyone to pay attention. I may be asking questions afterwards.'

She checked the flow of rocuronium one last time and then picked up the scalpel once again. She pushed her hand flat on top of Sophie's chest, her thumb moving back and forth in the space between the girl's nipples, pushing down hard so that the little shoulder blades were flat against the table beneath. Eyes wide open, she pushed the point of the scalpel into the little indentation at the base of Sophie's neck. A tiny pool of red fluid began to gather.

A noise. The sound of rubber on wood, followed by a grunt. Someone had tried to kick open the door to the room but had found it far more sturdy than they had imagined.

They would try again but in the meantime Matthews had all the time she needed to prepare. She filled a spare syringe with a dose of rocuronium and decided to stick with the scalpel as her other weapon. She moved to the middle of the room, ready to face her enemy.

Now it sounded as though at least two people were trying to kick the door in together. It took three attempts before the hinges finally buckled. Stanley and Woods tumbled into the room, closely followed by Collins.

All three looked down at Sophie, blood from the wound in her neck spilling over the sides of her tiny body. Stanley stepped forward.

'You fucking bitch, what have you done to my little girl? I'll kill you.'

It happened so fast that Collins didn't even have

time to speak. Stanley's right hand moved across his body and swung up into the air, no longer empty, holding something dark and shiny. A gun. He levelled the weapon at Matthews, who stood staring at him impassively just two feet away. There was no way he was going to miss. There was no way she was going to survive.

'No, Jack,' gasped Collins. 'You can't shoot her. For God's sake. Do you want us all to go to prison?'

Stanley hesitated. He turned to face Collins, his face pleading to be allowed to go ahead, to get justice in his own way. He had only just opened his mouth to speak when a scream emerged from his lips instead. The gun fell to the floor and Stanley grasped his forearm, which now had a six-inch blood-filled gash down one side.

Matthews was moving forward, advancing on Collins and Woods, the syringe pointing forward like a dagger. She broke into a run. She slashed at Woods with the scalpel and he barely managed to get out of the way, holding up a hand to defend himself and receiving a deep laceration on his left palm for his trouble.

Collins saw her chance and dashed forward, but Matthews was too quick. She raised the syringe high and brought it down with all her might. Collins saw the point of the needle moving towards her at high speed, but she was moving too fast, her momentum would not let her stop, she could not get out of the way.

Yet, at the last second, Collins stepped to one side. As Matthews brought the syringe down, Collins reached out with both hands and pushed down on the crazed woman's arm. The syringe continued its arc, moving down and down, until it finally came to rest in the flesh of Matthews's own thigh.

She looked down at what she had done and then up at Collins. Matthews began to speak but her words were lost as her mouth seized up, her body froze and she collapsed to the ground. Paralysed.

Collins rushed over to Sophie. There seemed to be so much blood, and she couldn't stop it. She pressed down on the wound with her bare hands, desperately trying to staunch the flow.

'Tony, call an ambulance,' she gasped, fighting back tears. 'Hold on, Sophie. Please hold on. Please hold on. I'm here, Mummy's here. You just need to hold on.'

Jack Stanley staggered up to the table and leaned forward over Sophie 'She's not moving. What's wrong with her?'

'She's been paralysed. It's a special drug Matthews has been using. I don't know how long it will take to wear off.'

Stanley reached across and held one of Sophie's hands. Collins did the same.

A clatter of heavy boots on the tiled floor made them both look up. DCI Anderson and a dozen officers in full riot gear had burst into the room. Two men immediately set about securing Jessica

Matthews with plastic cuffs while Anderson took charge.

'Jesus Christ,' he said as his eyes reached the shelves containing the jars of heads. 'It's like something out of a fucking nightmare.' His eyes continued moving around the room until they reached something dark and shiny on the floor.

'Whose gun is that?'

There was silence in the room for a moment. Then Stanley looked up. 'She had it.' He nodded towards Matthews. 'I managed to get it off her and then she cut me with the scalpel and I dropped it.'

Anderson looked at Woods, who nodded, and then at Collins. 'That's what happened, sir,' she said.

Anderson stared at Stanley hard, seeing him properly for the first time. 'And who the hell are you?'

'I'm Sophie's father.'

Seemingly at the sound of her name, Sophie's eyes began to flicker. As the drug wore off, she turned her head from one side to the other, smiling at her mother, smiling at her father, and then passing out.

28

Three Months Later

Two massive lines of protestors lined the street outside the Old Bailey on the day Jessica Matthews was due to arrive for her first directions hearing. The crowd was split neatly into two opposing camps. The first hailed Matthews as a hero for taking direct action against the scourge of paedophiles and included the parents of children who had been raped and murdered by sex offenders. The second group was composed of those who believed Matthews was a dangerous, insane psychopath who would have killed anyone who got in her way and needed to be stopped at all costs.

As the van with its blacked-out windows and escort of five motorcycle officers arrived, cheers and boos erupted from the gathered masses.

'Bit of a circus, isn't it?' sniffed Woods, as he and Collins made their way towards the court building. 'Can't believe some people see her as a hero. Murder is murder. There's no justifying it.'

Collins nodded towards one group of protestors. 'There are banners down there demanding that the government bring back the death penalty. I guess those people think it's okay to kill people just so long as it's official.'

'Yeah, well, that's the kind of moral dilemma that helps to make the world go around,' said Woods with a smile.

The two officers went through the revolving doors of the court and flashed their warrant cards to the security officer on the desk before taking the stairs to the entrance of Court Number 1.

It was by far the most secure court in the building and necessarily so. It wasn't that anyone thought Matthews had any chance of escaping. Rather that one of her supporters would attempt to free her. Or someone else might kill her.

It had been three months since Matthews had been captured and this would be the first time Collins had set eyes on her since then. She had heard rumours about the kind of state that she was in but nothing had prepared her for the sight of Matthews, flanked by a dozen court security officers, in the perspex box that served as the holding pen for the accused.

At first Collins thought that Matthews had been shackled at the legs; it would have explained her shuffling, shambolic gate. The truth was it was simply how she was walking. Matthews seemed to have aged about fifty years in the past few months. Her hair had become grey and matted; the flesh around her face had become sallow and languid. She was stooped forward and appeared to be having trouble keeping her balance.

Collins gasped and she and Woods exchanged glances.

'She's putting it on, she's got to be,' said Collins.

'I don't think so,' said Woods. 'Maybe it's the guilt; the bad karma has finally got to her.'

'You and your bloody psychology, you think that's the answer to everything, don't you?'

Woods cocked his head to one side. 'Well, yes, that's what it's supposed to be: the answer to all the things that go down in the mind of a human. This is completely classic. It's an amazing transformation.'

'Well, I don't believe it for a second.'

'Come on, Stacey. Her actions were never exactly sane, were they? Cutting people open when they were alive, keeping the heads in jars and talking to them? None of it is the kind of stuff that normal people do. She was clearly pretty deranged to start off with. The strain of going on the run and being caught, not to mention three months in prison, were probably just enough to finish her off. It makes perfect sense to me.'

As the judge called out her name and asked her to stand, Matthews began sobbing softly, covering her face with her hands.

The judge spoke solemnly. 'I have this morning received this submission from the Crown Prosecution Service. Can I ask if the defence has been consulted about this?'

A tall thin man in a grey wig sitting on the bench opposite the judge stood up to speak. 'We have,

Your Honour, but, like yourself, only this morning. However, we have no objections. I find myself in full agreement with my learned friend about Ms Matthews's state of mind. She is clearly not competent to understand the charges against her or assist in her defence. This is very clear from the doctor's psychiatric evaluation.'

Collins's brow furrowed deeply. 'What the hell are they talking about?' she whispered. 'One minute the woman is a top forensic pathologist, holding down an important job, dealing with people day in and day out, getting involved in complex scientific and medical studies, and then they want to say that the next day she's a gibbering idiot? It's doesn't make any sense at all. What the fuck is the CPS playing at?'

The hearing lasted only a few more minutes before a shuffling, shaking Matthews was led back down to the cells. The decision had been made. There would be no trial, there would be no further charges. The case against her would proceed no further.

The two dozen journalists who had crammed themselves into the press bench shot up at the earliest opportunity and made their way out into the corridor in order to begin filing their stories. The case had been covered by tens of thousands of column inches ever since it had first been made public, and it seemed that neither the press nor the public could get enough of it. This latest development had provided a fantastic new twist that would ensure the story remained in the public eye for weeks to come.

'I don't believe this, Tony, they're going to fall for it. She's faking and they're going to fall for it.'

Woods shrugged. 'It's not like they're going to let her back out on the streets or anything like that. She's going to end up in Rampton or Broadmoor, somewhere like that, and she'll be there for the rest of her life. You've got to admit, it was always a possibility that they'd find her insane and end up sticking her in an institution. It's probably the best place for her.'

'You don't understand, Tony. It's not the best place if she's faking it. She knows what she's doing. You have to remember, I got to know this woman. She made a deliberate effort to befriend me in order to keep tabs on what was happening with the case. If she's made this much effort to get herself into a mental institution, it's because she's up to something. And I mean to find out exactly what.'

The two of them waited in the court until the barristers, solicitors and clerks had all left before making their own way out into the cavernous hallway. From there they walked along the corridor towards the staircase. They were one flight from the ground floor when Collins suddenly broke off.

'Where are you going, guv?'

'I need to talk to her.'

'But the precedent – '

'Fuck the precedent. I can't leave it like this, I just can't.

'It's out of our hands; you have to.'

'No, not this time.'

'Well, I don't want any part of it. You're on your own.'

'Fine. I'll meet you back at the car.'

'I need to speak to Jessica Matthews. I was the officer in charge of her case. I need to see if there is any further information she wants to divulge to us before they take her away.'

'I'm not sure I can do that, ma'am, especially with a verdict of unfit to stand trial.'

Collins sighed. 'You have to understand, sane or not, there are several other unsolved murders, some of which have involved very young children.' Woods headed towards the exit of the Old Bailey, but Collins moved into the back office and showed her identification to the guard, who blocked the way to the tunnel that led to the cells beneath the court house. 'She may be the only chance of catching the people responsible. I've got kids myself. I don't know if you have but there is no way I could rest until I knew I had done my best. I know it means bending the rules a bit, but rules are meant to be broken, especially if they help us to track down those who are guilty.'

The man bit his lip, deep in thought. 'Okay, but you've only got a few minutes. She's in Number 17.'

Collins hurried down the narrow staircase in case the officer changed his mind. She made her way along the line of cells, examining the numbers outside each door, until she reached the third from the end.

Collins pulled up the flap on the front of the door and peered inside. Matthews, her face seemingly still wet with tears, sat on the edge of the bed in the far corner. The cell had been especially stripped to ensure she would not be able to take her own life. The bed was a low concrete shelf covered in a thick rubber mattress. Aside from the narrow toilet – designed to prevent inmates from fitting their heads inside – and a tiny sink area, it was empty.

Matthews started to rock back and forth, as if dancing to the beat of an imaginary drum. Collins scrutinized her carefully. Up close she looked even more ragged, more wasted. And Collins didn't believe a single word of it.

'I know you're faking it,' Collins said softly.

Matthews did not appear to react; she simply kept up her steady rocking, back and forth, back and forth.

'I don't know what you think you're going to get out of it. Okay, so you won't be in prison but there's not much difference between that and a secure unit. And at least in prison you'd have had a whole load more privileges than you're going to have in a secure hospital.'

Matthews continued to rock back and forth. Collins stared at her intently.

'There's nothing wrong with you. You're just playing the system. The way you always have done. It's what you do best and you think it's going to get you somewhere, but let me tell you something.

You're wrong. This case may be over but I'll be keeping my eye on you.

'You think you can get away with almost killing my daughter? You've scared her for life. And let me tell you something, you picked the wrong target. You made a big mistake when you took me on and I won't ever let you forget it.

'Mark my words: I'll be watching, and if I get one more shred of evidence, if we find one more body, if I get one hint that you're faking all this, I'll come down on you like a ton of bricks.'

Sophie had spent more than two weeks in hospital after the attack. The doctors told her mother that, although the physical scars to her chest and torso would eventually heal, the psychological scars that she suffered might never go away. Ever since she had beome quiet and withdrawn. More than ever she craved the company of her father. Having been there, having been injected with the same drug as her, she believed that he understood the way she felt and the ordeal she had been through better than anybody else in the whole world. All of Stacey's attempts to keep the two of them apart, to improve her relationship with her daughter, seemed to have backfired on her. Now they were further apart than ever.

It had not been an easy ride for Stanley either. He had been arrested on suspicion of carrying out the murder of Danny Thompson. He had, incredibly, been released after a lack of evidence – typical in his kind of case. Sophie refused to believe a word of it of course, dismissing the whole thing as a police conspiracy. She went further and cited it as further evidence of her mother trying to drive a wedge between father and daughter because of her jealousy.

Collins was breathing hard now. During the whole of her rant, Matthews had not reacted in the slightest. Even the rhythm of her rocking back and forth, back and forth, had not changed at all. It was almost as if Collins was not even there. She might just as well have been talking to a brick wall.

Perhaps Woods had been right after all. Perhaps Matthews had finally lost her mind. Perhaps the horror of what she had been involved in for the past decade, the horror of what she had experienced as a young child, had finally caught up with her. Perhaps, Collins thought, she did deserve some small element of sympathy after all.

Collins sighed deeply, lowered the flap and began to walk away. She managed only two steps before a distinctive voice called out from behind her.

'I haven't finished with you yet, Stacey Collins, or with that little brat of yours.'

Collins rushed back, snapped open the flap and peered inside. Matthews did not appear to have moved from her previous position. Even her rhythm was identical to what it had been before. But this time, as Collins looked in on her, Matthews very slowly, ever so slowly, turned her head and stared directly at her.

The eyes were blank; the expression was that of a face that gave nothing away – no emotion, no depth, no understanding. But Collins knew it was a mask. She knew that Matthews was just as dangerous as ever. Whatever game the killer was playing, Collins did not understand it. But she would be forever looking over her shoulder.

Epilogue

The officers from SOCA and the DPS, along with Commander Patterson, DCS Higgins and DCI Anderson, had been summoned together to discuss the future of DI Collins in light of the revelations about Jack Stanley and her daughter.

The corner office on the twelfth floor of New Scotland Yard was nicely shaded from the sun and comfortably furnished. The men who entered said nothing as they took their seats around the large rectangular table in the centre. They were all too aware that a major decision had to be made and none of them were in the mood for smiling.

'I don't think any of us can underestimate the seriousness of this situation,' said Higgins solemnly after they had all sat down. 'On the one hand we have an officer who identified and brought to justice one of the most dangerous serial killers we have ever come across. At the same time, we have someone who has flagrantly disregarded the rules and regulations and put God only knows how many lives at risk because of her relationship with a hugely important figure in the London underworld.'

The other officers around the table nodded slowly.

None of them could have expressed it better, and none of them relished having to make a decision about the best way to move forward.

Each man spoke in turn. Higgins reminded everyone that, although Collins was undoubtedly a maverick, she always got results. They had, as yet, no evidence that she had done anything illegal in her relationship with Jack Stanley, though she had in fact lied under oath.

DCI Neil Barker leaned forward. 'You can't dismiss that element of it. It's an absolute offence. Perjury is perjury.'

Patterson shook his head. 'But this kind of lie isn't one that's going to lead us to press criminal charges and that only leaves a disciplinary matter. The question is whether we kick her off the force, suspend her or do nothing. We can't have one law for those we prosecute and another for those who work among us. The same laws have to apply to everyone. There are mitigating factors, for sure, and we can take those into consideration, along with her track record, but that doesn't change the facts.'

'Well, doing nothing clearly isn't an option,' said Anderson. 'That would give the wrong signal to dozens of other officers out there who might be in similar situations. We need to make a stand that says that this kind of behaviour will not be tolerated by anyone on our staff, no matter how successful or able an officer they may be.'

'Then we are agreed on one thing,' said Higgins.

'That we must do something. Now the next question to be resolved is exactly what that thing should be. Who wants to begin?'

The meeting lasted for another two hours, and when it was over the men emerged mentally exhausted. They had debated and discussed every possible angle and every possible outcome. The final decision was one that nobody was entirely happy with, but was the one they felt they could best live with under the circumstances.

Collins was summoned into the room; she sat down in a vacant chair at the far end of the table.

DCS Higgins shuffled a sheaf of papers in his hands, cleared his throat and began.

'It has not been an easy decision but we have decided that it is in the best interests of everyone working in the division at the moment if you are suspended on full pay for the period of our internal investigation.'

'You've got to be kidding me,' gasped Collins. 'I haven't done anything wrong.'

'And if that is the case then you know you'll be welcomed back into your job with open arms. But, until then, it's best if you keep as low a profile as possible. And, to put it quite simply, it's going to be far easier for you to do that when you're at home than when you're in the office.'

Collins looked around at the long faces in the room around her. 'And that's what you've decided.

You've kept me waiting out there for all this time to tell me this.'

'That's the decision of the disciplinary board, yes.'

Collins rose. Her face did not betray a hint of emotion and she walked out of the room and closed the door behind her.

Twenty minutes later she was parking her BMW outside the house and walking inside with a smile on her face. It had been a difficult few weeks with the decision of the committee hanging over her. It was perfectly possible that they might have suspended her without pay or even ejected her from the force. Instead she had been placed on what was often referred to as 'gardening leave'. Time on full pay at home. It was like an extended holiday.

There was a definite spring in Stacey's step as she walked up the front path towards the door. Of all the things that could have happened, this was far from being the worst of them. It would give her proper time to spend with Sophie for the first time in months. It would mean she could be there for her every evening, every morning. She would even be around to pick her up from school and to attend every show, every recital, every performance.

For the next few months at least, Stacey Collins would be a proper mother.

She stepped in through the door and called out Sophie's name. When there was no reply, she made her way into the kitchen to put the kettle on. It was there that she saw the note, propped up in the middle of the table with her name on it in Sophie's distinctive handwriting.

She did not need to open it right away. She knew the contents would be painful. Instead of the kettle, she opened the freezer and made herself a vodka and tonic with plenty of ice and fresh lime. She then sat down at the table, opened the letter and began to read.

Dear Mum,

I do love you. It's important for you to know that. I know you have always tried to do your best for me and worked hard to give me the best possible start in life, but I truly believe that if I am going to be all I can be, that simply isn't enough.

We may not always agree about everything but I have never resented any decision you have made about my life. Until now. You have known for years how much I have longed to have my father in my life. The cruellest thing you have ever done to me is to deny his existence. The second cruellest was to introduce me to him and then snatch him away just as I was getting to know him.

The events of the past few months have brought my father and me closer than I would have ever thought possible. I know you came to rescue me, but in many ways you were simply doing your job, the same as the other officers who were there. To see my father there too was something different, an expression of true love. It moved me almost to tears.

The heartbreak I felt when that woman first jumped out and injected Dad with that drug, when I thought he was dying from a heart attack, is almost indescribable. Because of your selfish actions I have already lost out on thirteen years of having a father. I have no desire to miss out on any more. The time we now share together is so precious that I want to make the most of it. I will always be your daughter, but I have always been his as well.

For all the above reasons, I am sure it will come as no surprise to you when I say that I have taken all my belongings and that from now on I am going to be living with my dad. Please do not try to fight this. I have looked into the law and, although I am still too young to make my own decisions, the courts will take my views into account. I will make it very clear where I want to be, make no mistake.

You have been a great mum but I know you have always struggled to balance life and work in order to spend the right amount of time with me. I'm hoping this will make things easier. For both of us.

Love
Sophie
x

Stacey Collins was still reading the note when the sound of a key turning in the front door made her spin around. The door flew open and Sophie, her face bright red and wet with tears, stormed in. She glanced briefly at her mother before stomping her way to her bedroom, slamming her door shut behind her.

It had all happened in an instant, leaving no time for Stacey to say a single word. She remained speechless as the tall, lean figure of Jack Stanley entered the hallway, looked over at her and smiled warmly.

It took only another second for Stacey to compose herself. 'What the hell have you done to her?' she demanded, a host of worst-case scenarios running through her mind. 'What the hell have you done to my daughter?'

Jack raised both his hands, palms outward, a gesture of peace. 'I brought her home. That's all I've done. This wasn't right. This wasn't what I wanted. Honestly, I had no idea what she had in mind when she came round. None of this was my idea.'

Stacey collapsed on the carpet, tears streaming down her face. She had never felt more distant from her daughter, from all the people in her life that really mattered.

Jack walked over and placed a hand on her shoulder. She shrugged it off with a grunt. 'Get out of here.'

'No.'

Stacey looked up, her eyes burning with rage. 'Get out of here,' she said again.

'I can't,' said Jack. 'I'm her father, but you're the one who brought her up. I want to be a part of her life, but I don't want to take over. I think we need to sit down, all three of us, and work out a way to go forward.'

Stacey placed her head in her hands. She felt exhausted. She didn't know how much more she could take. 'Maybe.'

'Besides,' continued Jack, 'Jesus Christ, my phone bill's gone through the fucking roof since she started coming round. At first I thought it was me she was there for but that only lasted a couple of days. Now she doesn't talk to me, just to her mates. I feel like I have to send her a text to make an appointment.

'I mean, I want to be a good dad, I want her to have her freedom, but I don't want her to take the piss. Trouble is, I don't know if she is or not. I don't know any of her friends, I don't know any of her teachers or anything. I don't know what's going on. I don't even know how long something like this is going to last. I'm totally in the dark. I can't do this on my own. I don't think you can either. We need to do this together.'

Stacey looked down at the floor and smiled. She wiped away her tears, then slowly rose to her feet.

'Welcome to parenthood. She'll calm down in about ten minutes. I'll put the kettle on.'

Read on for a taster of
Kevin Lewis's first book

The Kid

Now a major motion picture by
Nick Moran

Starring:

Rupert Friend
Natascha McElhone
Ioan Gruffud

1. The Pink Tin House

I was born on 8 September 1970, so this is not a story from the 'bad old days', this all happened at a time when British society was priding itself on becoming enlightened. We had the welfare state and child-protection laws and an army of well-meaning people dedicated to making it a fair world for children born at the bottom of the social heap. But still they couldn't save me from the fate that awaited me in my own home.

On my birth certificate it says we lived in Gypsy Hill, near Crystal Palace in South London, but I only remember living on 'The Horseshoe' – a curve of houses on King Henry's Drive in New Addington, near Croydon in Surrey – so we must have moved there when I was still too young to take in what was happening. It doesn't really matter where we were living because any house that our family occupied would soon have looked the same.

That strip of the South London suburbs was a bleak and culturally desolate area. There was row upon row of twentieth-century social housing provided for those who couldn't afford to live in the city, mixed in with street after street of dreary 'affordable' housing for those who aspired to a more genteel suburban existence. There was no cultural history for the community to feel any pride about, no sense of belonging. In New Addington there was nothing to soothe the eye or the soul. It was just a place where hundreds of thousands of people lived until they could afford to move to somewhere nicer. Many of the families, just like ours, were never going to be going anywhere, trapped in a spiral of poverty, debt and desperation.

King Henry's Drive was a long, busy, depressing road lined by row upon row of tin houses, with the Horseshoe in the middle and tower blocks at the end, and roads either side leading nowhere. The Horseshoe, as the name implies, was a curved side road allowing the houses to be set back from the main road around a large patch of grass. If a private company was building the Horseshoe today it would be called a 'crescent' and would be prettily landscaped with trees, but all we had to look at on the grass was a public phone box and the houses opposite. All the houses around it were built of corrugated tin and were owned by the council. I don't know if the architects who designed them intended these houses to last for more than a few decades, but they are still there today, although some of them have now been improved with new tiles on their roofs and wooden cladding on the outside walls. In the early seventies they were all still just tin boxes for living in, cost-effective places to put families in order to stop them ending up on the street.

Every house in the row was painted a different pastel colour, probably in the hope of lifting the spirits of those who had to live in them and giving the area some sort of character. Ours was pink on the outside, which belied the filth and misery that existed inside those flimsy walls. Behind the house was a garden, which backed on to the car park and play-grounds of Wolsey Junior School.

Some of the neighbours had managed to make their homes look quite nice, with well-tended front gardens, tubs and hanging baskets, decorative fences and pretty curtains at the windows. Their efforts to add colour and life to their houses merely drew attention to the lack of colour and life all around.

Anything like that would have been completely beyond the abilities or imaginations of Gloria and Dennis, my natural parents. Just existing was almost more than they could manage. Gloria never bothered to change out of her dressing gown unless she was leaving the house to cash her Giro and it never occurred to her that she should even clean her own house, let alone decorate it or improve it in any way. Even today I can't bring myself to call them mother and father. On the rare occasions when I'm talking to one of my brothers or sisters, I always refer to her as 'your mother'. Some wounds are just too deep to ever heal.

Gloria was a giant of a woman, over six feet tall and lean, with all the physical strength of someone constantly supercharged by a powerful bad temper.

Dennis was physically strong and silent, whereas Gloria was loud – and she was violent. She never talked in a normal voice, only shouted. She was never calm, always angry. No one liked her, which made her angrier. The neighbours hated the way she was screaming at them one minute and scrounging from them the next; they hated how every other word that came from her mouth was an obscenity. It was a constant, ugly stream of the few most aggressive expletives the English language could supply, fired out by a jet of permanent spite. When she tried to be nice to people outside the family and make them her friends, which wasn't often, she was still too overpowering and they would shrink away from the onslaught of her personality.

Dennis was stocky and much shorter than her. He worked as a British Rail engineer, maintaining the tracks, one of those gangs of men you see sometimes from train windows, out in all weathers in their luminous jackets. He had jet-black hair and was naturally withdrawn. A life spent wandering the rail tracks, never having to deal with the public, must have suited him well. The passion of his life was the music of Elvis Presley. He was a desperately shy man, working every moment he could, sometimes out in the rain and snow or all through the night. But however many hours he put in, he could never make enough money to keep us at anything approaching a decent level. The pressure of it all seemed to be too much for him. The moment he got home from work he would shut himself in the kitchen with his tape machine, just playing Elvis songs over and over again while he stood at the sink, silently drinking. The music must have provided him with an escape from reality, something I later came to appreciate myself, but it certainly didn't give him any joy. It never made him smile or sing along, except when he'd had too much to drink, when he would join in with the most soulful songs. I don't know if the rock and roll even made him want to tap his feet. It was a sticking plaster for his damaged soul rather than a balm. I guess the drinking provided another means of escape, numbing the pain of failure and disappointment for at least a few hours each day.

As far as I know Gloria had never worked, certainly not in my living memory. She was always totally dependent on the welfare state for handouts, but who could blame her when she had so many children to look after? Every Monday she would be queuing up outside the Post Office in the dingy shopping precinct for her Giro with so many others and she would immediately spend it. That Post Office seemed to do more trade than any of the other shops around it. Now they sell lottery tickets as well, so people can buy a few rays of hope with their meagre handouts without even having to leave the premises. Gloria had no budgeting abilities whatsoever. Even if Dennis gave her money during the week, there would still be no food in the house by Friday. She never made any plans or harboured any dreams. She had no hopes of bettering herself or ambitions for us; she lived from one handout to the next without a thought to the future or even a plan to get us safely through to the following Monday and the next Giro.

If the Giro didn't arrive when it should we knew the pressures on us all would increase enormously. She would wait by the window for the postman to come. Very little mail came to our house and if the waiting became too much for her she would send me out, even as young as five, to find the postman in the neighbouring streets and see if he was on his way to the Horseshoe and would be willing to let me run ahead with our mail so she would get it a few minutes earlier so that she could cash it and spend it the moment the shops opened. If the postman didn't have it and I had to return to the house empty-handed I knew I would be in big trouble, and we would have to repeat the whole process when the next post was due.

As children we were always hungry, not able to dull our appetites with drink and cigarettes, as she and Dennis did. From an early age I knew my father liked drinking and smoking and although my mother never drank anything except tea, there was always a smouldering cigarette stuck to her bottom lip.

The house was always in chaos. Anyone glancing in through an opened door or uncurtained window would have known immediately that we were a family who couldn't cope. In fact they would have known before that from the piles of junk outside the front door. Our clothes were always strewn around the living area on any surface that was free and many that were already cluttered, great limp piles of them would encircle us as we sat on the sofa, or slide to the floor if we bumped against them, where they would remain to be walked across or kicked carelessly into corners. Nothing was ever put away into a cupboard or a drawer; nothing was ever cared for or cherished. The front room always looked like the last hour of a jumble sale, just before the unsaleable items are finally consigned to the tip. In the kitchen there was always washing-up waiting to be done and frying pans would be re-used with the fat of previous meals still clinging to them. Nothing was ever washed up. Everywhere you looked there was filth and disorder.

Gloria ruled the house like the tyrant she was. Some of the rules were completely irrational, but as a child you accept things the way they are. It's only later that you look back and see the gruesome absurdity of it all. We weren't, for instance, allowed to have lights in our bedrooms. Perhaps it was an economy measure, or perhaps they couldn't be bothered to install the bulbs, but looking back now I think it was more likely they wanted to exercise their power over us and let us know they were the masters and we were just mistakes. We may have been great when we were cute little puppies, but as young dogs we needed too much looking after.

The bathroom was on the ground floor with an outside toilet, but we weren't allowed downstairs in the night in case we stole whatever food there might be left in the fridge, so if we needed the toilet we had to use a bucket, which was left out at the top of the stairs. Because it was so dark upstairs we didn't always manage to hit the bucket, and the puddles were allowed to soak into the bare boards, creating a tacky patina of stains. Sometimes the smaller children didn't even make a pretence of using the bucket, they just peed wherever they felt like it. The whole house stank of urine.

There was no paper on any of the walls, or if there was it was hanging off in strips. If anything was broken or stained it stayed that way. The bedrooms were just bare, dingy cells where we tried to hide from Gloria's tempers. The walls were drawn on and sometimes smeared with human excrement, where small children had had accidents and no one had bothered to clear it up. The floors upstairs and downstairs were always sticky with grime and in the few areas where there were remnants of carpet, they were black with filth and ragged with years of wear and neglect. It was like living in a derelict house, one that was just waiting for the demolition crew to arrive or for homeless youths to move in and squat. But it wasn't derelict, it was our family home.

Electricity and gas were always a problem. We had to have meters installed because Gloria and Dennis never paid the bills, and even then they were always robbing the fifty pence pieces, breaking in and then wedging the fronts open. We'd sometimes go for days with no power at all because they'd broken the equipment or had run out of money and we'd have to wait till the following Monday for the same ritual of waiting for the postman to arrive. Since we never had any money, we always owed people. Whenever the gas, electricity or rent people came knocking we were told to hide, diving for cover behind the sofa, or simply pulling a pile of clothes over us, hoping that if they peered through the windows they'd just see a scene of deserted chaos. If that failed, and they managed to get into the house, there would always be a shouting match with accusations flying back and forth and Gloria boiling with righteous indignation at the unfairness of life.

Occasionally my older brother Wayne and I would pluck up the courage to steal from the fridge while our parents were preoccupied somewhere else in the house, driven on by the ache of hunger that constantly gnawed at our insides. We trained ourselves to creep downstairs in the dead of night, knowing what floorboards to avoid treading on in order not to be heard. There was never much to choose from, but anything we found we would cram into our mouths, swallowing it as quickly as possible in case we were caught and forced to spit it out. We'd wolf down raw sausages if that was all there was, or raw potatoes. Dennis had a liking for veal and ham pies and if he left one overnight in the fridge we'd try to get it, willing to brave the consequences in order to lessen the pain of hunger.

Like many small boys I used to wet the bed almost every night and I would call out to my mother, scared of telling her but not knowing what else to do. I soon learned not to tell Gloria because then she would smack me on my wet skin, which made the blows sting even more, and she would push me downstairs and force me to sleep in the bath with just a dirty towel as a blanket to teach me a lesson.

'You dirty, fucking cunt!' she'd scream into my sleep-fuddled ear in the early hours of the morning, furious at being woken up from her own exhausted slumbers, pushing and pinching and slapping at any part of me I didn't manage to get out of her reach.

I'd do as she told me as quickly as possible, lying in the cold, hard bath until she'd gone back upstairs, and then I'd creep out on to the bathroom floor, trying to find another towel to lie on as it was warmer than the cold metal of the bath. Desperate not to fall too deeply asleep, in case I didn't hear her coming back downstairs in the morning, I'd then doze fitfully for the rest of the night. The moment I heard her stirring upstairs I'd climb back into the bathtub and feign deep sleep. I soon learnt not to wake her when I had accidents if I could help it. I discovered that if I lay long enough on the wet patch the heat from my body would dry it. She would never notice the stain because she never changed the beds. The smell of dirt and urine permeated us as well as our surroundings, travelling with us to school the next day in our clothes and hair and on our skins.

My nights were often as frightening as the days, haunted by nightmares. I would sometimes wake up in the dark room and cry out for my mother without thinking, but as soon as I heard her stamping towards the room I would instantly regret it, curling up into a ball, pulling the covers over my head to counteract the inevitable blows that would rain down. I had to learn as early as possible to curb my natural childish instincts to turn to my mother when I was frightened or unhappy. I had to learn to hold the fear and misery inside, to cope with them myself, because if I annoyed her in any way with my problems I would simply make everything worse.

'You make another fucking sound, you fucking cunt,' she would scream at the top of her voice as I tried to hug her and tell her what had frightened me, 'you'll get the shit kicked out of you, and you'll be sleeping in the bath.'

Nightmares were punishable in exactly the same way as bed-wetting. She would drag me down the stairs by my hair to the bathroom. I learnt to cling on to her hands when she had hold of my hair, to take off some of the weight and lessen the pain. There are always tricks you can employ, usually instinctively, to increase the chances of survival in any situation. The more I screamed and pleaded for mercy the more furious she would become, so I learnt not to cry, to keep as quiet as possible. I reasoned that if I took the punishment in silence it would all be over quicker, but sometimes my silent acceptance of the punishment simply fuelled her fury. I would stand there flinching, my lip trembling and silent tears running down my face. She would see it as some sort of dumb insolence and keep attacking me until I was unable to stop myself from crying out in pain. I think she needed to hear the screams of pain to prove she was in control.

Her anger always and immediately erupted into violence; sometimes she'd lash out at us with her hands and feet, sometimes she'd grab a stick or a belt or anything else that came to hand in order to make the beatings more effective. If she hit me with her hand, the blow was so hard there would be a raised imprint of the palm and big fingers left on my skin for hours afterwards. In some of the worst furies she would be biting and scratching us in the sort of frenzy you might associate with a wild dog. The best way of defending myself was to curl up into a ball, guarding my face and vital organs. I was too young to defend myself, just pleading for mercy, 'Sorry, Mummy! Sorry, Mummy! Please no, Mum! Please no, Mum!' and on and on.

One night – I must have been no more than six years old – I woke from a deep sleep with an unfamiliar feeling. Someone was holding me, but it wasn't the usual sort of holding. I wasn't being restrained, or pulled painfully in some direction I didn't want to go. There didn't seem to be any anger involved or shouting. I was confused in my half-awake state, knowing that I felt comfortable and protected, but not knowing why. As I came round I realized the house was full of unusual activity. The arms I was cradled in were unfamiliar. They were a man's arms and although he was taking care not to alarm me he was hurrying. There was a sense of urgency and I could hear voices and the noise of running engines outside the house as we made our way downstairs. As we came into the illuminated night I saw that the man who was holding me was wearing a helmet and uniform, and I realized he was a fireman. I didn't feel frightened because he seemed so calm as he took me out into the street. I didn't appear to be in any danger.

There was a smell of smoke and a lot of noise coming from the fire engines that were parked by the curb, putting out the fire that had broken out in the tin house next door. I was sad when he put me down to watch the goings-on with the others. I'll never forget the feeling of being carried for those few moments by that fireman; I'd never experienced anything so gentle or caring before.

My brother, Wayne, was just a year older than me and, below us, were Sharon and Julie. Robert and Brenda came along later. Gloria always preferred Wayne to me, and Sharon and Julie were much quieter and less likely to annoy her. So it was me she hated with the greatest vehemence, until Robert arrived to share my role as her scapegoat. Brenda, the baby of the family, would always be her other favourite, along with Wayne. It was a situation we all understood and accepted. It was just the way things were.

Gloria didn't confine herself to physical bullying. As she punched and kicked, scratched and slapped me, pulling my hair and sometimes even biting me, she would also rain down abuse, telling me I was 'pathetic', that I was 'gay'. 'Kevin is a gay little bastard,' she would repeat over and over again. All the time she was telling me how useless I was, her face would be an inch away from mine, her teeth gritted in fury and the four-letter words punching into me. All the frustrations and hardships that were constantly building up inside her own head would spew out over me every time I came near her, every hour of every day. The aggression never relented. Her dislike for me was so intense that even when she was in a good mood she couldn't bring herself to speak kindly to me or to hug me or kiss me. I never heard a single word of praise or kindness pass her lips. Sometimes she'd become so incensed with me her false teeth would jump loose as she shouted. Whenever that happened I could never resist laughing, which would add even more fuel to her rage. To me this was normal life.

The moment Dennis came back into the house from work she would be screaming out lists of my misdemeanours. 'Your fucking son's done this, and that . . .' It was the same every single day. Her endless tirade would drive him straight through to the kitchen as she pelted him with hysterical complaints and abuse until he could get his tape machine going and a bottle open, to drown her voice out with Elvis and beer.

I don't remember what my crimes were in those early days. I was a lively, boisterous boy, so they could have been anything from breaking a cup to slamming a door or eating something that was forbidden, giving her a bad look or being overexcited because I was going outside to play. Sometimes it was nothing at all. It didn't matter what I did or didn't do, the reaction would always be the same.

There were social workers coming to the house now and then, but they never stayed for long, and if any of my marks or bruises were visible they could always be explained away with some invented accident or other. 'He fell over in the garden!' she'd say and they'd look out at the three-foot-high grass with the debris poking out of it and decide they had no reason to doubt her story. The moment they walked through the door she would be pouring out her tales of hardship and streams of bile against anyone who had upset her. You could see the panic in their eyes as they tried to get away from her barrage of complaints and grievances about us, about Dennis, about the neighbours, the council and anyone else who had touched her life in the previous few days or weeks. They couldn't wait to get back out of the house into the fresh air, so they didn't prolong their visits unnecessarily by talking to me or asking me how I was.

They could see she and I hated each other, but they had no proof that she was hitting me. If they did ask me how I'd come by a particular cut or bruise, I'd lie for her, because if I didn't I knew I'd be beaten to even more of a pulp the moment they were out of the door. She would be standing there, towering over me as the social worker knelt down to talk to me. I never knew why they came to us or what they did, but whenever they were there Gloria was on her best behaviour, like a child being good for sweets.

There was no escape for me. I couldn't outrun her. I couldn't hide from her. I had no choice but to continue to live in fear and stay silent about it.

Once Dennis was home and in the kitchen she still wouldn't allow him to listen to his music in peace. She'd be determined to involve him in the disciplining of his children. No one in the family ever spoke quietly. There were never any reasonable conversations. Everyone would be screaming at once and he would inevitably be dragged into the affray, his patience stretched as tightly as hers by the endless noise and foul language. Eventually, particularly once he'd got a few drinks inside him, he'd start hitting out as well. Because she wouldn't let up, going on and on about everything that was wrong in her life, everything that was wrong with him and with me, he would be unable to withstand the pressure any longer. After a long hard day, or night, of physical labour he would snap and they would start to argue. They would hit each other and, if we were within reach, they would both hit out at us as well.

Once tempers were lost we were all in real danger of being seriously hurt by both of them. Both lost all sense of judgement when their anger bubbled over. When Wayne back-chatted him one time, Dennis threw a knife at him. Wayne can't have been more than six or seven. We were all there in the room; Gloria, me and Dennis shouting, the girls watching in nervous silence. He could have thrown anything in his fury; it just happened to be a knife that came into his hand at the moment his temper snapped and he didn't have the control to stop himself. The blade dug into Wayne's leg and the blood immediately started to flow. A loud panic mixed with anger filled the house as they tried to work out what they should be doing and calm themselves enough to act responsibly. When they finally realized they couldn't treat the wound adequately themselves, they were forced to take Wayne down to the hospital to be stitched up. They must have been nervous that they'd be asked awkward questions. When the harassed doctor asked what had happened they told him it had been an accident and he accepted the explanation. It continually amazed me how people in positions to rescue us were always happy to believe whatever they were told by adults. It must have been obvious from the state we were in that things were out of control, but all the people we came into contact with were always willing to take whatever explanation Gloria or Dennis came up with. Maybe it was pressures of time or workload that made them so anxious to move on to the next problem, or maybe they didn't want to interfere, or maybe we were just too scary a prospect for most normal people to be able to face.

Dennis was a very strong man physically. When he was hitting me he would lift me up by my wrist, leaving my other hand free to frantically try to block the blows as I squirmed and wriggled in his grip, but it was impossible and my efforts at self-protection and my refusal to remain a stationary target only made him angrier. Wayne, Julie and Sharon would become afraid when he lost his temper with me, screaming at him to stop hitting me, but their noise would only annoy him more, like a dazed, confused bull being taunted in a bullring. Once he'd smacked me with all his strength he would toss me aside like a piece of dirty laundry. But his eruptions would pass, unlike Gloria's, and he would never scream abuse into my face or tell me what a useless little bastard I was. I got the impression he liked me, that I was his favourite, but he just couldn't handle the strain of the constant noise and the screaming and the anger. He just wanted to be left alone with his beer and his music.

The constant noise must have been like a torture for him, gradually driving him further and further inside himself. He became quieter and more withdrawn with every passing year. There were moments when we got glimpses of the sort of father he might have been if he hadn't been under too much pressure from us all. Once, when Wayne and I were squabbling about something, he gave us both boxing gloves and told us to fight properly if we were going to, believing that the only way to sort anything out was through violence and abuse. Sometimes, if I'd taken a real bashing from Gloria, I'd walk past him and he would put his hand on my shoulder, but he never said anything. When that happened I thought that everything would be all right, but it never was. I thought that he would protect me and look after me, but he never did.

As the years went by his drinking became worse. He moved from beer to gin, coming home every night with half bottles tucked into his pocket and staying in the kitchen until the small hours just drinking and listening to the music. None of us went in there; we knew he wanted to be left alone. The harder he drank the angrier and more depressed he became, withdrawing further into himself.

There was nothing in the house except anger and unhappiness, nightmares and rows, beatings and abuse. There were no saving moments of laughter or forgiveness, no kind words or encouragement for any of us. Life under those circumstances beats down a child's self-esteem and gives them no hope for the future. There is only endurance, never enjoyment. If something or someone else doesn't come along to save them, the children of such families have no hope of escape and merely repeat the pattern set by their parents.

KEVIN LEWIS

THE KID: A TRUE STORY

Kevin Lewis never had a chance. Growing up on a poverty-stricken london council estate, beaten and starved by his parents, bullied at school and abandoned by social services, his life was never his own. Even after he was put into care, he found himself out on the streets caught up in a criminal underworld that knew him as 'the Kid'. Yet Kevin survived to make a better life for himself. And this is his heartbreaking and inspiring story . . .

'Gripping, harrowing. A true triumph over tragedy' *Mail on Sunday*

'Devastating . . . Every parent must read' *Daily Mail*

'Incredible. A fantastic story' Fern Britton, This Morning

'By the end, your heart is overwhelmed' *Daily Telegraph*

KEVIN LEWIS

THE KID MOVES ON

Kevin Lewis wrote *The Kid* to exorcize the demons from a childhood of abuse and neglect at the hands of his parent, Gloria and Dennis.

But while his story became an instant bestseller, it did not free him from the past. He began to revert to habits that had sustained him during the years of abuse. And while battling his own fears, Kevin was horrified to hear that Gloria was trying to get her hands on his nieces and nephews.

The Kid Moves On tells how Kevin made the most difficult decision of his life – whether to confront Gloria and Dennis over their abuse – and how in making that decision he finally freed himself from the terrors of his past.

'Gripping, harrowing. A true triumph over tragedy. You may start Kevin Lewis's book in tears, but you finish exultant' *Mail on Sunday*

'Harrowing, chilling . . . with passages of heartbreaking frankness' *Daily Telegraph*

He just wanted a decent book to read ...

Not too much to ask, is it? It was in 1935 when Allen Lane, Managing Director of Bodley Head Publishers, stood on a platform at Exeter railway station looking for something good to read on his journey back to London. His choice was limited to popular magazines and poor-quality paperbacks – the same choice faced every day by the vast majority of readers, few of whom could afford hardbacks. Lane's disappointment and subsequent anger at the range of books generally available led him to found a company – and change the world.

'We believed in the existence in this country of a vast reading public for intelligent books at a low price, and staked everything on it'
Sir Allen Lane, 1902–1970, founder of Penguin Books

The quality paperback had arrived – and not just in bookshops. Lane was adamant that his Penguins should appear in chain stores and tobacconists, and should cost no more than a packet of cigarettes.

Reading habits (and cigarette prices) have changed since 1935, but Penguin still believes in publishing the best books for everybody to enjoy. We still believe that good design costs no more than bad design, and we still believe that quality books published passionately and responsibly make the world a better place.

So wherever you see the little bird – whether it's on a piece of prize-winning literary fiction or a celebrity autobiography, political tour de force or historical masterpiece, a serial-killer thriller, reference book, world classic or a piece of pure escapism – you can bet that it represents the very best that the genre has to offer.

Whatever you like to read – trust Penguin.

KEVIN LEWIS

FALLEN ANGEL

DI Stacey Collins has seen the darker side of humanity all too often. A single mum brought up on the grim Blenheim estate, she knows only too well what terrors the world can hold. But even her jaded eyes have never witnessed a crime of such unspeakable horror.

A body, broken and lifeless, is found in the gloom of a London church. Kidnapped and horrifically murdered, young Daniel Wright never knew his tormentor.

And it is only the beginning. Soon Collins finds herself both haunted by the demons of her past and battling in the name of innocence itself.

Some angels never find their path to heaven . . .

'Fans of Martina Cole will love this' *Heat*

www.penguin.com